The
GIRL
in the
SKY

Also by Suzanne Fortin

The Dance Teacher of Paris
The Lost Dressmaker of Paris

The GIRL in the SKY

SUZANNE FORTIN

embla books

First published in Great Britain in 2024 by

Bonnier Books UK Limited
4th Floor, Victoria House, Bloomsbury Square, London, WC1B 4DA
Owned by Bonnier Books
Sveavägen 56, Stockholm, Sweden

Copyright © Suzanne Fortin, 2024

All rights reserved.
No part of this publication may be reproduced, stored or transmitted in any form or by any means, electronic, mechanical, photocopying or otherwise, without the prior written permission of the publisher.

The right of Suzanne Fortin to be identified as Author of this work has been asserted by them in accordance with the Copyright, Designs and Patents Act 1988.

This is a work of fiction. Names, places, events and incidents are either the products of the author's imagination or used fictitiously. Any resemblance to actual persons, living or dead, is purely coincidental.

A CIP catalogue record for this book is available from the British Library.

ISBN: 9781471416385

This book is typeset using Atomik ePublisher.

Embla Books is an imprint of Bonnier Books UK.
www.bonnierbooks.co.uk

*In memory of Pilot Officer W M L Fiske III
otherwise known as Billy Fiske*

Part 1

East Anglia

England

Chapter 1

Cambridgeshire

July 1939

Geraldine Fitz-Herbert, Fitz to her friends, put her finger to her lips and winked at her younger brother, Michael, before slipping back behind the long velvet curtain that hung at the window of Badcombe House.

The hard heels of her governess clipped along the floorboards of the corridor, nearing the nursery of the country home where the Fitz-Herbert family had been in residence for generations.

'She's coming,' whispered Michael, Fitz's half-brother through their father's second marriage. Her own mother had passed away when Fitz was just eight years old. The new Mrs Fitz-Herbert was much younger than her husband and between them, they'd had Michael when Fitz was ten years old.

'Shh. Don't say a word,' replied Fitz, pressing herself further back against the wall and trying to control her breathing.

The door opened. Fitz heard Michael's chair scrape on the wooden floorboards as he rose to greet their governess.

'Good afternoon, Miss Stevens,' he said.

'Good afternoon, Michael,' came the reply. The footsteps came to an abrupt halt. 'Where's Geraldine?' Although Fitz was nearly twenty-one, while her father was away on business and an extended holiday, accompanied by his wife, Fitz had been left under the care of the governess. Fitz was less than happy about this arrangement. However, her father was due to return next week and, as a result, Fitz sincerely hoped she would be free of the governess's control.

'I don't know,' Michael replied.

'Is she sick?'

'I don't know.'

'Was she here for her lunch?'

'Yes.'

'And you don't know where she is now?'

'No.'

Miss Stevens let out an impatient sigh. 'I do hope she's not misbehaving again. She's not, is she? Speak up, now and tell the truth. Where is your sister?'

Fitz felt a wave of guilt. She didn't want to get Michael into trouble but, at the same time, she didn't want to stay for afternoon tea in the garden with the Dowager of Badcombe and the Dowager's friends from the local parish, where the conversation would be embroidery, flower arranging, the hymn choice for Sunday service and what nice young man they could introduce her to at the upcoming summer ball.

It was a glorious June afternoon, the sun was shining, the sky was a beautiful blue and the freedom this brought was calling to her. Fitz knew her mind. A mind she did not care to occupy with sewing and the like.

'I don't know where she is,' replied Michael.

Oh, how Fitz loved her brother for not giving her up. Hopefully, the old battleaxe of a governess would go and look somewhere else for her now. Fitz held her breath.

'I see. I shall have to waste my time trying to find her,' complained Miss Stevens. 'I don't know what your parents will say when they get back from their trip next week. Your sister has been nothing but trouble. Take out your reading book and read silently until I come back to take you down to greet the Dowager.'

The governess left the room, locking the door behind her. Fitz waited until Miss Stevens's footsteps had faded away, then she was bundling her way out from behind the curtains.

'Are you really going?' asked Michael.

'Yes. I am.' Fitz rushed over to the bookcase at the back of the nursery. It really shouldn't be called a nursery these days, as neither she nor Michael were babies. It really should have been renamed as the school room, or prison, as Fitz thought of it. A room where imagination was stifled, traditions were kept and stuffy rules implemented. A place certainly not for children. And if her father knew they were being locked in, she was sure he would be horrified. He and her stepmother had been away for three months now and they couldn't get back soon enough as far as Fitz was concerned. Then they could sack the dreadful Miss Stevens.

'When can I come with you?' asked Michael. 'Can I come today?'

Fitz gave her brother a sympathetic smile. 'Not today, but soon, I promise.' She turned back to the bookcase.

Much as Fitz hated living in such a traditional home, both in structure and in concept, she loved the secret passageways in the building. None of which Miss Stevens knew about, having only been employed for the last twelve weeks. Their previous governess had decided that teaching the Fitz-Herbert siblings was not for her – or rather teaching Fitz wasn't.

Fitz located the switch under the shelf and flicked it to one side. She heard the click of the locking mechanism release and then she pushed against the shelf which was, in fact, a hidden door.

'Be careful,' said Michael.

'I'll be back by supper time.' Fitz blew her brother a kiss and slipped through the opening into the passageway, before pushing the door back in place. Originally, the passageway would have been used by servants to move around the house unseen, and indeed some staircases were still in use, but this was one of the long forgotten and unnecessary passageways. Fitz took the torch from her pocket and lit the way ahead as she quietly descended the staircase, which ran alongside the main, much grander one. On reaching the ground floor, there was a passageway to the right which took her through to the scullery. All she had to do then was nip out through the scullery door into the garden.

She had just closed the door to the staircase when Annie appeared in the scullery.

She let out a gasp. Annie was the same age as Fitz and had been at Badcombe House for about six months. Her eyes widened at the sight of Fitz in front of her and she looked fervently over her shoulder back into the kitchen.

'Whatever are you doing, Miss Geraldine?' she whispered. 'Miss Stevens has been down here looking for you.'

'Please don't say anything, Annie,' pleaded Fitz, putting her hands together as if in prayer. 'I'll be back for supper. I promise.' She was already heading for the door to the garden. 'Please, Annie.'

'Oh, go on, then. Don't say anything, mind. You'll get me sacked.'

'Thank you, Annie. You're a darling.'

With that Fitz was out through the garden door and racing across the lawn towards the stables where the bicycles were kept. She jumped on the first one to hand and pedalled furiously down the drive of Badcombe House and on through the Cambridgeshire village to the airfield.

She was going to be late if she didn't hurry.

A few minutes later, she was skidding to a halt at the entrance to the airfield. From her pocket she pulled out a compact mirror and her most favourite bright red lipstick, which she deftly applied. Make-up was frowned upon by her governess who considered it unnecessary, but to Fitz, not only was it something she loved, but it reminded her of her mother who had always worn the same shade.

Fitz cycled through the entrance of the airfield and headed towards the hangars. She could see the figure of Johnny Fisher carrying out the last inspection of the Tiger Moth biplane.

'Ah, Fitz, there you are,' he said, as she anchored on the brakes, coming to a halt in front of him. Although Johnny was several years older than Fitz, the two of them had struck up a firm friendship over Fitz's love, or obsession, as her father called it, with aircraft. Johnny grinned at her. 'I thought you weren't going to make it.'

'Yes, sorry about that. Old Stevens was on the war path this afternoon. Had to sneak out.' She propped the bicycle up against the hangar. 'But I'm here now.'

'What are you going to do when your parents get back?' asked Johnny, closing the bonnet to the engine and wiping his hands on a rag. 'You're not going to be able to sneak out then.'

'For a start, only my father is my parent,' replied Fitz. 'And secondly, I'm going to be twenty-one in a few weeks' time so technically an adult and neither he nor my stepmother can tell me what to do.'

Johnny raised an eyebrow, an amused look settling on his face. 'Is that right?'

'Well, put it this way, I'm not going to give up flying, for anyone,' said Fitz, running her hand along the cloth of the biplane's wing. 'And I intend to make the most of my last week of freedom.' Although Fitz's father had paid for her to have flying lessons after she had non-stop begged him for nearly a year, it had been on the proviso she behaved herself. By that, her father had meant not upsetting the governess or her stepmother. So far Fitz had been unsuccessful on both counts, and she rather suspected Stevens was going to complain terribly about her to her father, and with that might come a possible grounding by withdrawing funds to pay for her flying lessons. Still, when her birthday came along soon, Fitz would have access to a small trust fund her mother had left her, and she had already decided she'd use the money to stay airborne.

'Best we get going, in that case,' replied Johnny, picking up a flying helmet and handing it to Fitz.

Fitz quickly pulled the helmet on and connected up the headset so she could communicate with Johnny up in the air. He'd been giving her flying lessons, in between his job as a flying instructor and a commercial pilot, for the past six months.

'Oh, look out, lads,' came a voice from across the hangar. 'Female pilot about.'

Fitz looked over as three aircraft mechanics wandered into the hangar. The one who had called out was Henry Simpson, who found it highly amusing to rib Fitz about her learning to fly. He never missed an opportunity to make fun of her. The other two men with him laughed.

'Take cover!' one of them called out.

'I hope you're insured, Johnny,' said Henry as they neared. 'I heard you both had a near miss last week.' He was referring to an incident where the control tower had cleared Fitz for landing but hadn't realised another plane was attempting to land at the same time, due to a misfiring engine. Fitz had caught sight of the wounded aircraft out of the corner of her eye and had pulled the Tiger Moth she was flying up, narrowly avoiding a mid-air collision.

'It was not a near miss,' retorted Fitz, unable to stop herself from responding. 'Anyway, it was the control tower that messed up.'

'Yeah, of course it was,' said Henry, winking at his mates who sniggered.

'Actually, if it hadn't been for Fitz's quick thinking, it would have been a collision,' said Johnny. 'She showed a lot of skill to avoid a nasty accident. I know plenty of men who wouldn't have used their initiative.'

Henry shrugged. 'You're best off sticking to your bicycle, love. Much safer for everyone.'

'Just ignore him,' said Johnny, before telling Henry where to go in no uncertain terms.

Fitz settled for scowling at Henry instead of giving him a piece of her mind. She really should ignore him like Johnny said. It wasn't the first time one of the men had been condescending about her flying and, sadly, it probably wouldn't be the last. Fitz would continue to do what she did best, and that was to prove them wrong by being a highly accomplished pilot, like Johnny said she could easily be. Henry could laugh all he liked – at the end of the day he was stuck under a plane while she was up in the skies.

They taxied their way down to the end of the small airfield in the Cambridgeshire countryside and made ready for take-off. Fitz's stomach fluttered with excitement as they began to build up speed, her heart beat hard against her breastbone and her pulse pumped fast through her veins. None of it was from fear, though. It was all from anticipation.

She loved that feeling of weightlessness when the wheels of the Moth no longer had contact with the ground and her stomach gave a small jump as her body caught up with itself. And then they were climbing up in the sky, above the tree tops, as the gap between plane and earth extended and extended.

Fitz glanced down as the buildings became less distinguishable and the fields a puzzle of all shades of green and gold. She grinned madly to herself. Nothing on earth could match this sense of freedom.

'You're doing great,' came Johnny's voice through the headset. 'Where are we going?'

'Oh, you'll see,' Fitz called back into the mouthpiece. She smiled to herself. She really shouldn't do this, but it was far too tempting not to.

She steered the Moth back around towards Badcombe village, dropping in altitude as first the church spire came into view and then the imposing building of Badcombe House and the fields beyond.

'What are you up to?' asked Johnny.

'Just going to say hello to Michael!'

'Why do I get the feeling I'm going to regret this?' came the reply.

Fitz laughed out loud, throwing her head back and grinning wildly. She took the Moth lower than she had before, her eyes fixed on the field ahead and the gardens of Badcombe House. She could see the afternoon tea party, that Stevens had wanted her to attend, had begun. She swooped in low and howled with laughter to herself as she turned the biplane around and took another fly-past. She could see Michael jumping up and down, waving madly at the Moth.

'All right, Fitz, that's enough,' said Johnny. 'You'll get me grounded at this rate.'

Fitz laughed again. 'Don't worry, I think I'll be the one getting grounded but it was so worth it.'

Chapter 2

'Honestly, Geraldine, it's totally unacceptable behaviour,' said Edward Fitz-Herbert, as he paced back and forth between his desk and Fitz.

Fitz looked down at the red and gold rug she was standing on. Her father had only returned from his trip abroad the day before and the reprimand she knew would be coming had arrived sooner than she expected. It must have been one of the first things Stevens had told him. Fitz knew she shouldn't have done the fly-past but at the same time she still didn't regret it. However, she knew better than to tell her father that. 'I'm sorry,' she said.

Edward let out a long sigh and came to a halt in front of her. 'Sorry. Are you, though?'

Fitz looked up. 'I'm sorry, I've upset you, Pa.'

He gave her an appraising look. 'Hmm. That's not quite the same as being sorry for your actions.' He gave another sigh and went around his desk, sitting himself down in the red leather chair. He indicated to the chair on Fitz's side of the desk. 'Sit down.'

Fitz did as she was told. 'I'll apologise to Miss Stevens and the Dowager,' she said, feeling contrite now. 'I'll write a letter.'

'No. Currently the Dowager has no idea it was you in the plane. Miss Stevens has assured me of that,' replied Edward. 'But you can write a letter of apology to your tutor, or rather, your former tutor. Not that it will do any good. She's given notice.'

Fitz's eyebrows shot up. 'She's leaving?'

'Yes, Geraldine. Miss Stevens is leaving at the end of the month. So that's another perfectly good governess you've managed to get rid of.'

'Are you going to advertise for a new governess?'

'I don't know, if I'm honest. You're nearly twenty-one and it really should be finishing school for you. Camilla wants to send Michael to boarding school so there might not be any need for a governess.'

'Boarding school? Does Michael know? I'm not sure he'd like that.' Fitz's own experience at boarding school had been short-lived, ending when the headteacher told her father that she'd be better off with a private tutor who could spend one-to-one sessions with her because Fitz clearly was still suffering the trauma of losing her mother. Fitz had never really agreed with that analysis, but it had meant she could leave behind the unhappy days of boarding school and the bullying she'd endured there for not quite fitting in. She'd never fitted in to the norms of society but it didn't bother her in the slightest. It was everyone else who had the problem – she was either too bossy, too opinionated, too reckless, too eager. Basically, too much.

'No, we haven't spoken to him yet, so don't go saying anything,' instructed Edward. 'The summer holidays are practically upon us so we'll decide before September.'

There was a knock at the door and in came Fitz's stepmother, Camilla. 'Oh, Geraldine, you're still here. I hope your father has made it clear how disappointed we are with the reports we've had from Miss Stevens.'

Fitz bit down the urge to answer back that it was none of Camilla's business; she didn't want to upset her father any more. It wasn't that she disliked Camilla, it was just that the two of them had never really hit it off. Cook said it was because Fitz was so like her mother,

Annabelle, the first Mrs Fitz-Herbert. Not only in looks but in temperament, too.

'Yes, I've spoken to Geraldine and explained to her in no uncertain terms how none of her behaviour reported to us by Miss Stevens is acceptable,' said Edward.

Fitz knew her father was pacifying his wife at this point and she couldn't help feeling guilty for putting him in this position. She smiled at Camilla. 'And I've apologised and promised Pa in future, I'll consider my actions before doing anything.'

Camilla raised an eyebrow, clearly not believing Fitz, then offered a tight smile. 'Very good. That is all we ask,' she said. 'Besides, I don't want Michael thinking that's how a person should behave. You do need to set a good example.'

'Yes. I agree,' said Fitz. 'Michael should have the right influences.' Fitz knew she was treading a fine line between insubordination and compliance, but she couldn't quite bring herself to bow down and conform.

Camilla went to reply, but Edward beat her to it. 'Right, well, that's that sorted,' he said briskly, clapping his hands together and getting to his feet.

Fitz didn't miss her cue. 'Thank you, Pa. I'll write that letter now.'

'Oh, there was one thing,' said Camilla. 'I've invited the Montagues over for dinner on Saturday. They're bringing their son, William, and I'd like you to be there please, Geraldine.'

Fitz's automatic reaction was to roll her eyes, but she caught a look from her father and managed to stop herself. She owed him after he'd just covered for her. She withheld the sigh that was threatening and turned to Camilla. 'Of course.'

William Montague was the son of the vicar and Camilla liked nothing more than to try to matchmake Fitz and William up. What was it with everyone trying to marry her off? Or was it they simply wanted to get rid of her, thinking marriage would quell her troublesome ways?

'And Geraldine,' called her father as she was about to leave the room. 'I expect to see you there. No excuses.'

'Yes, Pa.'

She left the room, closing the door behind her before then poking her tongue out and scowling at it. A stifled giggle behind her, had Fitz spinning around. It was Annie.

Annie looked down and went to scurry past. 'Sorry, Miss Geraldine.'

'Oh, Annie, it's all right,' said Fitz. 'Good job it was only you. I've got to attend a wretched dinner on Saturday evening and waste several hours being polite to William Montague.'

'I hear William Montague is quite a catch,' said Annie.

'For some, maybe,' said Fitz. 'But really he's a dreadful bore and will send me to sleep talking about the latest addition to his stamp collection.'

'There might be more to him than that,' said Annie.

'I doubt it. I'm sure my stepmother thinks he's suitable husband material.'

'He is rather handsome.' A small blush crept up Annie's neck to her face.

'You know, I wish we could swap places,' said Fitz. 'Then I could go to the pub with Johnny Fisher and have a much more agreeable evening.' Fitz sighed. 'Alas, I don't think we can pull that one off. So I must suffer for my crime of passion and love affair with the sky.' Fitz grinned at Annie. 'Ignore me, I'm being dramatic.'

Annie giggled but stopped abruptly as the door opened and out came Camilla.

'Is everything all right?' Camilla asked.

'Yes,' replied Fitz. 'I was just asking Annie if she could make sure my blue dress was clean so I can wear it on Saturday.'

Camilla looked between Fitz and Annie. 'Right. I'm pleased to hear that you're already thinking ahead. Now,

Annie, run along and do whatever it is you're supposed to be doing.'

Fitz spent the afternoon duly writing the letter of apology to Miss Stevens and resisting the urge to add a postscript that she wasn't sorry in the slightest. She wasn't sorry the old battleaxe was leaving, either. Her father had declared the summer holidays were to commence a week or two early so that it would give him time to appoint a new governess for Michael, to start at the beginning of September, if that was what they decided, or to enrol the boy in a boarding school.

Fitz had just finished her letter of apology when the door opened, and her father came into the drawing room.

'Ah, there you are,' he said. He ran his fingers around his chin, smoothing down his beard. A habit that Fitz recognised when her father was concerned about something.

She placed her ink pen in the well. 'Is everything all right?' she asked, getting to her feet.

Her father indicated to the sofa and for Fitz to sit down. He stood in front of the fireplace, his hands now behind his back and a frown creasing his forehead.

'It looks like bad news about a finishing school on the continent,' he said.

'Oh, really?' Fitz kept her face neutral. Inside she was mentally jumping up and down for joy. She'd love to go to Europe but not to a finishing school.

'Things aren't looking good with Germany. I'd sooner you stayed here in England, where you'll be safe.'

Fitz had overheard a lot of talk about Germany between her father and stepmother and then again at a dinner party last week. It seemed to be the main topic of conversation.

'What shall I do instead?' she asked.

'I'm considering the options,' replied her father. 'Camilla has suggested you go to stay with her relatives in Scotland.'

'Scotland! Why would I want to go there?' Fitz couldn't think of anything worse than being hundreds of miles away from home stuck up in Aberdeenshire with nothing to do, with a family she didn't know. Ugh. Perhaps that was the whole idea. Somewhere to keep her out of trouble.

'It was simply a suggestion,' said her father.

'One I don't much care for,' she found herself replying before she could check herself.

Her father frowned at her. 'Geraldine,' he said, in warning.

Fitz quickly apologised. 'Sorry.'

Her father gave a nod of acknowledgement before speaking again. 'I think while there is so much uncertainty, you should stay here at Badcombe House.'

Fitz breathed a sigh of relief. 'Thank you, Pa.'

'But on the condition you don't do anything reckless or anything to upset Camilla. And I mean it this time.'

Fitz realised she had been played. Walked right into the trap her father had set for her, maybe unknowingly. The brains behind the barter would, of course, have been Camilla. Fitz didn't want to make things difficult for her father and she reluctantly agreed to the deal.

She spent the next few weeks keeping a low profile and only went down to the airfield once a week for a quick fly in the Tiger Moth. As long as she didn't perform any more antics like before, she was safe.

As the summer holidays drew to a close, the tension between Britain and Germany was at its height. So much so that Fitz had been denied access to the airfield.

'I'm sorry,' said Johnny. 'But no civilians are allowed on the airfield now. The RAF are going to be taking it over.'

'Are things that bad?' asked Fitz, pushing back a wisp of hair that had escaped from the pins.

'Yep. Things are going to kick off any day now with Hitler. That's the word on the base anyway. You mark my words.'

Fitz had cycled back to Badcombe House utterly dejected, not only at the thought of war, but at the idea of not being able to fly.

Gazing up to the sky as she cycled along Church Lane towards home, she caught sight of a plane, the engine growing louder as, turning, the pilot lined the aircraft up with the runway. He dropped lower and lower as he brought the plane into land. Fitz wished she was up there in the clouds.

Johnny's prediction turned out to be accurate. It was a week later when Fitz had been out for a cycle ride in the morning and had arrived back at Badcombe House, having deposited her bike in the garage.

Fitz came in through the kitchen and was surprised to see there was no sign of Cook or Annie.

She could smell the chicken roasting in the oven and the potatoes were simmering on the stove unattended. How odd. She glanced at the clock, it was just gone eleven-fifteen.

Fitz left the kitchen and went through to the front of the house. From the sitting room, she could hear someone talking on the radio.

'This is London. You will now hear a statement from the prime minister.'

Fitz stepped into the room and was surprised for the second time that morning to see not only her father and Camilla sitting by the radio, but Cook, Annie and George the gardener were standing there, too.

Her father looked up at her but didn't smile. With his brow furrowed and his mouth downward, Edward looked incredibly worried, and fear coursed through her. His eyes were dark with consternation. The last time she'd seen such a grim expression on his face was when he had told Fitz her mother had died.

Neville Chamberlain's voice was the only sound in the room.

'I am speaking to you from the Cabinet Room of number ten, Downing Street . . .'

Edward silently beckoned her over. Fitz perched on the arm

of the chair, clutching her father's hand. She looked around at the others in the room. Every single one of them looked incredibly solemn as they focused on the radio broadcast. A few minutes later, it was over.

'Oh, dear Lord,' said Cook, her hand going to her throat. 'We're at war.'

Chapter 3

Fitz wasn't sure what she was expecting to happen once war had been declared. To begin with, essentially, nothing changed in her day-to-day life, but she felt on tenterhooks, as if she was waiting for something to happen. She just didn't know what.

With Michael's boarding school and, indeed, Fitz's finishing school now ruled out, the new governess came in mid-September and largely, Fitz had nothing to do with her. Miss Winters was there for the sole purpose of teaching Michael. Fitz's twenty-first birthday came and went in a very subdued manner. No frivolous party or extravagant meal. It hadn't seemed right to celebrate her entrance into adulthood now the country was at war.

To keep herself busy and to do what she could to aid the war effort, Fitz had joined the Women's Land Army and, much to her surprise, had earned some praise from Camilla. It wasn't often Fitz managed to do something her stepmother approved of. Her father had been even more pleased when she had gone to work at a local farm owned by Jack Howard, whose son had been called up, with Fitz taking his place.

'I thought you might end up in a different part of the country,' said her father when she'd told him where she had been assigned. Personally, Fitz wouldn't have minded a change of scenery, but she acknowledged there were advantages to being able to eat and sleep at her own home.

She'd heard some of the land girls were having it quite rough, with not very comfortable digs and apparently one of the girls from Badcombe village was having to sleep in a hay loft.

For the most part, Fitz enjoyed her work on the farm where she spent her days driving the tractor and moving bales of hay about for the animal feeds. The winter saw an extremely hard frost which lasted months rather than weeks into 1940, making getting up before dawn most mornings quite a struggle.

Fitz had to cycle in the dark down to Jack Howard's farm due to the blackout and on more than one occasion misjudged the roadside and ended up in a ditch or a hedge.

The warmer weather of spring, together with lighter mornings and evenings, couldn't come too soon for Fitz. It was now mid-May, and Winston Churchill had been elected as the new prime minister to take over from Neville Chamberlain. When Fitz arrived at the farm, she could tell straight away that Jack was not in the best of spirits. His frown was as deep as the furrowed fields.

'Morning, Jack,' said Fitz.

'If you say it is,' came the reply which confirmed her assessment of his mood.

'Is everything all right?' she ventured, taking off her regulation issue land-girl coat. The cycle ride to the farm had already warmed her up.

'No. I take it you haven't heard the news?'

Fitz shook her head. 'I went straight to bed last night.' She had been so tired; she'd had her evening meal and taken herself upstairs foregoing her usual habit of sitting by the radio with her father to listen to the latest news on the war.

'We're pulling out of Dunkirk,' said Jack. 'We're running from Hitler.'

'Really?' Fitz was surprised. From what she'd gathered from her father and, indeed, Jack, Winston Churchill was a no-nonsense fighting man and was determined to stand up to Hitler. 'Why are we withdrawing?'

Jack tutted. 'Underestimated the Jerries, didn't he? Old Churchill.'

The Germans had invaded France the previous week and with little resistance from the British Army, they looked set to storm their way right through to Paris in a short space of time. And then, as Fitz had heard people in the village shop saying, Hitler would have his sights set on Britain.

Although concerned, Fitz hadn't felt especially worried, and when she'd spoken to her father about it, he'd assured her that Britain would stand fast. She wondered now if her father had really believed that or was simply trying to protect her from the truth. It all sounded very real and not just village gossip.

'What's going to happen now?' she asked, hearing the uncertainty in her voice.

'Well, get our boys home, regroup and decide what to do next,' said Jack. 'I don't think sending the boys back over there is going to work, not when they've just sent us packing. It will have to be in the air we fight them.'

There had already been numerous German bombing raids on the country, but they had thus far been military targets. 'Will the Germans keep bombing us?' asked Fitz.

'Look, I don't want to worry you or anything, Fitz,' said Jack, 'but in my humble opinion as a farmer, yes they will. And it will only get worse from now on.'

As the days went by Fitz was glued to news of the Dunkirk evacuation as it began to filter in through the media. She couldn't help noticing the different tone in which they were reporting. Unlike Jack, who was all doom and gloom, the newspapers were making it sound like a positive thing and not the rearguard action Jack had come to call it.

Fitz never missed an opportunity to listen to the radio or read the newspapers – not through excitement like some of the young boys in the village who were running around with sticks and 'shooting' each other – but through a certain amount of fear and a desire to know. Possessing knowledge made Fitz feel more involved somehow, more aware so she could come to her own conclusions. It gave her a sense of control, in as much as anyone could have in the circumstances.

By the beginning of June, a truer picture of the withdrawal was beginning to emerge, along with stories of just how awful those days on Dunkirk beach really were, not to mention the enormous loss of life and the Navy destroyers, ironically, destroyed.

It was brought into sharp focus when Fitz was at the farm one day and Jack received the dreaded telegram informing him his son had been a casualty at Dunkirk and had died on the French beach on the last day of the evacuation.

The news had broken Jack and his wife, Peggy. Their grief was raw and visceral. Fitz understood grief enough to know that losing a child, no matter how honourably, was the worst possible thing for a parent to experience.

After that, the mood around the farm had been heavy, with Jack showing little to no interest in what needed to be done. His whole purpose in life lost. He'd once told her he was only keeping the farm on so his son had something to come back to after the war.

Fitz found herself increasingly left to manage the day-to-day running of the farm. It was a two-man job really and she was having to work longer and longer hours trying to do everything. She'd had to resort to seeking advice from a neighbouring farm as she had no idea about what crops needed sowing and harvesting.

In the end, the Ministry of Agriculture stepped in and appointed a manager to take over the running of the farm. Jack and Peggy packed their bags and took what few possessions they had to go to live with Peggy's sister in the West Country.

Fitz had been sorry to see them leave. They were more casualties of this war and it was so unfair.

* * *

The weeks rolled on and there was no sign of the war ending, in fact, it was only getting worse. The German Luftwaffe had started a sustained bombing campaign across the country. Air-raid sirens and running to the Anderson shelter in the garden had become part of everyday life for Fitz, just as it had for the rest of the country. The only pleasure Fitz derived from the war, was watching the RAF fly overhead. Plane spotting had become quite a pastime for her and Michael. He'd started up a journal and was recording the different types of aircraft he saw, and proudly showed Fitz each time he updated it.

Fitz had also become obsessed with spotting the Air Transport Auxiliary pilots flying planes around the country from one airfield to another or straight from the factory. She would love to do something like that, but when she had mentioned it in passing to her father, just to test the waters, one evening in late November, he had been adamant his daughter was not going to put herself in such danger.

'You know what they did to London,' he had said. 'They did the same to Coventry. Practically flattened the city and now Southampton is under attack. It's a firestorm there, by all accounts.'

It was true, the city was a prime target for the Germans. The Supermarine factory building where they manufactured Spitfires had been targeted earlier in the year, but it hadn't ended there. The Luftwaffe was regularly targeting the Hampshire city.

'I'll be delivering the planes to help the RAF. I won't be having dog fights with the Germans,' said Fitz.

'I don't want to discuss it any further,' said her father. 'Help the war effort by all means, but on the ground where I know you'll be safe.'

Fitz had managed to stop herself from arguing the point further with him. Even though she didn't want to go against her father's wishes, she debated whether she should simply go ahead with what she wanted to do in secret. By the time her father found out, it would be too late for him to do anything about it.

When a few nights later, Fitz overheard her father and stepmother discussing her, she knew she didn't have time to waste dithering over whether it was the right decision or not.

Fitz had been coming down the stairs and stopped mid-tread as the conversation between Edward and Camilla drifted through the open door of the drawing room.

'I know she's joined the Land Army,' Camilla was saying, 'but it's only at Jack Howard's old farm. I wondered if she could benefit from a change of scenery. She doesn't seem very happy these days. I think all this farm work is not good for her spirits.'

'But she's learning some life skills,' placated her father. 'She's doing her bit. I think she's happy as she is.'

He was wrong there, Fitz had thought. She obviously hadn't made it clear to him when she'd told him about wanting to join the ATA.

'Hmm, she could, of course, be doing something less . . . agricultural, shall we say,' continued Camilla.

'What do you mean by that?'

'I know you've ruled it out before, but you should reconsider. My elderly aunt could do with a companion. She's a very knowledgeable woman and would take Geraldine on any trips. I know it's not exactly finishing school, but you'd be surprised what a young woman like your daughter could learn from my aunt.'

Fitz scrunched her eyes tight shut at this turn in the conversation. She absolutely did not want to go to Scotland to be a companion to an old woman, aunt or no aunt to her stepmother. Fitz had already told her father this and she couldn't help being a little disappointed he wasn't more robustly refusing to entertain the idea. In fact, the silence told her he was mulling this over with more thought than she wished.

The Girl in the Sky

Camilla obviously felt she had him on the back foot as she rounded with another assault of persuasion.

'It will give her some more life experience,' she was saying. 'Scotland is a beautiful country and I know for a fact there are several eligible bachelors, with sizeable estates. She could do far worse than to find a husband in Aberdeenshire.'

'I'm not sure Geraldine is ready for marriage,' replied her father.

'Too bloody right,' Fitz whispered to herself.

'Whoever takes her on will have his hands full, that's for sure,' continued Edward.

'She just hasn't met the right young man, that's all,' said Camilla. 'Besides, she will be very safe in Scotland. Far safer than down here with all the bombings. Once Hitler has gained control of the skies, it will be an attack by land next. You said that yourself. Up in Scotland, Geraldine will be much safer.'

Fitz shook her head. Camilla was far more persuasive than she imagined. Using her father's own words against him.

'Maybe you and Michael should go with her?' suggested Edward.

'I'm not leaving you,' replied Camilla. 'My home is here at Badcombe House, and it will not do to run away, especially when not everyone in the village has the luxury of such choice. No, my duty is to serve the community in the best way I can.'

'That's very noble of you, darling,' said Fitz's father. 'You're a good woman.' He paused. 'What about Michael?'

'In times like this, a young boy needs his father more than ever,' replied Camilla. 'He will one day inherit Badcombe House, and he will need to understand its history and the history of the village. He's at a very impressionable age and you are the man to set the example for him. Sending him away to stay with my aunt is not going to make a man of him.'

Fitz had to clamp her hand over her mouth to prevent herself from gasping out loud. Camilla was a cunning fox. She simply wanted rid of Fitz, that was all.

'I'd never thought of it like that,' she heard her father reply. 'If you organise it with your aunt, I'll speak to Geraldine, and we can arrange for her to go in the new year.'

'Excellent. I'll do that at once.'

Fitz slid back into the shadows of the staircase as Camilla opened the door of the drawing room. She certainly wasn't wasting any time in contacting her aunt that was for sure.

Fitz felt a sting of unexpected tears prick her eyes. She wanted to be cross with her father but instead she pitied him that he had been so easily swayed by Camilla's scheming.

'Oh, darling,' came her father's voice. His wife stopped in the doorway and turned to him. 'Let me tell Geraldine.'

'Of course. Maybe tell her it was your idea. She'll accept it better that way.' With that Camilla bustled across the hallway towards the library. No doubt to contact her aunt.

It was just over a month later, the start of 1941, when Fitz's father informed her of the decision they'd made on her behalf. Fitz didn't argue or protest. She sat patiently on the sofa of the drawing room while her father explained his reasoning. She was only half listening. His speech was purely a formality. There was no discussion to be had.

She looked across the room and through the French doors of the first-floor sitting room which led out onto a veranda overlooking the grounds of Badcombe House.

The trees were bare of their leaves, the branches stark against the murky patchwork of the grey and white sky.

She had missed being airborne but knew it wouldn't be long before she was up in the sky again.

'Did you hear me?'

Fitz turned her attention back to her father and realised she had been daydreaming. 'Yes. Yes, I did,' she replied. 'You want me to go to Aberdeenshire as a companion to Camilla's aunt. And for my own safety.'

Her father eyed her with a mix of surprise and suspicion. 'And you're happy with that?'

Fitz smiled, as she mentally pulled the ace from her sleeve. 'Actually, it won't be necessary to send me to Aberdeenshire,' she said. 'Whilst I appreciate the thought it's been given, you won't need to consider me for much longer.'

Her father frowned. 'What are you talking about?'

'I've signed up to join the Air Transport Auxiliary service.' The sense of satisfaction at that announcement lifted her spirits. She didn't want to hurt her father but sure as eggs were eggs, she wasn't going to Aberdeenshire.

'What? You never said? You didn't consult me?' her father blustered.

'I wasn't consulted about Aberdeenshire,' replied Fitz. 'However, I'm twenty-two years old and, as such, I don't need to consult anyone.'

'Well, I won't let you go,' said her father. 'I don't agree with this ridiculous notion of joining the ATA. What on earth do you plan on doing there? I thought you enjoyed working as a land girl.'

'Look, I've been working as a land girl for the past year, working for the ATA is no different. Instead of tractors, it's aeroplanes. It would be such a waste of time and money not to put my skills as a pilot to good use.'

'But you can always fly after the war,' protested her father. 'At least working on the farm, you're safe and if you did go to Aberdeenshire, even safer.'

'You're not listening to me,' said Fitz. 'I don't want to go to Aberdeenshire. It would be my worst nightmare come true. I'd be bored silly and end up getting myself into bother trying to find something fun to do.' She met her father's gaze. 'I wouldn't want to embarrass Camilla.'

Her father raised his eyebrows. 'That sounds remarkably like blackmail to me.'

'Now, why would I do that?' Fitz gave her most angelic smile.

Edward gave a grunt. 'Why, indeed?'

Fitz leaned forward. 'Please, Pa. I really want to do this. I'm old enough to join with or without your blessing.'

There was a look of sadness on her father's face. 'You remind me of your mother at times like this,' he said, picking up the photograph of Fitz's mother that he kept on his desk, alongside one of Camilla. 'She knew her own mind, too.' He studied it for a moment before setting it back down. 'Truth be told, the thought of something happening to you . . .' His voice trailed off.

For a moment Fitz was taken aback by her father's openness. He rarely showed any vulnerability. She went around to his side of the desk and crouched down, holding his hand.

'I promise I'll be safe,' she said. 'I'm a good pilot. You know that. I won't do anything reckless. I need to do something more tangible than drive a tractor up and down a field. With the ATA I'll be on home ground; well, air and zipping about in planes.'

Her father was silent, and Fitz watched him mentally adjust his stance on the whole subject. His shoulders dropped and he let out a defeated sigh. 'I don't suppose I'm going to be able to change your mind.'

She shook her head. 'No. This is what I want to do,' she said, not unkindly. 'I'm not cut out to be a lady's companion.'

'You weren't surprised when I told you.'

'No. I overheard you and Camilla talking,' she confessed.

'She was only thinking of your safety,' said Edward. 'We both were.'

'I'd like to think that were true,' replied Fitz, choosing her words carefully so as not to upset her father.

Edward let out another sigh but also smiled. 'Well, I'd sooner you didn't join the ATA, but I also know the importance of not simply wanting to do your bit, but your need for autonomy. I suppose I must face the fact you're not a child anymore but a young woman with her own mind.'

Fitz hugged her father. 'Thank you, Pa.'

'Please be careful, though,' said Edward. 'No fly-pasts or looping the loop.'

'I promise I'll be on my best behaviour.'

He squeezed her hand. 'So, when do you start?'

'In a couple of months' time,' said Fitz, standing up. 'I have to report to Central Flying School in Maidenhead at ten o'clock on the fourth of March.'

Edward got to his feet and hugged Fitz. 'I'm very proud of you and you have my blessing. Your mother would be proud of you too.'

And that last sentence meant the world to Fitz.

Chapter 4

March 1941

'Don't be sad,' said Fitz, giving Michael a hug. 'I'll be able to come back and see you when I'm on leave and, you never know, I might be back here in Badcombe one day delivering a plane. I'll come and see you.'

'Promise?' asked Michael, looking up at his sister with teary eyes.

'Of course, I will. And I'll write to you anyway and tell you about all the planes I get to fly and all the places I'll be visiting.'

Michael gave a small smile.

'Come along, now,' said Camilla, placing her hand on her son's shoulder. 'Don't be crying. Geraldine has to leave now.'

'Goodbye, Camilla,' said Fitz, embracing her stepmother briefly. It felt odd to have this kind of personal contact with the woman.

Camilla patted Fitz's back and pulled away. 'Good luck,' she said.

'We need to go otherwise you'll miss your train,' called her father, getting into the driver's side of the car. He was taking her to Badcombe train station for the first leg of her journey to Maidenhead.

The Girl in the Sky

Fitz climbed into the car next to her father and waved from the passenger window all the way down the drive.

'Don't worry about Michael,' said her father. 'He'll be all right.'

'I know. I do feel a bit guilty leaving him,' admitted Fitz, although the excitement at joining the ATA far outweighed any sense of duty to stay in Badcombe.

The parting with her father was perhaps more emotional than Fitz had anticipated. He hugged her tightly and kissed her cheek.

'I will miss you,' he said, with a soft smile.

'I'll miss you, too,' she replied, feeling a genuine wave of sadness wash over her.

'You're not allowed to,' said her father. 'You're to go and enjoy what you're doing. All I ask is two things. That you'll keep in touch and write to Michael often.'

'Of course.'

'And that you'll be safe. Please stay safe.'

Fitz didn't miss the look of sadness in her father's eyes and she knew instantly what he wasn't saying was more powerful than his actual words. The unspoken message that he'd lost his first wife and didn't want to lose his daughter might as well have been signposted above him.

'I promise I'll be safe, Pa.' She hugged him again before clambering onto the train. Her father boarded with her to put her case in the overhead luggage rack before disembarking just as the platform guard blew his whistle and waved his flag at the driver.

Fitz stood at the door with the window slid down and waved furiously to her father as the train pulled out of the station. She would miss him. She knew she would, but she couldn't afford to dwell on those emotions.

She sat back down in her seat and smiled to herself at the start of her new adventure.

As the train steamed its way through Cambridgeshire, Fitz watched the passing countryside. The telephone lines running along the side of the railway line were hypnotic as they rose and fell in time with the rhythm of the train.

St Neots heralded a change of trains, and this one was rather busier than the one before. There were several carriages packed with service personnel where it looked to be standing room only. Fitz was lucky in that her father had bought her a first-class ticket and she was able to sit for the journey.

Eventually, the train pulled into the railway station. As Fitz slid down the window to open the door from the outside, she looked down the train and was surprised to see about twenty to thirty military personnel disembark further down the platform.

She stepped off the train and onto the platform, placing her suitcase down on the ground while she took a moment to work out where she was supposed to go. The letter had said there would be transport to meet her.

'Hello, there,' came a woman's voice. 'Are you here for CFS?'

Fitz looked at the young woman coming to a halt in front of her. She looked to be about Fitz's own age, maybe a little older, and had her brunette hair pulled back into a neat pleat. She was wearing a tweed styled suit.

'Yes, that's right. Geraldine Fitz-Herbert.' She held out her hand to the woman.

'Ooh, Geraldine Fitz-Herbert, now there's fancy,' replied the woman with a grin. She shook Fitz's hand. 'Elsie Sullivan. Single barrelled.'

Despite the obvious teasing, Fitz took an instant shine to the woman. 'Most people call me Fitz,' she said.

'Thank God for that. Much less of a mouthful.'

'Are you here to join the ATA?' asked Fitz.

'I most certainly am,' replied Elsie. 'I take it that's what you're here for?'

Fitz nodded. 'That's right.' From over Elsie's shoulder she saw several soldiers standing in a group, looking over at them.

One of them smoking a cigarette, put his finger and thumb in his mouth and let out a long high-pitched whistle as he openly looked Fitz and Elsie up and down.

'Hello, girls!' he called out. 'You look lost. Do you need help?'

Elsie rolled her eyes at Fitz and turned to face the group. Before she could say anything, Fitz called back to them.

'If we need any help, we'll ask one of the men.' She nodded towards three uniformed airmen striding down the platform. One of them heard her and slowed as he took in the scene before him and then made a beeline for Fitz.

'Sweetheart!' he called out, walking right up to her and kissing her cheek. 'Glad you got here safely.'

'Oh, darling, you're here,' replied Fitz. 'Oh, I'm so pleased to see you,' she said, continuing the farce. She couldn't help noticing how handsome the man was. And what was with the American accent? How odd. His dark hair was cut short, but the front left a little longer and combed back. He had the most amazing blue eyes, she'd seen, almost as blue as his uniform.

One of his companions put an arm around Elsie. 'Hello, baby,' he said. With his back to the Englishmen, he winked at Elsie.

Fitz looked over at the British soldiers who were watching the scene play out.

The American turned to the men. 'Can I help you boys with anything?'

'Boys? Sod off, mate,' said the soldier. He gave a derisory glance in Fitz's direction, before spinning on his heel and practically pushing his group out of the station.

'Thanks for that,' said Elsie. 'And sorry. I guess some of the British lads forget how to treat a lady.'

Fitz didn't miss the eye flutter her new friend offered the Americans and internally bristled at the notion she needed someone to look out for her. 'We did have that covered, you know. I could handle them myself.'

The American eyed her with amusement. 'Sure. I have no doubt, but I needed an excuse to come talk to you.'

Fitz raised her eyebrows. 'Is that so?'

'Certainly is, Ma'am.' He gave a quick salute. 'Flying Officer Sam Carter, at your service.'

'Well, Flying Officer Sam Carter, you've done your good deed for the day and we won't keep you any longer.' Fitz offered a tight smile to Carter and to the other airman, before picking up her suitcase and holding her head up high, walked towards the exit. After a few moments, she heard Elsie's footsteps clattering behind her as she hurried to catch up.

'What's the rush?' asked Elsie, falling into step alongside Fitz. 'I was quite enjoying myself there for a moment.'

'Maybe so, but I didn't want to encourage them. We're not pieces of meat that can be fought over.'

'Ooh, get you,' said Elsie. 'Lady Fitz-Herbert. Honestly, you can tell me, you've got to be a lady with a name like that and an accent like cut glass.'

It wasn't said with any malice and Fitz found herself smiling. She slowed her pace. 'Sorry to disappoint you but I'm not a lady.'

'But you're posh.'

'That's a matter of relativity,' said Fitz. 'Come on, we need to find our transport.'

They made their way through the ticket office. Something made Fitz glance back at Sam Carter. He was still watching her and gave her a wink. Fitz immediately looked away. She could feel the colour rising up her neck.

'Why have you got that silly smile on your face?' asked Elsie.

'I haven't.' Fitz forcibly schooled her face into a neutral expression.

They exited the ticket office and stood on the pavement, looking around for their transport to the CFS. There were five other smartly dressed young women congregated further along, each with a suitcase.

Fitz approached them. 'Hello. Are you for the CFS?'

'Yes, we are,' said one of them. 'Marjorie Timpson.'

They all made their introductions to each other, although Fitz wasn't sure she'd remember their names straight off but they all seemed a likeable bunch.

An army lorry started its engine and, packed with soldiers, pulled away from the pavement. Fitz noticed one of the soldiers at the back was the chap from the platform. He spotted Fitz.

'See you later, beautiful!' he called out, blowing a kiss in her direction, which caused laughter amongst the men.

'Is that your boyfriend?' asked Marjorie.

'You must be joking,' said Fitz, resisting the urge to shout something wholly inappropriate at the soldier. 'Wouldn't be seen dead with him.'

'Eyes up, girls,' said another of the women.

Everyone looked ahead as Flying Officer Sam Carter and his friend appeared from the ticket office. He glanced their way and made eye contact with Fitz and smiled at her.

Fitz held his gaze, not blinking, in a game of brinkmanship she didn't know why she'd entered. Goodness, he needed to stop looking at her like that. And as for that smile. He had no business to flash that around.

Sam did, in fact, break his gaze first and climbed into a waiting car, which drove them away.

Fitz let out a sigh of relief.

'Did you see that?' exclaimed one of the women.

'How could you not?' said another.

'Seemed like he had eyes for you,' said Marjorie to Fitz.

'You can't take any of them seriously,' replied Fitz, attempting to sound flippant.

'Well, if you don't want him,' said one of the women who Fitz thought was called Betty. 'You can send him my way.'

'You'd be very welcome to him,' replied Fitz, though not entirely sure she was being truthful.

The conversation was interrupted as a bus pulled up

alongside the group. The doors swished open and the driver called out to them. 'You for the flying school? Get on.'

Once at Central Flying School, things moved apace. Fitz and her newly found companions were officially enrolled, issued with their uniform and assigned their living quarters. It was ten of them on this intake and they all shared a dormitory, which was essentially a wooden hut.

'A bit different to what you're used to, I expect,' said Elsie, as they plonked their armfuls of uniform and luggage down on their beds.

'Probably a bit different to what we're all used to,' said Fitz. From their conversations travelling from the station, it was fair to say, all of the women had come from a more privileged background, having already had experience in flying. None of them were new to the skies and you only got that experience if you were lucky enough to have the money to do so. However, Fitz knew she was perhaps at the higher end of that financial privilege.

'I suppose so,' conceded Elsie.

'So, what made you sign up?' It was Marjorie, who had claimed the bed across the room from Fitz.

'I love flying and this is the only way I get to be in the sky,' said Fitz. 'Plus it's helping the war effort. What about you two?'

Marjorie shrugged. 'Pretty much the same thing. I wanted to do something useful, and this seemed the perfect solution. Besides, I have two older brothers and they are both in the air force. I didn't want to be the odd one out. I've never let them outdo me before, so I don't intend to start now.'

Fitz smiled. She liked Marjorie. Very no-nonsense.

'I couldn't bear the thought of milking any more cows,' groaned Elsie, opening her suitcase. 'If I never see another glass of milk again in my life, it won't be a moment too soon. Plus they are smelly bloody things. Eh.'

Fitz laughed along with Marjorie.

'Mind if I camp here?' came a voice. The young woman Fitz thought was called Betty stood by the bed next to Marjorie.

'Be my guest,' replied Marjorie. 'It's Betty, isn't it?'

'Thanks. Yes, that's right. Betty Anderson.' The redhead smiled at the trio. 'Nice to meet you all.'

As they unpacked their suitcases, the four women chatted amongst themselves, exchanging information on where they lived and what they had been up to prior to the war and since it had broken out. They, of course, all had the same thing in common – their love for flying and their sense of duty. Becoming a ferry pilot, ferrying the aircraft from one place to another, was the perfect role for them.

That night when Fitz went to bed, she had a sense of belonging. Something she wasn't sure she'd ever experienced before. She'd never felt she had fitted in well anywhere, and often felt the odd one out amongst her contemporaries. When her mother had died, the sense of being the odd one out was exasperated. All her friends still had both parents alive. Even from an early age, Fitz could see the pity in the grown-ups' eyes that she had only her father to look after her. It wasn't a feeling Fitz had enjoyed and in fact she had rebelled against it. She'd done everything she could to find happiness and to prove to them she didn't need their pity. She had dated several young men in the past few years, much to Edward and Camilla's disapproval, and had ignored their requests that she modify her behaviour and not skip from one boy to another. Fitz always found the start of a relationship fun and exciting but the thrill soon fizzled out, especially when the men seemed to be one step ahead of her and within a couple of months were talking marriage. Settling down was high on Camilla's agenda for Fitz, but Fitz didn't want that because with marriage would come responsibilities and babies, neither of which she was ready for. She wanted to enjoy life and be free of societal expectations. In the air, she'd always found that freedom, and she wasn't giving that up for anyone.

Flying had become her happy place.

And now she was amongst women who loved the skies as much as she did. She'd found her family.

Chapter 5

Training was just as much fun as Fitz imagined it would be. If not more. The first plane Fitz and the other ATA women were taught to fly was the de Havilland Tiger Moth and as this was Fitz's choice of plane prior to signing up with the ATA, she was perfectly at home in the cockpit.

'You made a decent fist of that flight,' said one of the instructors after her first time in the air. 'Need to clock up a few more hours, though.' He scribbled something on his clipboard that Fitz couldn't read. 'You also need to take that lipstick off. Can't have you flying into RAF stations all done up like a dog's dinner.'

'A dog's dinner!' Fitz could barely contain her outrage at the remark as she unfastened the chin strap of her leather flying helmet. She was well aware of the prejudices against female aviators from her time at the airfield, but she hadn't been expecting this level of chauvinism from a senior ranking airman.

The instructor looked up and pointed his pen at her. 'Before you say anything you'll regret, I suggest you read the handbook you were given. You may be a civilian ferry pilot but you are to abide by the rules and regulations just as a serving member of the air force does. And that includes no make-up.'

Fitz wasn't sure if that was strictly true but she didn't want to risk being sent home, that would be worse than not wearing her favourite red lipstick.

'Yes, sir,' she said dutifully, marvelling at her own restraint and how her father would be amazed at her deference.

That evening in the dining hall she voiced her outrage to her friends. 'And if he thinks I'm going to stop wearing my lipstick, he's another think coming.'

'Oh, Fitz, you're going to get yourself in trouble,' said Elsie. 'Are you always this rebellious?'

Fitz shrugged. 'Why is it a woman is rebellious but a man is a maverick?'

'Because it's a man's world, my dear,' said Marjorie.

'Well, it's wrong,' said Fitz. 'I mean, look how many women are doing men's jobs now there's a war. It just goes to prove we're as good as them.'

'It's a shame women don't get paid as much as men,' said Marjorie. 'Us women get ten shillings a week less for doing the same work. It's outrageous, but what can we do?'

'Complain, for a start,' said Fitz. 'We wouldn't be here training to be ferry pilots if we weren't essential. The ATA was only formed to ferry mail, medical supplies and personnel about but look at it now, we're moving planes about the country.'

'It's going to take more than a war to change the attitude of generations,' said Elsie.

'It doesn't mean we have to accept it, simply because that's the status quo,' said Fitz. 'Things are changing and people's attitudes will need to change. By people, I mean men in particular.'

'And you're going to change it, one lipstick at a time,' said Marjorie, taking a packet of cigarettes from her pocket.

The other girls laughed and Fitz found herself smiling, even though she was still determined to make her point and push back against the patriarchy.

The rest of the week passed and Fitz soon found herself in the rhythm of CFS: up early for breakfast, dressed in her flight gear and out on the runway by nine o'clock.

There were several hours of flying throughout the day,

with and without instructors, aeroplane type permitting. She found some of the exercises rather tedious but they had been told under no circumstances were they to perform any type of aerobatic manoeuvre or travel at any excessive speed. Their job was simply to fly the aircraft at the most efficient speed and height so as not to cause any undue stress or damage to it when it was delivered to the RAF.

It was with ease that, at the end of their first month's training, Fitz and the rest of her class all officially qualified as ferry pilots for the de Havilland Tiger Moths and were moving onto Magisters and Proctors next.

Most of the women were already at home in the Tiger Moths. During their evening conversations, Fitz learned that both Marjorie and Betty belonged to the Biggin Hill flying school while Elsie was part of the Brooklands club. Although Fitz hadn't been part of any of the prestigious flying clubs nearer to London, she didn't feel in the slightest bit intimidated. In fact, she revelled in her rather innocuous passage into the world of flying, albeit because her father was wealthy enough to support her passion. She was well aware that it was a privilege.

'I'd love for every girl, whatever her background, to be able to have the opportunity to fly,' she mused one night when they were sitting in the mess room, drinking their late-night cocoa. They had been at flying school for six weeks now and already halfway through their training 'How fantastic would that be?'

'The way this war is going, it might not be long before every girl can have the opportunity,' said Marjorie.

'Really? What have you heard?' asked Betty. 'I mean, I want the war to be over, of course I do. But selfishly, that means our flying days will be rather humdrum after all this.'

'I overheard one of the instructors talking to someone and saying there is going to be a big push to get people to join the ATA.' She looked over at Fitz. 'So, Fitz, darling, your dream of every girl in the sky might be closer than you think.'

'Did you hear that chap who was in the canteen earlier?' asked Marjorie. 'Complaining loud enough for me to hear about how women should stick to planting vegetables and making bread.'

'Anyway, enough of all this talk,' said Elsie. 'We should all get to sleep. We've got to be up early tomorrow for dawn flying.'

The following morning the women all reported to Hangar 202 at 0600 hours, kitted out in their flying gear, having had a very early breakfast.

'I could do with another coffee,' said Marjorie, as they waited for the instructor to appear.

'Me, too,' said Fitz. 'To think before I came here, I was a strictly tea and toast girl in the mornings. Now I'm coffee and ciggy.'

'Morning, ladies,' came the instructor's voice as he entered the hangar. 'Nice to see you all bright eyed and bushy tailed.' He stood in front of them, casting his eyes down the piece of paper attached to his clipboard. 'So, who fancies taking a Spitfire out for a spin?'

Fitz stood a little straighter. She loved flying the Spits.

'Right,' continued the instructor. 'Fitz-Herbert, you take the Spitfire out and familiarise yourself with the south of England. You, too, Anderson.' He took two sheets of paper and handed one each to the women. 'There are your stop-off points. Be back in time for tea.'

'Yes, sir,' said Fitz, feeling absolutely giddy with excitement.

'Thank you, sir,' replied Betty.

As they made their way over to the Spitfires, Fitz slipped her arm through Betty's. 'We're in the Spits!'

'I know, good stuff, isn't it?' Betty's excitement, as with all her emotions, was rather more contained than Fitz's. 'Where shall we go first?'

Fitz consulted the list of airfields they'd been given, which

The Girl in the Sky

essentially took them in a loop, starting with RAF Tangmere, then Hamble, Northampton, Essex and back to Maidenhead. 'What about Tangmere? It's nearest.'

'Good idea.'

Within thirty minutes, Fitz was in the air as the first rays of dawn stretched across the horizon, casting a warm glow through the translucent clouds. She could hear the growl of the Spitfire's engine as it echoed through the stillness of the morning. She knew Betty wouldn't be far behind.

The planes were fitted with minimal equipment and the key instructions on how to fly the plane were on a ring-bound notebook, not that Fitz needed to refer to it for the Spitfire. The notebook was a place for pilots to jot down anything that would help other pilots when it came to flying. Fitz had already been warned that she wouldn't necessarily have experience in every single type of aircraft. It would be a case of reading up on the notes and then straight away flying the aircraft. She wasn't daunted by the fact. If anything, it was a challenge she was quite prepared to take on. Some of the men might not have faith in the women pilots, but she was on a mission to put that straight, one lipstick at a time, as Marjorie had joked.

With that thought in mind, she dove into the pocket of her flight suit and retrieved the roll-up red Max Factor lipstick and applied it expertly without a mirror. Thank goodness she didn't have to use a brush and palette.

Fitz looked back over her shoulder and could see the silhouette of Betty's aircraft. The sun had truly risen now and the sky was clear of clouds. She couldn't think of a place she'd rather be.

The flight to Tangmere was over far too soon for Fitz's liking, and as the wheels touched down onto the runway she was already thinking about the next leg of the journey.

Fitz taxied the aircraft off the runway and over to the side where a mechanic was waiting for her. She took off her helmet and shook her hair free from the confines of the leather, and then fluffed her blonde waves into what she hoped looked a tidy affair. She had brought a day bag with her and reached down to pick it up before climbing out onto the wing, bag in one hand and helmet in the other.

She smiled at the mechanic who was staring up at her with his mouth half-open. Fitz lifted her bag. 'Here, catch!' She dropped the bag down to him and then climbed down herself.

'This is a pleasant surprise,' said the mechanic. 'Not quite what I was expecting to see.'

'We're only here for a quick pit stop,' said Fitz. 'Be a darling and tell me where the canteen is.'

The mechanic cleared his throat. 'Of course. Well, I can do better than that. I can show you.' He ran his finger around the neck of his overall.

'Help Betty taxi in and you've got yourself a deal,' said Fitz. She did enjoy flirting with the ground crew when she got the chance. Where was the harm in it? A dash of light-hearted flirting never hurt anyone. In fact, it practically boosted morale.

A few minutes later, Betty was standing next to Fitz. 'Cup of tea?' she enquired.

'Of course,' said Fitz. 'This lovely chap is going to take us to the canteen.'

'It's Bob Allan,' said the mechanic.

'Hi, Bob.' Fitz smiled broadly. 'I'm Fitz and this is Betty.'

Bob shook hands with them both. Fitz couldn't help giving a rather coy look from up under her eyelashes. 'Nice to meet you, Bob. Before we go over, just give us a second to get out of these flight suits.'

Bob raised his eyebrows but said nothing as both Fitz and Betty unfastened their jackets, removed their boots and slid their trousers down. Each was wearing their dark blue ATA uniform underneath. Betty had sensibly opted for trousers that morning, but Fitz was wearing a skirt and stockings. From her bag, she whipped out a pair of low-heeled shoes and slipped her feet into them. 'There. That's better.' She turned to Bob expectantly.

The Girl in the Sky

Bob visibly swallowed. 'Erm. Yes,' he said hesitantly, clearly caught out by the quick-change routine.

'Right, Bob, be a darling and take us to the canteen. We're gasping for a cuppa,' said Fitz.

As they followed Bob across to the canteen, Betty nudged Fitz gently in the ribs. 'Stop it,' she mouthed silently.

Fitz simply grinned and winked at her friend instead.

The mess hall was busy as it was mid-morning and a lot of the crew were having their elevenses. A momentary hush descended over the room as Fitz and Betty made their entrance.

'Tea and coffee is over here,' said Bob. 'What would you like?'

'Oh, we have company,' said a British airman, getting to his feet. 'Good morning, ladies.' It was as if he'd only at that moment noticed. 'Where did you two appear from?'

'We were just touring the area and dropped in,' said Fitz.

The airman looked confused. 'You can't just drop in.'

'Oh, they can,' said Bob. 'Believe me, that's exactly what they've done.'

It took a second for the airmen to realise what Bob meant. 'Attagirls?' he said, eventually.

Fitz smiled. 'Of course. Not that the uniform gives it away.' She took the cup of tea Bob passed to her. 'We landed the two Spits out there.'

'Oh, Christ,' said the airman.

'And they landed them with ease, despite the crosswind today,' came a voice that was distinctly not English. Maybe American.

Fitz turned around and nearly spluttered on the mouthful of tea. Leaning against a bookcase on the other side of the room was Flying Officer Sam Carter. The American she'd seen at the railway station when she'd stepped off the train at Maidenhead.

There was a small curve of amusement to his mouth and Fitz guessed the shock registered clearly on her face.

She swallowed her tea and composed herself. 'Well, if it isn't . . .' she paused and looked up to the ceiling, as if trying to recall his name. 'Sam. Sam Carter. Didn't expect to see you here. You're turning up everywhere like the proverbial bad penny.'

There was a small chuckle from Bob. 'That's Flying Officer Carter.'

'Oh, is it?' replied Fitz nonchalantly, although she was dying to ask how an American had joined the RAF. And what a coincidence that she should meet him again.

Betty saved her the trouble. 'How are you in the RAF if you're American? Or are you Canadian?'

Sam pushed himself away from the bookcase and tapped one of the men sitting by the fireside on the shoulder. 'Why don't you let the ladies sit down?'

The airman got to his feet, albeit somewhat reluctantly, but he didn't protest. Fitz got a sense that Sam was well respected among the British pilots. 'Thank you,' she said taking the now vacant seat.

The other chair was swiftly vacated for Betty by another pilot. Sam stood by the fireplace and offered Fitz and Betty a cigarette each, which they both accepted.

'You didn't answer Betty's question,' said Fitz, blowing out the smoke.

'How I came to be here?' Sam asked.

'That's the one,' said Fitz.

'American father and British mother,' he replied.

'He charmed his way in,' said Bob. 'He could charm his way into anything, couldn't you, Sam?'

Sam didn't answer. Fitz could sense a self-assurance that the flying officer didn't feel the need to explain himself to anyone. Although there was a quiet and reassured confidence about the man, there certainly was no sense of arrogance.

Fitz was aware that not all the RAF pilots welcomed the ATA girls. The idea that a woman could fly a plane as well as, or indeed better than, some of the male pilots was alien to them. Still, it wasn't the first time she'd come up against such resistance. It only served to spur her on even more and there was nothing she liked better than putting the men in their place.

'So what are you both doing here today?' asked Sam.

'Our assignment is to familiarise ourselves with the south of England,' said Betty.

'And what better place to start than with RAF Tangmere,' said Sam.

'Yes, the Millionaire's Club, as I understand it,' remarked Fitz, casually looking around the room.

Sam shrugged. 'I guess so.'

Bob laughed. 'Our American Anglo pilot is being very modest. You know he's an Olympian.'

Now that did surprise Fitz. 'Really? In what sport?'

'Rowing. Men's eight,' said Sam, matter of factly, as if it was no big deal.

'And did you win? I have to admit I know nothing about rowing,' confessed Fitz. She'd never wanted to get into a boat in her life but for some reason she was inexplicably fascinated by this American Olympian Anglo pilot based in Britain. She had no doubt he won.

'Of course, Sam won,' said Bob. 'Gold.'

'Wow. That's impressive,' replied Fitz.

'He also went to Cambridge,' added someone else from the other side of the room. 'Quite the golden boy, aren't you, Carter?'

'Someone has to be,' replied Sam.

Another ripple of laughter rang around the room. Fitz got the feeling that Sam was popular amongst his contemporaries. The ribbing was gentle and she could sense the ease among the men.

'What made you swap a boat for a plane?' she asked.

'It sounded like good fun,' replied Sam.

Fitz had the impression there was more to it than that, but Sam didn't want to talk about it.

'And why did you want to join the ATA?' asked Sam.

Fitz held his gaze for a moment. 'It sounded like good fun,' she replied.

Sam laughed and lifted his teacup up to her. 'Touché.'

'So, what's Tangmere like?' asked Betty. 'Seeing as it is the Millionaire's Club.'

'Oh, Tangmere is pretty quiet,' said Sam.

'Yeah, most of the village has been seconded by the military,' said Bob. 'Only a handful of villagers left. The houses and everything are needed for the likes of us. Well, mostly the officers.'

'Not much nightlife,' said Sam. 'There's the pub and the church. A few more pubs in Chichester. That's three miles down the road but that's about it.'

'There's a satellite airfield nearby, if I remember rightly,' said Fitz. 'Westhampnett.'

'Someone's been doing their homework,' said Sam.

'She's not top of the class for no reason,' said Betty with a motherly pride. 'Our Fitz here is one of the best pilots in our group.'

'I've only had clearance for class one aircraft at the moment,' said Fitz. 'Hoping to get onto the twin-engined planes soon.'

'Those Spits are pretty good fun, though, I imagine,' said Sam.

'Oh, absolutely,' gushed Fitz. 'We love flying them. They are super fast.'

They chatted for about another twenty minutes or so, mostly about the aircraft and the war. Fitz thoroughly enjoyed talking to Sam, who seemed to take an interest in her personally. Asking where she was from and what it was like growing up with a governess.

'Ghastly,' confessed Fitz. 'Although I think rather more ghastly for the governesses than for me. I did manage to go through seven of them in ten years.'

'That's quite an achievement,' said Sam.

'Probably not one I should boast about,' said Fitz. 'My father would be horrified.'

'Gosh, we'd better get a move on,' said Betty looking at her watch. 'We've got to get around three more airfields today.'

It was with a great reluctance that Fitz said her goodbyes to RAF Tangmere, Sam in particular.

'It's been great talking to you,' she said.

'Likewise,' said Sam, holding the door open for her and stepping out into the hallway. 'If you're ever here again, let me know.'

'I'll be sure to do that,' replied Fitz.

She couldn't help grinning to herself as she crossed the tarmac to her Spitfire.

'Gosh you look like the cat who got the cream,' said Betty.

Fitz just grinned even more. There was no point denying it.

Chapter 6

'I'll see you at Hamble, then,' said Betty as she shrugged on her flying suit and pulled the helmet down over her hair.

Fitz had slipped on her trousers from her luggage and yanked off her skirt, managing to maintain her dignity. She was aware that Sam was standing in the doorway watching her leave. Oh, well, it wasn't like he could see anything. 'All right, Betty,' she called back. 'See you there.'

As Fitz pulled on her flying suit, Betty started the engine of her aircraft. Unusually, the engine spluttered and it took Betty another try to get it going properly before taxiing towards the runway.

Fitz's Spitfire started first time without any problem and she gave a wave to Sam as the chocks were removed from under her wheels and she was given the all-clear to follow Betty towards the runway. She watched as her friend's plane took off into the air.

Fitz prepared her own plane ready for take-off and was about to open the throttle and speed down the airstrip when she noticed Betty's plane seemed incredibly low.

A swell of panic rolled up from the pit of Fitz's stomach. Betty needed to gain height and speed. What on earth was she doing? There must be something wrong with the plane. The deep growl of her own engine was too loud for her to hear Betty's Spitfire, which might have been able to give Fitz an indication whether everything was all right.

She looked across to the hangar and could see Bob standing watching Betty. He was too far away for Fitz to see his expression properly but his whole body stance looked on edge. Then from behind him, she saw Sam coming across to join him.

Fitz looked back at Betty's plane, which had just about cleared the trees and was climbing into the sky but not fast enough. She watched for several more seconds and could see Betty was fighting to keep the Spitfire in the sky. She was turning back on herself and must be trying to reach the airfield again.

Immediately, Fitz manoeuvred her own plane away from the landing strip to give Betty every chance to touch down safely and to keep her own aircraft out of harm's way. The last thing Betty needed was to have to think about avoiding a crash of any description.

Fitz taxied swiftly back to the apron of the airfield and cut her engine. She unbuckled her harness and jumped out of the cockpit, onto the wing of the Spitfire. With one hand shielding the sun from her eyes she tracked Betty's plane. The engine was spluttering.

'Sounds like a spark plug is misfiring,' called Bob.

Fitz glanced down at him and could see the apprehension in his expression. She looked back over to the hangar where a couple of other crew members had come out. They all recognised the sound of an engine that wasn't working as it should.

This wasn't good.

Fitz fixed her gaze back on Betty's plane. 'Come on, Betty, land it,' she said out loud. The plane was losing height and speed far too quickly. It was spluttering now like someone was choking it.

'Come on!' shouted Bob. 'You can do it.'

The words of encouragement were all they had. Fitz felt totally helpless. No one could do a thing to help her friend.

The aircraft was turning in towards the airstrip now. It

was dangerously low to the trees on the perimeter of the airfield, the wheels skimmed over the top of the tallest branches.

'She's not going to make it,' said Bob before swearing not so quietly.

'You can do it, Betty!' cried out Fitz. She could hear the crack in her voice. The aircraft's engine cut out. There was a silence that filled the whole airfield. Fitz couldn't take her eyes off the plane. She clasped her hands together. 'Please God,' she begged. 'Please God, let her land it safely.'

The plane was dropping faster and faster.

It hit the runway with a thud. One of the landing wheels collapsed with the force of the impact and the airplane skidded sideways, sliding along on its belly. Sparks flew up from the undercarriage and body of the plane and it spun violently towards the left. The wing dug into the grass alongside the landing strip sending the plane into a tumble and nose diving into the ground.

Fitz jumped from the wing of the Spitfire and was hurtling across the airfield towards her friend. She could hear one of the pilots shouting at her to stop, but she ignored them. She had to get to Betty. The stench of aviation fuel assaulted her nostrils. They had been flying with full tanks of fuel and had barely used a fraction of it, with Tangmere being their first stop.

Before she made it another twenty yards, there was a huge explosion and the Spitfire burst into flames. The force of the explosion knocked Fitz from her feet and she landed on the grass with a thud, winding herself for a few moments.

She could hear a scream and for one awful second thought it was Betty but realised she was screaming as the single engined plane was engulfed in flames.

Fitz stumbled to her feet, her legs were wobbly and she fell to the ground. She got up again. She had to get to Betty. A vehicle sped past her. It was the emergency rescue truck, swiftly followed by an ambulance. As she began to run again, she was suddenly caught by something on her arm and tugged backwards.

'Don't go any closer!' shouted a male voice. 'It's too dangerous.'

'Betty! My friend Betty is in there!' Fitz struggled to free herself from the grip of the man, but he was too strong for her. She realised she was crying. 'Let me go!'

She momentarily registered it was Sam Carter who had grabbed her.

'Fitz! Stop!' he yelled.

Before she could respond, there was another huge explosion from the Spitfire. The whole aircraft was up in flames. Fitz let out a cry of horror, grabbing hold of Sam's arm, wanting to look away, yet unable to move.

Sam wrapped his arms around Fitz and held her close to him, turning her away from the sight of the aircraft.

Still holding her, Sam walked Fitz back towards the hangar but that was as far as Fitz would allow herself to be taken. 'I'm not leaving her,' she said through tears.

'All right, but no running off,' said Sam gently. He unbuckled her helmet and lifted it from her head with one hand, all the while keeping his other arm around her.

Fitz watched in horror as the fire crew tackled the blaze and then, amazingly, she could see two of them at the cockpit, pulling Betty's body from the fire. All she could do was watch as Betty was placed onto a stretcher and then swiftly transferred into the ambulance.

The vehicle moved at speed across the uneven grass of the airfield, towards the medical centre.

'You can't go there,' said Sam, as if reading her thoughts. 'Let the doc see to her. You'll only be in the way.'

Fitz wanted to argue but she knew Sam was right. She allowed herself to be led away back to the mess room where Sam sat her down in the same armchair she'd been in not fifteen minutes ago. Someone handed her a drink. She thought it might be port but she couldn't taste it as she downed it in one. The warmth of the alcohol heated her throat but all she could taste in her mouth was smoke and aviation fuel.

Fitz wasn't aware of time as she sat there waiting for news. It could have been five minutes or five hours. All she could think of was Betty. She was aware at some point of Sam asking her if she wanted to take her flying suit off and she nodded, unable to speak. She didn't really care if she sat in the suit all day but she allowed Sam to help her take it off so she would be more comfortable. She smoked the cigarettes that were passed her way but she didn't taste them. She didn't enjoy them. She didn't want them. She could feel her mind closing, tunnelling vision, her thoughts only of her friend. Fitz felt as if she was in some lucid dream that she couldn't quite shake herself fully awake from.

It wasn't until the door to the mess opened and the doctor stepped into the room that Fitz snapped back to attention.

She got to her feet, throwing her cigarette into the open fireplace.

The doctor looked at Fitz. His expression was grim. His gaze went to Bob and Sam who were standing either side of her. She felt Sam's hand cup her elbow, as if ready to steady her.

'I'm very sorry,' said the doctor. 'I'm afraid there was nothing we could do to save her.'

'Nothing?' repeated Fitz. This couldn't be true. She must have misheard. There must have been something.

The doctor shook his head. 'She was too badly burned. She never regained consciousness. We did everything we could. I'm sorry.'

Fitz looked at Sam as if seeking confirmation. She went to speak but no words came out.

'Why don't you sit down?' suggested Sam.

From nowhere anger swamped Fitz. She felt the burn of fury in her stomach. It exploded up through her chest, bursting through her throat. 'I don't want to sit down,' she almost shouted. 'What good will that do?'

A part of her brain knew she was being irrational. She fought to calm her emotions. She couldn't let the RAF chaps see her break down, that would be exactly what they were expecting of a woman. No, she had to keep her emotions in check.

She looked the doctor in the eye and stood taller, pushing her shoulders back and lifting her chin up. 'Thank you,' she said. 'I'll make sure Betty's family know.'

'I'll let them know back at Maidenhead,' said the doctor. 'I think maybe you shouldn't fly any more today. We can arrange for accommodation for you for the night. Tangmere Cottage will have a spare bed, no doubt.'

Fitz took a deep breath. Much as she would like to curl up in a ball and cry her heart out, she was damned if she was going to do it here. 'Thank you but I'll be fine,' she replied. Whilst she appreciated that the suggestion came from a good place, she was sure male pilots would not be afforded the same sympathetic treatment.

'Perhaps fly back to ATA training headquarters, then,' suggested the doctor. 'I'm sure you'll be needed there for a debrief of the incident today.'

Fitz nodded. She'd agree to this. It felt wrong to be heading off around the English countryside on what was essentially a jolly when one of her friends had just died. 'If you could let Maidenhead know, I'd appreciate that.'

The doctor nodded and exchanged another look with Sam, before leaving the room.

'Are you sure you're going to be all right flying back?' asked Bob.

Before Fitz could answer, Sam spoke. 'Of course, she will.' He looked at Fitz. 'It's like falling off a horse. You need to get up and get back on straight away. It's what you need.'

Fitz studied Sam's blue eyes, as blue as the vast open sky on a summer's day. He understood her. Understood her need to experience the adrenaline rushing through her veins. It was what she lived for. She was addicted to that rush. She needed that surge to remind herself she was alive and that life was for living. It was a balm for her heart.

She had known from the start that she and Sam had a connection, but she'd not been able to articulate it or explain it before. And now she was certain that connection came from a place of pain. She wondered what heartbreak he was harbouring.

'You're right,' she said. 'It's exactly what I need to do.'

'Maybe we should get some fresh air first,' suggested Sam. 'You won't be able to leave just yet, anyway. They've got to clear the runway.'

Fitz nodded. Again, he knew exactly what she needed. 'Thank you.' She turned to Bob. 'Thanks so much. Please thank the emergency crews, too.'

She followed Sam through the hallway and out the back of the mess hut. 'There's not much to look at around here,' said Sam. 'But we can take a walk down to the church, if you like.'

'I'm not a religious person,' said Fitz.

'Neither am I, but there's a peacefulness there. A sort of calm.'

They walked along the main road and took the turning for St Andrews Church.

'Thank you for this,' said Fitz.

'Anytime.'

They walked on in silence, coming to a halt at the gate to the graveyard. Fitz leaned back against the wall, closed her eyes and lifted her face up to the sky, absorbing the warm rays of the spring sun. She took several deep breaths. 'All this feels like an awful nightmare.' She opened her eyes and squinted against the sun, before looking down at her feet. Tears filled her eyes and she fought hard to keep them at bay.

'You know that British stiff upper lip isn't always a good

thing,' said Sam softly. He rested his hand on her arm as if to underline his words.

The small act of sympathy was too much for Fitz. The tears breached the lids of her eyes and streamed down her face.

Then Sam was holding her again. His strong arms enveloped her and she had an unmistakable feeling of safety. She allowed herself to be held, unsure when it was she had last felt that human touch of kindness. The depth of her emotion at losing Betty surprised her and she quietly allowed the feeling to show itself through her tears.

After a few minutes, when her silent crying had subsided, Fitz pulled away, rummaging in her pocket for a hanky to wipe her face. Sam beat her to it and produced a crisp white handkerchief for her to use.

'Thank you,' she said. 'And sorry.'

'Hey, you don't have to be sorry. It's not good to hold all that emotion in. You gotta let it out sometime.'

'I just didn't want to do it back at the mess,' confessed Fitz. 'That would only reinforce some of the views from the men that women shouldn't be doing this job.'

'You shouldn't let small-minded people bother you.'

She smiled. 'I don't usually, and I know you're right.'

'I get it sometimes here even as a man,' said Sam. 'Not everyone is happy to have a Yank in their midst.'

'Even though you're half British?'

'Sometimes I think that's worse than being a full American,' said Sam. 'It means they have to kind of accept me even if they don't want to.'

'Oh, I don't know,' said Fitz. 'From what I saw back at the mess, you're very well liked.'

'I am now. Here with 601 Squadron but it hasn't always been like that. I guess my connection with some of the guys back at Cambridge and then through White's in London made it easier.'

Fitz raised her eyebrows at the mention of the exclusive London gentlemen's club. 'White's? Impressive.'

'To be honest, I don't always get the British snobbery thing, but I have to confess, knowing the right people and mixing in the right circles has made it easier to be accepted.'

Fitz smiled. 'I love the way you're playing the long game.'

'Don't let on to the fellas back at the mess. You'll blow my cover.' He winked at her and Fitz grinned back at him and then immediately felt guilty. Here she was chatting and flirting with Flying Officer Sam Carter when her dear friend Betty had died just a couple of hours earlier.

She looked down and shook her head, embarrassed at herself. Then taking a deep breath, she straightened up. 'Right, I really need to get back,' she said, her tone a little sharper than she intended. It didn't do well to let her guard down. 'I need to get back to Maidenhead.'

'Sure,' said Sam.

They made their way back to the airstrip where the remains of Betty's Spitfire had been removed from the runway. Several of the ground crew were performing a walk of the strip to make sure all debris had been cleared so as not to cause another catastrophe.

'All set when you are,' said Bob coming over to where Fitz and Sam were standing. 'Your gear is over in the office.'

'Thanks,' said Fitz. 'I'll get changed now.'

'I'll wait to see you off,' said Sam.

Fitz returned several minutes later, kitted out in her flight gear once more. It wouldn't have bothered her getting changed on the airstrip but Bob had been sweet to put her belongings in the office.

Sam was waiting outside the hangar for her.

'Thanks for earlier,' said Fitz. 'I appreciate it.'

'No worries,' said Sam.

'I'll get your handkerchief washed and back to you for the next time I'm here.'

Sam smiled. 'I'm glad there's going to be a next time.'

They shared a smile of unspoken communication. Fitz wasn't sure what the feeling was that zipped through her stomach but the thought that he would be happy to see her again, matched her own sentiment. Once more, in some unfathomable way, she felt a connection to Sam. Maybe because of what they had just witnessed. As pilots they were both very much aware of the risks.

The flight back to Maidenhead was one of the loneliest Fitz had ever taken. For some obscure reason, it was worse than when her mother had died. Maybe because it brought the fragility of life into sharper focus. Her mother's death all those years ago, seemed like another lifetime. One when Fitz was a child and which as an adult now she could escape from, but death had found her again. Someone close to her, someone she cared about. She may have only known Betty a short time but they, together with Marjorie and Elsie, had formed a tight-knit bond. And now the four were three.

When Fitz reached the ATA training school, she was immediately taken to be debriefed and she gave an accurate and full report of what had happened. She managed to keep her emotions under control by imagining it was a scene from a film or a book. That way she could take a step back and report as a viewer or a reader rather than a participant. It was a tactic she employed when thinking about her mother. It was easier that way and she now needed to use it again.

'Well done, Fitz-Herbert,' said the chief instructor. 'Now, I don't wish to sound brutal but it's imperative you don't go away from here all upset. It won't do morale any good whatsoever. The last thing we need is anyone cracking under the pressure.'

'Yes, Ma'am,' replied Fitz solemnly.

'Good. Dismissed.'

When Fitz arrived back at her billet she was met by Marjorie and Elsie, who were both as shocked and upset as she was, but they too had been given the lecture on not lowering morale among the other ferry pilots.

When they sat around the log burner with their cups of coffee that night, they poured an extra one for Betty and quietly shed a few silent and private tears for their dear friend.

Chapter 7

May–July 1941

The rest of training went through quickly and uneventfully. Although Fitz, Marjorie and Elsie had all been devastated by Betty's death, they knew it was a harsh reality of what they were doing, and each and every one of the ATA pilots faced these dangers daily. There had been a funeral for Betty back in her hometown, and Fitz, Marjorie and Elsie had been given leave to attend, although it came with another kind but firm talk about not letting the incident affect them. Death was something all pilots faced and they needed to get used to it. In private they had grieved for their friend, but out on the airfield and up in the sky they had to put that loss to one side.

May arrived and Fitz, Marjorie and Elsie soon found themselves settling into full active duty at Number 15 women's ferry pool in Hamble. It was close to the aircraft production factory in Southampton and many of their assignments involved picking up new aircraft from the site and delivering them to various RAF airfields around the south of England. They worked thirteen days on, followed by two days off.

Once they'd delivered an aircraft they were often tasked with taking another plane somewhere else and then another plane back again. At the end of the day, it was up to the ATA crew to make their way back to Hamble whenever possible. This could be by whatever means of transport available – plane, train, or bus. If it wasn't possible, then they stayed overnight until they could either get back or were given another assignment.

Fitz loved the freedom being a ferry pilot offered, not to mention the different aircrafts she flew during the day. She could start the day off with a Spitfire, then transfer to a de Havilland and end the day flying a Hawker.

Fitz was in her element and was becoming well known among the air crew. Her penchant for ruby-red lipstick, changing out of her flight suit and into her uniform and heels, ready for a quick drink in the mess, was becoming legendary.

'You've got quite a fanbase,' said Marjorie one day after they had both delivered aircraft to one of the RAF bases and were heading back to Hamble ferry pool by train. In the mess the previous evening, the pilots had greeted Fitz enthusiastically and, according to Marjorie, were practically queuing up to buy her a drink. 'You're terrible for encouraging them.' She laughed good humouredly.

'Oh, it's only a bit of fun,' said Fitz. 'They're all good sports.'

'You could have your pick of the bunch.'

'You sound like my stepmother trying to marry me off,' said Fitz. She winked at her friend to show she wasn't cross.

'Don't you want to get married one day?' asked Marjorie.

'Maybe one day, but not now. I want to enjoy life and be my own person. Not be shackled to the sink and up to my elbows in dirty nappies.'

'Good for you,' said Marjorie. 'But I'm sure you'll meet someone one day who will make you think completely differently.'

Fitz wasn't sure her friend was right, and for now she was happy as she was, doing the things she enjoyed. The only downside was it came at the expense of being at war. She was very much aware that, as an ATA ferry pilot, her experience of war was extremely different to the men fighting it out on the ground in Europe and Africa. It was very sobering to hear of people she knew from Badcombe who had been killed fighting for their country – such young men with so much of their lives ahead of them, tragically cut short. It made her all the more determined to enjoy and savour every minute of her life, despite the awful circumstances. Life could be snatched away at any moment, she knew that from bitter experience having lost her mother, so Fitz wasn't going to waste a second of her life.

'Post for you, Fitz,' said Marjorie one afternoon after they had been out flying on what was the last week of training. She dropped the two letters into Fitz's lap.

Fitz looked at the handwriting. 'One from Pa and one from Michael,' she said, choosing to open Michael's first.

Master Michael Fitz-Herbert
Badcombe House
Little Badcombe

Cambridgeshire

13th May, 1941

Dear Geraldine
How are you? Are you flying lots of aeroplanes? Every time one goes over the house, I always look out of the window and wonder whether it's you up there. I've been keeping a log of all the planes that fly over, the time and what type they are. Have you been over Badcombe? If you do go over the house next time can you tip the wings or dive down, just so I know it's you?
Are you coming home on leave soon? I asked Pa if

I could come and see you but he said he didn't think that was possible because you don't get many days off and you could be anywhere in the country depending on what planes you were delivering and where.

You should see the garden! It's all been dug up to grow vegetables. Mummy said everyone must do their bit. There are posters in the village saying Dig for Victory. We have so many potatoes, I've been cycling down to the shop and leaving them there so people in the village can have some. We have a lot of carrots, too.

We are going to have some children from London to stay with us. Mummy said we will have two children who are brother and sister, like you and me. The boy is a year younger than me and the girl is two years younger so I'll be the oldest for once. I heard Cook say to Annie that Mummy lost a little girl but I don't know what she meant by that. Do you know anything about a little girl? I asked Cook and she said I shouldn't have been listening to grown-up talk and I wasn't to repeat a word of it. So I still have no idea what they meant. Maybe you can tell me?

I should go now. It's teatime and Cook wants me to help Annie pick some fruit to make a pie.

I really hope you can come and visit soon. It's awfully lonely in the house now you've gone. Pa said I wasn't to make you feel homesick by telling you that I miss you, so I had better not say anything.

With love from your brother
Michael

Fitz stumbled at the part where Michael had overheard Cook and Annie talking. Of course, Fitz knew exactly what they meant but she had no idea that Camilla had lost a child. Was it a miscarriage or a stillborn? If it had been after Michael was born, then how had Fitz not known her stepmother was expecting another baby, or more to the point, how had she not known Camilla had suffered a loss? Fitz cast her mind back over the years since Michael had been born. She couldn't remember Camilla ever being ill or bedridden or taken to hospital. When had this happened? And how didn't she know?

Fitz felt awful. Camilla had gone through a terrible experience and Fitz had been totally oblivious. Could she have done something to help her? Oh, God, even worse, had she done something to cause more anxiety? An unexpected pang of guilt shot through Fitz – an emotion she wasn't used to experiencing where her stepmother was concerned. She felt ghastly.

She wasn't quite sure how to respond.

'Everything all right?' asked Marjorie from over the top of the letter she was reading.

'Yes, fine,' said Fitz quickly. She wasn't ready to unpick the implications of Michael's letter. She needed time to think about it.

She opened her father's letter, hoping for some more uplifting news.

Edward Fitz-Herbert
Badcombe House
Little Badcombe

Cambridgeshire

20th May, 1941

Dearest Geraldine
I do hope this letter finds you well and you have settled in nicely to your role with the ATA.
Michael has written you a separate letter he tells me. He took himself off to the post office with it so I hope it has reached you.

I have some rather sad news to tell you, my dear. I heard today that your friend and flying instructor, Johnny Fisher has been killed flying over France. He was on a night-time mission, the details of which I don't know. His aircraft was shot down and there were no survivors. His name will be read out at church on Sunday and I know you will want me to pass on your condolences to his family.

Fitz's breath caught in her throat and she stopped reading as tears filled her eyes. Johnny Fisher was dead.

'Oh, no,' she gasped.

'Fitz, what's wrong?' Marjorie put down her letter.

Fitz couldn't speak at first. She looked up at her friend and shook her head.

Marjorie shot across the room and put her arm around Fitz. 'Bad news?'

Fitz nodded. It was the second time in only a few weeks that someone close to her had been killed during the war and as before, it hit home very differently than hearing and reading about strangers dying.

'Johnny Fisher. He taught me to fly. He's been killed in action,' Fitz finally managed to say.

'Oh, Fitz. I'm so sorry,' said Marjorie, hugging her friend tightly.

Fitz was grateful to have someone there. She pulled her handkerchief from her pocket and wiped at her eyes so she could read the paragraph again.

'He was shot down over France on a night mission,' said Fitz, dabbing at her nose. 'That's some consolation, I suppose. He was doing what he loved. When my time comes, I hope I'm in the sky, too.'

'Don't talk like that now,' said Marjorie. 'I know what you mean, but even so, we mustn't think about that. It's tempting fate, even though I don't believe the bloody thing myself but you know . . .' She made Fitz a cup of tea, adding extra sugar. 'You can have my ration for the day,' she said. 'You need it for the shock.'

Then Marjorie had sat back down in her chair with her letter. Fitz appreciated the gesture. Marjorie was pragmatic, as ever, and they both knew that dwelling on death was not a good thing. So Fitz instead thought of all the good times she'd had with Johnny and how much she had enjoyed learning to fly with him. He had been one of the few men not to dismiss her desire to be a pilot. He had never once said it wasn't a place for women. He had always encouraged her to pursue her dream and she would be forever grateful for his patience and expert teaching. If it wasn't for him, she wouldn't be where she was now.

Fitz drew in a deep breath and exhaled slowly, vowing to make Johnny proud of her and her flying. She'd never forget him.

It was a while before she picked up her father's letter again to finish reading it.

So, my dear, moving onto better news, Camilla has volunteered to take in two children from London and they arrive tomorrow. Michael is looking forward to having two new playmates. We are also taking in two pregnant women whose babies are due in the next six weeks. Camilla has turned the two rooms at the top of the house into nurseries. I think she's rather enjoying it all and I'm pleased she feels she has a purpose.

The village feels quite strange these days with no young men about, only those who have been declared unfit for duty but there are lots of young women here taking up the slack. You know, Geraldine, you can always come back and work on the farm as a land girl any time you like. Although I don't suppose you will, I just wanted to remind you that you can.

I do hope you can call to see us soon on one of your days off, preferably by conventional travel and not a Tiger Moth.
Fondest love
Pa

Had Fitz not received Michael's letter, she might have skimmed over the part in her father's correspondence where he spoke of Camilla. She would have probably rolled her eyes and sighed at her father proudly talking about what his wife was doing. Today, however, Fitz did none of those things. With the knowledge she now possessed, inadvertently relayed by her brother, she had a very different impression of Camilla.

Not only was Camilla taking in two children, she was also taking in two pregnant women. Fitz couldn't help wondering if it was to do with Camilla's own loss. Some women would shy away from having contact with children and babies, but here Camilla was, opening the doors of Badcombe House to them.

It was bittersweet, though, if that was the right term. How could Camilla do that for absolute strangers but had never been able to do that for Fitz? It stung a little and that feeling of rejection stayed with her for the rest of the day, nestled amongst the grief for her flying instructor.

The pub was busy that evening, and Fitz was glad of the distraction. There were two ATA pilots there who she hadn't met before. Two men, one of them older and probably too old for conscription, but the other could only be in his mid-twenties.

'Oh, look, two new boys,' said Fitz, as she, Elsie and Marjorie reached the bar. 'Always good to see some new faces.'

'Hello,' said the younger man. He held out his hand. 'Harry Broome.'

They exchanged greetings and introductions. The older chap was Reg Collins and both men had delivered aircraft to Southampton that day and were making their way back to Whitchurch airfield near Bristol the following morning.

'Can we get you a drink?' asked Harry.

'I'll have a G and T, thanks very much,' said Fitz, ignoring the warning look Marjorie shot her way. After the news Fitz had received today, she very much felt like letting her hair down.

'Ladies?' asked Harry.

Elsie and Marjorie politely accepted the offer and while Elsie struck up conversation with Reg, who it turned out came from the same neck of the woods as her, Marjorie sat next to Fitz.

It was like having a chaperone, which only made Fitz act up more than usual. She felt a deep anger at the loss of her friends. She didn't want to be angry but the other option was to cry and she couldn't do that, either. Not here in the pub, anyway. 'So, Harry, what brought you to the ATA?' she asked the young pilot.

Harry grimaced. 'Dodgy leg. I had Polio as a child. So whilst I might not be fit for active duty, I can damn well do my bit in the ATA.'

'Good stuff,' said Fitz. 'I mean, I'm sorry about the Polio but it's good you haven't let it hold you back. That really would be a waste.'

'Indeed,' replied Harry. 'And what made you want to fly planes?'

'I don't like to be outdone by the boys,' said Fitz, taking a sip of her drink. 'That would also be a waste.'

'Anything the boys can do, the girls can do, too?' suggested Harry.

'Girls can do better, I think the term is,' said Fitz.

'Is that right?'

'Absolutely.' Fitz downed the remainder of her G and T.

'Now that sounds like a challenge to me,' said Harry, his gaze fixed on her.

Fitz felt a sharp kick in the back of her leg. It was Marjorie. 'Take no notice of Fitz,' said Marjorie. 'She's teasing you. She does this all the time.'

'Who wants another drink?' asked Fitz, getting to her feet. 'My round.'

She went to the bar and Marjorie appeared at her side. 'Go easy, Fitz.'

'You're not my chaperone,' replied Fitz and immediately regretted sounding so terse with her friend. 'Sorry. I'm being mean. I'm in a bad mood. I don't even know what I'm doing chatting to that chap.' She didn't want to mention to Marjorie that her thoughts had regularly strayed to Sam Carter in the past few weeks, and she'd found herself daydreaming about the pilot rather excessively. It was somewhat unsettling that had been the case when she'd been having a bit of fun chatting to Harry.

'You're grieving for your friend. You're sad and you're a little angry,' said Marjorie.

'I should also go home,' said Fitz. She didn't know if Marjorie was right but coming to terms with the loss of Betty and Johnny, whilst simultaneously having pleasant thoughts about Sam, was confusing to say the least. She took out a few coins and slid them along the bar to her friend. 'Drinks are on me.'

With that she headed for the door and out of the pub. She felt bad about walking out on Harry like that but Marjorie was a good stick and she'd smooth it over for her. Fitz would make it up to her friend.

When she got home, Fitz made herself a cup of warm cocoa and took herself up to bed. An hour or so later she was still awake but pretended to be asleep when Marjorie and Elsie crept into the room. She didn't want to talk tonight. Her emotions were all over the place and she didn't know how she felt about anything, least of all how she even felt about herself.

The Girl in the Sky

* * *

The following morning when Fitz woke, she only felt slightly better than she had after the pub.

She rolled over and Marjorie was already dressed. She was always the first one up. Elsie's bed was empty and Fitz assumed she was in the bathroom.

'Sorry about last night,' said Fitz, pushing her hands under her pillow.

'You don't have to apologise to me,' said Marjorie, checking her reflection in the dressing-table mirror.

Fitz sighed and pulled the blanket over her head for a moment, before shoving it back down. 'It wasn't very gracious of me to run out on Harry like that,' she said, remembering with clarity what had happened.

'He was somewhat perplexed.' Marjorie slid another pin into her hair. 'I explained you'd had bad news and he was all right in the end. In fact, he said next time he was here, be sure to catch up with him again.'

'Sorry about dumping that on you,' said Fitz, sitting up as Elsie came into the room.

'Oh, our resident heartbreaker is awake.' Elsie dropped her wash bag on to the bed. 'Another casualty you notched up last night.'

'Don't,' said Fitz. 'Anyway, Marjorie just told me he was fine.'

'Spoilsport,' said Elsie. 'He was very nice. In fact, you might have competition the next time he turns up.' She gave her friend a wink.

'Be my guest,' said Fitz with a smile.

'Yes. Don't let a nice lad like him anywhere near Fitz. She's more than a match for him,' said Marjorie. 'Now, Fitz, get ready, otherwise you're going to miss breakfast. You know how Mrs Temple is a stickler for mealtimes.'

Although Fitz's heart was heavy with the news she'd received about Johnny, she reminded herself of her promise to live life to the full and not to waste any days she had on this earth.

'It won't take me long to get ready,' said Fitz, hopping out of bed. She might always be the last one up, but she was never late and within ten minutes she was washed and dressed, following her friends downstairs to breakfast.

Fitz's day turned out to be a busy one as she ferried planes from Hamble to Essex and then on to Manchester. She was away for three days in all and was grateful to get back to the lodgings where she was billeted.

The few days away had given her a chance to think about the letters she'd got from home and that evening, she penned her reply to Michael.

Dear Michael

I hope this letter finds you well. Thanks so much for your letter. It was so nice to hear from you.

I haven't flown over Badcombe yet, but when I do, I'll be sure to let you know. Now that I'm qualified to fly, I've been billeted in a house near to the ferry pool in Hamble with two other girls – Marjorie and Elsie. My new address is as above so make sure you write to there in future.

My favourite plane to fly is the Tiger Moth and as you know I was already flying that before I joined the ATA so that has been very simple and straightforward for me. I've enclosed a photograph of me standing in front of the aircraft with my uniform on. I don't think I've ever felt so proud.

I promise as soon as I have a day free, I'll come and visit or if I fly into Bassingbourn airfield I might have time to see you at Badcombe. We only get two days off a fortnight so it doesn't leave much time I'm afraid.

Don't worry about what you heard Cook and Annie talking about. They do like a gossip sometimes. I wouldn't be surprised if it wasn't even about your mother.

The house will be jolly full with everyone who is coming to stay, but it will be good for you to have someone your own age to play with. I do hope it all works out well.

Anyway, must dash.
Love from
G

She hoped Michael would be appeased by her explanation of what Cook had meant about his mother. Fitz didn't want to make a big thing out of it and by simply explaining it away, she hoped Michael would forget all about it. She didn't want him worrying and it wasn't her place to explain what Cook meant, especially as she had no idea if it were true or not.

Nor did she mention Johnny Fisher's passing to Michael in case their father hadn't told him. She didn't want to burden the boy with anything else to fret over.

She folded the letter and slipped it into an envelope which she addressed and placed next to the one she'd already written to her father the day before while she had been away.

'Oh, there you are, Fitz,' said Marjorie coming into the bedroom that they shared. 'Elsie and I are going down to The Three Feathers, fancy coming?'

'Oh yes. I'll come. I need to post these two letters to Michael and my father so I can do it on the way.'

'Don't you ever write to your stepmother?' asked Marjorie, glancing at the two letters on the bureau.

Fitz looked up at her friend and gave a shrug. 'No, but then she never writes to me.'

'I suppose one of you has to write first.' Marjorie fixed her with a gaze. 'Why don't you like your stepmother?'

'It's not that I don't like her, it's more that she doesn't like me,' said Fitz, getting to her feet and checking her reflection in the mirror above the fireplace.

'You know that for a fact?'

'I do as it happens. She wanted to send me off to Scotland.

She couldn't wait to get rid of me. I was just glad I got in the ATA before that happened.' She smoothed down her hair and then applied her red lipstick. 'Anyway, what's with all the questions?'

'I just wondered,' said Marjorie. 'You don't talk about her much.'

'Well, now you know why.' Fitz pressed her lips together and dabbed on a little more lipstick. 'She's a lot younger than my father. Closer to my age, actually.'

'Maybe that's why you find it difficult,' said Marjorie. 'Maybe she finds it difficult. Maybe she doesn't know whether to be your friend or your mother.'

'She'll never be my mother,' said Fitz, becoming a little irritated at the questioning from Marjorie.

'Perhaps you should let her be your friend instead?'

Fitz turned to Marjorie. 'I don't want to be her friend, either. Now, can we stop talking about her? Otherwise it will put me in a bad mood.'

'Right you are,' said Marjorie, picking up Fitz's jacket and tossing it to her. 'Come on, they'll be ringing for last orders if we don't get a move on.'

As they made their way to the pub, Fitz's conversation with Marjorie nagged at the back of her mind. In particular, the comment that either Fitz or Camilla had to write first. Was Camilla waiting for Fitz to send her a letter as an invitation to write back? Surely, Camilla should initiate the communication. The more Fitz thought about it, the less certain she became of what was protocol.

It was something of a surprise to Fitz when, a couple of weeks after her conversation with Marjorie, she received a letter from Camilla.

She opened it with a certain amount of trepidation, initially worried that it might be bad news but as she read the flowing cursive writing, she found herself stunned, rather than shocked.

Camilla Fitz-Herbert
Badcombe House
Little Badcombe

Cambridgeshire

2ⁿᵈ June, 1941

Dear Geraldine
I hope you don't mind my writing to you but I'm not sure when we will see each other again and there's been something playing on my mind, that really can't wait.

The other day, when I was tidying Michael's room, I happened to see the recent letter you sent him. I wasn't prying but I said to Michael how nice it was you'd written to him. He eagerly showed me the letter. When I got to the final paragraph where you said Cook had probably been gossiping, I asked Michael what you meant. He must have forgotten about that part in the letter. He was very reluctant to tell me, but he did in the end.

I rather wished I hadn't asked him but there I was, faced with questions that needed answers and I feel it's only right that you know too.

What Cook said was true. I did indeed have a child before Michael, with your father. Tragically, I was unable to carry her to full term and she was stillborn at six months. A beautiful little girl who we named Isabelle. I was devastated, as was your father. Cook was very kind to me and I'm not sure without her strength and compassion I would have recovered so well.

You were only young at the time and I'd had a troublesome pregnancy. The baby was small, and I wasn't really showing, so we hadn't yet told you the news. Afterwards, we wanted to shield you from what we'd been through so never told you.

It is something we have never spoken about since. Despite that, the loss has weighed heavy on my heart since. We were overjoyed and felt blessed when Michael entered the world a healthy boy, but I have never forgotten Isabelle. And I never will.

Some people said I was lucky to have you, that you could be the daughter I'd lost but both you and I know, grief doesn't work like that. And I would never bestow that burden on you. A person, a deeply loved person, can never be replaced.

I wish I could have spoken to you about this before, but you were too young at the time and as the years rolled by, it never felt the right time to tell you. I'm so very sorry you found out this way and I hope you will understand why I never told you. I didn't want to burden you with more unhappiness.

Take care.
Fondest love
Camilla

P.S. I'd rather keep this just between us as I don't want to upset your father, so maybe best if we don't mention this again. I simply wanted you to know.

Fitz sat down on the edge of her bed as she took a moment to take in what she'd just read. Fortunately, she was alone that morning as it was her day off but both Marjorie and Elsie were working.

She had never expected Camilla to write to her, and never in a million years thought her stepmother would tell her about such a tragic time in her life. All Fitz could think was how terribly heartbreaking it must have been for her father and Camilla.

Fitz cast her gaze over the words again, carefully reading the paragraph where Camilla spoke about someone never being replaced. It was obvious she was not only referring to her own grief but to Fitz's, too. And Fitz had never given her credit for that sentiment. Gosh, she felt terribly selfish.

She deliberated for a good thirty minutes how to respond but in the end decided to respect Camilla's wishes not to mention it in a letter so as not to upset her father. She would have to wait until she saw Camilla again and thank her privately.

Chapter 8

Summer 1941

So far in the eight weeks she'd been on active duty, Fitz had been to Tangmere twice. The first time she went back after Betty's fatal accident had been more traumatic than Fitz had expected. As she came into land, images of Betty's plane hitting the tarmac and digging into the ground flashed before her. When she'd climbed out of the Spit she was delivering, Fitz's legs had buckled and Bob had somehow managed to catch her under the arm.

She found herself wishing it was Sam who had been there to comfort her, like he had that awful day. She had managed to regain her composure, though. It wouldn't do to fall apart in front of the men and Fitz certainly didn't want it reported back to the ATA. She refused to put her emotions out on show for everyone and blamed the near collapse on cramp in her leg.

Fortunately, the second time she flew into Tangmere, she was mentally prepared and had no such problem as before.

On neither occasion had she seen Sam Carter again, and she had to acknowledge she was a little disappointed. Bob had reliably informed her however that on one of the days, she had missed him by just an hour as he'd set off on a mission, and on her other visit it had been his day off and he'd headed up to London to see an old friend. Fitz wondered if the old friend was of the female kind but then silently admonished herself for even thinking that. It wasn't like her at all. She wasn't even looking for a romance, so why she was letting Sam Carter get under her collar, she didn't know.

Still, one morning when Fitz, Marjorie and Elsie were waiting for the bus to take them to the ferry pool, Fitz found herself wondering when or if she'd see Sam again. She took out his handkerchief from the pocket of her flight bag and refolded it. Maybe she'd never get a chance to return it to him.

'Ah, look at you,' said Elsie. 'I bet you're hoping you'll be sent to Tangmere today.' She nudged Fitz with her shoulder.

'I don't know what you mean,' declared Fitz, as the bus pulled up.

'You hear that, Marjorie?' said Elsie as the three women climbed on board. 'Fitz here doesn't remember a certain American airman with the most amazing blue eyes whose handkerchief she's been carrying around in her flight bag all this time.'

'Oh, really?' said Marjorie, as she headed down the aisle to the empty seats at the back. 'That is strange. Maybe we need to jog her memory?'

'You'll do nothing of the sort,' said Fitz.

'I wonder if he's been pining for you,' teased Elsie, settling into her seat.

'Every morning he looks wistfully up to the sky wondering if today will be the day the Attagirl with the bright red lipstick will return.'

'Well, Fitz, this could be your lucky day,' said Marjorie, sitting down next to Elsie.

'Stop it, both of you,' said Fitz, taking the seat in front of them. 'Besides, if he is there, it will be *his* lucky day.'

Marjorie leaned forward and slapped Fitz on the shoulder. 'Exactly. He is the lucky one.'

* * *

When they arrived at the ferry pool and Fitz was handed her chitties for the day, she was amazed to see her second delivery was indeed to Tangmere. Despite her declaration that it was Sam who should be thrilled, she couldn't help feeling excited herself that she could possibly see him.

Two hours later, after delivering her first Spitfire of the morning to Andover and getting a lift back to Southampton's Supermarine factory to collect another, Fitz landed her second Spit of the day at Tangmere airfield and taxied to the apron. She was pleased to see, once again, that Bob was there to meet her.

'Hello, there, Bob,' she said, climbing down from the cockpit. 'Good to see you.'

'And you, Fitz. Are you going over to the mess room?'

'I mostly certainly am, but you know me, I need to get ready first.' She smiled at the engineer and immediately began peeling off her flight suit. 'How're things here at Tangmere?'

'All good,' said Bob. He checked his watch. 'If you hurry you'll be in time for elevenses.'

Fitz by now had smoothed down her skirt and whipped her lipstick from her pocket. Using the small, hand mirror, she applied it to her lips. 'There. How do I look?'

'Perfect. Oh, we've got a couple of Frenchies in the mess today.'

Fitz frowned. 'Frenchies?'

'French airmen. They're being flown out tonight.'

'Right. I'll look forward to talking to them. It's been an age since I last spoke French.'

'You speak French?'

'*Bien sûr*,' replied Fitz.

'I might have guessed,' said Bob. 'See you over there.'

Five minutes later, Fitz walked into the mess room, casting her gaze around, she couldn't deny her disappointment that Sam wasn't there. She had so been hoping to see him. She did, however, notice the two gentlemen in civilian clothes sitting on one side of the room.

'*Bonjour*,' she greeted them. 'How are you both?' The two Frenchmen looked surprised but replied in French that they were indeed well. 'And you're looking forward to your trip overseas?' queried Fitz.

The two men exchanged a look and the older of the two replied. 'We really can't comment.'

'Oh, of course not. Silly of me. I take it you've come across from Tangmere Cottage?' asked Fitz amiably.

'That we can confirm,' replied the man. 'I must compliment you on your French. I can barely detect an accent. You're not French though, are you?'

Fitz smiled. 'Thank you. I'm afraid I have a succession of French governesses to thank for my language skills.'

The man looked impressed, but before he could say anything else, a deep American voice, one that Fitz had replayed over in her mind the past few months, broke through the conversation.

'Why am I not surprised you speak fluent French, Miss Fitz-Herbert?'

Fitz spun around. She wanted to fling herself into Sam's arms but even she wasn't that brazen. 'Oh, Mr Carter,' she said. 'Not just French but German, too. There is no end to my talents.'

This caused a snigger from one of the English pilots who was standing nearby. Fitz winked at him and looked back at Sam.

He shook his head. 'I don't doubt that for one moment.'

They grinned at each other. 'Hello, Sam,' said Fitz. 'I wasn't sure I was going to see you today.'

'Hi there,' replied Sam. 'I heard you were in town so thought I'd drop by.'

'I'm glad you did. You owe me a pub lunch I seem to remember.'

'And you owe me a handkerchief.'

Fitz produced Sam's handkerchief from her pocket not unlike a magician. 'Hey presto!'

'I'm impressed.' Sam took the cotton square from her.

'I do like to impress you,' said Fitz. 'Now, I've fulfilled my side of the deal, I do hope you're not going to renege on yours?'

Sam raised his eyebrows in mock indignation. 'Never let it be said I don't keep my promises.'

'Oh, God, you two need to get yourselves down the pub.' It was Bob who had come into the mess room unnoticed by Fitz. 'All this pussyfooting around. Go on. Off you go.'

Fitz wished the two Frenchmen well and then left the mess with Sam. He offered her his arm and she placed her hand in the crook of his elbow.

They walked through the village to the one and only pub which was more of a small hotel, simply named The Tangmere Hotel and Bar.

'It's not much to write home about,' said Sam apologetically. 'I figured taking you into Chichester when you're supposed to be on duty, it wouldn't go down too well with the top brass.'

'No, I don't suppose it would,' agreed Fitz. 'However tempting it might be. I confess I don't always abide by the rules, but nevertheless I don't want to be booted out of the ATA.'

The bar area was quiet for the time of day and Sam showed Fitz to a table in the window, before ordering them a drink each. Fitz stuck to orange juice. She knew she'd be hung out to dry if they thought she was boozing before getting into a plane.

'So, how have you been?' asked Sam.

Fitz knew he was thinking of Betty and the accident. 'I've been all right,' she replied. 'We try not to dwell on what happened but remember Betty for, well, the things we love doing ourselves. You know, flying.'

It was hard for Fitz to articulate how she felt about Betty when it was so very different to how she felt about her own mother's death.

The Girl in the Sky

'You shouldn't try to bury things, though,' said Sam. 'I know you British like to keep a stiff upper lip, but it's not always a good idea.'

'I don't know. It's served me well so far,' said Fitz. She stopped. She could have bitten off her own tongue for saying that out loud. She could see by the way Sam was looking at her, he was going to ask some awkward questions. And before she had a chance to say another word to divert the conversation, he spoke.

'What is it you're frightened of?' he asked.

Fitz took a sip of her drink to stall for time before she answered. 'Frightened of? I don't know. I don't believe in fear.'

'That makes you either brave or foolish.'

'Maybe I'm both.'

'When you're up in the sky, what is it you're looking for?'

Fitz swallowed. She'd never been asked this question. She knew the answer ran deep, maybe deeper than she fully understood herself. She wasn't one for talking about it to anyone, least of all an American pilot she barely knew and yet something made her want to open up to him.

'It's just me and the aircraft. It's exhilarating. It's freedom. Free of responsibility. When I'm flying I don't have to rely on anyone else or worry about anyone else.' She paused. 'It all sounds rather selfish and self-indulgent when I say it out loud. I'm not sure any of it makes sense. All I do know is my mother was taken away far too soon.' She could hear the bitterness in her voice and it shocked her. She usually kept these feelings locked away.

'You're angry that she died. That she took that risk and left you without a mother.'

'Is that right?'

'I think so,' said Sam in that confident yet casual way of his. 'You fly without fear because you're seeking power and control over a situation, that as a child, you had zero control or power over. You're attempting to gain a sense of closure and your childhood self might have been attempting to rewrite the outcome.'

Fitz scoffed at the last suggestion. 'It sounds rather fanciful, don't you think?'

Sam shrugged. 'True, it might be a less common reaction to childhood trauma, but it's not unheard of.'

'Golly. That's all rather deep,' said Fitz not feeling comfortable at all with the psychological analysis Sam had just offered. 'Well, I hate to disappoint you or suggest that your degree at Cambridge is wasted, but none of that applies to me. I simply love flying. I do love the adrenaline, that's true but it's a love my mother had and passed on to me. It's in my blood. Anyway . . . enough about me. What about you?' she asked, switching the subject away from herself. 'What makes you take to the sky? Are you after that rush of adrenaline, too?'

'You won't be surprised to learn that I've thought about this before,' said Sam. 'And, yes, I am seeking the rush of adrenaline, but that's because growing up my life was very rigid and very safe. Don't get me wrong, I had a good home life and childhood. My father is an international banker. He likes order. Planning ahead. Sticking to a well thought-out plan.'

'And that's not you.' Fitz might not know a great deal about the Anglo American sitting next to her, but she'd worked that one out pretty early on.

'Most definitely not me. I guess I kicked out against it. I wanted to test myself.'

'Finding your limits can be dangerous,' said Fitz.

'True, but I've not found them yet, so I'll keep pushing,' replied Sam. 'I'd always thought I'd like to fly and when I met some of the pilots at White's and was invited out with them one day, I was hooked. But I like speed of all kinds. Not only in the air. I got myself a motorbike. A Brough Superior. She's a beauty.'

'Really? I love motorbikes,' said Fitz. 'I used to take a Triumph out for a spin around the airfield sometimes. It belonged to Johnny Fisher. He was an absolute sweetheart. He taught me to fly, you know.'

'Sounds like I have competition,' said Sam. He fixed his gaze on Fitz.

She didn't look away. Wouldn't have been able to even if she had wanted to. His eyes looked particularly blue today. More Mediterranean than West Sussex blue. 'Competition?' she said, her voice low. 'I'm not sure that's possible.'

For all her extrovert ways, Fitz's heart was hammering in her chest. Her pulse was pumping far faster than it should. She was fully aware this visceral reaction to Sam was for him and him alone.

Sam leaned in closer to her, his face merely centimetres away. 'I'd hate to have competition,' he said in almost a whisper.

Fitz offered a small smile as the loss of Johnny struck her again. 'He died in service not that long ago.'

'Ah. I'm sorry,' said Sam.

'As I say, Johnny was a sweetheart,' said Fitz, and then adding to lighten the mood. 'So you have big boots to fill and might have to up your game.' She raised her eyebrows. Flirty. She could do flirty with Sam. Anything else was dangerous. But then, she loved a bit of danger. She needed to get back in control of this conversation. 'Maybe you need to thrill me on your Brough Superior.'

'That will do for starters,' said Sam. 'Thrills are my speciality.'

He was dangerously close to her now. She could feel his breath on her skin. 'You'll have to prove that you're not all talk,' she managed to say.

With that, Sam leaned in and kissed her on the mouth.

Fitz's whole body reacted to that tender and fleeting meeting of their lips. She gasped at the ferocity of the feeling. She certainly had never experienced anything like that before. And judging by Sam's sharp intake of breath, it was new for him, too.

This time she didn't wait for him to initiate the kiss. And when he kissed her back, she couldn't help let out a small moan of pleasure.

The sound of the barman giving an exaggerated cough had them pulling apart. Fitz and Sam giggled like naughty teenagers being caught out. She didn't care. If just his kiss could do that to her, then heavens knows what she'd be like if anything else happened.

'Next time you're here, I'm taking you out on the Brough.'

'I'll hold you to that,' said Fitz.

Chapter 9

September 1941

Over the coming weeks, Fitz found herself calling into RAF Tangmere far more than she ever had before. She wondered whether that was by design or coincidence. Surely the ferry coordinator wouldn't be sending her to Tangmere on purpose, or would she? Either way, Fitz didn't mind, it meant she got to see Sam on a regular basis. Of course, he wasn't always there. His job did involve a lot of sitting around at times, waiting to be scrambled. Being on the south coast the airbase was something of major importance. The previous year, Tangmere had played a vital role in defending Britain against the attacks from the German air force. Sam had been involved in all those battles and although they had lessened, he was often out on regular patrols of the south coast.

A few times by sheer good fortune, Sam's days off had coincided with Fitz's down time, and he had indeed kept his promise that he'd take her out on his motorbike, promptly turning up at the house where she was billeted on his bike and whisking her out for the day.

It had been heavenly. Fitz had climbed on the back and slipped her arms around Sam's waist. He had squeezed her hand and then patted her thigh. 'Hold on tight!' he called revving the engine before releasing the throttle and tearing off down the road.

Fitz had laughed in delight all the way. The feeling of the air rushing over her head and across her face wasn't unlike being up in the sky. She loved holding tighter than necessary to Sam, her thighs squeezing against his. If she couldn't be in an aeroplane then being on a motorbike with Sam was the very next best thing.

That night, Sam had booked them into a hotel and they'd slept together. Sex with Sam had been tender and beautiful. Fitz had never experienced such a depth of emotion, positive emotion, before. It was immense and overwhelming. And it was terrifying.

Because much as she wanted to love Sam, Fitz also didn't want to. Her heart beat fast in her chest as something akin to panic surged through her.

She wasn't supposed to be falling in love with him. She was just supposed to be living life and having as much fun as she could, while she could. Sam was only meant to be fun but Fitz was fully aware she was on the brink of their relationship transitioning into something far more serious.

As she lay in Sam's arms, a tear tracked its way down her face and onto his chest.

'Hey, hey,' said Sam, moving his arm and turning on to his side so he could see her. He gently hooked her chin with his finger, tilting her head slightly so he could see her face.

Fitz brushed away the tears but couldn't stop more swiftly following. 'Ignore me,' she said. 'I'm being silly.'

'You, silly? Never,' said Sam. He stroked away another tear with his thumb. 'You gonna tell me what's wrong or do I have to work it out myself? Which I will, but it might be easier all round if you just talk to me.'

Fitz took a breath. 'I'm scared,' she said at last.

'Of what?'

'Of what's happening between us. It's all going rather

fast.' There. She'd managed to order her thoughts into a coherent sentence or two.

'But I thought you liked speed.' He gave a small smile and she knew he was trying to put her at ease with humour, but there was also concern in his eyes and she hated being responsible for that.

'You know what I mean,' said Fitz.

He held her gaze and the smile slipped away. Outright sorrow took its place. 'Sadly, I do know what you mean, Fitz,' he said softly, trailing his forefinger across her damp cheekbone. 'And what's even more sad, is I know why you mean it.'

'Don't say anything . . . please,' whispered Fitz. She didn't want to break what they had at this point. Any declaration of love would irreversibly change their status quo. Things would be different and she didn't know if she could cope with that change.

'Don't hit the brakes, baby,' said Sam. 'Not yet. Stay with me. Trust me.'

Fitz nodded, gulping back another surge of tears that were welling up. She blinked them away. She mustn't let the moment get to her. She took a deep breath to steady herself and closed her eyes for a couple of seconds.

When she opened her eyes, Sam was still looking at her. Gosh, she couldn't cope with that. She sat up, flinging the covers back and then grappling for her dress which she slipped over her head. 'Just need the bathroom,' she said. She glanced back at Sam who was watching her from his position on the bed, propped up on one elbow.

'Fitz . . .' he began.

She shook her head and dashed into the bathroom, locking the door behind her, before sinking down to the floor and resting her head on her knees.

It took her a few minutes to compose herself. She splashed some water on her face and brushed her teeth. She couldn't hide out in the bathroom all night and she didn't want to – she just didn't want to have any deep and meaningful conversation with Sam. It was too much for her.

When she went back into the bedroom, Sam was lying on his back. He smiled and pulled the cover back for her. 'The night is still young,' he said with a wink.

Fitz relaxed. This was the happy-go-lucky Sam she could deal with. 'And so are we!' she declared and with a flourish whipped off her dress and hopped back into bed, relieved to be back in chartered waters.

That had been three weeks ago, and Fitz had resolutely refused to even visit the conversation she'd had with Sam about their fast-moving relationship in her head, let alone discuss it with him. To her relief, he hadn't brought it up either. They were simply enjoying the moment as much as possible. She had admitted to herself that it was a barrier, but she didn't care to look beyond it.

'Lucky you, you're off to Tangmere again,' said Elsie as they looked at their chitties. 'I've got Farnborough first thing and then on to Biggin Hill and then Detling.'

It was mid-September and the demand for aircraft was increasing by the day. In fact, four days earlier the Luftwaffe had carried out an assault on Fighter Command's forward airfields and radar stations across Kent, Sussex and the Isle of Wight.

'Lucky in that she'll see her sweetheart,' said Marjorie. 'Things are hotting up in the air. I think we're going to be busy for the next few days.' She looked at her chitty and reeled off the three airfields she was ferrying planes to and from.

'Of course, I want to see Sam,' said Fitz, 'but it's literally drop the plane off, and straight off again. I've got to take a high-ranking officer from Tangmere to Farnborough.'

'You'll probably be back here for tea,' said Elsie. 'Not sure if I'll make it back tonight.'

'Well, good luck, girls,' said Marjorie as she fastened her flight helmet. 'First one home puts the coffee on.'

For the first time in a long time, Fitz felt apprehensive as she climbed into the Supermarine Spitfire she was to deliver to Westhampnett, a satellite airfield to Tangmere, then she was to get herself back to Tangmere, then on to Hamble to collect a Hurricane and bring it back to Tangmere. It was a lot of back and forth that day but Fighter Command was keen to get all the right planes in the right places. Fitz assumed there had been some sort of intelligence come in that the likes of her wasn't privy to. She simply had to do her job and not ask questions.

The bombing raids by the Luftwaffe a few days ago had unsettled everyone. They had been told to keep their eyes peeled and to make themselves scarce pretty damn quick if they spotted enemy aircraft. In reality, they knew they wouldn't stand a chance. They were civilians trained to fly not fight.

As it happened, Fitz had a very uneventful flight across Hampshire and into Sussex, landing at Westhampnett. It was less than a fifteen-minute flight and she was pleased to touch down. There was a whole line of Spits lined up ready to take to the skies at a moment's notice. At times like this when the crew were on standby, they took to sitting in their squadron group on garden chairs, listening to music on a gramophone and sipping tea or coffee. It looked more like an afternoon tea party, than a group of elite pilots ready to defend the nation.

'I need to get down to Tangmere,' she said to one of the ground crew once she'd handed over the aircraft and completed the necessary paperwork. 'Anyone going that way?'

'Fitz, isn't it?' said the chap.

'Er, yes,' said Fitz, surprised that he would know her name. 'Has transport already been arranged?'

'You could say that. Take a seat over in the mess room. I'll give you a shout when it's here.'

Fitz hadn't been to Westhampnett before and was impressed with how efficient it appeared. She made her way over to the building, stopping at the toilets to apply her lipstick and fluff her hair. If she was going to arrive in style at Tangmere and see Sam, she wanted to look her best for him.

The mess room was fairly quiet and the pilots there were very polite, making her a cup of tea – one of them even managing to find a biscuit for her. It was all very civil. One could have been forgiven for imagining the war wasn't going on.

She had just finished her tea when the door opened and a pilot popped his head around the door. 'Ah, you must be Fitz,' he said.

'Amazing powers of deduction,' said one of the pilots. 'Seeing as there aren't any other women in the room.'

Fitz got to her feet. 'Is my lift here?'

'Yes. Come this way please, Miss.'

Fitz followed the chap out, waving goodbye to the pilots as she went. She was a little surprised to find herself being walked out to the gate and wondered whether she was catching the bus rather than actually being picked up by someone.

'There you go, Miss,' said the airman.

Fitz stopped in her tracks. There on the edge of the road was Sam, astride his motorbike. He held up a crash helmet for her. 'What are you waiting for?'

Fitz sauntered over to him. 'Well, you're certainly a sight for sore eyes,' she said, planting a kiss on his mouth, not caring whether the guards on the gate or anyone else were watching. She took the crash helmet and slipped it onto her head, sighing inwardly at how it would flatten her hair once again but at least Sam had seen her beforehand.

Sam revved the engine and after ensuring Fitz was safely on the back of the bike with her arms around him, he sped away from the airfield. Fitz had to hold on with one arm and grip her flight bag tightly in the other hand. It felt ridiculously dangerous as Sam zipped his way along the winding country lanes towards Tangmere. Fitz whooped and squealed in delight as Sam took the roads at speed, leaning the Brough over frighteningly close to the ground and then accelerating hard out of the bends and along the straight, with a canopy of trees above them.

All too soon they arrived at Tangmere and although Sam had eased off the throttle, he still travelled down towards the airfield at an alarming rate. One gentleman had to step back from the road to avoid the oncoming motorcycle.

He waggled his walking stick in the air to show his vehement disapproval. Fitz would have waved an apology but holding onto the overnight bag with one hand and Sam with the other prevented her.

Within a minute, they were pulling up at the airbase.

'You're crazy, Mr Carter, do you know that?' said Fitz, as she climbed off the motorcycle.

'Crazy for you, Miss Fitz-Herbert.' He unfastened her helmet and took his own off, before kissing her.

Fitz laughed the reply away, pretending she didn't know what he meant.

'Right, well, I'm going for a cuppa,' she said. 'What are you up to now?'

'I'll be over as soon as I've put this baby away,' said Sam, patting the fuel tank.

Fitz went to turn but stopped. 'Are you supposed to be on duty?'

Sam winked. 'I snuck out for ten minutes. It's all right. I cleared it with Teddy first,' he replied, referring to the squadron leader. 'He said I had fifteen minutes and by my reckoning, I've used precisely twelve of those.'

Fitz had no idea how he got away with it, but she was delighted nonetheless that he had made a special effort to pick her up from Westhampnett. She looked across the airfield where the squadron were sitting out in wicker chairs, reading newspapers, dozing in the sun, chatting to each other, looking terribly relaxed. Their Hurricane aircraft were beyond them on the field, all ready to go at a moment's notice.

It was then she saw Bob, whom she'd become good friends with over the past few months. He jogged over to them. 'Might want to get yourself back there, ASAP,' he said.

'Trouble?' asked Sam.

'West Malling has just been hit,' informed Bob. 'Two squadrons of Junkers got through. They thought it was a feint.'

Fitz understood the term. A feint was designed to give the impression of a mock attack to draw the enemy out. 'What's the situation now?' she asked.

'We're all on high alert,' said Bob.

Sam swore under his breath. 'I'd better go,' he said to Fitz.

She nodded. 'See you back here for a cuppa later,' she said, trying to sound bright and breezy but missing the mark.

Sam held her gaze for a few seconds, his unspoken words of reassurance communicated to her in his eyes. Fitz couldn't help thinking they had a blue-grey colour to them today, rather like an ominous rain cloud. 'Make it a strong black coffee and I'm all yours,' he said, throwing her a grin before starting the engine and driving off in the direction of the hangar.

As she hurried over to the mess room, the lightness Fitz had felt earlier had all but disappeared. She was anxious and she hated feeling like this. The risk of losing someone she cared about was almost too much a price to pay. Surely it was easier not to love, and then she wouldn't have to lose.

She glanced back at the squadron where Sam was now standing talking to one of the other pilots. It was time for her heart to retreat. She was so silly to have allowed herself to get emotionally attached to him. She should have kept Sam Carter at arm's length, exactly like she had every other man. That way her heart was safe.

She hadn't been in the mess room for more than half an hour when the sound of the squadron being scrambled rang out across the airstrip. Fitz jumped to her feet and darted over to the window where she could see the ground crew sprinting towards the stationary Hurricanes. The pilots were shrugging on their flight jackets and helmets whilst simultaneously running over to their aircraft that were already being warmed up by the engineers.

She went to the door and stepped out onto the airfield. The sound of the engines rumbling into life filled the air, and the smell of aviation fuel took Fitz right back to that awful day when Betty had died.

The anxiety was now racing through her. She took several long deep breaths. This wasn't like her at all. She did not go to pieces in an emergency.

'Get a grip of yourself,' she muttered.

She watched the Hurricanes begin to rumble their way towards the runway in groups of three. Within seconds the first trio were hurtling down the tarmac and taking off, heading out towards the south coast. Seconds later, another trio, and then another. The next group contained Sam's plane and she watched as it lifted into the air, not taking her eyes off it until it was out of sight.

'Please come back, Sam,' she whispered. 'Please come back.' She purposely didn't ask him to come back to *her*. She had no right to ask that. He didn't belong to her. She didn't want that responsibility – she was no good at that sort of thing. It was a selfish trait she was aware of but didn't like to acknowledge. However, today, she realised the most unselfish thing she could do, was to not ask for Sam to come back to her. He just had to come back and she'd settle for that.

Due to the confrontation going on in the sky, Fitz knew without having to check that she was grounded until it was safe for her to continue her assignment or receive further orders to return to Hamble.

She tried to settle in the mess room, tried not to worry about Sam, but she found it impossible. Her emotions were like some macabre merry-go-round, with every complete cycle, she changed from confident, to fearful, to terrified. She wanted to go over to the control tower, to hear what was going on but she knew they wouldn't let her in. The same with the command room. It was out of bounds to her. Instead, she was stuck in the mess room with absolutely no idea of what was going on as 601 Squadron defended the south coast.

Fitz wasn't aware of time but it couldn't have been more that fifteen or twenty minutes when the sound of aircraft approaching was heard before she could spot it. She tuned in her ear. It wasn't Hurricanes. She'd recognise their distinctive sound anywhere. No this was something different.

The air-raid siren began to sound and she could hear the station tannoy warning.

'Take cover – take cover, Stukas sighted coming towards Tangmere – take cover.'

Chapter 10

Fitz ran towards the air raid bunker. Ground crew were scattering across the concrete desperate to get to the shelter. The roar of aircraft engines overhead was deafening. Fitz looked up to the sky and gasped in horror at the sight of three German Ju 87 'Stuka' dive bombers heading straight for their airfield.

Everything else happened in such a blur and frenzy, Fitz had barely time to register it all. Bombs were being dropped all over the airfield. There were huge explosions from the hangars and great balls of black smoke billowed into the sky.

The Stukas were diving down, dropping their cargo of incendiaries before swooping back up into the sky, turning and lining up for another attack.

'Take cover!' shouted a voice and someone shoved her in the shoulder. She realised she had come to a complete halt as she surveyed the carnage around her. She was shoved again and this time she began to run for the bomb shelter.

Explosions rang out all around her, the noise deafening her momentarily. Debris flew up in the air and crashed back down onto the airfield.

As Fitz raced across the tarmac towards the shelter, she cursed herself for wearing heels and a skirt which only slowed her progress. She could hear the change in the engine noise of the Stukas, the rumble turning into a wail as the aircraft dived downwards before releasing their bombs.

There was the sound of a huge explosion behind her and an almighty force punched her in the back, sending her crashing down onto the concrete. She couldn't breathe. It felt like someone was standing on her chest, crushing the air from her lungs. All around her the noise was muffled. She could still hear the Stukas but they sounded distant and far away. She managed to roll onto her side, releasing the pressure that was constricting her ribcage and she gasped for breath. She'd been winded. With a rush her senses burst back into life.

She could smell smoke and burning, hear the Stukas clearly again and she could hear groaning. She looked around. There, only a few yards away from her, was an engineer sprawled out on the ground. His left ankle was at an impossible angle and must be broken.

Fitz managed to get to her hands and knees and then her feet. She could hear the enemy aircraft approaching for another bombing run. She and the engineer were right in their path.

Adrenaline overtook her and she ran towards the prone body of the engineer. From somewhere, Fitz had no idea where exactly, another engineer came running over and they reached the injured man at the same time.

'You get one side,' shouted the man. 'I'll go the other.'

Together they hauled the semi-conscious engineer up and hooked his arms over their shoulders.

The scream of the Stuka was getting louder and closer by the second. 'Quick!' shouted Fitz.

They somehow managed to get themselves and the injured man to the safety of the air-raid shelter just as the next cargo of bombs were despatched across the airfield.

The attack lasted less than ten minutes but the damage was immense. After the noise had abated and the Stukas had turned for one final time away from the airfield, Fitz could hear the sound of people shouting and emergency-vehicle sirens wailing. And then came the all-clear sound.

The Girl in the Sky

Fitz was out of the bomb shelter in no time. She squinted as she came out into the light. All around her was carnage. There was barely anything left of the airfield. Buildings were on fire, the hangars ablaze as the fire crew attempted to put out the flames. Someone shouted that the sick quarters had taken a direct hit. She could see the chimney breast had collapsed and standing amongst the rubble, up to his waist in debris, was Dr Lloyd.

Fitz sprinted over to the sick quarters and scrambled over the rubble of bricks and mortar, tiles and debris to help the doctor escape.

'Are you all right, Doctor?' she asked. 'Your head's bleeding.'

Lloyd whipped a handkerchief from his pocket and dabbed at his forehead. 'Just a scratch,' he said. With that he began issuing orders to the service personnel to set up an emergency sick bay so he could treat the injured.

Fitz's ears were still ringing from the bombing, but spurred on by Lloyd's dedication she set about helping to salvage as much equipment from the bombed sick bay as she could find. At least she was doing something tangible and it helped stop her thinking about Sam.

It wasn't until sometime later, when Dr Lloyd was treating a pilot who had been shot down, that Fitz took a moment to catch her breath.

She looked up to the sky. All she wanted to see was the British Hurricanes flying back to land. She wanted Sam to be home. But the sky was silent. Fitz spent an agonising thirty minutes waiting for any sign of 601 Squadron. Helping the doctor set up an emergency room was a good distraction and when she finally heard the sound of the Hurricanes returning to base, her heart was leaping around inside her chest like a Jack in the box.

She stood out on the apron of the airfield watching the planes come in to land. Some on their own and some in pairs. Certainly not the formation they went out in.

She silently prayed they would all make it back to base safely. There had been several deaths today and a sombre mood cloaked the airfield. Their families and loved ones would soon be delivered the tragic news and their lives would never be the same again. She knew that feeling all too well.

And then Fitz saw Sam's plane, she recognised the number on the side, and she thought her legs were going to give way with relief. A fresh swell of tears gathered in her eyes, but she brushed them away. And yet, in a strange way, she felt guilty being relieved and, yes, happy, that Sam was safe.

And then came the anger. Unexpected and roaring like an inferno. She hated being put through this emotional wringer. She couldn't cope with it. She'd experienced loss before, and she had been on the brink of experiencing it again. The feeling of utter helplessness was excruciating. The fear overwhelming

There was no way she could cope with this. She had dropped her defences and the fear that brought was unbearable. She couldn't put herself in that position again. Wouldn't allow it. She had to put a stop to it now before it was too late. She thought of her mother, and Betty and Johnny. She'd cared about them, and they were a constant and painful reminder of what could lie ahead for her if something was to happen to Sam. It only hurt because she cared. If she didn't care, then there'd be no pain. It was that simple.

She watched Sam's plane taxi its way through the bombed-out airstrip. Red flags had been placed to warn them of unexploded incendiaries and craters in the tarmac.

He wove his way through, bringing his plane to a halt on the apron. Then he was out and after a few words with his ground crew, he was striding over towards her.

His smile was warm and reassuring. He opened his arms and wrapped them around her, kissing the top of her head.

'Jesus, Fitz,' he said into her hair. 'I was so worried about you when I heard the airfield had been bombed. Thank God you're all right.' He pulled away to look at her as if he needed to see with his own eyes. Then taking off his flying gloves, he wiped her cheek with his thumb.

The tears came again. 'Hey, it's all right,' continued Sam. 'Don't cry. I'm not hurt. You're not hurt. We're good.'

Fitz shook her head and took a step back. She could hardly bear to look at him. 'I'm sorry,' she said.

Sam looked confused. 'Sorry? For what?'

'I can't do this, Sam,' she said. 'We can't do this. Worrying about each other all the time. Wondering if the other is all right. Our minds not on the job properly. That's dangerous. One of us will end up making a fatal mistake.'

'What the hell?' The confusion and hurt settled on his face. 'I have no idea what you're talking about.'

'Listen to me, Sam,' said Fitz. 'We can't love each other. Not now. It's the wrong time.'

He stood there for a moment, stunned as he took in what she was saying. 'You can't speak for me,' he said, his jaw tight. 'You've no right to tell me what I can and can't do. I can love you if I want to. Hell, Fitz, I love you because I can't not love you. I thought you felt the same.'

She shook her head. 'No. I don't. You thought wrong.' Fitz couldn't believe saying those words would be so difficult. She refused to acknowledge that, even to herself, she was not telling the truth.

'That's the biggest crock of shit I've ever heard,' said Sam.

'I'm sorry.'

Before Sam could answer, one of the ground crew was calling him. He looked around. 'Sam! Hey, Sam! You're needed. The boss wants you. Now.'

Sam turned back to Fitz. 'I've not finished this conversation. I'm not going to let you walk away from us.'

'You can't stop me,' said Fitz.

'SAM!' came the engineer again.

'Look, I gotta go, but we need to talk about this some more,' he said. 'I love you, Fitz. We're worth fighting for. Don't you forget that.'

Fitz didn't reply. She watched him jog over towards the hangar, where he paused and looked back at her. 'Don't you forget that!' he shouted out before disappearing into the hangar.

Fitz stood there for a long moment. She'd never forget that. Never. But it didn't matter. She wasn't going to let herself love him back.

Chapter 11

October 1941

It had been two weeks since the attack on Tangmere airfield and the Germans had intensified their bombing campaign. Fitz had been ferrying planes every day as the factory tried to keep up with demand.

She hadn't spoken to Sam in that time. He had tried to telephone the house she was billeted at twice now, but each time she had declined to take the call. It was cruel, she knew. There was nothing more she wanted than to speak to him, but she knew if she heard his voice her resolve would crumble. He had even turned up on two nights unannounced on his Brough but she had been away on an overnight assignment.

'He stayed outside on his motorbike for three hours,' reported Marjorie the next day. 'I went out to him but he was adamant he'd wait just in case you returned. In the end he had to go, Mrs Temple said she didn't want him hanging around outside the house as it wasn't good for her reputation. Something about the neighbours would think it was a house of ill repute.'

Fitz wanted to laugh at the idea of their landlady worrying about her house being one of ill repute, but it wanted to make her cry more. The thought of Sam desperate to see her was almost too painful to contemplate.

'I don't know why you don't just speak to him,' Elsie said.

'The man is clearly head over heels in love with you,' said Marjorie, as they boarded the bus that was taking them to Hamble ferry pool. 'I'm with Elsie on this, you should at least hear him out.'

Marjorie and Elsie sat down on a double seat and Fitz took the empty seat in front of them. She turned to face her friends. 'I can't speak to him,' she said. 'It will be too hard to turn him away a second time.'

'But why? What has he done?' asked Elsie. 'I would die to have a chap as gorgeous as Flying Officer Sam Carter. An American who is handsome as hell too.'

'And don't say it's because he's not your type, either,' said Marjorie. 'He is absolutely your type.'

'I told you,' said Fitz. 'I'm not the settling down sort. I want to have fun, especially when this war is over. I refuse to clip my flying wings and I refuse to clip my social wings either.'

Sitting on a bus on her way to the ferry pool wasn't quite the place she imagined having a heart to heart with the girls. Fortunately, the bus wasn't too busy and most people seemed engrossed either in their own conversations or reading a newspaper.

'You can still be in love without clipping any wings,' said Marjorie.

'Look, this fling with Sam, was purely that. A fling. It was never anything serious. Not on my part, anyway.'

'Are you sure about that?' asked Elsie.

'Poppycock,' declared Marjorie, folding her arms as if to underline her utter disbelief.

Fitz let out a long sigh. 'If you must know,' she said quietly. 'I can't love him. I don't want to love him. Not now. It's the wrong time. Maybe if I was to meet him in ten years' time when the damn war is over, then maybe things would be different. But not now.'

Fitz turned to face the front, not able to look at her friends in case they saw the tears in her eyes. She was grateful neither of her friends pushed for any further explanation. She didn't want to talk about Sam, even after a couple of weeks, it still felt as raw as it had that day back at Tangmere.

The bus rattled on towards the ferry pool. Marjorie and Elsie talked about the cake Mrs Temple had promised to make for Elsie's birthday later that month. Food restrictions were very much in effect now and with butter being rationed since the beginning of the year, Mrs Temple said she was keeping some back each week. She was also going to barter with her neighbour with the eggs her two hens produced each day.

'Exchange is no robbery,' Mrs Temple was fond of saying.

Soon enough the bus pulled up around the corner from the ferry pool. Fitz paused to fix the strap on her gas mask box that had worked itself loose. Marjorie and Elsie were ahead of her and she broke into a little run to catch up with them. As they turned to walk into the airfield, Fitz stopped in her tracks.

Sam Carter was sitting on his Brough motorbike just like he had been that time at Westhampnett.

Marjorie and Elsie had also stopped. The former turned to Fitz. 'Give the poor man a chance,' she said. 'He's desperate to speak to you.'

'Did you know about this?' demanded Fitz.

'Of course not,' said Elsie.

Fitz wasn't sure whether she believed her friend or not. She hung back as Marjorie and Elsie went on through the gates to the airfield, then slowly she walked over to Sam, trying to work out how she was ever going to cope with speaking to him. He looked as handsome as ever but there was such sadness in his eyes. The very same eyes she had seen in her dreams every night.

'Hello, Sam,' she managed to say, rather more cheery than necessary.

'Hey, Fitz.' He hooked his leg over the fuel tank and stood in front of her.

'You shouldn't be here,' she said after a few seconds.

'Why? Because it makes it difficult for you?'

Wow. He wasn't going to tackle this gently. She looked up at him and plastered on a smile, followed by a chuckle. 'Whatever makes you say that? It's jolly nice to see you. How have you been keeping?'

Sam frowned. 'Not too good as it happens.' He sighed and looked away before looking back at her. 'I've missed you.'

Her heart was thudding and she was sure he could hear it but she forced herself to keep up the nonchalant stance. 'Oh, that's sweet. I would have thought you'd have been too busy fighting the Germans or got yourself another girl by now.'

'Why the hell would I want to do that?'

'I'm sure you could have your pick of the Attagirls,' continued Fitz. 'Whisking them off on your bike.' She nodded at the machine. 'I'm surprised you've had time to even think about me. Anyway, it's been awfully nice to see you, but I really have to get to work. Got a plane to fly.'

She went to walk around him, but he stepped into her path. 'Why are you being like this?'

She blinked hard as if she were perplexed by the question. 'Being like what?'

'Jesus, Fitz. You're acting like you don't care about me. About us.'

'Sam, I thought I made it clear before,' she said. 'There is no us.' She wanted to cut her own tongue out of her mouth.

'You're lying.'

'Sam, please,' she said, her resolve beginning to weaken.

'Don't you miss me at all?' he demanded.

Of course she missed him. She missed him more than she ever imagined possible but to confess to that now was only paving the way for heartbreak. She had to remind herself of what was at stake.

'I don't mean to sound brutal,' she said. 'But I've been too busy.'

'Too busy?'

'I've got a new boyfriend,' she said. 'He's a squadron leader. Jolly nice chap, too.'

Sam's eyes narrowed. 'A new boyfriend?'

'Yes, that's right.'

'Do you love him?' A muscle twitched in Sam's jaw.

Fitz swallowed. Now was not the time to fall to pieces. 'It doesn't matter.'

'It matters to me,' snapped Sam. 'Do you love him?'

'I need to go,' said Fitz, not able to meet his gaze.

Again, Sam blocked her path. 'Do you love me?' His voice was quiet, this time. 'Did you ever love me, Fitz?'

'Sam, please.'

'Answer the goddam question.'

Before Fitz could answer, though, the duty guard came over. 'Is everything all right here?' he asked, eyeing Sam up.

'Just fine, buddy,' replied Sam, his gaze still fixed on Fitz.

'Miss?' queried the guard.

'Everything is fine, thank you,' replied Fitz. This time Sam didn't block her path as she hurried on through the gates. She didn't turn around despite being aware of his gaze still tracking her. She didn't want him to see the anguish and tears on her face.

Fitz didn't have time to dwell on her encounter with Sam. Despite Marjorie and Elsie trying to quiz her, she refused to discuss it. The sooner she was in the air and away from everything and everyone, the better as far as she was concerned.

Half an hour after receiving her chitties for the day, Fitz was landing a Spitfire into Westhampnett. She had been given an assignment to deliver to the satellite airfield with an immediate onward trip to Biggin Hill, delivering a high-ranking officer back to his station. She was glad there was no hanging around at Westhampnett, just in case Sam turned up. Although in her heart of hearts, she knew he wouldn't this time.

Soon enough she was landing the aircraft and her passenger at Biggin Hill.

Fitz climbed out of the plane, followed by the officer.

'Thank you,' he said. 'You're Fitz, aren't you?'

'Erm, yes, sir. Geraldine Fitz-Herbert.'

He studied her for what seemed like an age before he spoke. 'Could you come with me please? I'd like to talk to you.'

'Yes, sir.' Fitz's mind was racing. What on earth had she done to warrant a talking-to from an officer? She followed him into the station and down a corridor, before entering what she assumed was his office.

'Sit down,' he said, indicating to the chair. 'Don't look so worried. You're not in trouble.' He perched on the edge of the desk. 'I'm Flying Officer Henley. I've heard a lot about you.'

'Have you?' Fitz didn't think this was a good thing and didn't really know how to respond. She opted not to say anything else.

'You're quite a pilot, so I understand,' continued Henley. 'In fact, pretty damn good by all accounts.'

'Thank you, sir.' Fitz hoped this was a good omen. He did say it wasn't anything to worry about but she wished he'd get to the point.

'Also, you're pretty good with the French language. Speak like a native, I'm told.'

'I had three French governesses,' said Fitz.

'Yes, I heard through the grapevine you had a nice chat with a couple of Frenchmen at Tangmere recently.'

'It's nice to use it when I get the chance,' replied Fitz, wondering where on earth the conversation was leading to.

A knock at the door interrupted them. 'Come in,' called out Henley.

'Good morning, Henley,' came the voice of another man.

Fitz turned to see a man in civilian clothes of a suit and tie enter the room. He shook hands with the officer and then looked at Fitz. 'And you must be the infamous Fitz, I've heard so much about.'

'Yes.' Fitz got to her feet and shook the outstretched hand of the man.

'My name's Wilding, I'm with the Joint Technical Board. We oversee certain foreign operations,' he explained. He sat down in the seat opposite Fitz, while Henley took his place on the other side of the desk.

Fitz sat down, too. She had no idea what the Joint Technical Board was. She was sure she'd never heard of them.

'Mr Wilding is looking to recruit some new staff,' said Henley. 'It's come to our attention that you might have the specialist skills he is looking for.'

'I see,' said Fitz. 'And, if I may ask, what sort of position did you have in mind?' She couldn't imagine what they wanted her for other than to fly planes, unless it was her language skills and they wanted her to liaise with some of the French operatives that were in England.

Henley and Wilding exchanged a look, before the latter spoke. 'I can't say too much about the position just yet. It's all rather delicate. Anything I say now is said in the utmost confidence. You are not to repeat this to anyone.'

Now Fitz's interest was really piqued. 'Of course not.'

'We're looking for a young woman such as yourself to undertake a top-secret assignment,' said Wilding. 'That's about all I can say.'

'And you've picked me above anyone else?' Fitz wasn't sure who Wilding represented but surely there must be other females he could choose from.

'We need someone who can speak fluent French and fly a light aircraft,' said Wilding. 'That's all I'm prepared to say right now, other than it will be a highly dangerous mission.'

'Don't answer immediately,' cautioned Henley. 'Have a few minutes to think about it. I mean really think about it. If you're not up for it, we can pretend this conversation never happened and move on. No one will think any the worse of you. As Wilding said, it's highly dangerous.'

'We're looking for an attractive young woman such as

yourself to act as a bit of a decoy,' said Wilding. 'I won't lie and pretend it's not risky work. It is. It involves you being dropped into enemy territory and carrying out instructions. Again, it's highly dangerous. Quite simply, it could cost you your life.' He looked at Fitz, as if weighing her up. 'Do you think you're up for something like that?'

Fitz looked from one man to the other, as she considered what she was being asked. 'I take it the enemy territory is France.'

'Indeed. With your linguistic skills, you'll fit in perfectly as a native. The Germans won't be able to tell you're English. That's what I've been told at any rate.'

'I had no idea anyone had monitored my French so closely,' said Fitz.

Henley gave a smile. 'It's been noted by the right people.'

Fitz didn't really need to think about it for very long. What did she have to lose? The danger didn't particularly scare her. She had lost everything dear to her, if she didn't include her father or her little brother Michael. And maybe she was better off out of their lives, anyway. That way she'd be no bother to her father or her stepmother. Not that she had any particular desire to die but it didn't frighten her.

'I accept,' she declared.

Part 2

Southern Britanny

France

Chapter 12

Winter 1941

When Fitz had agreed to join the Joint Technical Board that day at Biggin Hill airfield, she hadn't known what to expect. All she knew was she had entered into the secretive world of the SOE(F) Special Operations Executive (France).

After being interviewed officially in London at the Baker Street headquarters of the SOE, Fitz had only five days to say her goodbyes to Marjorie and Elsie and all the other colleagues at the Hamble ferry pool.

'I can't believe you're leaving us,' bemoaned Elsie as she had helped Fitz pack her bag.

'Just the two of us left now,' said Marjorie.

'You will keep in touch, won't you?' said Elsie.

'Of course. As much as I can,' replied Fitz, inwardly wincing at the lie. She would not be permitted to communicate very often with her friends for fear of giving away what she was up to. She didn't know if she'd be needed for further assignments once she was back from this one. Assuming, of course, she made it back. Fitz was very aware of the dangers. They had been spelled out at her interview in London so she was under no misunderstanding about what she was doing. It wasn't the time for rose coloured glasses she had been told.

Even though Fitz knew what she was undertaking was dangerous, and that she had lost Betty and Johnny to the war, it was still hard to truly, deep down inside, believe she could lose her life. Whether her mind was trying to protect her, she didn't know, but the thought of dying didn't frighten her. However, she was all too aware this was totally at odds with her fear of Sam dying. That she couldn't even contemplate.

'You know Fitz is going to be far too busy doing lots of exciting stuff,' said Marjorie.

'Oh, I wouldn't call being an air-taxi service exciting stuff,' said Fitz.

Marjorie fixed Fitz with a long look. 'Darling, Fitz,' she began. 'The three of us know full well that you're not going to be a taxi service. You don't get called up to London out of the blue like that and then have to hot-foot it out of here in a few days with very vague information of where you're going and what you're doing.'

Fitz bit her lip. 'I really can't comment.'

Marjorie smiled and stepped forward to hug her friend. 'No. I shouldn't ask, so I'm not going to.'

'We will miss you, Fitz,' said Elsie. 'Whatever you're doing, know that you'll be in our thoughts and prayers.'

Marjorie made a scoffing noise. 'You'll be in my thoughts at least. If I did pray, then you'd be in those, too; but as I don't . . .' She left the sentence unfinished as Fitz hugged her this time.

'Take care both of you,' she said. 'I'll miss you both and with fair weather and a tail wind I'll be back very soon.'

She blew kisses from the gate, before climbing into the waiting taxi.

Initially, Fitz had no idea where she was going, only that she was to pack for all weathers. So secretive was the branch, she was first taken to what was termed as Preliminary School where they were assessed for the suitability for whatever it was they were going to be requested to do. Neither Fitz nor the other candidates had any real idea what the branch actually did. Every day, at least one or two candidates were deemed unsuitable and swiftly sent home.

During her first three weeks of assessment Fitz learnt far more than she imagined, weapons handling, unarmed combat, elementary demolitions, map reading, field craft and basic signalling. She passed that without any problems and was then sent to Paramilitary School in Scotland for further training and then on to Manchester for parachute training. This came easy to Fitz, after all, it was an essential skill to have as a pilot.

After that it was Beaulieu in the New Forest for what was called Finishing School. Fitz wasn't sure this was the type of finishing school her father would have wanted her to attend, but she was certain it was far more up her street than a Swiss boarding school. It was in the New Forest where she was educated in the art of being a spy. It sounded all very exciting and Fitz thoroughly enjoyed learning about personal security, clandestine life, communication in the field and how to maintain a cover story.

She wished she could tell Marjorie and Elsie what she was up to, they would be thrilled to know she had entered the world of spying.

It was also at this point that the recruits who had made it this far were told about SOE and what they were about to undertake once they had completed the training programme. Fitz had been sworn to secrecy even to her colleagues, friends and family. Under no circumstances was she to breathe a word of what she was doing. Very few people knew about the SOE so Fitz had to come up with a cover story that she had been asked to work for the Joint Technical Board as a pilot – the department was a totally fictitious one of course.

Fitz felt dreadfully deceitful not being able to tell even Marjorie or Elsie what she was up to but she knew it was for the best. It wasn't only to protect herself, it was to protect all the other operatives in and out of the field.

After three months of intensive and highly secretive training, and Christmas fast approaching, Fitz knew the details of her assignment off by heart, and was about to be flown out to France by the next full moon and dropped behind enemy lines. Wilding had been to see her two days before with the details of the mission.

'The mission is to kidnap a highly regarded Colonel Rolf Hoffmann of the Wehrmacht. He has certain information we need and it's a good bargaining chip for us. You'll be tasked with . . . well to put it bluntly, seducing him. Getting him on his own in the right place at the right time, so the rest of our operatives can kidnap him.'

'When you say seducing him . . .' began Fitz.

'Whatever it takes to have him where we need him.' Wilding eyed her. 'You do understand what I'm saying, don't you?'

'Whatever it takes?'

'Yes.'

Fitz took a moment to consider this. Truly consider what this could mean. She'd certainly have to flirt with him – that in itself wasn't something that troubled her. She would probably have to cuddle up to him and kiss him. Not terribly appealing, but she could do that.

Then, of course, there was what came next. She might have to have sex with the German officer. That, most definitely, was not appealing. Could she do it?

She ignored the little shiver of distaste that ran through her at the thought. She'd have to somehow shut down emotionally. Disconnect herself from what she was doing. A fleeting moment of guilt ran through her as she thought of Sam. She pushed it away. She couldn't let her mind go there. Sex with a German officer was totally different – incomparable. It would be done out of duty and nothing more. If that's what she had to do, then she'd bloody well do it.

She looked up at Wilding. 'Is that all?'

He gave her a look that said he already knew she wouldn't back down from the mission. 'Your skills as a pilot will be imperative to fly him back to England. There will be an aeroplane waiting for you. In fact, it's Colonel Hoffmann's private aircraft. It will be fuelled and ready to go. You'll be back to Blighty, tucking into your Christmas turkey before you know it,' said Wilding. 'You think you can do that?'

'Seduce a German officer? Help kidnap him? Fly him back to England in time for Christmas dinner?' Fitz lifted her chin. 'I'm sure I can.'

'Yes, we thought this would be up your street,' said Wilding. He took an envelope from his desk and passed it to her. 'You will be Claudine Bardot, the daughter of a wealthy businessman in Paris who has been sent to the Brittany countryside to stay with her cousin at Josselin Castle for the Christmas period. Colonel Hoffmann is visiting there for three nights, arriving on the twenty-third. On Christmas Eve, he will be attending a drinks evening and piano recital. You will make yourself known to him and encourage him out into the garden at 2100 hours. You're to take a walk alongside the north wall. Once there, you will be greeted by the resistance and Hoffmann will be ushered into a waiting car. You're to go, too. You'll be driven to an airfield and the waiting aircraft that has been conveniently diverted from Vannes for the Colonel's flight back to Paris.'

It all sounded exciting and a little scary but she embraced the idea of danger. It's what she thrived on. This challenge was exactly what was needed. It would help her to stop thinking about Sam. Much as she'd tried to put him to the back of her mind, it had proved impossible.

The day finally arrived for Fitz to begin her mission into occupied France and to seduce the German officer. She was sent to Bignor House to stay overnight with Barbara Bertram and her family. It was hard to believe this house tucked away in the West Sussex countryside was a safe house for transferring SOE operatives into France.

At the house was a Frenchman, André, who was going to be working alongside Fitz in Brittany. She didn't know what his real name was, only his cover story, or at least enough of it so if they were questioned by the Germans, she would be convincing as a friend of the family.

Fitz had been given the codename Nathalie though her undercover name, in France, was Claudine.

After spending the night at Bignor House, Fitz and André were transferred down to RAF Tangmere. It felt strange coming to the airfield dressed in civilian clothes and being taken to Tangmere Cottage where they were to receive a final briefing before being flown out that night on the full moon.

Fitz couldn't help wondering if she'd see Sam. Part of her hoped not. She didn't need any distractions before going out on a mission but another part of her – her heart – desperately wanted to see him. She had to ignore her heart. It hadn't healed as she hoped it would. Despite being incredibly busy and tired throughout her SOE training, Sam had never been far from her thoughts. He had been her first thought in the morning and her last thought at night. Whoever said, 'out of sight, out of mind', clearly had never been in love.

Wilding, and another army officer, headed up the briefing where they went over the final details of the mission but only in as much as what Fitz and André needed to know right at that moment. They were being flown in behind enemy lines that night, the 21st December, where they were to make contact with a local resistance group in Josselin. All Fitz knew, was that her contact was a woman called Margot and they were to meet at the well behind Château Josselin at noon the next day, the 22nd. Margot would identify herself with the agreed code word.

'If for any reason you're unable to make the rendezvous

that day, you're to try again the following day, on the twenty-third,' instructed Wilding. 'Try not to mess it up, though. Miss the second rendezvous and you're on your own. You'll have to use your initiative to contact Margot. Whatever happens, the kidnap has to happen on Christmas Eve, without fail.'

'We won't get another chance like this,' said the other officer.

'If all goes well, you'll be back on the plane to England in time for Christmas dinner,' said Wilding with a smile.

'Right, so is that all clear and understood?' asked the officer.

'Yes, sir,' replied Fitz. André confirmed his understanding in the same way.

'Good,' said Wilding. 'Now, get yourselves over to the mess room and someone will call you when it's time to leave.' He paused and looked from Fitz to the Frenchman. 'Good luck, and see you back here in a few days with our guest.'

A jeep whisked them from Tangmere Cottage across the airfield to the mess room. Fitz's heart was thudding hard. Not because she was frightened of the mission, but because she could well bump into Sam now.

There were only a couple of pilots in the mess room. It was mid-week and an apparently quiet evening. Fitz didn't know whether to be disappointed or relieved Sam wasn't there. She had so many conflicting feelings about him, she felt in a permanent state of unrest. She really needed to focus on the mission. She couldn't be distracted by thoughts of Sam.

She had been keeping her mind occupied by reading a book for the past hour when the door opened and she looked up to see Bob coming into the mess.

'Ah, F—' He managed to stop himself when she quickly put her finger to her lips.

Fitz got up from the chair and indicated to the door.

'Hello, Bob,' she said once they were outside. 'How are you?'

'Fitz,' said Bob. He didn't return her smile and his expression looked serious.

'Is everything all right?' asked Fitz, wondering if there was something wrong with the aircraft which meant the mission couldn't go ahead.

Bob rubbed the back of his buzz-cut. 'I've got something for you.' He fished into his pocket and brought out an envelope.

Fitz looked down at the airmail letter, which military personnel used to send letters home. This one had no stamp, though, just Fitz's name. She knew instantly it was from Sam.

She looked from the letter to Bob. 'I don't know if I should open it,' she said. 'What do you think?'

Bob shrugged. 'I wasn't sure, but when I saw you sitting in there, I realised it was you being flown out tonight. I thought you should at least have the opportunity to decide before you left. In case . . . well, you know.'

'In case I don't come back,' said Fitz.

Bob nodded. 'Sam gave it to me last week. He said to give it to you the next time I saw you. He didn't think you'd want to speak to him so he wrote a letter instead.'

'Where is Sam now?' asked Fitz, looking around, half expecting him to emerge from the hangar like he had done before.

Bob looked down at the ground, not meeting her eye.

'Where's Sam?' she asked again, this time her voice quieter.

Bob shook his head before looking up at her. He took a deep breath. 'We're not sure,' he said eventually.

'Not sure? What does that mean?' asked Fitz. Her heart had picked up its pace now.

'He took a plane out to France last night. A drop-off.'

'A drop-off? What was he doing flying a drop-off?' Her voice sounded tight in her throat.

'Last minute they needed a pilot. The pilot, Micky Jenkins, got ill. Sam volunteered. There wasn't time to get anyone else. Jenkins was literally sick just as he was about to climb into the cockpit.'

'And Sam stepped up. Oh, God. What's happened?' asked Fitz.

'He was shot down. That's what the reports are we're getting from across the channel anyway,' said Bob.

Fitz was sure the whole world stopped for several seconds as she took in the news. Sam was missing in action. Was he presumed dead? She shouldn't be entertaining such an idea. Not when she was about to be dropped in France herself.

She looked up at Bob. 'Whereabouts in France did the plane go down?'

'Not sure, exactly, but central Brittany. He was flying a VIP out there for a meeting. It was all hush-hush. Couldn't be delayed and that's why Sam stepped up.'

'Stupid, stupid man,' said Fitz, her voice cracking completely. She blinked hard. She didn't want to cry. She had no right to cry. She had spurned Sam and now he could be captured, lying injured somewhere . . . or indeed . . . dead. The tears sprang from her eyes at that thought and she quickly brushed them away.

'I didn't know whether to tell you,' said Bob. 'But I thought you should know.'

'Thank you, Bob,' replied Fitz. 'I appreciate you telling me.' She looked down at the letter. She wouldn't be able to take it with her. They weren't allowed any personal effects, just in case they were captured. It would blow her cover in seconds if a love letter was found.

But she didn't want to read it and then hand an opened letter back to Bob. Whatever Sam had written, it was private between the two of them.

Bob held out a box of matches to her. 'You could read it and burn it afterwards,' he suggested as if knowing what she was thinking.

It was a tempting solution, but Fitz didn't know if she could bear to burn a letter from Sam. What if it was the last letter she was ever to receive from him?

She shook her head at the box of matches. 'I don't want

to burn it,' she said and held the unopened letter to Bob. 'I'll read it when I get back.'

Bob eyed her for a moment before taking the letter from her. 'You sure?' She nodded. He pushed the letter into his pocket. 'All right. I'll make sure it's safe until then.'

Chapter 13

The noise of the engine rumbling away would normally have thrilled Fitz, but she barely noticed it. She was only faintly aware of the vibration of the aircraft against her back. For the first time in her life, she found no comfort from being in the air.

Her mind was stuck on her conversation with Bob and what had happened to Sam. The thought that he was missing, possibly dead, was an utter nightmare. Despite the risks of being a pilot, Fitz had always thought of Sam as invincible but now the reality was hitting home hard.

A nudge to her shoulder brought Fitz from her thoughts. It was André.

He leaned in and raised his voice to be heard above the engine. '*Ça va? Tu es prête?*'

Fitz started and gave herself a mental shake. She needed to focus on the mission. If she messed up, she didn't really care about herself but she knew the implications would be far-reaching and other people in the field were depending on her.

'How long until we land?' she called back to André in French.

'Ten minutes.'

She gave him the thumbs-up before going through her final checks, ensuring she had all her documentation, her false identity, her papers, some French francs in her purse, an old shopping list and a hankie stuffed in her pocket. All little things to help with her cover to make her seem authentic, should she be stopped and questioned.

She could feel the aircraft banking to the left and guessed the pilot had spotted the landing lights and was lining the plane up for its descent.

Within a couple of minutes, the plane was landing on the makeshift airstrip – a field the resistance had identified as a good landing point. The Lysander bumped and lifted, bumped and lifted, before juddering its way along the field and coming to a halt. It would only be on the ground for a matter of seconds, enough time to get passengers off and then on for the return trip to England. Then it would taxi to the end of the field, turn and take off.

The door was yanked open and a hushed but distinctly French voice ordered them to disembark quickly.

'*Dépêchez-vous*.' The man had a hunting rifle hooked on his shoulder and hurried Fitz and André off the plane. Two British pilots appeared from the darkness, both looking rather bedraggled.

In the light of the moon, Fitz searched their faces, hoping beyond hope that one of them was Sam. Neither of them were. They nodded briefly at Fitz as they started to climb aboard but no words were spoken.

Fitz knew she wasn't supposed to say anything but she couldn't let the opportunity pass. She grabbed the first pilot's arm, forcing him to stop.

'Flying Officer Sam Carter, American. Have you seen him?'

The pilot hesitated, surprised by the question but then shook his head. 'No. Sorry.' He climbed into the aircraft.

Before Fitz could even ask the second pilot, he was already shaking his head. 'I'm sorry,' he said.

'Stop wasting time,' ordered the Frenchman. He bundled Fitz out of the way, so he could close the door to the Lysander.

Next thing she knew, André had grabbed her by the shoulders, spinning her around to face him.

'You need to think about your mission and not about your boyfriend,' he hissed. 'You are a liability to us all otherwise. If you don't think you can, then you need to get back on that plane now.'

'I . . . I'm sorry,' stuttered Fitz, as shame washed over her.

'Are you going to be able to do this?' demanded André.

'Yes. I promise.' Fitz knew she was blushing with embarrassment and was thankful it was dark.

'Good. Let's go.' André bundled her towards the edge of the field, shoving her without any care.

Fitz hurried along, trying not to stumble on the uneven ground. She glanced behind as she heard the plane taxiing to the end of the field. She would not humiliate herself any more, she promised. Whatever had happened to Sam was out of her control. She couldn't do anything to change that or anything to help him, but she could help herself and those around her.

They were in the surrounding woodland now and the resistance members had all left the field and joined them among the trees.

'What happens now?' asked Fitz.

'You will come with us,' said the man who had opened the door to the Lysander. He appeared to be the one in charge. 'We will take you to Josselin, where you will make contact with another member of the group.' He looked at Fitz's suitcase. 'What have you in there?'

'Just a few items of clothing. I've come to Brittany from Paris to stay with my cousin, Philippe,' she said, keeping to the cover story she had learned off by heart.

'You have travel papers?'

'Yes,' replied Fitz, trying not to be irritated at the questioning. 'Everything has been covered.'

The man looked like he didn't necessarily trust her. 'I hope so. Last time one of you came, they had been given the wrong papers,' he said. 'They were shot as spies on the spot.'

Fitz swallowed. Of course, she had heard of things like that happening, but it was a stark reminder of how dangerous their mission was.

'We need to get moving,' said one of the other men.

'*Alors*,' said the leader. 'Follow me.'

Fitz and the two Frenchmen set off through the woods, while the rest of the welcoming party went in the other direction, their part of tonight's mission complete.

Ten minutes of trekking through the woods, with the faintest of light from the moon to show the way, meant Fitz was relieved when they stepped out onto a track. They were staying off the main roads as much as possible to avoid any German patrols, but now needed to break cover from the trees in order to get to a safe house for the night.

They tramped along the unmade dirt track for several minutes until they finally reached a farmhouse surrounded by several outbuildings.

A dog barked to announce their arrival and darted out from the open doorway of a ramshackle-looking shed. Fitz went to jump back but the dog came to a sudden halt and continued its somewhat half-hearted barking. She realised it was tethered on a long rope to a post outside the shed.

The Frenchman practically barked back at the dog, telling it to be quiet. The dog gave a final bark before skulking back into the shed. Fitz felt sorry for the poor animal and wondered when was the last time it had been able to run free.

The door to the farmhouse opened and an elderly woman appeared, her silhouette lit by the light from inside the building.

She spoke in rapid Breton that Fitz found difficult to follow. She had been schooled in French by Parisian governesses, so the local patois of this region was alien to her.

The old woman gave a cursory glance in the direction of Fitz and André, then waggled her walking stick towards the outbuildings adjacent to her house.

The Frenchman, who for security reasons, hadn't introduced himself or his comrade, thanked the woman who then went back indoors.

'Follow me,' he instructed as he and the other man strode off across the muddy courtyard and disappeared around the corner.

André followed the man as did Fitz, but she stumbled on the uneven cobbles.

'My shoelace,' she said, noticing it had come undone. She knelt to fasten it. André made a tutting noise, clearly not impressed, and proceeded to carry on walking. Gosh, he was going to be fun working with, mused Fitz as she hurried to tie her shoelace.

As she stood up, the sound of a German voice shouting cut through the air. Fitz froze.

Voices were coming from around the side of the barn. Then there was more shouting from the Germans, but this time in French.

Fitz darted across the courtyard on tiptoes so that no one could hear her heels on the cobbles. The sound of gunfire rang out, followed almost immediately by return fire.

Without thinking, she bolted into an open doorway, pushing herself back into the shadows, trying to control her breathing.

Then she heard the low rumble of a dog's growl.

'Damn it,' she muttered. She'd only taken refuge in the dog's shed. 'Good boy,' she whispered. '*Bon chien*.' It would be just her luck if she was mauled to death by a bloody dog.

The dog continued its low-level growling.

Fitz was debating whether to make a dash for it out of the shed in the hope of finding somewhere else to hide, when the sound of booted feet on the cobbles outside stopped her.

There was more shouting. Fitz tuned into the German language, listening to the commands being issued to the soldiers to search all the outbuildings. They were looking for another woman. She heard footsteps hurriedly approaching the shed.

The dog let out a fierce bark and Fitz nearly jumped out of

her skin. She slapped her hand to her mouth, to stop herself from squealing in fright.

The dog was in full barking mode now, as if it knew the Germans were the enemy. One of the soldiers shouted at it to shut up and another called out that someone should shoot it.

'It's on a rope,' called back the soldier. 'I'm not killing it.'

'Just leave it,' came a third voice. 'There's no one in there, anyway, the dog would be going crazy.'

Fitz let out a slow shallow breath. The dog had stopped barking and had retreated back to the doorway where it was just offering the occasional growl now.

More shouting, and Fitz could hear the sound of a door being opened and closed.

'I'm here on my own.' It was the old woman's voice.

'Then who are these?' asked a German.

The rumble of an engine as what sounded like a truck approaching drowned out the voices. Very slowly, Fitz edged her way along the inside of the shed towards the front, where there was a small crack between two planks of wood. All the time, she eyed the dog, who fortunately didn't seem the slightest bit interested in her as it guarded the entrance to its territory.

The noise of the truck was louder now and as Fitz reached the gap in the wood, the vehicle pulled into the courtyard, the headlight beams sweeping across the building as it did so. She pushed herself back into the corner until the light passed over the shed.

Doors opened and slammed and the sound of more booted feet. Fitz watched from the crack as several soldiers jogged around to the front of the vehicle. She couldn't see clearly but another soldier had climbed out from the cab of the truck. As he came to stand in front of the headlights, she could see he was a captain. The circle of soldiers in the courtyard parted and Fitz saw André, the old woman, and the two French resistance members all kneeling on the cobbles with their hands behind their heads.

She watched as the German officer inspected the papers, as one of the soldiers shone his torch onto the forged documents. The officer shoved them into the hand of the soldier and walked over to the group kneeling on the ground.

'Where is she? *Où est-elle?*' he asked. Fitz was unsurprised to hear him speaking French. Many of the German officers would have been taught French at school as their foreign language, often alongside English.

Fitz's breath hitched in her chest.

There was silence from the group of four.

The officer prowled around them like a wolf stalking its prey. He stopped behind the old woman and leant down so his mouth was near her ear. Fitz couldn't hear what he was saying, but guessed he was repeating his question.

The old woman shook her head.

The officer straightened up and removed his pistol from the holster and walked along the line, past André, past the Frenchman who had appeared to be in charge, before coming to a stop behind the other resistance member.

'I will ask again,' said the officer, his voice loud. 'Where is the other woman?'

Fitz swallowed hard. They must have been betrayed. How would the officer know someone was missing and it was a woman otherwise?

Without warning a single shot rang out, making Fitz jump in fright. Her eyes felt like they were popping out of her head as she saw the Frenchman fall face-first onto the cobbles. Blood pooled out across the ground, seeping between the stones like water in a gutter.

She clamped her hand over her mouth once again but then immediately took her hand away, fearful that it would amplify her heavy breathing as she fought to remain calm. She closed her eyes for a moment and forced herself to steady her breathing. She needed to stay in control.

'I will ask once again,' the German's voice rang out. 'Where is the other woman?'

Fitz opened her eyes and looked through the crack. The officer was pacing back and forth behind the remaining three. He stopped behind the woman, cocked his gun and held it to the back of her head.

'I know you're here!' he shouted out. 'Come out now and the woman will be spared.'

Fitz watched him look all around the courtyard, his eyes sweeping the buildings, coming to rest on the shed. She was sure he was staring right at her. She daren't move. He couldn't possibly see her, but he might notice a change in the shadows. For several horrifying seconds she stared straight into the eyes of the German officer.

Finally, his gaze moved on. Fitz could barely breathe. She felt lightheaded and her legs weak. But somehow she remained standing.

'If you don't come out in five seconds then the blood of this woman will be on your hands,' announced the officer. Fitz was certain he didn't know she was in the shed or that she was even there. She didn't doubt that he meant what he threatened, though, whether she was there or not. If she stepped out, they would all be killed. If not immediately, then later, once they had been interrogated and tortured. But would he let the old woman go? She doubted it. And although she knew she wasn't responsible for the woman's death, it still felt like it.

'One. Two. Three,' the officer began counting. 'Four. Five.' Fitz remained where she was. 'Very well.'

Another single shot rang out and the old woman slumped to the ground.

Fitz blinked hard. What would happen now? Would he execute André and the other man? And when she still didn't come out, what then?

The dog gave a low rumbling growl and backed into the shed. Fitz remained perfectly still. She didn't want the dog to suddenly remember she was there and then attack her.

She flicked her gaze back to the courtyard. The two

Frenchmen were being dragged to their feet by several soldiers. She watched as they were shoved towards the truck. Fitz could hear orders being issued but couldn't work out what was being said. She guessed they were being put in the back of the truck to be taken away for interrogation.

'This is your last chance to come out,' called the German officer. 'I have been very patient but now it is at an end. It is your choice.'

Fitz didn't move.

The officer issued some more orders and several soldiers hurried out of sight, returning shortly carrying petrol cans. Fitz watched as they began to douse the farmhouse doors and windows with the liquid. They worked their way around the courtyard. Soon they would be at the shed.

She had no choice but to back away from the spy hole otherwise she'd be smothered in petrol, too. The dog gave a growl but didn't move. Fitz backed away some more. And then some more, until she had reached the rear of the shed.

It was dark in the shadows and she couldn't make anything out. With her back to the wall, she felt with her hands and one step at a time, moved along, trying to feel for any way out of what was about to become an inferno.

As she moved along, to her surprise, she realised the back wall had ended. There was an opening into another room.

More orders from the courtyard were shouted and as Fitz edged through the opening, she glanced back to see the farmhouse was already ablaze. The flames lapped up the petrol, and the whole place was bathed in an orange glow from the fire.

Chickens squawked as they fled from one of the outbuildings and Fitz could hear the bleat of a goat. The dog began to bark and pull at his rope. This time not with fierceness but with fear. It retreated back into the shed.

The figure of a soldier appeared in the doorway at the front of the shed, silhouetted by the orange glow of flames behind him. Fitz ducked back from the opening and pushed herself against the wall of the back room she was now in. She could hear the soldier say something about getting the dog.

Another soldier's voice came. 'Leave the thing to burn,' he snapped. Fitz could hear the slosh of petrol being splashed into the shed.

She crouched down and stole a glance around the opening. There was only one figure there now. He took out a box of matches and struck one. It broke and he swore in German, before taking another match from the box, and struck it on the side of the box. It fizzled into life. The soldier tilted the match a fraction so the flame crept up the stick. Then he took a step back and slung the lighted match into the shed.

There was a whooshing sound and the fuel ignited a second later.

All Fitz could do was watch the flames eagerly lick the wooden structure. She was going to die in a shed in the middle of the Breton countryside and no one would know what had happened to her. She didn't feel sorry for herself but she felt sorry for her father.

Chapter 14

The wood crackled and smoke billowed. The heat was already intense and Fitz backed further into the rear of the shed. The dog followed her, whining and offering the occasional bark. The animal sounded desperate, just like Fitz felt. The smoke was beginning to fill the back of the shed and the roof at the front was now on fire. The timber cracked and the flames angrily spat splinters of wood about.

The dog approached Fitz, whining and pulling on the rope. She could feel the animal at her legs and if there had been anywhere to escape to, Fitz would have but she realised the dog was shaking. She reached a hand down, touching the matted fur. She felt the rope around its neck. If she couldn't save herself, she might at least be able to save the dog.

'Come here, boy,' said Fitz. She pulled at the knot but it was too tightly fastened. 'Hold still.' After some tugging and wiggling, Fitz managed to pull the loop over the dog's head. 'There you go, boy. Go on, then,' said Fitz as tears began to fall down her face.

The initial burst of fire had died down a little and now all the petrol had been burnt, the flames had only the wood to feed their hunger.

It might just give the dog enough time to escape. But the animal didn't move towards the door, instead it went over to the far corner and began scratching at the wooden panel.

Fitz could hear the voices of the Germans outside and

wondered if they were waiting to see if she made a bolt for it. The thought was tempting but she wasn't quite done yet.

The dog was still scratching and whining. Fitz scurried over to it.

To her surprise there was a latch. The shed had a rear door. Just a small one. Big enough for the dog. She managed to free the latch and lift it. The door opened inwards.

Immediately, the dog was out. Fitz knew she had only seconds before the Germans spotted the dog and guessed there was another exit. They would be after her in no time.

Without thinking, she scrambled on her hands and knees through the doorway. The fresh air took her breath away for a moment and she gratefully breathed in a lungful of it.

She took a furtive look around. She remembered coming into the farmyard from the left, where the forest was. Her skills of flying planes without radar, relying on landmarks and a good sense of direction, had never been more important than now. They could cost or save her life.

She looked up at the moon to confirm her bearings and with one last look around, she bolted from the cover of the bushes behind the shed towards the trees that bordered the property.

She didn't stop, didn't hesitate, didn't look back. She just ran. She half expected someone to shout at her to stop. Or there to simply be the firing of a rifle. Or maybe she wouldn't even know she had been shot at. Maybe the bullet would kill her instantly.

As she stumbled across the muddy ground, she wondered if this was the last second she'd ever know on this earth.

She reached the wire fencing and scrambled under it.

Still no one shouted. No shots. No pain of a bullet. She could see the dark tree line ahead of her. It was less than fifty yards away. The branches swayed in the night breeze, cheering her on, waving for her to come to them.

And then she was there, running through the trees. Her breathing coming hard and fast. She had to sit down for a minute and slumped behind the trunk of a large Douglas fir.

She looked back around the tree. The whole farm was ablaze. Orange and black shadows danced in the moonlight.

The sound of leaves rustling behind her, made Fitz startle. She spun around expecting to see a German soldier pointing his rifle at her.

Her heart missed a beat with relief. She found herself laughing. It was the bloody dog. He sat down a few feet away from her. All the earlier aggression born out of fear had disappeared.

'Oh, come here, you silly thing,' said Fitz, holding her hand out towards the dog. 'Come on, boy.'

The dog rose and padded over towards her, but remained out of reach.

Fitz looked back at the farm, which was well and truly ablaze now. She really should put as much distance as possible between the place and herself. It might be the Germans came looking for her.

She got to her feet and the dog followed suit. 'Gosh, I suppose you're coming with me, then,' she said. 'You really should have a name. I think I'll call you Scout.' He reminded Fitz of an old, tatty teddy bear she had at home. One of the few remnants she had from when her mother was alive. It had been a Christmas present from her parents. And in the days and weeks following her mother's death, Scout had brought Fitz much comfort. The only other person in Fitz's entire life who had been able to engender that kind of reassurance was Sam. A wave of longing for human comfort washed over her and Fitz closed her eyes, and shook her head, to rid herself of the emotion. 'What on earth is wrong with me, I'm getting awfully sentimental?' she said to the dog as they began to pick their way through the forest.

Fitz knew that Josselin was thirty kilometres south-west from their landing strip. That much she had been told at her briefing before they left. The original plan was to spend the rest of the night in a safe house and then travel by truck to a small village on the outskirts of Josselin the following day, where they would then walk into the town for their rendezvous with the local resistance.

Fitz hadn't been told the details of where they were to meet the truck, and she couldn't risk wandering around aimlessly in the hope of bumping into someone from the resistance. For all she knew, the Frenchman who'd taken them to the farmhouse, and who was now in the hands of the Germans, may have been the one to drive them to Josselin. Fitz had no choice but to make her own way to the town on foot. She had to make one of the rendezvous, otherwise she'd be stuck in France with no contacts and no means of communication. She wouldn't be able to hide among French people for very long without being arrested.

With a renewed sense of hope and purpose, not to mention urgency, Fitz made her way through the woods for another hour, ensuring she didn't stray too near to the road. She needed to keep her ears open for the sound of any German patrol. She didn't know if they were looking for her, or if they really believed she existed. She probably had two days at the most before either André or the Frenchman cracked under interrogation. It wasn't a case of if someone cracked, it was simply when.

Before any of that, though, Fitz needed some sleep before it got light again. Confident she was deep enough in the trees, she nestled down against a large fir tree, and patted the ground beside her. 'Scout, come here. There's a good boy,' she said softly. The dog came close, but not within touching distance and lay down. 'I guess that's an improvement,' said Fitz, resting her head back against the bark of the tree. She closed her eyes and allowed herself the indulgence of sleep.

It was the cold and damp that woke her. The morning light was poking its way through the forest canopy.

At some point in the past few hours, the dog had shuffled a little closer to Fitz but hadn't quite been able to touch her.

She shivered. The damp ground had seeped into her bones.

She got to her feet, checking around to make sure there was no one about.

Confident that she hadn't been discovered and no one was lying in wait for her, she set off in the general direction of the town of Josselin.

She estimated it would take her three hours to get there. She didn't want to arrive too early. The rendezvous wasn't scheduled until midday and hanging around at the well for too long would only attract the wrong kind of attention.

Her stomach rumbled and she wished she'd been able to bring something to eat with her, but if she'd been caught it would have been harder to explain why she had food provisions. Not having André with her also meant her cover wasn't as good as it otherwise would have been. She had to just hope she didn't run into any German patrols or was stopped and questioned at any point between now and reaching Josselin.

The dog was following her, which, although she was comforted by, it also meant it could put her in more danger. How was she going to explain a semi-wild dog as her travelling companion? If any of the Germans from last night stopped her, they were bound to realise the dog was from the farm. She didn't want to have to leave the poor animal tied up again somewhere.

While she mused what she was going to do about Scout, Fitz carried on through the forest. The trees were beginning to thin out now and she assumed she was coming to the edge of the woodland.

Within a few minutes she was on a dirt track, similar to the one they had used to get to the farm last night. Keeping to the edge so that she could dive for cover if needed, Fitz made her way along the track. These were like the English public footpaths and generally connected villages and communes together. Sooner or later, she'd come to a village or a farm and maybe she'd be able to get some food there. She had been issued with a ration book, a forgery, of course, but good enough not to raise suspicion and it would allow her to at least eat without having to use someone else's rations.

Fitz carried on along the track until it came to an end at a road. There was the distinct smell of smoke in the air, and having stepped out onto the road she could see a small stone house a little further along. At first she assumed the smoke must be coming from its chimney but as she cautiously approached the building, she could see it was seeping out from the doorway and windows. All the glass had broken. The whole cottage was burnt out.

Fitz carried on walking, aware of the eerie silence around her. There weren't any birds singing and, indeed, none flying in the sky. She looked back at the dog who was still following on behind her. Its ears were flat against his head, and he was stooping as he walked. He had clearly picked up on the odd atmosphere.

As Fitz rounded the corner, she stopped in her tracks. The village was ahead of her, and she could see smoke curling its way up into the sky from several of the buildings.

And there was another smell filling the air. An obnoxious, putrid smell that she couldn't quite recognise. The village looked deserted and as she passed house after house, each was burnt out, some more so than others.

Where on earth was everyone? She headed towards the centre of the village where the church was situated in the square.

There were several shops in the centre, but they too had been burnt – one or two were still on fire. Whatever had happened here, had happened recently.

Fitz reached the entrance to the church and tried the iron ring on the door. It lifted and she pushed open the heavy oak. She was immediately hit by a stench that made her want to gag. She clasped her hand to her mouth and nose.

As her eyes adjusted to the dark interior of the building, it took her a moment to realise what she was looking at.

Sprawled across the altar and the first few rows of pews were bodies. Men, women, children. None of them moving. Some had their eyes closed, while others stared wide-eyed but seeing nothing. All of them were dead.

Fitz let out a cry and rushed out of the church, gagging so much she thought she was going to be sick but only brought up bile from her empty stomach.

Dear God, what had she just seen? She slumped down against the wall of the church, holding her head in her hands.

The whole village had been massacred. It had to be the work of the Germans. She had heard about such atrocities when she was training with SOE. Being told about them was one thing, but witnessing them first hand was another.

When she was finally able to open her eyes, she saw the dog sitting at the foot of the stone steps, watching her. It gave a little whine before lying down.

Fitz got to her feet and gently closed the door to the church. 'God have mercy on your souls,' she said quietly.

Slowly, she made her way down the steps. Her stomach cramped in hunger and she looked over towards the shops. Maybe she'd be able to salvage something to eat from what was left of the bakery, which stood apart from the row of shops and didn't look so badly fire-damaged.

The glass was blackened by the smoke and as she stepped through the doorway, ash covered the floor. The ceiling had collapsed from the fire but amazingly the rafters remained intact. Fitz wasn't sure how stable it was but she was desperate for some food. Anything, until she made it to Josselin. She looked back at the dog who was waiting on the path outside. He was probably hungry, too. She wondered when he'd last been fed.

The counter was partially damaged by the fire, charred and burnt at one end, but still more or less intact. She could see a wicker basket that had miraculously escaped being burnt, sitting on the shelf alongside the remains of others.

Luck was on her side. Inside the basket were two loaves of bread. Fitz grabbed them and tore off the end to one of them, hungrily stuffing it in her mouth. It didn't taste great – faintly of smoke, but she didn't care. She just needed food.

She searched the rest of the bakery but there was no other food and she wondered if the Germans had taken what supplies there had been before setting the shop alight. When she went through to the rear of the shop, it had been totally burnt out and some of the timber was still smouldering.

Back out on the street, she broke several pieces of bread up for the dog, who gulped them down at lightning speed. She had no idea if bread was good for a dog or not. The next thing she needed was water. She walked around the church and found the village water pump. She could have done with a canister of some description to take some water with her, but again that would have aroused suspicion had she been stopped. Instead, she had to pump the water with one hand and catch as much as she could in her hand where she sloshed it into her mouth. It was a thankless task. What she needed was a cup of some description.

She went back to the bakery and amongst the debris in the shopfront found a metal scoop, used for weighing out flour. This proved a much more efficient method and she was able to satisfy her thirst.

'Are you going to drink now?' she asked the dog. She filled the scoop and held it out towards the dog who had steadfastly remained out of touching distance from her the whole time.

Of all the things Fitz thought she might be doing on this mission, looking after a dog hadn't been one of them. The dog looked warily at Fitz and she felt sure he must be thirsty but she still hadn't managed to gain its trust yet. Propping the scoop up against the stone base of the pump, Fitz took a few steps away.

The dog eyed her and then hurried over to the water, lapping it up immediately. As Fitz stood there, her gaze drifted back to the church and thoughts of all the innocent dead inside. She realised her body was shaking and she was crying. Big uncontrollable sobs erupted from her throat and she once again sank to the ground. She allowed herself to cry for several minutes, but at the back of her mind she knew she couldn't stay where she was.

If the Germans came back, she needed to be out of here.

She picked up her bag and taking a minute to get her bearings again, she headed down the road towards the town of Josselin. The dog fell into step alongside her, which was an improvement on it following behind by several feet.

As she went down the street, every single house had been burned. The smell of smoke and ash hung heavily in the air as some of the buildings still smouldered. Again, Fitz noticed the silence. She couldn't begin to imagine the terror of the villagers as the Germans rounded them up. Had they known they were going to their deaths in the church? Had they sought refuge there, even? Only to be killed, slaughtered by a hail of bullets. At least they hadn't met their deaths by fire. That would be unimaginable.

Fitz paused at the end of the road to look back at the village. She wanted to remember this. If she ever got the chance to come back to France when the war was over, she'd come here and pay her respects to the villagers.

She thought she could hear the sound of a cat mewing. It was soft and floated through the still air. She looked around trying to pinpoint the direction of the noise. It was coming from the house on her left.

Fitz pushed open the gate and walked up the path to the single-storey stone cottage. She had no idea why she was going to look for a cat, as if she was gathering animals for Noah's ark, but something was drawing her towards the sound.

This house wasn't as burnt as some of the others and Fitz pushed open the wooden front door, stepping into a severely smoke-damaged room.

She nearly jumped out of her skin at the sight in front of her.

She had been expecting to find a cat, but instead there was a child. A little girl of about eight or nine years old, standing in the middle of the room, looking at Fitz. The child's face was tear-streaked and dirty, her blonde hair was tied back in two plaits. In one hand she clutched a teddy bear. She stared at Fitz.

Chapter 15

Fitz stared back at the little girl for a long moment while she gathered her thoughts. The child was such a sorry sight. '*Bonjour*,' Fitz said softly, offering a reassuring smile. '*Ça va?*'

The little girl didn't say anything.

Fitz's gaze looked beyond the girl. What if this was some sort of trap? Or were there other villagers who had somehow escaped the massacre?

She took a step closer and knelt, so she didn't seem overbearing to the girl. '*Comment t'appelles-tu?*'

Still the child said nothing. Fitz tried a different approach. Perhaps the child was hungry. 'Are you hungry? *Tu as faim?*' She continued in French as she pulled out the loaf of bread from her bag and tore off a chunk which she held out in front of her. 'Here, eat,' encouraged Fitz.

There was a little flicker of alertness in the girl's eyes before she reached out and grabbed the bread, stuffing it into her mouth. 'Eat slowly. *Lentement*,' said Fitz. 'You'll get tummy ache. Are you thirsty?'

Again the girl said nothing, but the eagerness in her eyes told a different story.

Fitz rose and went through into the what was left of the kitchen. There was a cup on the floor, which she picked up and was pleased to see that the china sink, together with the taps, hadn't been affected by the fire. The water glugged out and Fitz rinsed the cup before filling it with water. She handed the cup to the girl who drank steadily. She had probably been able to get water herself, Fitz concluded, but maybe not food.

Fitz opened the door to what she guessed was the larder, but there was barely anything on the shelves. The floor was covered in flour, smashed eggs and what looked like milk. She wondered if the Germans had destroyed the provisions just for the sake of it and taken anything worth saving.

'Are you here on your own?' asked Fitz, turning back to the girl. Still no reply. 'Have you been hiding?' The girl looked out towards the back garden. 'Out there?' asked Fitz. 'Can you show me?'

She followed the girl out to the garden, and through a gateway into an orchard. The girl went over to the corner which was filled with brambles and squeezed her way between the bush and the hedge. Fitz winced as one of the thorns caught her leg. There wasn't much of a gap, but she pushed her way through, catching herself several more times on the thorns.

Behind the brambles, hidden from sight was a well. Fitz watched in amazement as the child climbed over the stone surround and grasping hold of the rope slid down out of sight.

'Wait! *Attendez!*' Fitz rushed to the well and peered over the edge. She gave a sigh of relief. The girl was sitting on a little ledge a few feet down, holding onto the rope to stop herself from falling into the water far below. 'You hid here?' asked Fitz in amazement. 'I assume you can get out of there easily enough?'

The girl proceeded to show Fitz how she did it, using the uneven brickwork as footholds and the rope to support herself, she made her way out of the well.

'How did you know to hide there?' asked Fitz. Unsurprisingly, the girl didn't answer. Fitz wondered if the girl had hidden in there before, perhaps in a game of hide-and-seek. Or whether the mother had hidden the child, in the hope that she might survive and be able to come back for her daughter. And now the mother was probably among those bodies in the church and the child was all alone with no one to look after her.

Fitz took in a deep breath as she realised she'd need to find someone to take care of the child. But who and where, she had no idea.

She beckoned for the girl to come out of the well and helped her back onto the ground, before sending the bucket back down for some clean water. 'You're very clever,' said Fitz, kneeling and using her handkerchief to clean the dirty tear-streaked face. 'Now, do you have any papers? With your name on?'

The girl nodded and taking Fitz's hand, led her back into the house where she pointed to a rather singed leather satchel hanging on the larder door, next to a child's coat, presumably hers. Fitz took the bag down and looked inside. She was amazed and somewhat relieved to see the child's identity papers.

'So, let's see who you are,' she said, opening up the papers which hadn't been touched by the fire. 'Yvette Moreau.' She looked up and smiled at the child. 'Born twenty-fourth January, 1932. So you, Yvette, must be nine years old.' The child nodded. 'And my name is Claudine,' continued Fitz, remembering at the last moment not to use her real name. 'I'm going to look after you until we get to the next town.'

Yvette appeared uncertain. Her grip tightened on her teddy. She looked up at the mantelpiece. Fitz followed her gaze. There, spared from the fire by the brick chimney breast, was a photograph of a man and woman with a small child. Fitz took the photograph down. 'Is that you?' Yvette nodded. 'And Mama and Papa?' Again Yvette nodded and her eyes filled with fresh tears, which then slid down her face. Fitz wasn't sure her heart could take such pain as the sight of this little girl crying for the loss of her mother. A child who could so easily have been Fitz at the same age, experiencing the same loss.

She couldn't allow herself the indulgence of grief, though. She was supposed to be on a mission and having a child in tow wasn't part of the plan. For now, though, Fitz would just have to look after her. It shouldn't be too hard. Yvette wasn't that much younger than Michael and it was only until the next village, where Fitz could leave her with someone.

'Come here, my darling,' she said, going over to Yvette and wrapping her arms around her tiny frame. After a few moments, she pulled away and wiped Yvette's tears with her thumbs. 'Now, listen, Yvette. We have to go on quite a long journey and we need to pretend that I'm your aunty.' She took the satchel and slipped the photograph inside, together with Yvette's identity papers and hooked the strap over the child's shoulders. 'If anyone asks us, we have to say I'm taking you to stay with my cousin, who lives in Josselin. Do you think you can remember that?' Fitz wasn't sure if Yvette would be capable of answering, but she had to at least ensure they stuck to the same story. She wasn't of course going to take her as far as Josselin, but Fitz had no idea of what any of the villages on the way were called. It would be safe simply to say Josselin if they were stopped.

Yvette sniffed and wiped her nose on her sleeve. She nodded her understanding.

'Right, well, let's get on our way,' Fitz said, with more cheer than the situation warranted. She took the coat from the door and helped Yvette put it on, buttoning it up for her. The lining was singed, but the heavy outside fabric had avoided any fire damage. It smelt of smoke but with any luck, the fresh air would get rid of that. 'Do you like dogs?' asked Fitz. Again, another nod. 'That's good, because I have a dog outside called Scout. He's coming with us.'

Yvette's curiosity was piqued as she looked eagerly through to the front of the house. Fitz held out her hand. 'Ready?'

Yvette slipped her hand into Fitz's and the two of them went out onto the street.

Scout was on the other side of the road sniffing around, but as soon as he saw them, he trotted over, stopping a few feet away, as was his custom. 'He's a bit shy,' said Fitz. 'Rather like you. We'll start walking and he'll follow us.'

They must look an unlikely trio thought Fitz to herself as they headed down the road. She certainly hadn't been expecting this when she boarded the plane the previous night. First a dog and now a child. Life hadn't prepared her for this. And certainly, no amount of SOE training had either!

The trek to Josselin was going to take at least twice the time Fitz soon realised. Yvette wouldn't be able to keep at Fitz's pace for long. If she'd been issued with a fake permit to use a bicycle she might have been tempted to look for one in the village, if only so that Yvette could sit on it while she pushed it. Fitz just hoped they'd soon come across a village where she could leave the child.

The sky was looking very dark with rain filled clouds which Fitz was sure were on the brink of bursting. They needed to find somewhere to shelter from the weather. They should head for woodland which the Breton countryside provided in abundance. At least there the trees would afford some sort of shelter.

They hadn't long left the village when Fitz heard the sound of an engine in the distance. Not a truck but a car. 'Quick, this way,' she said, beginning to run to the gateway she had seen up ahead. The sound of the car was getting louder. It was coming fast and would soon be on them. They weren't going to make it to the gateway in time. 'Down here!' said Fitz urgently, almost dragging Yvette into the bracken-filled ditch on the side of the road. 'Duck down under the leaves. Scout! Here, boy. Here.' The dog however wouldn't come. 'Come here,' called Fitz, aware it was only seconds before the car would be whizzing around the corner. A stray dog standing in the road was bound to cause some level of curiosity.

Without warning, Yvette had jumped up. 'Scout! Come here!' she called in French.

Fitz was momentarily stunned to hear the child's voice and then stunned a second time as the dog did as it was told and trotted over. 'Good boy,' she said, amazed at the obedience of the animal. 'Lie down.'

The dog settled down next to Yvette and Fitz quickly rearranged the foliage before ducking down herself. She heard the car coming around the corner, changing gear and then accelerating. She closed her eyes and held her breath. Both actions pointless but she did them all the same. *Please don't stop. Please don't stop*, she said over and over again in her head.

The car continued to accelerate away from them. She looked at Yvette and put her finger to her lips. She wanted to be sure the car wasn't turning around and coming back anytime soon. She had to assume its destination was the burnt-out village. Maybe to check for any survivors.

'We can't stay on the road,' said Fitz. 'We need to use the trees as cover.' She climbed out of the ditch and helped Yvette out, too. 'Come on, we need to run, in case the car comes back.'

Within a few minutes they were in the safety of the trees, just as the first few spots of rain began to fall. Fitz looked down at Yvette who was once again holding her hand. The little girl looked up at her. There was so much trust in her eyes, Fitz was both surprised and slightly perturbed.

The trek through the woods slowed their progress even more. The ground was uneven and now and again one of them would stumble but they carried on and Yvette didn't complain once. Fortunately, the rain hadn't lasted too long and, although they were wet, neither was soaked. Fitz had tried to get Yvette to speak again by asking questions, but she had lapsed back into silence. Scout walked behind them mostly, though every now and again he would trot on ahead, only to turn to look at them as if to make sure they were still there.

It wasn't until they had been walking for an hour that Fitz finally felt it was safe enough to stop and take a break. She was glad she had managed to find a bottle to fill with water and she passed it to Yvette. 'Only take a few sips,' she instructed. 'We have to make it last.' Fitz closed her eyes and pictured the map of the area she had been told to memorise.

Fitz tried to remember what villages were in the area, but she felt slightly disorientated after trekking through the woods. She supposed there was always the option of finding somewhere to hide Yvette and Scout while she went onto Josselin by herself, though she wasn't sure if it was a good idea. She didn't like the idea of leaving Yvette on her own. The child was bound to be traumatised by what had happened in her own village.

As she looked down at the child, Fitz could see her eyes were already closing as tiredness overwhelmed her.

Chapter 16

Fitz hated having to wake Yvette. The little girl was obviously exhausted, probably mentally as well as physically. Fitz couldn't help worrying about the long-term effects of what she had witnessed or experienced. Thank goodness Yvette had had the sense to hide, or someone had hidden her in the well.

When they'd sat down, Yvette had sat between Fitz and Scout, who'd positioned himself on the other side of her. As Yvette had sunk towards Fitz when she nodded off, Scout had moved closer to the little girl, as if offering his protection and body warmth. Fitz had been a bit wary of the dog at first, but with each hour that passed, her confidence in him was increasing. Gradually they were all beginning to trust one another.

'Yvette,' said Fitz softly, stroking the child's hair. 'Time to wake up. We need to start walking again.' Yvette gave a sleepy groan and snuggled into her. 'You really need to wake up,' encouraged Fitz. 'Come on.'

Yvette sat up and looked around her and then at Fitz. Her brow furrowed and as realisation of who she was with dawned on her, her small shoulders slumped and she looked down at the ground.

Fitz felt for her but there wasn't time to dwell on the situation. She was reminded of Cook who was fond of saying things like, 'Chin up. Worse things happen at sea' when either

Fitz or Michael had been disappointed or feeling sorry for themselves about something.

She spared Yvette the quote but chivvied her along, nonetheless. They needed to keep moving. Fitz held Yvette's hand as they made their way on through the trees, aware that the forest was spanning out in a northern direction, which was contrary to the way they needed to go in order to reach Josselin. It meant they would have to break cover and risk taking the open road.

Fortunately, the Breton countryside was sparsely populated, and the road was quiet. They passed the occasional house or entrance to a property, but there was no one about. Fitz was hoping to find someone who could take Yvette in but was having no such luck. The road undulated its way across the area – a combination of long straights and then twisty turns.

They had been walking for some time, when in the distance Fitz could see a cluster of buildings and beyond that, poking up from behind a hill, was a church spire.

Maybe this was where she could find a safe place for Yvette. But then a thought struck her. Walking into a village where she was obviously a stranger, with a girl and a dog, would cause a lot of unwanted attention. Someone might take Yvette in, but they might also report Fitz to the Germans and then she could be in deep trouble. The Germans would realise Fitz had escaped last night. Damn. She hadn't thought this through properly. It meant she was still stuck with Yvette.

They somehow needed to work their way around the village. The countryside was littered with small tracks that wove their way through trees and fields. If Fitz could find one before they reached the village, they might be able to easily work their way around without being seen. Fitz still held out hope that they'd come across a secluded farmhouse where she could deposit Yvette.

They carried on walking and as they rounded a bend in the road, Fitz's heart plummeted. She had got careless and blasé, for now they were faced with a checkpoint ahead, manned by two soldiers. It was too late to turn back or to hide out of sight, they had been spotted. She forced herself to carry on walking, reminding herself she had been trained for these kinds of situations. She could do this. She had to.

One of the soldiers nudged the other and nodded in Fitz's direction. The second soldier chucked down the cigarette he was smoking and crushed it underfoot. He lifted his rifle a fraction.

'Papers,' he demanded as she, Yvette and Scout came to a halt in front of them.

Fitz handed over both sets of identity papers.

The soldiers took a long time examining the documentation. Fitz fought to keep her breathing even. Now was not the time to panic and give herself away. Yvette slipped her hand into Fitz's and Fitz looked down and smiled at her.

A car approaching the other side of the barrier, had both soldiers looking up. It was a black Citroën – the car of choice for the Gestapo and officers.

Fitz's mouth dried and she swallowed hard. All she had to do was to hold her nerve.

There were two occupants in the car. A driver and a German officer. He looked back at her through small round glasses, before saying something to the soldier.

The car moved through the checkpoint and Fitz was just about to breathe a sigh of relief, when the car stopped next to her.

The officer got out of the car and gestured for the guards to hand him the documentation, which he proceeded to inspect for what felt like hours. He beckoned Fitz over to him.

'Mademoiselle Bardot,' he said, reading from the documentation.

'Yes, that's right. *Oui, c'est vrai*,' replied Fitz.

'And this is Yvette Moreau?' he continued in French. He looked at Yvette who remained silent.

'She's shy. *Elle est timide*,' said Fitz.

'I wasn't talking to you,' snapped the officer. He lifted

The Girl in the Sky

Yvette's chin up with his leather gloved finger. 'You are Yvette Moreau? Speak up, child.'

Yvette nodded. Fitz was willing her to speak. She squeezed the little girl's hand gently. 'You need to answer the gentleman,' she said. The last word tasting bitter in her mouth.

There was a tense silence, and just when Fitz thought the officer was going to run out of patience, Yvette finally spoke. '*Oui, monsieur.*'

'That wasn't so difficult,' muttered the officer. He turned to Fitz. 'What relation is she to you?'

'She's my niece. My sister's child. Sadly, my sister has passed away. We are going to stay with my cousin in Josselin,' Fitz said, elaborating on her official cover story.

The officer looked thoughtful. 'You have come from the village of Saint Pierre?'

Fitz's heart quickened as she tried to think of an explanation. 'She came with me to visit relations in Pontivy first. That's where we've been the last few days. We're now making our way to Josselin.'

'And she is your niece, you say?' asked the officer.

'That's right,' replied Fitz.

The officer placed a hand on Yvette's shoulder and moved her away from Fitz. He whispered something in Yvette's ear and after a little coaxing, Yvette replied. Fitz couldn't hear what was being said. The officer turned back around and moved Yvette in front of him, facing Fitz.

He looked Fitz straight in the eye as he spoke and then put his finger to his lips, before taking his pistol from its holster and pointing it at the back of Yvette's head.

Fitz gasped in horror but then seeing the questioning look on Yvette's face, she forced herself to smile at her instead.

'Keep looking at me,' said Fitz, her voice cracking slightly. 'That's it, Yvette. Just at me.'

'So, a little game,' said the officer. 'I have asked your dear niece what her favourite colour is. I'm going to ask you what that colour is, and you have one chance to get it right or you lose a life.'

Fitz's stomach churned with fear. What sort of man did this? She had no doubt he wouldn't hesitate to pull the trigger. In fact, he looked to be enjoying himself, delighting in her distress at the situation.

She looked at Yvette who was clasping her teddy, her fingers flicking the little red ribbon around its neck. Fitz wanted to cry. A poor innocent child – how could someone be so cruel? In fact, cruel was too kind a word. This was barbaric.

The small curve of the officer's mouth repulsed her. 'Are you ready?' he asked.

Fitz wasn't sure if her legs were going to hold her but she couldn't show the fear she felt. She didn't want the last thing Yvette to see was fear. She smiled again at the child. 'I'm ready.'

'Good. So, remember, one chance otherwise you lose a life.' The officer paused dramatically and then posed his question. 'What is Yvette's favourite colour? Now think very carefully before answering.'

'Favourite colour,' repeated Fitz. She looked at Yvette who was worrying the ribbon between her finger and thumb. She was staring straight at Fitz, her eyes wide as if she was trying to tell her the answer. The poor child, if only she could somehow convey it to Fitz.

'Hurry up,' said the officer. 'I haven't got long.'

'Erm . . . p—' Fitz went to say pink but something stopped her. Yvette was tugging at the ribbon on the bear. The red ribbon. Was Yvette actually trying to tell her the answer? No, surely not? Fitz glanced up at the officer and back at Yvette.

'You have five seconds to give me an answer,' said the officer. 'Five. Four. Three—'

Fitz took one last look at Yvette. 'Red!' she shouted out just before the German had finished counting. 'Red. Her favourite colour is red.'

The officer raised his eyebrows. 'I'm impressed,' he said. 'I'm also a man of my word.' He replaced the pistol in its holster and then pushed Yvette towards Fitz. It was then he appeared to notice the dog. 'Is that your animal?'

'Yes, he's with us,' said Fitz.

'Strange, one of my men said something about a dog in the village of Saint Pierre last night. Wasn't very welcoming apparently.' He took a step towards them and immediately Scout's hackles went up. The officer once again took the pistol from its holster.

'He's very protective,' said Fitz, quickly. 'Just not very good with strangers.'

'But fine with you two because he is, after all, your dog, yes?'

'Erm, yes.'

'Maybe you could prove to me he's not dangerous,' said the officer. 'Go on, both of you. Pet the dog.'

Fitz took Yvette's hand and slowly turned towards Scout. She said a silent prayer that the dog wouldn't be scared of them. 'Hello, Scout,' she said, as she took a few steps closer to him. She purposely placed herself ahead of Yvette. If the dog did try to attack them, which she knew would be out of fear rather than aggression, then she could protect Yvette from harm.

Scout stood his ground. Fitz was in front of him now. She reached out her hand, hoping the officer wouldn't see she was shaking. Scout sniffed her fingertips. There was no sign of aggression from him at all. 'Good boy,' said Fitz. She slowly moved her hand to the dog's head and stroked him a couple of times before taking her hand away.

She looked around at the officer. 'He's a bit nervous, that's all.'

'Now the child. I want to see her hug the dog. You move away.' He indicated with his pistol. Fitz had no choice but to let go of Yvette and move to the side. She watched intently, ready to jump in if anything went wrong.

The assured confidence of a child who didn't know the danger was apparent as Yvette stepped towards the dog and kneeling, put her arms around Scout's neck. She ruffled his fur before standing up and looking back at Fitz.

The officer looked surprised. 'Well, what can I say?' He gave a shrug. 'You're free to carry on your way.' He handed back their papers.

'*Merci*,' said Fitz. Not wasting any time, she took Yvette's hand and with the dog following on behind, hurried under the raised checkpoint barrier.

'Oh, Mademoiselle Bardot!' called the officer.

Fitz paused and closed her eyes for a second before turning around. 'Yes?'

'I will see you in Josselin! I'll be there later today once I've attended to some business. We can perhaps meet again, more sociably.' He gave a salute and got back into his car.

Chapter 17

Fitz fought to control her breathing as an adrenaline rush of relief swarmed through her body. She had to force herself not to break into a run as she walked away from the checkpoint. She could hear the officer's car disappear into the distance and it wasn't until they were out of sight of the checkpoint that she allowed herself to relax for a moment.

She looked down at Yvette. 'You were so clever,' she said. 'So very clever, to fiddle with your teddy's ribbon. Well done.'

She put her arm around Yvette's shoulder and gave her a brief hug and Yvette rewarded her with a warm smile.

As they neared the village, Fitz spotted one of the narrow tracks she had been looking for and guided Yvette off the main road. She relaxed a little, feeling marginally safer taking the path along the edge of the fields. Her earlier plan to rest had now been relegated. Her main aim was to get to Josselin as soon as possible and make contact with the resistance.

Two hours of walking and they hadn't covered half the ground that Fitz would have liked. The cold and damp December weather made Fitz shiver. She paused to fasten the top button on Yvette's coat. For the next hour or so, as they trudged along the road, their speed slowed as Yvette grew more and more tired.

'We'll find somewhere to settle down for the night,' promised

Fitz, aware that if she wore Yvette out too much today, the child mightn't be able to make the final leg tomorrow. It was vital they made the rendezvous.

It took another twenty minutes or so of walking before Fitz spotted somewhere. A solitary barn was standing in the corner of the field and beyond that was woodland. Tucked away from sight of the road, it was a perfect place to stop.

Despite the remoteness, Fitz needed to make sure the barn was empty.

'Right, what we're going to do,' she said to Yvette. 'We're going to head over to the woods and watch the barn for a while. I want to make sure no one comes out or goes in.'

They waited among the trees out of sight until it was dusk. Fitz watched the barn and the track leading up to it for several hours until she was satisfied it was safe and there was no sign of the farmer who owned it. She didn't want to have to persuade him to allow them to sleep the night there. With the promise of extra food or a special concession from the Germans, turning in a fellow countryman was a tempting offer for anyone. Fitz had heard stories of the French turning against each other, not so much out of disloyalty but out of the need to survive.

Not for the first time, she wondered where *her* boundary was. If she was ever put to the test, at what point would she give in? What prize would be worth betrayal? So far, she hadn't come up with a definitive answer and she had no desire to test her limit, if she could help it.

Once dusk had truly fallen and evening arrived, Fitz, Yvette, and Scout crept out of the woods and into the barn. There was an old tractor parked inside, which didn't look like it had been used recently. The mud on the wheels was dry and cobwebs hung across the steering wheel like Christmas decorations. Several hessian sacks were piled on the seat of the farm machinery and might be useful to keep them warm in the night.

Bales of hay were stacked at the rear of the barn. Fitz ignored the fact that the place was probably a hotbed of mice and rats, and having Scout with them, might deter the furry creatures from venturing too close while they slept. It was a shame she couldn't light a fire, but the straw and sacks would help keep them warm.

It wasn't long before Fitz had made them both a nest of hay to snuggle into with the sacking over their legs and bodies as blankets.

'There, I know it's not exactly a hotel, but it will do for the night,' said Fitz, pleased when Yvette snuggled into her and closed her eyes. She fell instantly into a deep sleep.

The temperature had dropped notably and Fitz was glad for the sacks, even though bits of straw poked through from underneath them. Yvette moved in her sleep, seeking a more comfortable position and Fitz put her arm around the child, so Yvette's head rested against her.

She wondered what Michael would say if he saw her now. He'd probably think it was jolly good fun sleeping in a barn. She smiled fondly as she thought of him and imagined him tucked up in bed listening out for any passing planes overhead.

A sudden feeling of loneliness washed over her, taking Fitz by surprise. She wasn't the homesick type but right then she felt vulnerable and responsible both at the same time.

If Fitz could have one wish right there and then, it would be to be back at Badcombe House where it was safe, familiar and warm. Funny how she thought the house was cold in the winter, at least she had the luxury of a hot water bottle. Here in the barn, it was just hers and Yvette's body heat to stave off the cold. What Fitz would do now for a warm bed, cotton sheets and a couple of logs burning in the fireplace. She closed her eyes imagining the mug of hot cocoa her mother would have made her and allowed her to have in her room. Her mother would have wrapped a hand-knitted shawl around Fitz's shoulders and sat on the edge of the bed to read a story.

Fitz didn't always permit herself to visit such memories, as they were sometimes too painful, but tonight they brought her comfort and she prayed that she would one day be fortunate enough to see Badcombe House again, to see Michael and her father. She even found herself thinking of Camilla. Gosh, she really must be missing home.

Fitz allowed herself to relax enough to fall asleep, too. She hadn't realised quite how tired she was.

She didn't know how long she'd been asleep but at some point in the night, when it was dark and cold, she was woken by the sound of Yvette crying. Not big heaving sobs but gentle, pitiful murmurs and sniffles.

'It's all right,' soothed Fitz. 'Don't cry now, sweetie.' She held the child a little tighter.

'*Je veux Maman*,' came Yvette's muffled voice.

Fitz's eyes snapped open. Yvette had actually spoken of her own accord. That was something of a breakthrough.

'I know you want your mother,' replied Fitz softly. 'I wish I could find her for you.'

'She was at home,' said Yvette. 'Where is she now? Why hasn't she come for me? Are we going back for her? She'll be worried about me. Does she know I'm with you?'

It was as if Yvette had been storing these worries up and the dam of silence, holding them back, had broken. The questions came pouring out. Where did Fitz even begin answering them? She didn't want to lie but at the same time, the truth was so brutal.

'I don't know where your mummy is,' she said eventually. 'But when we go back to Saint Pierre, I'm going to look for her.'

'I'm frightened,' said Yvette. 'I want my mummy.'

'Don't be scared.' Fitz dropped a kiss onto the child's head. 'You've been so brave and so clever. Not only did you trick the German, but you were so clever in hiding from them in your garden.'

'I was told to hide there,' said Yvette.

'By your mother?' asked Fitz. Now that Yvette was finally talking, there was no stopping her. Fitz didn't want to dissuade her, even though they could both do with getting some sleep.

'No. By the man,' replied Yvette.

'What man was that?' Fitz's eyes grew heavy and she could feel her mind beginning to wander into that half dreamlike state just before falling asleep.

'He flew aeroplanes.'

Fitz sat bolt upright now. 'He was a pilot?'

Yvette looked a little alarmed and Fitz forced herself to relax again. 'Did he say what his name was?'

Yvette shook her head. 'His leg was bleeding.'

'But he could walk?'

'A bit.'

'What was he wearing?'

Yvette shrugged. 'Brown coat with fur here.' She pointed to the collar of her coat.

She was describing what sounded like a flight jacket. Something that was standard issue for RAF pilots. 'What was he doing at your house?'

'*Maman* was cleaning his leg,' said Yvette. 'She put a bandage on it and then some other men came.'

'They came in the house?'

'*Oui*. They spoke to the man.' Yvette looked down at her hands and fiddled with the frayed edge of the sack.

Fitz could see the memory was upsetting Yvette, but she needed to know what happened next. 'Were they friends of the man?'

'*Oui*. But then . . .'

Fitz swept a stray strand of hair from the child's face. 'Then what?' she asked quietly.

'Everyone was running around, saying they needed to hide. The men left. *Maman* looked very scared.' Yvette sniffed and wiped her nose. 'She kissed me and told me to go with the man.'

'With the bad leg?'

'*Oui*. She said to hide in the well and wait for her. The man took me and said wait there, sweetheart and then he went.' Yvette paused to take a breath, before speaking again. Her voice was full of anguish, confusion and fear as her words tumbled out, one after the other. '*Maman* said she'd come back for me, but she didn't.' Big blobs of tears ran down Yvette's face. 'I want *Maman*.'

Fitz held the little girl tightly, not knowing what to say or how to comfort her. She thought of all the things adults had said to her when her own mother had died. Promises that everything would be all right. That her mother loved her and was up in heaven looking down on her. Even at that young age, Fitz knew they were just words, what she now knew to be platitudes the grown-ups said to try to make her feel better. How they ever thought she'd be reassured, she didn't know. She'd never believed them about heaven, but she also knew it made the grown-ups feel better if she played along with it. Fitz didn't want to make impossible promises and say silly things to Yvette, so she said nothing and did what she had herself found most comforting – to be held and to feel cared for. To feel someone loved her after her mother had died.

It was some time before Yvette's sobbing faded and her breathing became steady and deep as sleep took her, Fitz hoped, to a restful place where she'd dream of happier places and times.

Meanwhile, what Yvette had told her about a man helping her hide in the well had been plaguing Fitz ever since and it was only now that she could fully consider it.

Her heart was jumpy simply at the thought that the pilot could have been Sam. Was that too fanciful? Was it purely wishful thinking?

His plane had come down in the area, she knew that much from Bob. If it was Sam, then who were the other men? They were trying to help him; they must be resistance members.

Could that mean Sam was still alive and he had been here? It was a crazy idea. What would the chances be? Slim but not zero. Dare she hope that it was true or was that asking too much of the universe?

Fitz wanted to get up and walk around, as the more she entertained the idea, the more nervous energy she felt building up inside her. But her arm was well and truly wedged under Yvette and when she tried to move, Yvette stirred, whimpered and snuggled in tighter to her.

It was no good, she was going to drive herself mad thinking and rethinking whether it had been Sam who had helped Yvette earlier. If she was to stand any chance of getting some sleep, she needed to put the whole idea out of her mind.

She made a conscious effort to think of Marjorie and Elsie. They wouldn't believe she was curled up in a barn with a little French girl and a dog, hiding from the Germans. It was so different to anything any of them had ever done. In a way Fitz found it hard to believe herself. She felt a certain detachment from the whole situation as if it wasn't really happening to her. She didn't know if that was a good or a bad thing.

Fitz had eventually fallen into a light sleep, and it felt like only minutes had passed when she woke early the following morning, as the first rays of sun were poking their way over the hills, shining into the barn.

As she opened her eyes, she gave a yelp of surprise. Standing over her and Yvette was a man, dressed in corduroy trousers, a grubby looking once-white shirt and a jacket which had definitely seen better days.

Fitz sat upright, her eyes darting towards the doorway and then back down at Yvette. Surprisingly, Scout wasn't making a sound.

'I'm not going to hurt you,' said the man.

At this point, Yvette stirred and opened her eyes. She let out a cry of alarm and huddled into Fitz.

'We just needed somewhere to stay for the night,' said Fitz, starting to get to her feet and pulling Yvette up with her. 'We're leaving now. We haven't taken anything. I promise.'

'Come with me,' ordered the man.

'Please, *monsieur*, we'll leave now. Please let us go.'

'You need something warm to eat. Come inside. My daughter will cook you some eggs.'

At the mention of eggs, Yvette tugged on Fitz's arm. 'Please?' she said.

'Bring the dog, too,' said the farmer before turning and heading towards the doorway.

'Please,' said Yvette again.

Fitz was a little bewildered by the wake-up call but the thought of being able to offer Yvette some small comfort even if it was just food, was too tempting. '*Allez*,' said Fitz, holding Yvette's hand and breaking into a small run to catch up with the man who she assumed owned the barn.

'The dog can come inside,' said the farmer, opening the door to the farmhouse. 'He looks like he needs feeding, too. He is yours?'

'Not really,' said Fitz, unsure how much to share with the man. 'He sort of adopted us.'

Fitz heard a woman's voice from inside the house. 'Who are you talking to, Papa?'

'We have some guests,' said the man. 'They are in need of food and a drink. Use the eggs.' Fitz and Yvette followed the man into the house, the door opening straight into a kitchen.

Standing at the sink was a woman, probably not much older than Fitz. She didn't look especially startled to see her guests and Fitz wondered if this was not the first time the family had extended their hospitality to strangers.

'My name is Yves and this is my daughter, Vivienne.' He indicated to the wooden table in the middle of the room. 'Please, sit.'

'*Bonjour,*' said Vivienne.

'*Bonjour,*' replied Fitz. '*Je m'appelle—*'

She went to speak but Yves shook his head. 'It's best if we do not know your names.'

'*Oui.* Of course,' said Fitz, feeling embarrassed she hadn't thought of that herself.

Scout was still hovering in the doorway and Yves took a bag from under the sink. He scooped a handful of dog biscuits and dropped them into a metal bowl. 'We used to have a dog,' he explained. 'He died a few months ago.'

'A dog,' said Vivienne, her eyes lighting up as she noticed the animal for the first time. 'Oh, he is beautiful. What is his name?'

'I don't know his name, but I've been calling him Scout,' said Fitz.

Yves took the bowl over to the doorway and placed it on the floor. 'What sort of name is that for a French dog?' he said not without humour. 'He is a very handsome dog. A little on the thin side and looks like he could do with a wash. He needs a more suitable name.'

'He should be called Beau,' said Vivienne, crouching down and tapping the bowl to encourage the dog into the kitchen.

Hesitantly, the dog moved into the house and after sniffing the contents of the bowl, eagerly began eating. Vivienne stroked his head and Fitz was amazed the dog didn't bat an eyelid.

'Now leave the dog alone,' said Yves. 'We need to feed our guests. I suspect they are in a hurry to be somewhere.'

'Of course,' said Vivienne, getting up and busying herself at the stove.

Within a few minutes both Fitz and Yvette were tucking into fried eggs and bread. 'Thank you so much,' said Fitz when they had finished. 'You have been very kind.' She looked at Yvette who was mopping up her egg yolk with the bread. If Fitz was going to leave Yvette with anyone,

Yves and his daughter might be the best option. Who knew if she would get another chance? 'Monsieur,' she began. 'I was wondering if it would be possible for the child to stay with you?'

Yves frowned and exchanged a look with his daughter. 'Why do you want to do that?'

Before Fitz could answer, Yvette jumped in. 'I don't want to stay here. I want to stay with you.' She grabbed Fitz's forearm with both her hands. 'Don't leave me here.'

Fitz looked at Yves and Vivienne. If she thought she was going to get some back-up, she had sorely misjudged them. They both remained silent. Fitz tried again. 'I have things I need to do in Josselin and it's not the best place for a child. Please. It is not safe for me to take her.'

'No!' cried Yvette. 'I'm not staying.'

'Yvette, that's enough,' said Fitz, rather more sternly than she intended. She tried to extract her arm from Yvette's grip but Yvette wasn't letting go. 'It's not safe for you to come with me.'

Yves held up his hand. 'Enough,' he said. He looked at Fitz. 'She doesn't want to stay.'

'She's only a child and doesn't understand,' protested Fitz. Gosh, she couldn't look at Yvette, it was making her feel guilty. Of course it was better if Yvette stayed here. Why didn't anyone see that? She turned to Vivienne. 'Would you be able to look after her?'

Vivienne's eyes widened a fraction. 'I'm sorry, but it would be even more dangerous for her to stay here. For her and for us.'

Yves cleared his throat. 'We have a German officer billeted here. No, don't be alarmed. He's not here now. He's away for two days but he will be back and how could we explain a child suddenly appearing?'

Fitz dropped her gaze. Yves was right, of course. There was no way she could leave Yvette here. She patted Yvette's hand. 'It's all right. You're coming with me.'

The Girl in the Sky

Yvette's face lit up. 'I am?'

'Yes,' said Fitz, feeling strangely relieved herself.

'You're not leaving me?'

'No.' Fitz smiled at Yvette who clung even more tightly to her.

The embrace was so full of emotion, Fitz could feel the relief sparking out from Yvette like an electrical charge, zapping her right in the heart. Yvette sat up, unhooking her arms from around Fitz, but refusing to let go of her hand. Fitz gave her hand a little squeeze. 'We should really leave now.' She was conscious that they had little time to make it to Josselin. Her stomach gave an anxiety-ridden roll at the prospect of missing the rendezvous.

'Where are you going?' asked Yves.

'Erm, it's probably best if I don't say,' said Fitz, not wishing to compromise herself.

Yves nodded his understanding. 'If I was to tell you I was going to a village near Josselin this morning with my horse and cart, would that be of help to you?'

Fitz glanced at Vivienne, who nodded encouragingly. She looked back at Yves. 'That would be very helpful, indeed.'

'*Alors*. We will leave shortly.' He looked down at the dog who was now settled at his feet. 'It may be difficult for you to take the dog with you to Josselin. Would you like to leave him with us? That I can explain far more easily to the German officer.'

Fitz hesitated before she replied. 'I might not be able to come back for him,' she said carefully.

'He can stay with us for as long as is necessary,' replied Yves.

'Thank you,' said Fitz. Although she knew this was the right thing to do, she couldn't help feeling a little sad that they would be continuing without Scout – or Beau, as she suspected he was going to be known from now on. 'That is very kind of you.'

'It will be good to have a dog around again,' said Yves, reaching down and ruffling the dog's ear. 'Do you think that is good, Beau?'

Chapter 18

Fitz was sorry to leave Scout behind, but she was also relieved. It would be better for her and Yvette and so much better for the dog. Yves and Vivienne seemed like genuine people who would take good care of him. She couldn't imagine he would be tied up to a shed and neglected. It reminded her that there were good people about and although only a small act of kindness, it felt like something much bigger, and it warmed her heart.

The journey into Josselin went without any hitches. Sitting on the back of the hay cart with Yvette alongside her was a blessing for their legs, especially Yvette's. The cart lolloped and bumped its way down the uneven track but the going was much smoother once they were on the main road.

Fitz had already agreed a cover story with Yves should they get stopped. He was going to a village near to Josselin to see his brother with some provisions and had spotted Fitz and Yvette on the road and given them a ride. A very normal thing to do, which shouldn't arouse any suspicions.

Fitz allowed herself to relax for a while and as she took deep breaths of clean Breton air, her mind drifted to thoughts of Sam. She had asked Yves if he knew of any Allied pilots who had been downed in the area, but he had shaken his head and moved the conversation on. She wasn't sure if he knew more than he was prepared to tell her or simply didn't know.

The cart came to a halt at a crossroads. Yves turned around to speak to Fitz. 'I have to go this way now,' he said, indicating to his left. 'You need to go straight on. Josselin is just down around the corner and down the hill.'

Fitz hopped off the back of the cart and helped Yvette down. 'Thank you so much for your kindness,' she said, shaking his hand. 'Take care.'

'Good luck,' said Yves. And then to Yvette. 'Don't worry about the dog. He will be happy with us.' He gave Fitz one last look before flicking the reins and, making a clicking noise, he drove the horse on.

Josselin really was just around the corner. Fitz could see the canal below and the huge castle walls running alongside the water. She knew from studying the map that the canal ran from Brest to Nantes. In any other circumstances, it would have been wonderful to walk alongside the canal or even take a boat, but with giant red Nazi flags draped from the windows of the château, the fairy-tale image was downgraded to one of a horror story. Even the bridge crossing the canal and leading into the town had been adorned with a Nazi flag.

From her vantage point at the top of the winding hill, Fitz could see a checkpoint on her side of the bridge. There was no other way across the canal to the town – she would simply have to run the gauntlet again.

Luck was on her side as the guards appeared to have little interest in her or Yvette, due to a woman at the checkpoint who was giggling and openly flirting with them. The soldier merely gave Fitz's papers a cursory glance before waving her through.

She and Yvette walked along the canal path. The château was even more impressive close up. It must be at least one hundred feet from the ground to the top of the tower. The town itself was built on the hillside, and from what Fitz had been told and the maps she had studied before leaving

England, the entrance to the château was on the other side at street level.

Around the side of the château, halfway up the hill that led to the centre of the town, Fitz spotted the well – the rendezvous point. They were early and she didn't want to hang around too much in case they aroused suspicion.

'Let's see if we can get something to eat,' she said to Yvette.

A few minutes later they were in the centre of the town where Fitz suspected, prior to the invasion and occupation, this had once been a bustling market. Today, however, it was empty. She spotted a boulangerie where there was a short queue from the doorway. Food was rationed here in France just as it was in Britain and during her SOE training Fitz had been advised that the black market was very much alive and thriving.

They tagged onto the back of the queue. Fitz didn't mind that it moved slowly, it was a good way to kill time and to blend in with the locals. It also gave her the opportunity to scope out as much of the town as she could see. What she could learn now, might just save her life in an emergency.

She hoped she wouldn't need a back-up plan, though. All she wanted was the kidnap plot to go ahead without any hitches. She wasn't entirely sure what she was going to do with Yvette yet, but hoped one of her contacts at the château would be able to help.

Eventually they reached the head of the queue and were able to obtain a small block of cheese and two slices of ham. Fitz had found a quiet spot at the top of the street, where they could eat their food away from any spying eyes before they made their way back to the rendezvous point.

They were there a few minutes early. Fitz rested her bag on the wall of the well and pretended to rummage inside it for something. She had a hanky in her hand, ready to produce should any Germans ask her what she was doing.

It was exhausting having to think about every action and ensure she had a valid reason, one that wouldn't get her into trouble and would be accepted. She had been trained for all this but putting it into practice when the danger was very real was so much different to exercises and hypothetical scenarios back in England. No matter how hard SOE training tried, they couldn't prepare someone fully for the real thing.

The December sky looked dark and ominously cloudy. Fitz hoped it wouldn't rain before they met their contact, as they would look very suspicious standing in the street getting soaking wet. Fortunately, they had only been waiting a few minutes when Fitz noticed the woman from the checkpoint approaching. She smiled at Fitz and waved.

'Oh, Claudine, there you are!' She kissed Fitz on each side of her face and then enveloped her in a hug. 'A Christmas feast awaits you at the château.'

It was the coded message Fitz had been told to expect. She answered with the prearranged response. 'As long as there are chestnuts roasting and mulled wine warming, Margot.'

'Of course, plenty for you to take home with you.'

Margot looked down at Yvette. 'How lovely to see you, too,' she said, before giving Fitz a quizzical look.

'My niece,' said Fitz.

'You are alone? Where is André?' asked Margot looking around.

'He was captured by the Germans,' replied Fitz, keeping her voice low so as not to be overheard. 'We were ambushed at the farm. Someone ratted on us.'

The woman's eyes widened. 'Well, it will be someone from your side. No one from the resistance would do such a thing.'

Fitz gave her a challenging look. 'You sound very sure. On "my side", as you put it, only four people knew about the arrangements. The mole has to be here in France.'

'You don't know what you're talking about.'

'Well, let's see what Philippe says,' replied Fitz.

Margot made a scoffing noise. 'First the child and now an ambush. It is strange how you managed to escape.'

Fitz had no mind to argue with the woman any further. 'This needs to be discussed somewhere safe,' she said. 'Are you going to take me to the château or do I have to go there myself?'

Margot pushed herself away from the wall. 'Follow me.' And then pasting on a smile for anyone watching, she slipped her hand through Fitz's arm. 'The child was not in the plan,' she said quietly.

'I had no choice,' replied Fitz.

This earned her a reproachful look from her contact, but she didn't care.

They walked through the cobbled streets and around to the entrance of the château, passing through the red wooden gates where two German soldiers stood on guard.

'Philippe's cousin,' said Margot nonchalantly, not breaking stride. Fitz kept up with her and was surprised when again they weren't asked for their papers.

'My cousin must be very influential,' commented Fitz once she was certain they were out of earshot.

'Oh, he is,' replied Margot. 'He has friends in high places. Now, there are several German officers residing, at your cousin's invitation, in the château. Please remember that at all times. There are also three officers here as guests for the party tomorrow night.'

It all seemed so bizarre, talking about guests and a party as if the country wasn't under occupation. Fitz couldn't imagine how some people were seemingly going about their daily lives, almost welcoming the Germans. But then, she guessed, some were playing a very dangerous game – like the man who was pretending to be her cousin.

'We are in the west wing of the building and the Germans are all in the east wing,' said Margot, as they ascended the sweeping stone staircase to the first floor.

A German officer passed them, trotting down the steps, he slowed to bid them both good afternoon before continuing on his way.

Another surreal encounter. Fitz would have to get used to this for the next thirty-six hours. She followed Margot down the hallway, where she knocked on the door of one of the rooms, before entering.

'Ah, my dear cousin, Claudine,' said a man, getting to his feet and walking over to Fitz. He greeted her with kisses and Margot closed the doors behind her.

'We have an extra guest,' she said, gesturing to Yvette. 'And we have another absent.'

Philippe frowned. 'A child?' he whispered. 'No one told me about this.'

Fitz reined in a sigh. Patiently she explained how she'd found Yvette and how she couldn't possibly leave her.

'And her mother?' asked Philippe.

'I haven't been able to find her yet,' replied Fitz, raising her eyebrows at the Frenchman, hoping he'd understand what she wasn't saying. She was very conscious that Yvette still didn't know the true fate of her mother.

Philippe made a huffing noise. 'Very well. I'm not happy, but she's here now.'

'Exactly,' said Fitz. 'And she is my charge. I don't expect anyone to have to look after her.' The words came out before Fitz realised what she was saying. She had just taken on sole responsibility for Yvette.

'I'll hold you to that.' Philippe returned to the desk he had been sitting at. 'I take it you know what the plans are for the party tomorrow?'

'Yes,' replied Fitz. 'We don't have André with us. We were ambushed.'

Fitz relayed the events at the farmhouse to Philippe. She was aware of Margot making tusking noises and sighing in exasperation as she listened, but Fitz ignored her.

'She was the only one to escape,' said Margot, in a way

that left Fitz in no doubt, the Frenchwoman did not believe her story.

'André was alive when he was taken?' asked Philippe.

'Yes. Both he and the resistance member who was in charge.'

'Bernard,' said Margot to Philippe, who nodded.

He rubbed his chin with his fingertips as he considered the information. 'Hmm. They need to hold out another day or so.'

'Let's hope they can do that,' said Margot.

'They know the details. I am certain they won't give us up,' said Philippe. 'Not Bernard, anyway. He won't say a word. I guarantee that.'

'Then let's also hope the rat isn't André,' said Margot.

'Enough talk of that now,' instructed Philippe.

'We should call the plan off,' said Margot, leaning against the fireplace as she lit a cigarette. 'We've been compromised.'

Philippe frowned and silence filled the room as he contemplated the scenario. 'No,' he said finally. 'The plan will go ahead. The people of the area need to know that we are fighting for them. That we won't allow Hoffmann to continue with his barbaric punishments. The community needs a morale boost otherwise we will lose support. Things are not going to get better for a long time and we need these people behind us from the start. Otherwise we have no hope of defeating the Nazis.'

'But it is just one act. We can do it another time,' argued Margot.

Philippe shook his head. 'We don't know when we will get another chance like this. We are being handed the general on a plate.'

Margot pushed herself away from the fireplace. 'Are you doing this for the good of the country or for your ego?'

Fitz watched the exchange between the two resistance members. She saw the rage sweep over Philippe's face but his response was controlled. 'Never question my integrity again,' he said, his voice cold and hard. 'Everything I do is for France. I have already lost so much. This is not about me; this is about freedom and equality.'

There was a pause before Margot spoke. 'Very well. You are in charge,' she said, clearly not happy about the decision.

Philippe turned back to Fitz. 'You should get some rest now.'

'I'll show you to your room,' said Margot. 'I can make a spare bed up on the sofa in your room for the child.'

'Oh, there is one thing,' said Fitz. She moved closer to the desk so she could speak quietly. 'Have either of you heard about an American pilot, flying for the RAF, being shot down? He might be injured or working with the resistance. Or he might be in a safe house.'

Philippe gave Fitz a long hard stare before replying. 'I have no idea what you're talking about,' he hissed. 'And you will do well to remember not to ask such questions. You will put yourself and others in danger. Do you understand?'

Fitz looked down at her feet. She could feel a flush of embarrassment hit her cheeks. She shouldn't have asked. How stupid of her. 'I'm sorry,' she said. 'I didn't think.'

'Clearly,' snapped Philippe. 'You need to make sure you do start thinking. We can't afford any mistakes.'

'Yes, of course. It won't happen again. My apologies.'

As Fitz followed Margot out of the room and up to the next floor where her room was waiting for her, she felt suitably humiliated. She knew she shouldn't have asked but she hadn't been able to stop herself. The idea that Sam might be out here, helping the resistance just wouldn't leave her. She wasn't given to such fanciful ideas normally. What on earth was wrong with her?

'You will be expected to join Philippe for dinner this evening,' said Margot. 'Colonel Rolf Hoffmann will be there, and you will be seated next to him.' She glanced at Yvette, before addressing Fitz again. 'All you have to do this evening, is make him like you. Don't be too keen, though. You need to leave him wanting. Understand?'

'Yes,' said Fitz. She couldn't deny the churning of her stomach at the thought of flirting with a German officer, but it had to be done. She'd already had this conversation with herself about how far she was prepared to go and each time had come to the same conclusion. As far as it was necessary. This mission wasn't about her. What she had to do was a small sacrifice compared to what others had already lost. 'I understand perfectly.'

'Good. The child will need to stay up here in the room out of sight,' said Margot. 'I will make sure someone brings her something to eat.'

'That's fine,' said Fitz. 'Yvette will be very good. I promise you.' It irritated Fitz that Margot was even suggesting Yvette would be anything other than well behaved.

'There are clothes in the wardrobe that will be suitable,' continued Margot, crossing the room to the large mahogany armoire. She opened the doors theatrically and pulled at the one of the garments. It was a black evening dress. 'Wear this tonight.' She eyed Fitz up and down. 'It should fit you. At least you have a nice full bust – Hoffmann has a penchant for large breasts.'

Fitz shrugged. 'Good. Then that will make my job a little easier.' She got the impression Margot was testing her in some way. If she thought Fitz was worried about showing a little more cleavage than was perhaps necessary, she could think again. 'Make-up. Is there make-up here?'

Margot pointed towards the dressing table. 'As requested. Think yourself lucky, we don't usually pull the stops out for things like make-up. Especially the very specific request of bright red lipstick.'

Fitz smiled and went over to the dressing table, opening the drawer where all the make-up was neatly laid out. She ran her fingers across the cosmetics, resting on the lipstick and picking it up. If nothing else, she was looking forward to applying the lipstick. Without it she felt naked. Wearing it made her feel alive. And she would need all the help she could get tonight and tomorrow to succeed with the plan. 'It's a good day for red lipstick,' she declared.

Chapter 19

It had been a long time since Fitz had worn an evening dress and she felt mildly guilty for enjoying the indulgence. She loved flying planes, but she also loved being feminine – fixing her hair nice, wearing dresses, doing her make-up and, of course, her bright red lipstick. For a few hours she would feel like the carefree young woman she'd been before this dreadful war.

'You look pretty,' said Yvette, from her position sitting on the bed. She had a bowl of soup resting on her lap. It was nice to see her eating. The potato and vegetable soup would do her the world of good. 'I like your hair.'

'Thank you,' replied Fitz. 'Would you like me to do *your* hair now?'

Earlier that afternoon, Fitz had run a bath for Yvette and washed her hair. She had managed to get rid of the ground-in dirt under the girl's fingernails. A long soak with a bar of soap and some hot water had transformed the child.

'Yes, please,' said Yvette.

Fitz had never felt she had missed out on having a younger sister to play with or to look out for, but sitting on the bed, plaiting Yvette's now dry hair was almost therapeutic. It was rewarding in a strange way to see Yvette's appearance transformed. Was it pride Fitz was experiencing? It must be how parents felt about their children.

A wave of sadness washed over Fitz as she had an

unexpected memory of her mother doing the same to her hair when she was a child. A rather less welcome memory followed, of Camilla attempting to do Fitz's hair. She couldn't quite put a time on it, but she knew she'd been young and Camilla hadn't been married that long to her father. Camilla had attempted to brush her hair one night and Fitz had made such a fuss, screaming and yelling how it was pulling and hurting. She even swiped the hairbrush away, knocking it out of Camilla's hand. Camilla had gasped in shock and when she stooped to pick up the brush, Fitz had yelled at her again. She remembered Camilla rushing from the room.

Gosh, why hadn't Fitz ever remembered that before? She had been utterly beastly to Camilla. Thinking back, she couldn't recall Camilla ever attempting to do her hair again.

'*Ça va?*' Yvette's voice broke Fitz's thoughts and she looked up at Yvette's reflection in the mirror.

She smiled at her. 'Yes, I'm fine. I was just remembering my mother brushing my hair like this when I was your age.' She was too embarrassed to tell her about the Camilla incident. She dropped a kiss on the top of Yvette's head which now smelt of rose water.

'Where is your *maman* now?' asked Yvette.

Fitz hadn't been expecting that question. How was she supposed to answer that, considering the possibility that Yvette's mother had been killed?

She couldn't bring herself to lie to Yvette. '*Alors*,' she began, running her finger and thumb down each plait. 'My mother died when I was a young girl.'

'How old were you?'

'About your age,' said Fitz. She watched carefully as Yvette considered this.

'Is my mummy dead?'

'Oh, my darling, I don't know,' said Fitz, struck by the directness of the question. Had she been so matter-of-fact when her mother had died? If she had, she was sure she'd have wanted an honest answer. Yvette deserved honesty, too. 'As soon as it is safe, we will look for your mother. I promise I will find out what has happened.'

'What if she forgets about me?' The previous matter-of-fact tone had left Yvette's voice, replaced with genuine fear.

'She would never do that. You will be in her thoughts every single day. And even though she's not here right now, her love for you will always be in your heart and in your mind. Exactly like you will always love her. She will always love you. I promise you that.'

Yvette didn't answer. She pulled her teddy bear to her and Fitz put her arms around her. She hoped her words would offer some sort of comfort to Yvette.

'Do you still love your mummy?' asked Yvette.

Fitz hesitated. It wasn't a sentiment she examined too closely. She preferred to keep those sorts of feelings well and truly locked away, but it was proving almost impossible. How could she offer words of comfort without opening her own heart?

She realised Yvette was looking at her, waiting for an answer. 'Yes, of course I do,' she said breezily. She got up from the bed. 'Now, I should go downstairs otherwise I will be late for dinner.'

'You are coming back, aren't you?'

'Absolutely,' said Fitz. 'I promise you that. Now, settle down in bed. You can sleep in with me if you want. And when I get back, I'll tell you all about the evening, although to be honest, I think it will be very boring.'

She tucked Yvette into the double bed and switched off the light. 'See you soon,' she said at the door and blew a kiss. 'Catch it. Put it under the pillow for later.'

As she stepped out into the hallway, closing the door behind her, Fitz couldn't help smiling to herself at the warm exchange.

'I was coming to see where you'd got to.' Margot appeared at the top of the stairs. 'You need to stop fussing over that child.'

'I was just making sure Yvette was settled,' said Fitz, noting again how irritated she was by the woman who seemed to have no care for Yvette whatsoever.

'And is she?'

'Yes. You don't have to worry about her.'

'Good.' Margot looked Fitz up and down for the second time that day. 'Glad to see the dress fits. Colonel Hoffmann will appreciate that.'

Fitz couldn't help feeling like a prize cow or some sort of livestock, the way Margot had assessed her.

They went downstairs and along the main hallway to a large and extremely luxurious sitting room where several German officers were standing near the fireplace with whisky glasses in their hands, talking and smoking. Three women were standing with them and another two were sitting on the sofa talking to Philippe.

All conversations came to a complete halt and the officers at the fireplace turned to look at her.

To Fitz's horror, one of them was the German officer who had questioned her at the checkpoint.

'Claudine, there you are,' said Philippe. 'We thought you might have fallen asleep.'

Fitz smiled at the man who she had to remember was her cousin. 'Oh, I was just putting the finishing touches to my hair,' she gushed.

'Let me introduce you,' said Philippe and proceeded to walk her around the room, informing her of the names of the guests. She really did feel like cattle being paraded in the auction ring.

'This is Captain Engel,' said Philippe. 'Engel this is my cousin, Claudine Bardot

'We have already had the pleasure of meeting,' said Engel. 'Had I realised that Mademoiselle Bardot was your cousin,

I would most certainly have brought her here in my car earlier.' He turned to Fitz. 'Mademoiselle Bardot.' He took her hand and brought it near to his lips without actually making contact. 'My apologies.'

'No need to apologise, Captain,' said Fitz.

'Please, call me Walter.'

Fitz nodded. Philippe coughed. He seemed keen to carry on with the introductions. 'Now, Claudine, this is Colonel Hoffmann.' He ushered Fitz towards the German. 'Colonel, my cousin, Claudine.'

Hoffmann looked to be in his late forties to early fifties. A tall, thin man with angular features and high cheekbones. Fitz knew this was her time to play the part she had been trained for. She gave a coy smile at the German, glanced down and then back up at him again. 'Very pleased to meet you, Colonel,' she said, moving her black lace scarf to the side so he had an uninterrupted view of her and the rather tight-fitting dress.

'The pleasure is all mine,' said Hoffmann, taking Fitz's hand and kissing it. Unlike Engel, he made contact with her skin, pausing for a fraction of a second longer than necessary as he looked up at her.

Fitz met his gaze, and this time didn't look away. Gosh she felt sick at the pretence but reminded herself this was simply a job. All she had to do was to play her part.

'The colonel is our guest for the next few nights,' said Philippe.

'How lovely,' said Fitz. 'Will you be here for the piano recital tomorrow evening?'

'That is my intention,' replied Hoffmann. 'And you?'

'Oh, yes. I'll be here,' said Fitz. She was aware from her peripheral vision that Engel was still standing there, observing her interaction with the colonel. It was unsettling. She wasn't sure Engel was as easily drawn in by a woman as the older German officer was.

As they made their way through to the dining hall several

minutes later, her concern was compounded. Engel fell into step alongside her. 'You have made a very good impression with the colonel,' he said.

Fitz smiled. 'He's a charming man.'

'Indeed,' agreed Engel. 'Tell me, Claudine, when you were walking to Josselin yesterday, did you see a young woman, probably about your age walking along the road?'

Fitz maintained her composure. 'No, I don't believe I did.'

'Shame. I've been trying to find her.'

'Is she a friend of yours?' asked Fitz, as Engel paused to allow her through the doorway ahead of him.

'She has some information I need,' said Engel. 'If you had been on your own, I might have thought it was you.'

Fitz's throat constricted at the comment and she could barely breathe. She forced a laugh as if the idea that Engel had been looking for her was ridiculous. 'Oh, you would have been very disappointed if you'd arrested me, Walter.' She looked up at him from under her eyelashes.

'I don't know if disappointed would be the right word,' he replied.

'And what word is the right one?' Fitz touched his arm and this time managed to produce a flirtatious giggle.

Engel smiled and raised his eyebrows. 'I'd like to think satisfied would be the right word.'

His hand rested between her shoulder blades as he guided her into the dining room.

Before Fitz could offer any reply, her attention was taken by Philippe coming over to her. 'Claudine, I'm sorry to drag you away from Engel, but let me show you to your seat.'

Engel nodded and with that Fitz was whisked over to the table and found herself, unsurprisingly, next to Colonel Hoffman.

She glanced down the table to where Engel had been seated. Did he know she was the woman he was looking for or was he simply guessing? No, surely if he knew, he would have her arrested there and then, Fitz decided. She would have to be very careful now. She needed to get on the right side of the colonel. He outranked Engel and that would mean Fitz was safe for a while.

She had to force herself to concentrate on what the man was saying. Engel's words rattled around in her head on a constant loop as she tried to decipher them and second guess if there was a double meaning. One that put her in a very dangerous position.

Throughout the meal, Fitz made more flirtatious conversation with the colonel. At one point, he brushed her thigh with his hand as he smoothed out the napkin on his lap. The first time, Fitz thought it was a genuine accident but after the third time, she knew otherwise.

The wine flowed as they ate their way through three courses of the most delicious food – lobster bisque, steak and then a chocolate gâteau. Fitz couldn't deny how delectable it was but the experience was tarnished when she thought of how the people of France were being rationed for their food. This meal was extravagant and left a bitter taste in her mouth.

'Is there something wrong with your food?' asked the colonel as she pushed away a barely touched dessert.

'No, nothing, at all. In fact, it's the most delicious food I've tasted in a long time,' said Fitz. 'But I couldn't possibly eat any more. I'll burst out of this dress if I'm not careful.'

The colonel shifted in his seat and made some sort of noise in the back of his throat. 'I don't know if that will be a bad thing.' He reached his arm out and rested it on the back of her chair, his thumb caressing her shoulder.

Fitz pretended to look embarrassed. In reality she wanted to vomit at the feel of him touching her bare skin. 'So, Colonel,' she said, looking to move the subject. 'Tell me, what do you think of Josselin? It's a very beautiful town, don't you think?'

The colonel shrugged. 'The château is impressive but I have seen just as beautiful, if not more so back in Germany.'

His eyes lingered on Fitz. 'But, of course, nothing can match the beauty in front of me now.'

'That's very kind of you to say,' said Fitz, feigning embarrassment. She felt confident she had the colonel where she needed him. Tonight was purely a teaser – an appetiser. Tomorrow would be the main course.

The rest of the evening passed in very much the same vein. Fitz flirting with the colonel and reeling him in little by little with each giggle, each eyelash flutter, and each swell of her bust. She had made sure she didn't drink more than one glass of wine, despite the colonel's efforts to try to get her to indulge more.

'I need to keep a clear head,' she said, placing her hand over her glass as he lifted the wine bottle. 'I'm saving myself for tomorrow evening.'

By the end of the evening, Fitz felt exhausted with all the role playing and was relieved when the men retired to another room, and she was able to say her goodnights.

Margot accompanied her up to her room, stopping outside the bedroom door. 'Tomorrow, be ready at ten o'clock,' said the Frenchwoman. 'Just you. Not the child. She'll be looked after by the cook.'

Fitz knew better than to ask questions. 'All right. See you then. Goodnight, Margot.'

'You did well,' she said. 'Hoffmann is enchanted by you.' With that, she headed back down the hallway.

Fitz crept into the room, not wanting to wake Yvette. She turned the key in the lock and then went into the bathroom where, despite the cold water, she washed and scrubbed every inch of her body to rid herself of any trace of Hoffmann's touch. He had indeed been very charming all evening, but she knew what he was really like. A callous, cold-hearted barbarian who was known for exercising the most vengeful acts of torture on the Bretons. He was undoubtedly behind the order to raze the village of Saint Pierre to the ground and to execute the villagers. She wondered what had prompted such action. She might be able to ask Margot tomorrow when they went off to wherever it was they were going. She suspected it was a meeting with the resistance to discuss the plans for tomorrow evening and the kidnap. She would very much enjoy luring the colonel into a trap.

Once she was washed and dried, she slipped into the blue flannel pyjamas she had brought with her. Yvette was breathing steadily. The moonlight cast a white glow across the room and Fitz slid carefully into bed not wanting to disturb the child.

'You came back,' whispered Yvette as she snuggled into Fitz.

'Of course I came back,' said Fitz softly. 'You should be asleep by now.'

'I will now.'

'Goodnight, Yvette.'

'Goodnight, Claudine.'

Fitz felt a little pang of guilt at not being able to tell Yvette her real name. Deceiving the colonel was one thing, but it felt wrong to lie to Yvette. They had formed some kind of bond or connection which was a new experience to Fitz. But also one she felt at ease with. What an odd friendship they had established, she thought with a smile.

Soon Yvette was fully asleep, and her gentle rhythmic breathing was the only sound in the room. It wasn't quite so easy for Fitz to fall asleep. She went over the evening's events, Engel's comment and Hoffmann's greedy eyes and eagerness to see her the following evening. She was relieved he had been enchanted as Margot had put it. Margot's praise had been somewhat begrudging, but Fitz felt an inexplicable amount of pride that she had finally done something worthy of Margot's approval. All Fitz had to do was to be just as enticing tomorrow and then she would be winging her way to England to enjoy her Christmas dinner, as Wilding had promised. She stopped short of savouring the idea. She still needed to make some sort of arrangements for Yvette. It unexpectedly tugged at her heart to think that after tomorrow, they probably wouldn't see each other again.

Chapter 20

'Where exactly are we going?' asked Fitz as she followed Margot out of the château and through the town.

After breakfast in her room with Yvette, and then leaving her with the cook, Fitz had met with Margot. The latter still hadn't shed any light on what they were doing that morning.

'Stop asking questions,' said Margot. 'You just need to follow me, that's all.'

They walked down the hill back towards the well. At first Fitz thought they might be meeting some more resistance members, but Margot carried on, turning left before she reached the canal.

A few minutes later, it became apparent as Margot pushed open the gate to the cemetery. Silently, Fitz followed on until they reached the back of the grounds. There were two fresh graves, marked by newly dug soil formed in mounds. Two wooden crosses marked their spot and each cross was engraved with a number.

Fitz looked up at Margot with a questioning look.

'You asked about a RAF pilot,' said Margot, her voice unusually soft. 'Four nights ago, a plane came down just outside the town. The locals tried to help but it was too late. One of them survived, but only for a short while.'

Fitz took a moment to comprehend what Margot was implying. She looked back at the graves. Her mind racing as she tried to make sense of the barrage of thoughts. 'Two graves,' she said, remembering Bob had told her Sam was flying out a VIP.

Margot took out a packet of Gitanes cigarettes and offered one to Fitz.

Fitz's hand shook a little as she accepted the offer. She used her own lighter and drew on the cigarette. The French black tobacco was stronger than she was used to, but she needed it today. 'Do you know their names?' she asked after a moment. 'They would have been wearing identity tags.'

'I don't. The tags would have been taken by the resistance. They will find their way back to England.'

'You said one was still alive,' said Fitz. 'Did he speak at all? The man I'm looking for was American.'

'Apparently all he said was *thank you, Ma'am*. Isn't that what Americans say?'

Fitz wasn't ready to believe this was Sam. No, she needed more proof than that. 'He could have been trying to say Madame,' said Fitz, resolutely. 'Maybe the person who found him, didn't hear right.'

Margot gave a small shrug. 'It is possible but we were only expecting one aircraft that night. If it is the same night as your pilot, then it makes sense.'

Fitz shook her head. 'No, that can't be right. There was a pilot who hid Yvette. He called her sweetheart. That's what Sam would say.'

'The child might easily be mistaken,' said Margot. 'Besides, if she is right, who is to say he wasn't downed another night?'

'What type of aircraft was it?' asked Fitz.

Margot made a dismissive sound. 'Pfff. How would I know? I am not an expert in aviation.' She threw down her cigarette and ground it out under her foot. 'I just thought you should know. Or at least prepare yourself for when you get official confirmation. We need to get back. I'll wait over there for you.'

Fitz looked down at the grave. Was it possible it was Sam?

No. It couldn't be. She'd know if it was. Somewhere deep in her heart, she'd know if Sam was buried there. He was still alive, she just knew it.

'Rest in peace,' she said as she touched the top of each cross.

Fitz wasn't sure why Margot had chosen that morning to show her the graves. Was it because she knew Fitz would be leaving tonight? Or was she testing her resolve for some reason? Was she trying to break Fitz to prove to Philippe that she wasn't up to the job? Why would she want to sabotage the kidnap plot?

As they walked back to the château, Fitz became more and more aware of her strange, unsettling feeling about Margot.

'When you go tonight,' said Margot as they walked up the gravel path to the main entrance. 'You will leave the child with us.'

Fitz's stomach churned over at this news. 'Leave her with you. I . . . I don't know. I mean, what will happen to her?'

'There is a family Philippe knows. They will take her in,' explained Margot.

'What about Yvette's family?'

'What about them? She has none. Look, you have no idea how hard it is here now. No doubt, you have some romantic idea about finding the girl's mother. Well, listen to me. It is not possible. We have better things to worry about. The child will go to the Martin family.'

'Do the Martin family have children?' asked Fitz. Somehow it mattered very much to her who she was leaving Yvette with.

'No. But they will look after her. She will help around the house, and she will have a bed to sleep in and food on the table.' Margot eyed Fitz. 'That is more than some children have.'

They had reached the entrance to the château now and Fitz knew they couldn't talk about it anymore.

* * *

Fitz spent the rest of the day with Yvette. It was unlike any Christmas Eve she had ever experienced. She wished she could do something to make it special for Yvette, but it seemed frivolous given the circumstances. She decided the best she could do was to sneak some cake back for the little girl. She couldn't stop thinking about the fate that lay ahead for Yvette, and how treacherous she herself felt about leaving her, even though it was the right thing to do. Yvette was French. She needed to stay in France. What was Fitz supposed to do? Whisk her off to England in the plane that night? It was a ludicrous idea.

Ludicrous, yes. But not impossible. No. Fitz dismissed the notion. She would not entertain it for another second. Yvette belonged in France.

Fitz thought of Yvette's mother. What would she be thinking of Fitz if she knew what she was about to do? Yvette's mother hadn't chosen to leave her child. Fitz imagined the woman's last thought would have been about her daughter and whether she was safe.

Had her own mother had such thoughts and feelings right before she died? Had her last thought been of her daughter?

They stayed in the bedroom, out of the way, playing cards and drawing pictures. Fitz had always been fond of sketching and was soon filling the pages with requests from the little girl. Dogs and cats featured heavily. Fitz noticed Yvette didn't ask her to draw any houses or families, something she was sure little girls liked. They moved on to flowers and trees, then bigger, more exotic animals. Cars and buses came next. Once they had amassed a wide selection of pictures, Yvette set about colouring them in. Fitz carried on doodling on the paper and was surprised at the feeling of contentment she was getting from simply watching Yvette enjoy herself.

'What are you drawing now?' asked Yvette.

Fitz turned the paper around for her to see. 'An aeroplane.'

'I've never been in an aeroplane,' said Yvette. 'Have you?'

'Yes, I have. In fact I can actually . . .' Fitz managed to stop herself from blurting out that she could fly one.

'Can what?' asked Yvette.

'I can remember seeing my friend fly his plane,' said Fitz quickly. 'Oh, have you seen the time?' she said looking at the clock on the mantelpiece. 'I need to start getting ready.' She shuffled the papers together in a pile and placed them on the dressing table. 'Do you want to help me fix my hair?'

'Yes please,' said Yvette, dropping the coloured crayon back into the pot.

'We can do yours too,' said Fitz, glad the child was easily distracted. She silently scolded herself for nearly spilling the beans about being able to fly.

Once Fitz was ready, she settled Yvette in the room. 'Someone will be back later to make sure you're all right,' she said. 'Now be very good and quiet and stay in the room. The guests will be arriving soon.'

'Will you be gone all night?' asked Yvette. There was that glimmer of anxiety in Yvette's eyes. How could Fitz possibly leave her? Even though there was the promise of a French couple to look after the girl, would they be kind to her? Would they love her? Fitz wasn't sure.

Fitz put her hand on Yvette's cheek. 'Not all night. I'll be back.' She stopped short of saying she promised. If something went wrong and she was caught, she didn't want to have Yvette's last thought that Fitz had broken her promise. Fitz picked up the teddy bear and tucked it under the covers alongside Yvette. 'I'll be back for both of you.' She kissed Yvette on the forehead. 'Always know that you are loved,' she whispered.

She left the room before she choked up with tears. How on earth had she become so attached to the little human in her bed? The weight of responsibility was still there but it had been replaced by desire rather than duty. And was Fitz really going to do what she thought she was?

The little idea she had tried all evening to ignore? Damn it. Apparently so.

She straightened herself when she saw Margot waiting for her at the top of the stairs.

'Everything all right?' asked the Frenchwoman. 'Have you told the child about the Martins?'

Fitz shook her head. 'No. There's no need to upset her now. We don't want any distractions for this evening.'

'Good. That is wise.'

This time Fitz didn't feel any joy or sense of pride from receiving Margot's praise.

Philippe came up the stairs. 'Everything is in place,' he said. 'At eleven-thirty, the waiters will bring around a glass of champagne for everyone so I can propose a toast. You are to take the glass on the left-hand side – your left – and ensure Hoffmann drinks it.'

'The one on the left,' repeated Fitz.

'Yes, it will be laced with something to help Hoffmann relax,' said Philippe.

'Don't get muddled up and drink it yourself, will you,' said Margot.

An unnecessary comment which Fitz decided didn't even merit a reply. She ignored Margot and addressed Philippe.

'And a car will be waiting outside soon after that?'

'Tell Hoffmann you are going to take him to Madame Mimi's,' said Margot. 'I'm sure you can use your imagination about what happens at her house. Men are all the same. Governed by what's between their legs, rather than the brains between their ears.' She glanced at Philippe. 'It's true.'

It was Philippe's turn to ignore Margot now. 'Be outside at quarter to twelve. The car will be there.'

Margot spoke again. 'And then once in the car, you will have to keep him occupied. Make sure he doesn't look out of the window. I'm sure you can think of a way to do that.'

'Of course I can,' replied Fitz. 'What about the checkpoint on the bridge?'

'Don't worry about that,' said Margot. 'There will be distractions for the guards. Some very pretty ones.'

'Are you sure that will work?' Fitz wasn't convinced that the lure of a female was enough to take a guard away from his post.

Margot made a huffing noise. She looked incredulously at Philippe. 'Did you hear that? She is questioning me?' Philippe gave a philosophical shrug as Margot turned back to Fitz. 'Not that I need to explain to you, but I will, purely to stop you asking any more stupid questions.' She paused and when Fitz didn't reply, she continued. 'Two female agents have been working towards this point for the past ten days. Very soon they will arrive at the bridge with alcohol and promises. They are not just flirting like you. They are actually prepared do everything necessary to make this plan work. Am I making myself clear?'

'Margot, please,' said Philippe. He made a shushing noise.

'I will not be quiet. She needs to know she is not the brave one. My girls are.'

Fitz felt suitably admonished. She didn't want to argue with the woman. 'They have my utmost respect for what they are doing,' she said. 'But please be assured, I too am willing to give everything I need to, in order for this mission to succeed.'

'Let's hope you mean that,' said Margot.

'There is one thing you must do for me, though,' said Fitz.

Philippe frowned. 'What?'

'You must ensure Yvette is waiting on the other side of the bridge.'

'What are you talking about?' said Philippe.

'It's impossible,' said Margot.

'I am not leaving without Yvette,' insisted Fitz. 'She comes with me. That's the deal.'

'This was not part of the plan,' hissed Philippe.

'Make it part of the plan,' said Fitz. There was no way on earth she was leaving Yvette here to be dumped on a couple who didn't even have any children. How would they look after her when all they wanted was an extra pair of hands to help around the house? No. She wasn't leaving Yvette to that fate.

'And if we don't?' asked Philippe.

'Then I am not going anywhere, either.'

'But you will be arrested and interrogated,' said Philippe.

'And then she will talk,' said Margot. She glared at Fitz. 'Maybe we should leave you to Engel. I am sure he will be happy to question you. Then what will happen to Yvette?'

'I would have thought your main concern should be what will happen to the network?' said Fitz, standing her ground.

Philippe held up his hand to silence the women. 'The child will be there but after that she is your responsibility. If this goes wrong and something happens to her, then it will be down to you.'

Fitz nodded. 'Thank you.'

As they went into the reception room, Fitz was well aware of the responsibility she had just committed herself to.

Chapter 21

Hoffmann greeted Fitz with much enthusiasm when she came into the room. He kissed her either side of her face this time and slipped his hand across her lower back, giving her waist a squeeze. 'You look stunning tonight, Claudine.'

Fitz was wearing a bright red dress. She had no idea where Margot had obtained the gown, but once again it was a perfect fit. It had an open cowl back to it, with tiny spaghetti-like straps tied at the back of her neck. The dress was very fitted and a long split ran up to her mid-thigh allowing her just enough room to walk.

'Colonel . . .' began Fitz.

Hoffman held up his finger. 'Ah, ah, ah,' he scolded good humouredly. 'It's not Colonel. Remember, it's Rolf now.'

'Of course, I just didn't want to be presumptuous,' said Fitz with a giggle. Her stomach churned and she thought she was going to vomit for a moment. She could smell his aftershave and see a small nick on his jaw where he'd caught himself shaving. He wasn't unattractive in looks, though, and Fitz found herself wondering if it wouldn't be that bad having to sleep with him if necessary. She thought of the women who were distractions for the soldiers on the checkpoint. If they were prepared to do whatever it took, then she was, too. She leaned into the colonel. 'I've been looking forward to seeing you again, Rolf,' she said quietly, but offering a seductive smile. 'Much more of you.'

She could see the German puff his chest out a fraction at the overtly flirtatious comment. 'And I of you,' he said.

As she sipped her drink, Fitz glanced around the room, catching sight of Margot. The Frenchwoman gave a small nod at Fitz and returned to her conversation with one of the women.

Fitz spent the meal sitting next to Hoffmann and fawning over him as much as was decent without it seeming too over the top, but certainly offering the right encouragement to him. This time, when he reached down for the napkin on his lap, he rested his hand on her thigh, his fingertips sliding open the split of her dress so he could stroke her stocking top.

There was no mistaking his intentions for later that evening and Fitz felt somewhat reassured. She sipped rather more wine than she had the previous night, in a bid to settle her nerves or to cover them. Any slip up, she could put down to the alcohol.

After dinner, rather than the men retiring to another room, they remained in the dining hall. Fitz was aware the atmosphere was more boisterous than it had been the previous evening. One of the officers was leaning back in his seat, with a woman each side cuddled up to him. He had loosened his tie and undone the top button on his shirt.

Fitz glanced down at Engel and was disappointed to see he looked as composed as he had when he'd first arrived. Fortunately, he hadn't spoken to her other than to say hello and she hoped this was a good sign. But when his eyes locked on hers, an involuntary shiver ran down her spine. Hoffmann might have a reputation for his barbaric actions, but Engel's cool and calm demeanour was equally chilling. She was sure making an enemy of Engel was far worse than it would be of Hoffmann. Engel smiled at her and raised his glass.

Fitz smiled back with a confidence she didn't feel. She was just happy he wasn't anywhere near her.

However, her respite was short-lived and very soon Philippe ushered his guests through to the ballroom where a string quartet was playing, and more alcohol was on offer.

'How are you at dancing?' asked Hoffman, taking Fitz's hand in one of his and placing the other around her waist. Before she could even answer, he had whisked her into the centre of the room and straight into a waltz.

Thank heavens for the Badcombe House summer balls thought Fitz as she glided effortlessly around the dance floor. It wasn't long before other couples joined in with the dancing. The chandelier sparkled overhead, and soft lighting illuminated the dark corners of the room. A fire had been lit in the large fireplace and a decorated Christmas tree stood next to it.

Fitz wasn't sure her dress was ideal for twirling around for too long and was pleased when after only three dances the colonel seemed out of breath and in need of refreshment.

'Don't wear yourself out too soon,' she said, running her hand down his arm. 'We have a long night ahead of us.'

'We do?' Hoffmann kissed the side of her face. 'I'm pleased to hear that.'

'In fact,' continued Fitz. She leaned into him to whisper in his ear. 'If it gets too dull around here, we could go and see Madame Mimi.'

Hoffmann looked surprised. 'Madame Mimi?'

'Oh, don't tell me you haven't heard of her?' said Fitz.

'I have not,' said Hoffmann. 'Who is she?'

'Let's just say, she knows how to look after a man and his needs,' said Fitz. 'I'm sure a man like you will be able to handle the both of us.'

A deep guttural sound came from Hoffmann and he ran a finger around the inside of his collar. 'I like the sound of Madame Mimi very much.'

'Oh, good. It will be a fun evening after all,' whispered

Fitz. 'These dinner parties are all right but they can be a little dull.' She slipped her arm through Hoffmann's and cosied up to him. This was going far more smoothly than she had anticipated. She'd thought Hoffmann might be resistant to the idea, but no, he was definitely game for it. Thank goodness.

She checked the clock. She had an hour to get Hoffmann out of the château and into the waiting car. As planned, a waiter approached them, carrying a silver tray with two champagne flutes on it. He offered it to Fitz first, who took both glasses. The one on her left was the one she had to give to Hoffmann. It was laced with some sort of drug that would impair Hoffmann's co-ordination and thought process, so much so, it would make him open to suggestion and incapable of resisting. To the casual onlooker, he would appear very drunk.

Fitz handed the glass to Hoffmann, hoping that whoever had laced the drink hadn't got muddled up, or it would be her who was rendered useless rather than Hoffmann and who knew what sort of trouble she could end up in.

'Thank you,' said Hoffmann, accepting the glass of champagne. He looked around as Philippe stood on a chair.

'A toast!' called out Philippe, holding his champagne flute in the air. 'To our special guests this evening, Colonel Hoffmann. *Heil* Hitler!'

Echoes of Hoffmann and '*Heil* Hitler!' rang out around the room as everyone raised their glasses and then drank the champagne. Fitz wasn't taking any chances and took the smallest of sips. She watched as Hoffmann gulped his down in one go.

'I just need to use the bathroom,' said Fitz, handing Hoffmann her full glass.

'I'll look after this for you,' said Hoffmann with a laugh and proceeded to consume Fitz's drink.

'Oh, Rolf, I shall have to get myself another drink now,'

she said, pretending to pout but smiling at the colonel. She tapped his arm playfully. 'Naughty boy. I shall have to take you to Madame Mimi's and she will scold you herself.'

Hoffman's eyes lit. 'I can't wait to meet Madame Mimi,' he said, slurring his words a little. 'When are we going?'

'Oh, very soon,' replied Fitz. 'But first, I need to use the bathroom. Don't go away, will you?'

'I wouldn't dream of it. Don't be long,' said Hoffmann and to Fitz's surprise patted her bottom.

She giggled again. 'Now, now, Rolf. Not here,' she said, giving him a wink as she walked across the room. She knew he was watching and she gave an extra sway to her hips. She glanced at the clock. Only another hour and then she could get this insufferable man in the car and away from here. When she came back, she'd tempt him with some exaggerated stories of what to expect at Madame Mimi's house. She tutted to herself at the ridiculous name but if it worked, then she really didn't care.

Fitz loitered in the cloakroom for as long as she thought she could get away with, retouching her lipstick, which amazingly was almost the exact shade as her dress. What a shame she was wasting the gown on someone like Hoffmann.

An unexpected thought of Sam came to her, of when he had presented her with a red silk scarf one day, just before they were going out on his motorbike.

'When I saw it, I thought of you,' he'd said. 'The colour is a perfect match for your lips.' He had draped the scarf around her neck, pulling her into him, before kissing the life out of her. She blinked back the tears. The pain that she might have lost him was already slicing her heart in two. Why had she pushed him away? He was the best thing to have happened to her and yet, she had been too frightened to let him into her life fully. And now it might be too late to try to put that right. What an idiot she was.

She took a tissue from her purse and dabbed at her eyes. This was not the time to get maudlin about Sam. She was going to do whatever it was she needed to, to get Hoffmann out and into the car. She'd make Sam proud of her, even if he might never know.

After checking her make-up and reapplying her lipstick, Fitz left the cloakroom. As she crossed the main entrance hall, Engel appeared in front of her, blocking her path.

'Oh, Walter,' she said, plastering on a smile. 'You startled me.'

'My apologies. I wouldn't want to do that,' said Engel. Fitz went to step around the officer, but he moved in front of her again. 'I wanted to speak to you,' he said.

'Really? Can it wait until tomorrow?' said Fitz. 'Only the colonel will be wondering where I've got to.'

Engel raised his eyebrows. 'Will he? He seems rather inebriated to me. Almost like his drink has been spiked.' His eyes locked with Fitz's.

She held her nerve. 'Why would someone do that?' she said, attempting to sound perplexed.

'To take advantage of him,' replied Engel. He clasped his hands behind his back and looked up to the ceiling, as if deep in thought. 'Maybe they wanted to get him so drunk, he would simply go with them. Whoever this person is.' He made a rolling gesture with his hand. 'Of course this is all hypothetically speaking. Isn't it, *Claudine*?'

Fitz didn't like the way he emphasised her name. 'Yes, hypothetically,' she agreed, wary of where the conversation was heading. Engel was leading her blindfold down an alley, and any minute now he was going to ambush her, she was sure of it. But she had no choice.

'I do wonder why they would want to take him, though,' continued Engel. 'Can you think of any reason?'

'No. I can't.'

'I mean, no one would have the audacity to try to kidnap the colonel, now would they?'

Fitz gulped. 'Kidnap? I can't imagine anyone would attempt such a ridiculous idea.'

'Absolutely,' said Engel. 'I'm glad you agree. Can you imagine the consequences for anyone making such an attempt? Besides getting themselves shot by a firing squad, they and their loved ones would have to be made an example of.'

Fitz had no idea where Engel had got this idea from. He couldn't just be hedging his bets, could he? She noticed he was smiling and his gaze flicked to somewhere above and behind her. He gave a brief nod.

Fitz turned to follow Engel's gaze.

There on the gallery landing was a German soldier. Standing in front of him was Yvette, clutching her teddy in her hand.

Fitz let out a gasp, swiftly followed by another as she watched in horror as the soldier picked Yvette up and sat her on the edge of the balustrade. Yvette's feet dangled in thin air. She waved down at Fitz.

'Claudine, look at me!'

Fitz was horrified but tried not to show her alarm to the child. She waved back before spinning around to face Engel. 'She's only a child. Don't hurt her.'

'Don't worry. She is perfectly safe,' said Engel. 'That is until I give the command to let go of her.' He gave a long whistle as he pointed his finger to the banister and then down to the ground.

'Please, I beg you,' said Fitz. 'Don't do that.' She could hear the crack in her voice. She didn't doubt that Engel would carry out his threat.

'I'm sorry, I didn't mean to upset you,' he said. 'I didn't realise how fond of the child you are.' He waved at the soldier who hoisted Yvette back to the safety of the landing.

Fitz let out a sigh of relief. She watched as the soldier led Yvette back down the hallway. 'Bye, Claudine,' she called.

'*Bonne nuit*,' called back Fitz, blowing a kiss to the child.

Yvette put her hand up in the air, making to grab the kiss. 'Caught it!' she called, smiling broadly, before disappearing out of sight.

'How very touching,' said Engel. He turned to look at Fitz, his face deadpan. 'I hope I'm making myself clear,' he said. 'And just so that there is no doubt. If anything was to happen to the colonel, then the next time you see the child, you will wish you hadn't. Understand?'

Fitz hesitated. To nod her understanding would be to admit her involvement. She was still sure Engel was working on a hunch rather than any hard evidence. She schooled her face into a frown. 'I'm not sure I know what you mean, but I'm sure the colonel is very safe here surrounded by his men and as a guest of my cousin.'

Engel gave a snort. 'I'm glad we understand each other. Now, as you say, you'd better get back to the colonel. He is anticipating a rather fun night, I believe.'

When Fitz walked back into the room, she saw Margot look at her and then look at Engel who was following on behind her. She looked neither surprised nor concerned, Fitz observed. Again that feeling of mistrust washed up in Fitz's consciousness. She couldn't work out Margot's part in all this, never mind what her motives were.

Before she had time to consider it further, Hoffmann was upon her. The smell of alcohol on his breath was strong and he was unsteady on his feet. The drug that had been slipped into his drink had certainly taken effect. She looked at the clock above the mantelpiece. Very soon she would have to get Hoffmann outside and into the waiting car.

'Let's have one more dance,' said Hoffman, wrapping his arms around her waist and pulling her towards him. Fitz slipped both hands around his neck and they began to sway from side to side in time to the music.

She caught sight of Engel over the shoulder of Hoffmann. He returned her look with a cool stare and mouthed one word at her.

'Yvette.'

Chapter 22

Fitz felt paralysed with fear. She was sure Engel knew of the kidnap plot, but if so, why was he waiting to act? Surely he should be arresting them. Or was he doing this just for fun? Enjoying watching her dilemma. Enjoying toying with people's lives. If anything, the incident back at the checkpoint proved that. He didn't have any care or value for life. He was prepared to kill a child.

'When are we going to Madame Mimi's?' drawled Hoffmann in her ear. Fitz had minutes to act. 'Let's sit down for a moment,' she said, propping Hoffmann up and taking him to sit in a chair near the door. She motioned to the waiter for some water.

'Come here,' said Hoffmann, pulling her by the hips and forcing her to sit on his lap. He ran his hand up and down her leg while trying to ply her with kisses, but only able to reach her neck. 'We don't have to go to Madame Mimi's,' he was saying between kisses. 'I'd happily settle for just you and my room tonight.'

Fitz was about to say no, when she had an idea. She allowed Hoffmann to continue to make a fuss of her and pretended to be enjoying it, while she ran through the idea in her head. It was a risky plan, but it could work. The kidnapping could still go ahead, and she and Yvette could still escape. She didn't trust Margot and trusted her even less to get Yvette to the car as planned.

It really was the only choice she had. 'I think that's a rather good idea,' she said to Hoffmann. 'It would be a shame to have to share you with anyone else. Not on our first night, anyway.'

Hoffmann mumbled his agreement into her neck, something along the lines of what were they waiting for?

'Just give me one moment,' said Fitz. 'I need to get something from my room first.'

'Don't keep me waiting too long,' said Hoffmann, his eyes touring her body from head to toe.

She smiled over her shoulder at him and went over to Margot.

'Change of plan,' she said, smiling as if they were sharing a joke. 'I'm taking Hoffmann out down the servants' staircase. I'll be bringing Yvette with me. Don't argue. That's what is happening. Make sure the car is at the west entrance.'

With that she turned and went back over to Hoffmann before Margot had time to protest. She had no doubt Margot was boring holes in her back with her glare.

'Come along, then, Rolf,' she said, helping the colonel to his feet. 'Time for us.'

As she expected, Engel appeared. 'Where are you going?' he asked.

'We're finished here for the night,' said Hoffmann, his words slurring together.

Engel turned to Fitz. 'I do hope you remembered our conversation.'

'Of course,' replied Fitz. 'The colonel and I are going upstairs to his room. Aren't we, Rolf?'

'We are. Now, goodnight, Engel. I don't wish to be disturbed.'

With Hoffmann's arm draped over her shoulder, and Fitz's arm supporting him around the waist, they made their way out of the room and across the hallway to the staircase.

A soldier standing on guard at the entrance door stepped forward offering his help but Fitz assured him she could manage. It took some effort but they made it to the landing without mishap. Hoffmann's co-ordination was affected not just by the alcohol but by the drug. Fitz glanced down to the entrance hall as they walked along the gallery landing and saw Engel standing in the doorway, wine glass in one hand, his other hand in his pocket, monitoring her and Hoffmann's progress with those beady rat-like eyes of his.

Fitz was glad when they were out of sight. The château was long and thin in its construction, with one main corridor running from east to west over several floors. She knew Hoffmann's room was on the opposite side of the building to hers.

'Which room is yours?' she asked.

Hoffmann stopped and squinted as he looked at the doors. 'It's down the end here,' he said leaning forwards before his feet were ready to move. He almost fell flat on his face, but Fitz managed to grab hold of him.

'Steady now,' she said. They made it to the room and went inside. There was a large four-poster bed with heavy embroidered curtains in various autumnal colours. Very masculine in its appearance. There was a door leading to the bathroom and on the other side of the fire breast was a dressing room, where the servants' staircase was located.

Fitz had to time this perfectly. She led Hoffmann over to the bed and sat him down. He was like an obedient puppy now. The drug was well into his system and rendering him useless to make any conscious thought or decision.

'Wait here,' she said. After locking the door from the inside, she went through to the dressing room and opening the small door, stepped onto the narrow servants' staircase. She couldn't risk being spotted by Engel when she crossed the gallery landing to get from one side of the château to the other.

The servants' staircase spiralled down to the ground floor and up to the next two floors. Fitz climbed up to the second floor. It was a gamble but she hoped there was either no one staying in the room above or they were downstairs enjoying the party.

Before stepping out into the dressing room directly above Hoffmann's, she paused, listening for any sound of an occupant. When she was confident there was no one there, she made her way through the dressing room and the adjoining bedroom and out into the hallway.

This floor hadn't been decorated quite as elaborately as the floor below and she guessed that it wasn't used that often. Dashing along the red carpeted hallway, she reached the other side of the château and the room above her own.

Fitz tapped on the door and was relieved when she got no answer. In she went, through the bedroom and dressing room to the staircase. A minute later she was in her and Yvette's room.

'Yvette,' she called softly. 'It's me, Claudine.'

'Claudine?' She heard Yvette's surprised and slightly concerned voice.

'I'm here,' said Fitz, coming out of the dressing room.

Yvette's eyes widened in surprise. 'I didn't know you were there.'

Fitz grinned. 'It's a secret passage. Do you want me to show you?'

Yvette jumped off the bed. 'Yes please!'

'You must get dressed first,' said Fitz grabbing the clothes on the chair and hurriedly swapping the night garments for the day ones. 'Now, this is a bit of a game,' said Fitz. 'We have to be really quiet so no one knows what we're doing. We don't want to be spotted. You have to be as quiet as a dormouse. Do you think you can do that?'

Yvette nodded enthusiastically. 'I'm good at hiding.'

The comment made Fitz pause. Of course, the poor child had had to go undetected before. She ruffled Yvette's hair and smiled. 'There is one thing, though,' she said. 'When we get to one of the rooms, there is a man in there. You're not to be scared but we are taking him with us.'

'A man?'

'Yes. A German soldier,' said Fitz. She didn't want to say too much to Yvette, in case they were caught. She shuddered at the thought. 'But don't worry about him. You just follow me. *D'accord*?'

'*Oui*.'

'Don't forget teddy,' said Fitz. She took the little girl's hand and hurried back to the servants' staircase.

A few minutes later, they had reached Hoffmann's dressing room. 'Now, wait here,' Fitz instructed Yvette. 'When I come back with the man, you just follow us.'

Hoffmann was still sitting in the exact position Fitz had left him. His eyes were open but were gazing blankly at the carpet. He didn't even look up and acknowledge Fitz.

She went over to him. 'Come on, Rolf,' she said. 'Time to go.' She managed to get him to his feet. He was looking at her, but without focus. 'This way.'

As they went through the dressing room, Hoffmann didn't appear to register Yvette there. Fitz smiled at her and gestured with her head to follow.

The spiral staircase took some negotiation especially as Hoffmann's co-ordination was impaired, but they finally made it to the lower ground floor and into the laundry room. All she had to do now was to get the three of them across the lawn and out through the side gate where, she hoped to God, the car was waiting. She was aware they were already a few minutes behind schedule.

The side gate was no more than a door's width and was used as a short cut for the staff to exit to and from the château without having to use the main entrance. Set in a stone wall which was adorned in climbing and rambling roses, it was inconspicuous. So irrelevant, she had noticed yesterday that it was unguarded.

'So now, we need to go as quickly and quietly as we can across the grass,' whispered Fitz. 'Ready?'

With a nod from Yvette, Fitz began to walk the colonel

across the lawn. It was darker on this side of the château. The lights from the ballroom shone out across the other side of the château. There was a small terraced area with open doors from the ballroom and she could hear the string quartet playing a foxtrot.

They were about fifty yards from the château gate now. 'Keep walking,' encouraged Fitz. 'Come on, Rolf, we're nearly there.'

She was grateful he was incapable of speech at this point and she wasn't even sure he comprehended what she was saying but he was keeping up with her, if staggering every so often.

They were within a few yards of the gate now. Fitz looked back over her shoulder and could see a figure silhouetted by the lights from the ballroom.

'Hurry,' said Fitz, as they reached the gate. They were protected here from the shadows cast by the oak tree, and she propped Hoffmann up against the trunk, resting one hand on his chest so he didn't go anywhere. She drew Yvette closer to her. She glanced back again to the château and could see the flare of a lighter as the person lit their cigarette.

A soft hoot of an owl sounded out – it was the call sign of their pick-up. Fitz didn't have time to wait until the person had finished smoking their cigarette and return to the party. She would just have to risk it.

She took Hoffmann by the arm and stepped out from their hiding spot towards the gate. She was waiting for the person to shout out at her, but there was nothing. Her pulse was racing, and her breathing was coming fast. She lifted the latch on the gate and pulled it open, peering through the gap.

'*Dépêchez-vous*,' came the urgent voice of the driver as simultaneously the rear door opened, and another man jumped out. Another appeared from somewhere in the street.

Fitz pulled Hoffmann through the gateway and he was immediately collected by the two resistance members and bundled straight into the back of the car.

'He's drugged up to his eyeballs,' observed one of the men. He looked back at Fitz. 'Are you getting in?'

'Hang on.' She darted back through the gate to get Yvette but to her horror she wasn't there. Panic ripped through her. She looked back across the lawn and could see the girl running towards the house. 'Yvette,' Fitz called in as loud a whisper as she could. What on earth was she doing? Why hadn't she stayed by the tree.

'We have to leave.' The man was at the gateway.

Fitz looked at him and then back at Yvette. 'Wait. Please.'

The man followed her gaze. 'A child?'

'I'm bringing her with me,' said Fitz.

'We can't wait,' the man insisted.

Fitz looked from the man and back to the little shadowy figure of Yvette. To save herself and the mission or to save Yvette? The greater good or a single child? Why was Fitz even questioning herself? There was no way on earth she was leaving without Yvette. She'd never been aware of a maternal bone in her body up until that point. Yvette might not be her child, but Fitz was bonded to her as if she were her own flesh and blood. In the exact same way she wouldn't dream of deserting Michael, she was absolutely not going to abandon Yvette.

Fitz broke into a run, racing across the lawn after Yvette.

Chapter 23

Fitz stretched out her long legs, gaining ground on Yvette with every stride, desperate to reach her before she got too close to the house.

The person on the terrace had their back to them. Fitz wished she'd changed out of her ridiculous evening gown. She hoisted the skirt of the dress above her knees so she could run faster.

Yvette came to a halt and bent down to pick something up, before turning around. It was her teddy. She must have dropped it and only just realised when they were at the tree.

'Yvette! Quickly,' whispered Fitz. The little girl ran to her, and Fitz caught her by the hand, speeding her back towards the gate. The now closed gate. The man must have gone back to the car.

Fitz was dragging Yvette so fast, the little girl stumbled. Fitz managed to lift her up to stop her falling while still moving. They got to the gate. They were both panting furiously.

'I dropped teddy,' said Yvette.

'It's fine. Don't worry now,' said Fitz, between puffs of breath. She opened the gate and stepped out onto the path where she came to an abrupt halt.

The car was gone.

She looked down the hill and saw the taillights disappearing around the corner. They had left her. Deserted her.

Fitz stared in disbelief. How could they do that?

'What are we doing?' asked Yvette.

That was a very good question. Fitz had to think fast to work out what to do next.

They'd have to go back to the château. She could hardly try to escape dressed in a bright red evening gown; she'd be stopped the moment she was spotted.

'We need to go back to our room,' she said.

Yvette looked confused. 'Why? And where is the man?'

'He had to go,' said Fitz. 'Now, do you think we can creep back just as quietly as we did coming out here?'

'Is this a game?'

'Kind of.'

'It's a silly game.'

Fitz couldn't argue with that. 'Sorry,' she said. 'Right, let's go.'

They made it back to the room unseen by anyone. Somehow, Fitz needed to let Margot know what had happened. Fitz was in danger now. As soon as it was discovered Hoffmann was missing, she'd be the first person they would come looking for. She was the last person seen with him.

She considered her options. Sleep in Hoffmann's bed and wake up pretending to be confused as to where he was. Sleep in her own bed and say she'd left him sleeping this morning or had woken up and he wasn't there.

Yvette was yawning and had snuggled down under the covers. Fitz sat next to her and brushed her hair from her face. 'Try to go to sleep,' she said.

Anxiety was eating away at her stomach and Fitz was sure she was going to be sick as her mind flitted from one solution to another – none of them ideal.

As far as Margot and Philippe were concerned, she and Yvette had escaped with the colonel. No one knew they were still here. At what point would Margot be made aware of the change in plan? Fitz couldn't rely on the Frenchwoman coming to their rescue.

If Engel looked for her tonight and couldn't find her in

Hoffmann's room, then he'd come here. The thought sent a shudder through her body. She couldn't let Yvette witness her being arrested by Engel. The poor child would be terrified.

Fitz needed to go back to Hoffmann's room and wait there. She might be able to keep Yvette safe from harm if she wasn't with her. Someone might have the foresight to get to Yvette first.

She got up from the bed and went over to the writing desk in the corner. Taking a sheet of paper, she wrote a message for Yvette.

Darling Yvette
 I'm so sorry I had to go. I wish it could have been different.
 You are a wonderful girl, and your mummy would have been so proud of you. As am I. Please know how much you are loved.
 Am leaving kisses for you to keep in your pocket.
 Claudine.

Fitz folded the note in half and slipped it into an envelope, before sealing it. She tucked it under the ribbon around the teddy bear's neck, then, kissing her fingertips, she gently touched Yvette's forehead.

'Stay safe, darling girl.'

Chapter 24

The knock at Hoffmann's bedroom door came earlier than Fitz had expected. It was still dark outside, and the dawn was yet to break. How wrong Wilding had been when he said she'd be home for Christmas dinner.

Fitz had ruffled the sheets on both sides of the bed and dented the pillows, so it looked as if two people had spent the night there. She'd messed up her hair somewhat, smudged her lipstick and flung her stockings onto the floor, along with her shoes. She'd also used the towel in the bathroom and lifted the toilet seat. She wasn't sure it would fool Engel, but she had to at least try. If anything, it would buy some time and Hoffmann would be on a plane to England before anyone realised he was missing.

She waited for the second knock before going over to the door.

'Who is it?' she asked without opening it.

'Captain Engel. I need to speak to the colonel.'

'He's not here,' called Fitz through the door.

'Open the door before I shoot the lock,' commanded Engel.

Fitz turned the key, and the door was immediately barged open. She jumped back out of the way as Engel strode into the room, his pistol in his hand. Two soldiers followed him in. One of them trained his gun on Fitz.

'He's not here,' repeated Fitz as she watched Engel take

in the room, before striding over to the bathroom and then the dressing room.

He marched back out and stood in front of her. 'Where is the colonel?'

'I don't know,' said Fitz. 'He was here earlier. But when I woke up, he was gone.'

'Liar,' snapped Engel. Without warning, he raised his hand and struck Fitz hard across the face, almost sending her off her feet.

She let out a small cry. It stung, rather than hurt. Engel grabbed her jaw, squeezing her face between his finger and thumb. 'I will ask once again. Where is the colonel?'

'I don't know where he is,' she repeated.

This earned her another slap on the other side of her face.

Fitz could hear the sound of feet and voices. It sounded like Margot and Philippe.

'What is going on here?' Philippe strode into the room. 'It's Christmas morning, for goodness, sake, Captain. My cousin is a guest of mine.'

'Stay where you are,' ordered Engel. 'Mademoiselle Bardot is under arrest. Guest or not. I'm the one who gives the orders.' He nodded at the soldiers who stepped forward and at gunpoint grabbed Fitz by the arms.

'At least have the decency to allow her to get dressed into suitable clothing,' said Margot.

'The colonel will not be happy to learn you've treated Claudine in this way,' said Philippe.

Engel narrowed his eyes. 'That is the problem, though. We do not know where the colonel is and I have reason to believe Mademoiselle Bardot does and she is withholding the information with the intention of delaying locating the colonel.'

'Even so,' said Philippe. 'You might be wrong. He might have been called away for some reason.'

'And you think I wouldn't know about that?' Engel gave a snort. He looked at Fitz's clothing and then turned to Margot. 'Get her something else to wear.'

Margot hurried off and returned shortly with Fitz's clothes. 'Get changed,' ordered Engel as Margot handed her the garments. 'No, not in the dressing room. Here.'

There was a glint in Engel's eye and Fitz knew he was enjoying the thought of humiliating her in front of everyone. Well, he had underestimated her if he thought that.

Very slowly, she slid the thin straps off her dress from her shoulders and slipped her arms out. Philippe turned away and Margot looked down at the ground. Fitz looked at each of the soldiers in turn, but neither batted an eyelid. Her gaze moved to Engel and she locked eyes with him.

She lifted her chin and then reached around and undid the side zip and stepped out of the dress. Then she put on her own clothes, taking her time to fasten the buttons on her cardigan and smoothing down her hair.

'Very nice,' said Engel. 'Take her away.'

The guards grabbed her by the arms and marched her out of the room, down the stairs and out to the front of the château where Engel's black Citroën was waiting.

Philippe had protested at Fitz's arrest and had been so convincing in his disbelief and the injustice, that Fitz had almost believed him herself. Unsurprisingly, it had been to no avail and Fitz had been whisked off in Engel's car to Saint Martin's Clinic – a property in the north of the town, now taken over by the Gestapo as a place of interrogation.

Engel didn't speak on the short drive to the clinic as he sat beside her in the car. The car was accompanied by two motorcycle outriders who then stood at the entrance to the property as Engel and Fitz climbed out.

There was no point even thinking about trying to flee, Fitz knew she wouldn't get very far and, if anything, it would only signal her guilt.

She followed Engel up the steps to the entrance of the building, and the two soldiers walked closely behind her. At the front door, Fitz paused briefly, looking upwards, squinting at the cool wintery sun. Would this be the last time she'd see a crisp clear sky? Would she ever get to experience flying up above the clouds again?

She drew in a deep breath, savouring the moment, envisaging herself in the cockpit of a Spitfire, dashing through the sky, looking down at the greens and browns of the land below her.

Then she was being jostled into the building where it was just as cold, if not colder, than outside and the shutters kept out the light. It wasn't only the dip in temperature within the building that made Fitz shiver – there was something else, a chilling, malevolent sensation that wrapped itself around her, squeezing her ribcage, tightening her windpipe, and making her heart thud.

A clinic before the war, Fitz didn't allow her imagination to conjure up all the instruments available to the Gestapo to persuade a person to talk. Instead, she thought of all the people she'd loved in life, her mother, her father, little Michael, darling Sam, and dear sweet Yvette. She wouldn't let them down. She'd be brave and face whatever was coming to her. She could and would endure her fate.

To her surprise, Fitz was taken into a room that appeared to be an office. Engel indicated for her to sit at a chair on one side of a large walnut desk, while he opened the shutters and flooded the room with light. One side of the wall was lined with bookshelves and opposite were three filing cabinets. Fitz assumed she was in what would normally be a consulting room.

Engel took the seat opposite and lit a cigarette. He offered one to Fitz, but she declined.

'So, Claudine Bardot,' began Engel. 'Do you want to start by telling me your real name?'

'Claudine Bardot is my real name,' replied Fitz. She was sure Engel was just taking a shot in the dark on this. It was one of the first questions she had been coached in replying to at SOE training.

Engel waved his hand as if shooing a fly away. 'Very well,

we don't have to waste time on the little game of your name. I will find out soon enough.' He smiled but not in the way that conveyed any kind of sympathy. Quite the opposite. 'So, as I'm sure you are aware, Colonel Hoffmann is missing.' Engel paused.

'I wasn't entirely aware,' replied Fitz. 'I did think it was strange he wasn't in his room this morning but assumed he had been called away and hadn't wanted to disturb me.'

'He was last seen with you,' said Engel. 'Going up to his room.'

Fitz nodded. 'Yes. We decided to retire from the party a little early. Rolf . . . I mean, Colonel Hoffmann, was keen to get back to his room and requested I accompany him.'

Engel gave a chuckle. 'You make it sound very civilised.'

Fitz offered a slightly confused expression. 'It was exactly that. Colonel Hoffmann is a very charming man.'

'And when you arrived in Hoffmann's room, what happened?'

'Pardon?'

'I don't mean that,' said Engel. 'I mean, what happened? How did you lure Hoffmann away from his room? Who helped you?'

'I didn't lure him with anything,' said Fitz. 'We went to sleep quite soon after getting back to his room.'

Engel jumped to his feet and slammed his hand down on the desk, causing Fitz to flinch. 'Stop playing games,' he shouted. 'Either you tell me or I will make you tell me. What happened to Colonel Hoffmann last night?'

'I honestly don't know,' replied Fitz. She didn't have to inject a nervous wobble into her voice, it came naturally.

'You can make this as pleasant or as unpleasant as you like,' replied Engel. 'It doesn't matter to me.'

'I don't know any more than you do, Herr Engel,' said Fitz. 'If I did, I would of course tell you. I'm very concerned about Colonel Hoffmann if he is missing.' She wondered if she'd overplayed it with the last sentence.

The Girl in the Sky

'You are very fond of the child, aren't you?' said Engel, catching Fitz off guard at the turn in conversation.

'Yes, of course I am.' Fitz tried to remain relaxed. She hadn't expected Engel to bring Yvette into this quite so soon. She could only hope that someone had taken Yvette to safety already. Maybe the family who Margot mentioned before.

'We are currently looking into her identity and exactly how she is related to Monsieur Philippe Tebow. I'm concerned that she might have been travelling with you under false pretences.'

Fitz shrugged. 'I can assure you, *Herr* Engel, that you will be wasting your time. Everything will be in order just as I said before.'

Engel gave a small smile. 'Let's hope so.' He sat down at his desk again, his anger appeared to have been replaced by a more settled countenance. 'A few days ago we picked up two members of the resistance, Bernard Gareau and André Dacier. They came into the country with a woman who, thus far, we haven't found, but I suspect we are very close.'

Fitz maintained her impassive expression. Inwardly, her heart was racing. 'You did mention that at dinner the other night,' she said.

'We've interviewed both men at length. Here, actually,' he said. 'They've been very forthcoming with the information they've shared.' He took a fob watch from the pocket of his jacket. 'In fact, they'd like to meet you.'

Fitz's mouth dried at the words. Engel certainly liked to play games with people and this is all it was to him, a game. The German got to his feet. 'Would you come this way, please?'

Fitz rose from the chair and reluctantly followed Engel out of the room and into the entrance hall. Engel nodded and a soldier opened a door at the back of the space.

Fitz couldn't help the gasp that escaped as the two men she'd last seen at the farmyard were dragged into the hallway. They had been beaten so badly, their faces were swollen and bruised. One of André's eyes was completely closed up and dried blood coated his face. He couldn't stand and was supported by a soldier on each side. They let him go and he crashed to the floor with a groan.

The other man, who she now knew was called Bernard, hadn't fared any better, but he was standing of his own accord. He was barefoot and Fitz could see both big toenails were missing, the flesh fresh, pink and bloodied.

Fitz made eye-contact with the man. She realised too late what Engel's game was. He wanted the men to believe Fitz had collaborated with him, divulged their secrets. How could she convey to the Frenchman that so far she hadn't said a word? And how could Bernard let her know exactly what he had told the Germans?

'Your friends or your foe?' asked Engel. 'Who has said what?' Another sadistic smile played at the corners of his mouth.

Fitz wasn't about to be beaten in a battle of the minds. She made a big show of recoiling from the man, before she turned to Engel. 'I would say foe. I've never seen these men before in my life.' She hoped by saying this loud enough, Bernard would understand. If they had betrayed her, then she was certain Engel would already be interrogating her, presumably by the same methods used on Bernard and André. She couldn't let her mind go there and think what might happen to her. Now, she was purely surviving minute by minute.

'Is that so?' mused Engel. He nodded at the soldiers who had dumped André on the floor. They had obviously been given instructions on how this was going to play out, and without question they hoisted André to his feet and dragged him back down the hallway and through the rear door. 'Please follow,' ordered Engel.

With the Frenchman ahead of her, Fitz followed the party through the room at the back of the house and into a courtyard. She watched in horror as the two prisoners were forced to kneel, facing her. André could barely keep upright and swayed to one side but was swiftly booted back into a central position by one of the guards.

Both Frenchmen had their hands tied behind their backs, which Fitz thought was ridiculous. It was clear neither of them was in any position to put up a fight.

Engel walked behind the prisoners and held his pistol at the back of André's head, just as he had done with Yvette.

'Mademoiselle Bardot,' said Engel. 'I will ask you again, where is Colonel Hoffmann?'

Fitz shook her head. 'I don't know,' she replied.

The words had barely left her lips when a shot rang out and André thudded to the ground, blood seeping out from the fatal gunshot wound. Fitz flinched but refused to turn away.

Engel looked in utter disdain at the motionless body of the young Frenchman who, only a few days ago, had sat in the mess room with Fitz, waiting to board the flight to France. The fragility of life especially at the hands of someone like Engel was not lost on Fitz.

'I hope his mother can forgive you for not saving his life,' said Engel.

Fitz had to force herself not to respond. She wanted to race across the courtyard, grab Engel by his lapels and shout in his face that she was not responsible. It was him. He was the murderer.

Engel now had his pistol pointing at the back of Bernard's head. 'I will ask the same question and if you give the same answer, then my action will be the same,' he said simply. 'Are you happy to have more blood on your hands?'

Fitz looked at Bernard. They both knew that no matter what she replied, Engel was going to murder him. If Fitz confessed now, then their deaths really would be in vain. If she could hold out for as long as possible, it would give Yvette a chance to survive. She couldn't do anything for the Frenchman now and they both knew it.

Bernard closed his eyes slowly and opened them again.

He had accepted his fate and was in effect forgiving Fitz for what was about to happen.

She held his gaze for a moment longer, before switching it to Engel. 'As I said before, I do not know this man and I have no idea what happened to Colonel Hoffmann.'

She couldn't be sure, but she thought she saw a look of satisfaction on the Frenchman's face before he too was shot at point-blank range and met death instantly.

Engel let out a sigh and, holstering his pistol, walked over to Fitz. 'Maybe we should continue our conversation inside.'

This time, Fitz wasn't taken to the comfort of Engel's office, but to a room at the back of the house. Inside was a table and two chairs in the centre of the room. Fitz gulped at the sight of various tools and medical instruments laid out on the table. The tiled floor was wet and although smelt of disinfectant, the metallic odour of blood was undeniable.

She didn't need telling this was where André and Bernard had been interrogated and she was about to get the same treatment.

Chapter 25

No amount of SOE training could have prepared Fitz for the ordeal she underwent at the Gestapo house over the next twenty-four hours. She knew she was strong-willed but the pain she endured was almost unbearable, and apparently, according, to Engel, he was going easy on her because he liked her.

She'd been stripped to her underwear and tied to a chair, left for hours – either alone and blindfolded in darkness or with someone in the room. She didn't know when the next assault would begin or where it was coming from.

She had drip-fed her interrogators information, some of it false and some of it true – the latter being information that would be useless by the time it was acted upon, like, the trains which were marked for sabotage, or the communication lines destined to be cut by the resistance. All rehearsed pieces of information which were designed to make her captors feel she was co-operating. It would buy her a day or two if she was lucky.

Fitz's main concern was Yvette. Everything she was doing was not only to give Philippe and Margot more time to reorganise any of their plans, but to keep Yvette safe. She wasn't one for praying, but she did that night, tied to the chair, blindfolded, with her hands in agony where she'd had her fingernails pulled out earlier that day. She had passed out with the pain and had been brought around with a bucket of ice-cold water being thrown over her. And now the little clothing she was wearing was still wet and she could feel the cold night air seeping into the room. She guessed a window had been left open, with the intention of making her as uncomfortable as possible. She dreaded to think what she looked like. Engel had taken great pleasure in dishing out several blows to her face and the threat of teeth being pulled out with a large pair of plyers he had brandished in front of her was what she had to look forward to next.

Exhausted from this onslaught, Fitz allowed herself to drift into a semi-conscious state. Her head bowed, she sensed she was alone in the room and could try to doze if nothing else. The pain in her fingertips was immense and her back was very sore from where she had been struck with a leather strap. She needed to rest. To sleep.

It wasn't a deep sleep, though. As soon as she heard the door to the room open, she was wide-awake again. At the thought of what she was going to have to face today, her empty stomach churned. She had been deprived of food since she'd been brought here and been given a minimal amount of water – just enough to keep her alive she assumed.

The blindfold was removed from her eyes, and she squinted as the daylight dazzled her. Being blindfolded had heightened her other senses and she knew Engel was in the room by the smell of his pine-scented aftershave.

She flinched as someone touched her arm. She realised it was a soldier and he was untying the straps that had kept her wrists in place.

'Good morning, Mademoiselle Bardot,' said Engel. Fitz's eyes finally adjusted to the light. And although she was not able to open them fully, she could make out Engel standing in front of her. 'I'm sorry to say, your stay here has come to an end.'

Fitz had been fully prepared to die but to hear Engel's words made the reality suddenly very stark. She took a deep breath, refusing to allow herself to cry. She'd be taken out to the courtyard and executed like André and Bernard. Maybe no one in England would ever know what she had gone through, but she would die knowing she hadn't betrayed her country and with hope that Yvette was safe. She was certain if Engel had hold of Yvette, he would have used the child to get Fitz to talk. Fitz always knew that if that ever happened, then she would tell Engel everything he wanted to know. She would have done anything to save the child. Anything.

Her clothes were placed on the table in front of her, together with her shoes. At least she'd have the dignity of being dressed when they came to reclaim her body. She wondered if she'd be buried next to the airmen in Josselin cemetery. If Sam was buried there, then she would rest in eternal peace.

She got to her feet and immediately collapsed to the ground. Her legs were weak. Her body was exhausted. She felt the hands of the soldiers on her as they stood her up. She held onto the table for support. She did not want them to touch her.

It took Fitz what little energy she had to dress herself. Fastening the buttons on her blouse was especially difficult with her sore fingers. She had no idea what her face looked like but judging by the pain in her cheekbone and the swelling on her lip, she guessed she looked pretty damn awful. Still, though she might look totally broken on the outside, Engel hadn't destroyed her spirit. That she still had.

She smoothed down her skirt and patted her hair, trying to tuck a few loose strands into place with the two fingers which still had their nails intact.

She wouldn't look at Engel. She knew he'd be sniggering at her. She didn't care. She stood up straight, looking at a point beyond his shoulder.

'I shouldn't worry too much about how you look,' remarked Engel. 'Where you're going, no one will care.'

Where she was going? She wasn't sure what he meant. To her death? Or somewhere else? She wanted to ask but wouldn't give him the satisfaction of knowing she cared.

'Goodbye, Mademoiselle Bardot,' said Engel. 'I am sorry we didn't meet under more favourable circumstances. I'm sure we would have got on very well indeed.'

Fitz remained silent. She didn't want Engel to be the last face she looked at before she died. She'd already decided that her final thoughts would be of Yvette and Sam. People she cared deeply about. Her only regret was she hadn't acknowledged the strength of her feelings for them sooner. For her to die and never have been able to tell either of them how much she cared – how much she loved them – that was the greatest tragedy of this whole sorry affair.

The soldier took Fitz's arm and walked her out of the room. To Fitz's surprise, instead of turning left to the rear garden and place of execution, the soldier shoved her towards the front door. Fitz was still unsteady on her feet and stumbled but grabbed hold of the banister.

'Move,' ordered the soldier in German.

Fitz concentrated hard, putting one foot in front of the other. Was she being set free? A glimmer of hope filled her heart. Maybe they were going to let her go.

The soldier moved in front of her and opened the door and as Fitz stepped out onto the doorstep the glimmer of hope was snuffed out.

There was a military truck waiting outside and she was ordered to climb in the back. Each side of the truck, the benches were lined with mostly men, about fifteen of them and three women, who shuffled up so Fitz could sit with them. Two soldiers sat at the end nearest the back of the truck.

Fitz looked around at the faces. Some had suffered the same fate as her, judging by the bruising and injuries. While others simply looked broken, the light in their eyes extinguished. She realised with a sickening feeling in her stomach that she wasn't being released at all. She might have been given a stay of execution that morning, but she was by no stretch of the imagination free. They were all prisoners. The truck

The Girl in the Sky

trundled on through the town heading in the rough direction of Rennes.

'Where are we going?' Fitz whispered to the woman next to her, who looked to be in her mid to late thirties. She had a black eye but other than that, looked unscathed. Fitz couldn't help wondering what she had done to be on the back of a truck.

The woman looked at her as if she was stupid.

It was a man sitting opposite who answered. 'You really don't know?'

Fitz shook her head. 'No.'

The woman made a scoffing noise. 'She thinks she's going on holiday, maybe?'

This earned a chuckle from the people either side of them. The man leaned forward. 'You've heard of the internment camps being set up across the country?'

Fitz clamped her mouth tightly closed, to stop her bottom lip trembling. This was not the time to start crying. If the man was right, then she was to be interned in some sort of detention camp. She knew the Nazis were already sending people there, most of them who the Nazis termed 'nomads', but also some Jews and non-French nationals. A place where people were just detained, they weren't put on trial or sentenced, they were simply held there for as long as their captors wanted.

Silence fell across the truck as it continued on its journey. Fitz was jostled against the people either side of her as the truck swayed over uneven ground. As she looked around at the dejected faces of her fellow travellers, she noticed one thing – acceptance of fate. All hope had gone from their eyes.

Over the next couple of hours, the truck stopped in several different towns to collect more prisoners. Every one of them looked dirty, and they smelled. Fitz guessed she was no different to the others. She certainly hadn't been offered any soap and water before she was released from Engel's custody. Yet, despite the bodily smells, they all huddled together in a bid to keep themselves warm in the cold December air.

After collecting more prisoners, the truck was rammed full and some of the new pick-ups had to sit on the floor, three abreast. Then the rain began. Small infrequent drops to start with, but then larger heavier blobs, falling fast from the sky. The soldiers pulled a plastic sheet over themselves, but there was no shelter for Fitz and the others.

Fitz welcomed the rain, at least she had a chance to get some of the filth and dried blood from her skin. She lifted her chin up to the sky, just as she had done before she'd stepped inside the Gestapo house. She relished the fresh water, the feeling of being alive. She had seen the sky again, when she thought she wouldn't. There was still hope. She wasn't sure exactly what she was hoping for in the short term, but long term, she hoped she survived this war and was able to see her family again. And, of course, that somehow Sam was still alive, somewhere out there. Maybe he was trying to find his way back to England. She had to cling onto that hope. If she didn't, what was the point? What did her mother used to say? Where there's life there's hope. If that's all Fitz had, then she would take it.

The rain didn't show any signs of easing over an hour later. If anything, it was as if the grey rain-filled clouds were following them. Everyone was drenched and as the day wore on and the sun sloped lower in the sky, with it came the cold.

When the truck drew to a halt, Fitz thought they must be stopping for the night, but looking around from the back of the vehicle, all she could see were trees either side of the road. Then voices came from the cab and doors opened and closed as the driver and co-driver disembarked. The two motorcycle outriders and the jeep that was escorting the truck all stopped a little way ahead. Something was happening. Fitz leaned back and could just about see around the cab. In front of them was another truck like the one she was travelling in, except it had a canvas canopy which was open at the back, where two guards were seated.

There was a brief conversation between drivers and then both trucks began to move again in convoy.

They trundled on through the French countryside in an easterly direction, the heavy rain making the journey laborious as they stopped in several more villages, collecting more prisoners. Fitz estimated they had at least fifty people across the two vehicles. Sometimes it was a person on their own, other times it was whole families.

At one point, they stopped near a forest, and in groups of ten the prisoners were allowed to disembark and relieve themselves in a drainage ditch. Fitz hated the way they were being treated as if they were sub-human. As she climbed out of the ditch, she glanced across to the other truck where there were more women with children.

And there amongst the group climbing out of the truck, she saw her.

The blonde hair still tied in the plaits. The teddy clutched under her arm.

It was Yvette.

Fitz gasped. Her instinct was to call out to Yvette, but she managed to stop herself. She didn't want to draw attention to them and what if Yvette broke away and tried to run over towards Fitz? The guards might think she was trying to escape and shoot her. All these thoughts rushed through Fitz's mind in a second.

'Hurry up!' shouted a guard, jabbing his rifle in her direction.

Fitz scrambled up the grass bank and took another quick, but discreet, glance at Yvette. The initial joy and relief of seeing the little girl was quickly replaced by sadness and fear. Yvette hadn't got away. Had Margot and Philippe been arrested and was Yvette with them at the time? Or had Margot taken her to the family she mentioned and for some reason they'd given Yvette up to the authorities? Were they there on the truck or was Yvette alone?

Fitz tried to see if anyone appeared to be looking after

Yvette but she lost sight of her in the group as they slid down the bank into the ditch.

Once she was in the truck, Fitz couldn't see the other vehicle properly. As she sat down on the wooden bench, she tried to work out a plan to get to Yvette. Maybe she could get her on this truck with her. She was desperate to take care of the child. It was her fault Yvette had been caught. Fitz felt a great wave of responsibility for Yvette and equally a huge burden of guilt. She had let the little girl down. She wasn't sure she could live with herself. She had to find a way to get to her. At least then Yvette wouldn't be alone.

Thirty minutes later, the trucks were on the road again. The rain had not stopped, and large puddles were forming as the water made its way to the lowest point. With the occupation, the maintenance of the land and the ditches hadn't been a priority for the Germans and the excess water had nowhere to escape to other than across the roads. The grass verges were sodden.

As dusk began to fall and the last of the daylight was fading, the trucks finally pulled off the road and into a field which bordered dense woodland. Everyone was ordered off the trucks and escorted to the trees where they were made to crowd together with only the pine trees as cover. They had been kept in two separate groups and Fitz had not had the opportunity to get anywhere near Yvette. She had caught sight of her every now and again through the groups of people, but Fitz still couldn't work out if Yvette was alone or not.

The prisoners all huddled down on the damp forest floor, and Fitz wished she could wrap her arms around Yvette to reassure her and to keep her warm. As they sat there, Fitz did consider her chances of escaping. There were twelve guards altogether, with six on duty and six sleeping. She wondered how far she would get and where she would run to?

'Don't even think about it,' said a voice in her ear.

It was the man who had sat opposite her on the truck.

'Think about what?' said Fitz. It was best to be on her

guard, she didn't know who she could trust here. Admit to nothing for as long as possible had been a piece of advice she'd been given back at SOE training.

The man sitting next to her raised his eyebrows. 'They wouldn't hesitate to kill you. Or some of us as punishment.'

Sadly, it was true. Reprisal executions were a very effective deterrent.

'I'm not planning on trying to escape,' replied Fitz. And it was the truth. Breaking free was just a fantasy. Nothing more than a romantic idea to keep her spirits up because, ultimately, she couldn't escape without Yvette.

The rain stopped at some point during the night, but by the time morning came, it had started again. The two parties were escorted back to the trucks. The field was like a sponge as they picked their way across the uncut grass, before climbing into the trucks.

Now back on the hard, wooden bench, Fitz waited as the drivers brought the engines to life and prepared to move out.

The engines revved high and the trucks protested at being required to cross the boggy grass through the gateway and out onto the road. As the first truck got to the gateway, Fitz could hear the engine being worked hard to drive the vehicle through the mud, it sounded like it was wheel spinning. After a few fruitless minutes of trying to get any traction, Fitz and the rest of the prisoners in her truck, were ordered out to push the first one.

The mud was deep and squelchy, coming over her shoes, the act of just lifting her foot out of the mud wasn't easy. Under the orders of the guards, they tried as hard as they could to push the truck forwards but it wouldn't budge. Several prisoners were escorted back to the forest to gather branches to place under the tyres and the passengers on the first truck were ordered out. The rain was driving down now and thunder clapped in the sky. The guards had to shout to be heard over the noise of the weather. In the commotion, Fitz had managed to shuffle near to the back of the truck and as the passengers disembarked she watched like a hawk, waiting for Yvette. As soon as Fitz saw the blonde hair of the child, she pushed her way forwards and grabbed Yvette's hand.

Yvette didn't look up and Fitz dragged her back into the crowd, before crouching in front of her. 'Yvette,' she said, lifting the child's chin up. 'It's me, Claudine.'

Yvette's eyes widened like two saucers. She gasped for breath, burst into tears and then threw herself at Fitz, wrapping her arms around her neck and holding on so tightly, Fitz almost lost balance. Gently she prised Yvette's hands from around her. Yvette moved back and studied Fitz's face. She lifted a hand and her fingertips lightly touching the bruised cheekbone. 'What happened to your face?'

Fitz realised she must look a frightening sight with her injuries. She smiled reassuringly. 'It's all right. It will soon get better.' She wiped the tears from Yvette's face. 'Don't cry now,' she soothed. 'Everything is all right. We'll stay together.'

Chapter 26

Eventually and after much effort, they managed to get enough pieces of wood under the wheels enabling the truck to gain traction and lurch forward out of the boggy hole.

When everyone climbed back into the trucks, Fitz made sure Yvette came with her.

'There's not enough room,' complained the woman next to Fitz.

'She's only little,' said the man opposite. 'Swap places with me if you need more room for your behind.'

The woman glared at the man and begrudgingly shuffled up so Yvette could squeeze in next to Fitz. The man gave Yvette a wink. '*Merci*,' mouthed Fitz to the man. This little act of support gave her hope that all was not lost for humankind.

The track the convoy drove along was no better than it had been the day before, with more flooding it was hard to see where the road ended, and the grass verge began.

They had only been travelling ten minutes or so, when the truck Fitz was in suddenly lurched to the right and everyone was thrown to one side of it as the cab landed in the ditch, causing the rear of the vehicle to jack-knife and topple on its side. Screams and cries were swallowed up in the chaos as the truck hit the unforgiving bank with a thud. It took Fitz a moment to realise what had happened. She was trapped under a tangle of legs and arms. She could hear people shouting in French and German voices. People were trying to free themselves from one another, others were groaning. Water had filled part of the truck bed but fortunately the size of the vehicle meant that it was wedged only so far in the ditch.

Someone shoved their foot in Fitz's face as they clawed their way out. She frantically looked around for Yvette, pushing people off her as they scrambled to get out of the overturned truck and climb up the bank of the ditch.

'Yvette! Yvette!' Fitz could feel the panic setting in but then spotted a little hand clasped around a teddy bear. She scrambled over to her, shoving people to the side so they didn't trample on the child who was half under the bench seat. She pulled Yvette out backwards by her ankles and thankfully she seemed all right. They clambered out of the truck and jostled their way up the bank and away from the overturned truck.

People were still calling for help, crying out in pain, while others tried to free them. The guards were barking orders, trying to make themselves heard above the growing frantic shouts and cries from the prisoners.

There was a sense of disorder. One young-looking German soldier was shouting and waving his rifle around, trying to get people to move away from the trucks, while another was shouting equally as loud, sending them back to help. At one point the two soldiers were shouting at each other.

The prisoners were scared, not knowing what to do or who to listen to. A shot rang out in the air, causing everyone to scream and take cover, holding their hands over their heads in futile protection against a bullet. More shouting from the soldier on the bank ensued. The regular German soldier hadn't had the same education as that of an officer and didn't have the benefit of another language. It was obvious not many of the prisoners understood German and were terrified, having to guess what they were being ordered to do.

The frustrated soldier lifted his rifle and jabbed the butt between the shoulder blades of an elderly man who fell at his feet. The soldier was standing over him, shouting at him

The Girl in the Sky

to get up. He kicked out at the man and when someone else tried to get the man to his feet, they too were jabbed with the rifle.

Fitz pulled Yvette in towards her, wanting to shield her from what would happen next. Another shot. Fitz flinched. The man had been shot in the head at point blank range. More screams and cries from the nearby prisoners as they scurried about trying to obey the confusing and conflicting orders.

It was only then as Fitz took a moment to survey the chaos before her, she realised that the urgency from the guards was because the driver and another soldier were trapped in the submerged cab of the truck.

It was clearly becoming a desperate situation as frantically, the soldiers themselves joined in with trying to free their comrades. One of them shouted across to the two soldiers watching over Fitz and the rest of the prisoners.

One of the soldiers ran over to the submerged truck cab, joining in with the efforts to free the men before it was too late.

Fitz looked around, her eyes scanning the situation before her. The remaining soldier was by her side, but his attention wasn't on her or the rest of the prisoners, it was on the cab. He took a few steps closer, craning his neck to get a better look, glancing momentarily at the prisoners before his attention was back on the frantic rescue bid.

Fitz squeezed Yvette's hand. 'Very slowly, move back a little,' she whispered in her ear. In unison, they shifted themselves away from the main group of prisoners. One shuffle at a time as one step at a time, the soldier guarding them moved towards the truck.

The guards were shouting and yelling at each other and to the men trapped in the cab. It was all looking very desperate for them.

Fitz checked and double-checked no one was watching them. If they could make it to the other side of the road and through a gap in the brambles she had spotted, then they could disappear into the woodland. It was the only chance they were going to get.

'Hold on tight to your teddy,' said Fitz. She couldn't risk another cock up like before. 'When I say go, we're going to run around to the other side of the truck. And then across the road. *D'accord?*'

Yvette nodded. '*Oui.*'

Fitz made a final check that everyone else was preoccupied. She got to her feet and took Yvette's hand. 'Ready? Go.' They sprinted around to the side of the truck. It only took seconds but it felt like minutes. Fitz was waiting for the hail of bullets. But none came. They had made it without being noticed. There was no time to lose. 'And again. Run. Now!' she whispered, the desperation in her voice was clear.

Yvette didn't hesitate and they both bolted across the road, charging through the gap in the bushes. They kept running, into the forest.

Running as fast as they could.

All the time Fitz was listening out for shouts or gunshots, expecting the Germans to be hunting them down. She didn't look back. She kept hold of Yvette's hand and was almost dragging the child off her feet as they ducked and swerved their way through the trees.

It wasn't until Yvette collapsed and couldn't get up, that Fitz stopped to catch her own breath. She slumped down on the cold damp ground beside Yvette. They lay there on the forest floor panting furiously, looking up through the tree canopy at the small shafts of grey light filtering through.

Yvette was wheezing heavily which started off a coughing fit. Fitz sat her up and patted her back. She wished she had some water to offer her.

'I feel hot,' said Yvette.

Fitz put the back of her hand to Yvette's forehead and worryingly she did indeed feel like she was on the brink of developing a temperature.

'Just sit here and rest for a moment,' said Fitz. On the one hand she felt relieved they had escaped as she was sure a sick child wouldn't be looked upon too favourably by their captors. On the other hand, Yvette developing an illness which Fitz was totally unequipped to deal with was worrying.

'Where are we going?' asked Yvette after her cough had subsided.

That was a very good question. Fitz had tried to maintain her bearings on the journey, looking out for landmarks and any signposts to give her a clue as to where they might be, but it had all been minimal. She knew they had travelled east and she suspected they were still in France, but only just.

Location wasn't their immediate problem though. Safety was the priority. Finding someone who could help them. It was a risky business knocking on random doors. There was no guarantee she could trust anyone not to report them to the authorities. How could she possibly tell who was to be trusted, until it was too late?

Before that though, they needed food and water. That was their second priority. They were no good to anyone dead through starvation or dehydration.

Not wanting to stay where they were for much longer in case the Germans sent out a patrol to look for them, Fitz urged Yvette to her feet.

'We're going to head through the forest and look for food and water,' she said. 'The ground is sloping down and if there's a stream, that's where we'll find it.'

'And food?' asked Yvette. 'My stomach hurts.'

'We'll look out for berries,' said Fitz. Although, she wasn't entirely sure what they'd find in the middle of winter.

Fitz decided to head south, rather than continue east, as she thought there would be more activity and patrols the nearer they got to the border. Heading south, she might be able to get them into Vichy France where it would be easier to move around. How she was going to make contact with the resistance she hadn't yet worked out but she knew she had to remain optimistic. Hope was the only thing they had right now.

It was harder in the forest to keep her bearings. Everywhere looked the same. She was also losing track of time and Yvette was finding it hard to keep up.

'I'm so tired,' said the little girl, before succumbing to another bout of coughing. 'I can't walk any further.'

'You have to try. Just a bit further,' encouraged Fitz. 'We'll soon be out of the forest and then we might be able to find a farm. I'll be able to get us something to eat then.' She had already decided that if it meant stealing, then she would. It went against her principles but at a time like this, when it was life or death, she had to ignore those morals.

The trees were definitely thinning out and it wasn't long before Fitz could see the edge of a field. 'Look, Yvette,' she said enthusiastically. 'We've made it through the forest.'

They stood at the edge of the trees looking down a valley. There was a stone cottage on the other side of the field and beyond that a small village.

'Can we get some food now?' asked Yvette standing beside Fitz and looking down at the buildings.

'We have to be very careful,' said Fitz. 'We don't know if there are any soldiers about. Stay with me. Don't let go of my hand.'

Fitz had considered leaving Yvette at the edge of the forest and scoping out the village on her own but she was frightened that if she was caught, then Yvette would be left all alone and no one would know she was there. More than that, though, Fitz couldn't bear the thought of leaving Yvette again. She'd done that once before and look what had happened. It was only by luck they were reunited. She wasn't sure she'd be so lucky a second time. Her newly discovered desire to protect Yvette was riding high and although the strength of such emotion was a little unnerving, Fitz had no intention nor wish to run from it.

The Girl in the Sky

The rain had eased but their clothes were still damp. Fitz hadn't felt warm for days. She was chilled to the bone. Yvette was coughing every minute or so now and her complexion was very grey. Fitz hoped she wasn't developing a chest infection which could easily lead to something like pneumonia if left untreated. They were both in desperate need of dry clothes, hot food, and a good night's sleep.

They followed the edge of the field that took them out onto a narrow road about a quarter of a mile from the cottage she had seen earlier.

'I'm too tired to walk,' complained Yvette, sagging to the ground.

'Not much further,' said Fitz. 'Come on, try to stand up now.'

'I can't.' Yvette began to cry which started off her cough again.

Fitz crouched down in the road next to the child. 'Just a little further,' she said. She took a hanky from her pocket and dabbed at the beads of sweat forming on Yvette's brow. She definitely had a fever now. As if to underline this diagnosis, Yvette's eyes rolled back in her head and she slumped to the side.

'Yvette!' cried Fitz, managing to thrust her hand under the girl's head before it hit the ground. 'Yvette. Wake up.'

Yvette gave a weak moan. Her eyes were half open but Fitz could tell she wasn't focusing on anything. Panic swept through Fitz. Yvette was ill. Very ill. She needed a doctor.

Somehow Fitz managed to pick Yvette up in her arms, and get to her feet, before hurrying down the road towards the cottage.

Fitz had underestimated just how tired she was herself. She staggered up the path to the cottage and hoped to God the occupant would be sympathetic to their plight.

Before Fitz had even reached the front door, it was pulled open by a woman, probably in her forties. She took in the sight before her.

'Help me, please,' said Fitz, surprised to hear her voice cracking with desperation. 'She's not well.'

The woman took one more look at Fitz and Yvette, before opening her door wide and ushering them inside. 'Come. Quickly,' she said. 'Here, let me take her.' She took Yvette from Fitz and carried her through into the living room, shooing two young girls from the sofa. 'You're both soaking,' she said as she placed Yvette down on the cushions. She turned to the children. 'Monique, go upstairs and bring me one of your clean nightdresses from the cupboard. Amelie fetch two blankets from my bed and a clean towel.'

The children scurried off as instructed.

The change in air, coming into a warm room with a small fire alight in the hearth, must have set Yvette's cough off. The woman placed a cushion behind her head so Yvette was in a more upright position. 'How long has she been like this?' she asked.

'I'm not sure. Maybe a day or two with the cough,' said Fitz. 'But the temperature came on this afternoon.'

The woman nodded and telling Fitz to sit down, left the room, coming back a few minutes later with a bowl of warm water and a flannel.

'My name is Jeanne. I am a nurse.'

Fitz could hardly believe her good fortune. She wanted to weep with relief. 'Claudine Bardot,' she said. 'Thank you for helping us.'

The children returned with the dry clothing, bedding and clean towel. 'Go into the kitchen and warm some soup for our guests,' Jeanne instructed her daughters.

'You're too kind,' said Fitz.

'It is the least I can do,' said Jeanne. She put the flannel to one side and with the help of Fitz, they changed Yvette into the dry nightgown and covered her with a blanket. Jeanne got to her feet. 'Come with me. You need some dry clothes, too. And a wash.'

Fitz inwardly winced. She hadn't considered what a sight

they might look. When they went into Jeanne's bedroom, Fitz caught sight of herself in the mirror and let out a cry of alarm. 'I'm sorry,' she said, inspecting her bruised and battered face closer. 'I didn't realise. I haven't seen myself like this.'

Jeanne stood beside her and put her hand on Fitz's shoulder. 'You don't have to explain. It is obvious what has happened to you and God has brought you to my door for a purpose. I will get some medicine for the child in the morning. I am on good terms with the doctor. Also, I have friends who can help you both. Tomorrow I will speak to them. You can stay here tonight. You're safe now.'

The kindness from the woman was too much for Fitz and she sobbed in Jeanne's arms like a child.

Chapter 27

Looking in the bedroom mirror, Fitz was horrified to see the extent of bruising to her face. Jeanne came into the bedroom with a bottle of vodka and a pot of some sort of balm.

'Please, can I clean your wounds? You don't want them to become infected.' She had dabbed Fitz's face with the vodka and then applied what she explained was a homemade arnica balm to the bruising. 'This will help to soothe the skin,' she said. 'Is it just your face?'

Fitz shook her head. She slipped the towel from her back and heard Jeanne give a sharp intake of breath. 'You poor thing,' said the Frenchwoman.

Fitz winced as Jeanne applied the alcohol and balm to her back. 'Thank you,' she said afterwards. 'Is it bad?'

'Some of the skin is broken,' said Jeanne. 'You might have scarring,' she added gently.

Fitz didn't really care. She was at this point simply grateful to be alive. 'You're very kind to take us in like this,' she said to Jeanne, who was now looking through her wardrobe and placing some clothes on the bed.

'How could I not? I'm glad you came to my door,' replied Jeanne. 'Here are some clean clothes for you. They might be a little big.'

'Thank you,' said Fitz again. She felt overwhelmed by the kindness of this woman, but she didn't want to keep crying. She needed to be strong. She wouldn't be able to stay here for long, it would be putting Jeanne in too much danger. 'How is Yvette?' she asked.

'She's not well,' said Jeanne. 'If her fever doesn't break tonight, I will have to ask the doctor to visit. He is a good man.'

Fitz had known Jeanne less than an hour and already she knew she could trust the Frenchwoman. 'I should sit with her in case she wakes up. She'll be scared and I promised I wouldn't leave her.'

Jeanne held up her hand. 'You need to rest, too. Please, use my bed. I'll bring the child up to you. Yvette, you say her name is?'

'Yes. She's been through a lot,' said Fitz. She wanted to tell Jeanne, but she also knew she couldn't. 'I wish I could tell you more.'

'I know, it is too dangerous. I understand,' said Jeanne. 'Now, please, rest while you can. Here's a nightgown you can wear tonight. I'll be back shortly with the child.'

Fitz slipped on the flannelette nightgown and climbed into Jeanne's bed. It may not have been the kind of cotton sheets and quilted eiderdown she was used to back in England, but after the last few days, it was pure luxury. Jeanne soon returned with Yvette in her arms and placed her in the bed beside Fitz.

'I will come in to check on her but if you need me at all, I will be downstairs.' She pulled the bedclothes up over both Fitz's and Yvette's shoulders. 'Rest now. You're safe for tonight.'

Fitz knew she was tired, but she hadn't realised quite how exhausted she had been.

She was woken in the morning by Yvette thrashing around in her sleep. Fitz sat bolt upright and took one look at Yvette and jumped out of bed, calling for Jeanne.

Yvette was sopping wet with sweat and yet she was shivering. She was writhing around like she was having a bad dream.

'Jeanne?' Fitz called out, stroking Yvette's damp hair off her face.

Jeanne appeared within seconds. She felt Yvette's forehead and then put her fingers to the child's wrist, checking her pulse. 'I'll go and fetch the doctor now,' she said. Although she was calm, there was a sense of urgency in her tone.

'What shall I do?' asked Fitz.

'See if you can get her to drink a little water. Use a cool cloth on her forehead.' Jeanne was already out the door as she called out her instructions.

Fitz went around to Yvette's side of the bed and, putting her arm under Yvette's back, she got her to sit up. The change of position seemed to bring Yvette out of her disturbed dream. She opened her eyes, but they darted around the room, unfocused. 'Yvette, please try to drink some water,' said Fitz. 'You were having a bad dream.' She lifted the glass to Yvette's lips and encouraged her to take in some fluids. Yvette only managed a few sips before her eyes closed and she was drifting back to what seemed a calmer state of sleep.

Fitz wasn't sure which she preferred – Yvette lying motionless on the bed as she was now or flailing around in distress.

It was raining again outside and it was lashing against the windowpane. Whilst Yvette was asleep, Fitz got dressed quickly. She didn't know how long they could stay here, but taking Yvette out in the treacherous weather really wasn't an option. Every hour they stayed here, though, put Jeanne and her family in more danger.

It was another twenty minutes before Jeanne returned with the doctor. He nodded an acknowledgement at Fitz. '*Bonjour, mademoiselle,*' was all he said before turning his attention to the patient. Both Fitz and Jeanne stood by the window, watching the doctor examine Yvette. Fitz was silently willing Yvette to be all right. She couldn't bear it if anything happened to her now. She'd feel completely to blame if anything did.

The Girl in the Sky

Eventually, the doctor completed his examination. He clipped his black medical case shut. 'She's going to be all right,' he said kindly.

'Oh, thank goodness,' said Fitz. Her heart fluttered in relief.

'She's very unwell, but she is lucky that the cough hasn't developed into an infection. I can give you something to help soothe the cough. Also, if you have a peppermint balm to rub on her chest, that will help clear the airways for her. Keep her in a slightly sitting-up position. Plenty of fluids. If the fever hasn't broken in the next twelve hours, you will need to come and get me again.'

'Thank you, so much,' said Fitz. She suddenly thought about the cost of the medication. 'Can I pay you?' she asked. 'Where's my skirt? I have some Francs sewn into the hem in case of emergencies.'

But the doctor was already waving his hand. 'Not at all. I don't want paying. You might need that for a real emergency,' he said.

Fitz noticed a look pass between the doctor and her host. Jeanne spoke. 'The doctor can help you get to safety,' she said quietly.

'Really? But what if that is not here in France?' Fitz was hesitant to give away too much detail.

'It can still happen,' said the doctor. 'Especially if it was somewhere like England. Would that be somewhere you'd like to go?'

Fitz gulped back a ball of emotion. 'Yes,' she said. 'It would very much be somewhere I'd like to go.'

The doctor patted her hand. 'It will take a few days to organise.'

'And Yvette?' she added.

'She can't be moved until she's better,' said the doctor.

'I can't leave her,' said Fitz. 'I won't go until she's well enough to travel with me.'

The doctor cleared his throat. 'It can be arranged. Normally, I wouldn't advocate such action. Taking a child from her homeland but in these times of occupation, I believe she will be safer in England.'

'She will. I promised her I wouldn't leave her,' said Fitz. 'She has no one as far as I know.'

'You have to promise me one thing, though,' continued the doctor.

Fitz nodded. 'What is it?'

'After the war, when it is safe to do so, please bring her back to France. Try to find her family. She deserves to be reunited with them.'

'I promise,' said Fitz solemnly. 'You have my word.'

The doctor studied her for a moment. 'Yes, I believe I do,' he said finally.

By the following morning, after another disturbed and restless night, Yvette's fever had broken, much to everyone's relief. The doctor had been back to check on her and was pleased to find her sitting up comfortably in bed. Still very weak, but awake. Fitz spent the next two days barely moving from Yvette's side, as she tended to her every need. Thoughts of going home to England were never far from her mind, but her priority was Yvette's health.

New Year's Eve came and went. Fitz was barely been aware of the days going by, as she fretted over Yvette. On the third morning, she had gone downstairs to help Jeanne with the breakfast and was pleased, if not surprised, to see Yvette at the foot of the stairs.

'You're up,' she said, going over to her and hugging the nine-year-old. 'But look, you've nothing on your feet. You'll make yourself ill again.'

'I'm hungry,' said Yvette.

'That is a good sign,' said Jeanne. 'We don't have much, but I'm making porridge and just for today, you can have breakfast in bed. Now go back upstairs.'

'Go on, shoo,' said Fitz, good naturedly. She watched Yvette scuttle back up the stairs. 'It's amazing how quickly children recover,' she said going back to the stove where she was stirring the porridge in a pot.

'I know,' agreed Jeanne. 'One minute she was at death's door and now, look at her, skipping up the stairs.'

'I'm so relieved she's recovered,' said Fitz. 'Although she was still coughing this morning.'

'She'll have that cough a while,' said Jeanne. 'But she is certainly over the worst of it now.'

Fitz lifted the pot from the heat. 'I suppose that means I will be able to go home soon.'

'Yes. It probably does,' said Jeanne, taking the pot from Fitz and scooping porridge into the waiting bowls lined up on the table.

A knock at the door interrupted the conversation. Fitz grabbed two bowls from the table and quickly went upstairs and into the bedroom. 'Shh. You have to be very quiet now,' she whispered to Yvette. 'Sit very still and don't make a sound.'

Fitz listened to Jeanne opening the door. 'Oh, Madame Cussac. What can I do for you?'

'I was wondering if everything was all right?' came the visitor's voice. Madame Cussac sounded maybe the same sort of age as Jeanne, and Fitz wondered how friendly the two women were.

'Everything is fine, thank you,' replied Jeanne. 'And I trust you are well?'

'Pfft. As well as anyone can be,' she replied. 'I saw the doctor visited you. Have you been ill?'

Fitz wondered how anyone would be able to see Jeanne's cottage from the village. Maybe there was another house nearby where Madame Cussac lived.

'One of the children has a cough, that's all,' replied Jeanne. 'Thank you for your concern.'

Fitz noted the lack of warmth between the two women and the thought made her nervous. She adjusted her idea that they were friends.

'They must be ill if you've had the doctor here,' continued the woman. 'Which child was it?'

'Monique,' replied Jeanne. 'She's much better now, thank you.'

'Monique? And I thought I saw her out collecting eggs from the farm yesterday.'

'It must have been her sister you saw,' replied Jeanne.

A creak of the floorboards in the hallway, had Fitz looking up. Monique had come from her room and was obviously listening to the conversation, too. She looked across the landing at Fitz and Yvette. Fitz put her finger to her mouth.

'I was sure it was your older daughter,' persisted Madame Cussac.

At that moment, Yvette coughed. She tried to smother it with her hand, but it was too late. She coughed again and then a third time.

Fitz reached over to the bedside table and grabbed the glass of water, passing it to Yvette in a bid to prevent the onset of a coughing fit.

'Oh, is that Monique now?' asked Madame Cussac.

'It must be,' Fitz heard Jeanne reply.

The next thing, Monique began coughing. Fitz looked up in alarm. She wanted to tell her to stop. If they weren't careful that nosey woman downstairs would be up here like a shot. She watched as Monique went to the top of the stairs, coughing every now and again.

'Maman,' croaked Monique. *Cough. Cough.* 'Can I have some water, please?'

Fitz closed her eyes and lifted her head towards the ceiling. The girl was a genius.

'I need to go,' said Jeanne. 'As you can see, Monique is still unwell.'

'Yes. And it wasn't you who I saw at the farm getting eggs yesterday?' Madame Cussac called out to Monique.

'*Non, madame.* It wasn't me,' replied Monique.

Honestly, the child should be on the stage. She was giving

such a great performance. Fitz willed the Cussac woman to leave, just in case Yvette started to cough again.

'Goodbye, Madame Cussac,' Jeanne was saying.

Fitz heard the front door close and then Jeanne's footsteps on the stairs as she came up to see them.

'That woman,' Jeanne said in exasperation as she entered the bedroom. 'She is such a gossip.'

'Monique did well,' said Fitz. 'Quick thinking. Well done.'

'I'm sorry,' said Yvette. 'I couldn't stop it coming out.'

'Don't worry,' said Jeanne. 'We must be very careful now. Once that woman is on the scent of something, she is like a bloodhound. I shall have to try to speak to the doctor. We might have to find another safe house for you.'

'You think she'd report you?' I asked.

Jeanne shrugged. 'I don't know but it's not worth the risk. Now, bring the bowls down and let me give you some porridge to eat. It was good thinking to take them upstairs. She was trying to look over my shoulder the whole time. I had to stand on the doorstep to stop her.'

Jeanne was making light of it, but Fitz knew that was probably for the children's benefit. Underneath her calm exterior, she had no doubt, Jeanne was worried. And rightly so. Much as she hated the thought of leaving this kind woman, she was very much aware of the danger put upon Jeanne's family by her and Yvette's presence. If they had to move to another safe house, then so be it.

They spent the rest of the day upstairs in the bedroom with the curtains drawn, in case Madame Cussac decided to pay another visit or, indeed, if anyone else called by. Yvette wasn't sleeping so much now she was feeling a lot better. Monique and Amelie had brought in a book for Fitz to read to Yvette and they all sat together on the bed listening to Fitz tell the story.

Later when the children had all gone to bed, Jeanne invited Fitz down for a coffee. The shutters were all closed and the doors bolted. A small fire flickered in the hearth and Jeanne had placed a chair either side.

'I shall miss you when you leave,' she said, passing a cup of coffee to Fitz. 'It's been nice to have some company for the last few evenings.'

'You've been very kind to open your house to us,' replied Fitz. 'I shall never forget your kindness. You saved Yvette's life.'

Jeanne smiled. 'You are very fond of the child, aren't you?'

'Yes. I am.'

'Why is that?'

Fitz took a sip of her drink and looked at the flames flicking around the log. 'She reminds me of me,' she said after a while. 'I lost my mother when I was about her age. I know how that feels. In fact, I don't think that feeling of utter devastation has ever gone away. Not when I think about her.'

'What about the rest of your family?'

'There is my half-brother, and my father – he remarried within a year of my mother's death. I found that hard.'

'You felt you had lost your father, too,' said Jeanne. 'Your mother had left you and now your father had. Or at least that is how it felt?'

'Yes. I felt all alone in a world I had no control over. No autonomy. It was frightening. And I saw that same fear and confusion in Yvette.'

'She was vulnerable, like you. No?'

'Exactly, that,' agreed Fitz. It was so refreshing to find someone who understood how she felt. 'I hated feeling like that and I think a part of me didn't want Yvette to feel like that, either.' She sipped her coffee as she sifted through her thoughts. 'It's hard to explain, but I've never had to look after anyone before, only myself. I didn't want the responsibility but now it's like I can't choose to opt out. It feels embedded in my heart.'

Jeanne reached over and placed her hand on Fitz's. 'You feel like that because you care about her. Caring about a person other than ourselves is what makes us human. Love and compassion we have no control over. Don't try to fight it. Embrace it.'

Fitz didn't know how this woman could be so insightful.

Before she could reply, there was a rapid knocking at the back door. Jeanne jumped to her feet, spilling her coffee. 'Quick. Upstairs,' she whispered, snatching Fitz's cup from her hand and rushing over to the sink, tipping it away filling it with cold water.

Fitz darted up the stairs, thankful she had taken her shoes off earlier. She waited on the landing, out of sight.

The knocking came again. 'Jeanne. Open up. It's me, Frédéric.'

Fitz heard the door open and then urgent whispered voices that she couldn't make out.

Next Jeanne was hurrying up the stairs. 'Quickly,' she said. 'You and Yvette must leave now. There is a patrol on the way. That horrid woman, Cussac, must have reported me.'

Fitz rushed through to the bedroom and woke Yvette. She didn't bother taking off the nightdress but pulled the clothes on over the top. The extra layer would help keep her warm. Fitz didn't know where they were going or who with. She hadn't even heard Jeanne mention anyone called Frédéric.

Fitz and Yvette hurried downstairs, pausing in the doorway. 'What will happen to you? Will you be all right?'

'Don't worry about me,' replied Jeanne.

'Thank you,' said Fitz, hugging Jeanne tightly. 'I shall never forget your kindness.'

'We have to go,' hissed Frédéric.

'Go,' said Jeanne. 'And may God go with you, too.'

Frédéric hurried them out through the back of the property, Fitz glanced back one last time, but the door was closed. The sound of a vehicle's engine coming along the lane cut through the night air. Fitz caught glimpses of headlights flickering through the hedgerow.

'Hurry!' urged Frédéric. He picked Yvette up and threw her over his shoulder like she was a sack of potatoes and broke into a run, along the hedge, heading away from the house. The moon was out and Fitz could see him ahead of her. They needed to get into the trees before the Germans spotted them.

It was only fifty yards or so and as she darted into the woodland, she looked back again and could see all the lights on in Jeanne's house. The Germans must be inside searching for her and Yvette.

'They will be all right,' said Frédéric, setting Yvette down on the ground. 'The Germans have only the word of a silly old woman who tends to get muddled. Or at least that is what the doctor will say.' He gave a nonchalant shrug. 'Old age, it comes to us all. Now come, quickly. We must get to the safe house.'

'How far away is the safe house?' asked Fitz, as Yvette ran over to her and clung onto her hand.

'Just a mile,' replied Frédéric, already walking away.

Fitz and Yvette jogged to catch up with him. At least they would have somewhere to sleep for the rest of the night. 'After that?' she asked.

'You ask a lot of questions.'

'I don't like to be kept in dark if I can help it.'

'You will be pleased to know there is a plane coming tomorrow night. It is bringing in supplies. And you and the child have a place on it for the return journey.'

'A plane? Back to England?' Fitz could scarcely believe what she was hearing.

'Where else do you think you are going?' The Frenchman shook his head. 'You just need to make it through the next twenty-four hours and then you're going home.'

Twenty-four hours. One thousand, four hundred and forty-eight minutes. That was all they had to stay safe for. The relief and excitement rushed through Fitz's veins, sending tingling sensations to her fingertips.

Oh, please, God, let them make it. She had only been in France for two weeks, but it felt like forever. Now she knew what hell would be like, she never wanted to experience that again.

Fitz had never known time drag like the following twenty-four hours had. She had barely been able to sleep the previous night, despite feeling physically exhausted. Frédéric had taken them to a safe house, and they had slept in the hayloft of the adjacent barn. On the 3rd January, when daylight finally broke and the cool, hazy sun rose, Fitz was still awake.

For the rest of the day, they had to stay hidden in the hayloft. It was too dangerous to venture out in daylight in case any German patrol was out looking for them.

Every time Fitz heard the sound of an engine, whether it was in the distance or passing by the farm, she could feel herself breaking out into a sweat. To be caught now would be devastating. They had come this far, they deserved to make it home.

Finally, the time came for them to leave the safety of the hayloft and make a short hike across the fields to the rendezvous point. Fitz would have liked to have known exactly where they were going in case they were somehow separated from Frédéric, but he said he was under strict instructions not to divulge any information in case they were caught before they had made it. That way the Allied plane was still clear to make their drop-off.

Fitz was glad to be moving. Her nerves were nearly shot to pieces with the anticipation of going home. At least the physical exertion, albeit painful at times due to the injuries she was carrying, helped to channel those nerves in a positive way.

By the time they reached the field, which was the designated landing strip, Fitz thought she was going to be sick. Her stomach was churning like a tombola at a church fete and any minute now she was going to throw up.

They were greeted by a small group of resistance members and ordered to stay hidden in the nearby woods until the plane had touched down. Only then were they to break cover to board the aircraft.

'You will only have one minute,' said Frédéric. 'They will barely stop.'

Fitz nodded. She knew the drill.

She clutched Yvette's hand. 'Don't let go,' she said to her. 'Whatever happens, don't let go.'

The sound of the aeroplane rumbled in the sky, getting louder and louder. Fitz got to her feet.

'Not yet,' ordered Frédéric.

'I'm just getting ready,' replied Fitz. She could barely stand still, sitting still was impossible.

She watched as the resistance welcoming party lit the torches in the field to guide the pilot down onto the grassy runway. Fitz knew that the Germans would already be sending soldiers out to find them and round them up before they could take off. She'd heard of shoot-outs on landing strips and people being killed just as they were about to board the plane. Nothing was guaranteed until the plane touched down back in England.

It seemed an age before the plane came in to land. And then suddenly Frédéric was commanding her to run. For a moment, Fitz didn't think her legs were going to respond. She had lost all semblance of co-ordination.

But Yvette pulled at her hand and then she was back in control. Racing across the field, lengthening her stride, towing Yvette along with her. How they made it across the open field without falling, she didn't know but then the door of the plane was opening and two men exited the aircraft.

She didn't have time to see their faces. They were off into the night within seconds.

'Get in!' shouted the co-pilot who was at the door. 'Now!'

Frédéric grabbed Yvette and practically threw her into the aircraft, which was beginning to move and pick up speed as it readied for take-off.

'Claudine!' cried Yvette from the doorway. The little girl

The Girl in the Sky

stretched out her hand, before the crew member, pushed her away from the door.

'Run!' shouted Frédéric.

Fitz broke into a sprint. Where she found the energy from, she had no idea but she was not going to be left behind. She launched herself at the doorway and for an awful moment, thought she was going to be dragged back out but the crew member grabbed her and pulled her into the plane, before slamming the door shut.

'Glad you could make it,' he said, rather too cheerily for Fitz's liking.

Yvette threw herself on top of Fitz, sobbing in relief.

Fitz cuddled the child tightly. They had made it. They were on the plane. She was going home.

Part 3

England

Chapter 28

January 1942

As the Lysander bumped down onto British soil, Fitz let out a long sigh of relief. Was it really only two weeks ago that she'd been about to set off on her mission to France? So much had happened in that time. Her whole world had been turned upside down. And she'd returned home with an orphaned French girl. If someone had told her what was in store for her, she would never have believed them.

She climbed out of the aircraft and one of the crew lifted Yvette down. A car was already on the tarmac waiting for them and they were whisked away to Bignor Manor.

Barbara Bertram ushered them into the kitchen where a pot of soup was warming on the stove ready for their consumption. It was most welcome after twenty-four hours with only fruit and bread to eat.

That night, although tucked up in a warm bed with clean, crisp bedlinen and Yvette sleeping soundly in the bed next to her, Fitz found it hard to get to sleep. Her mind was still on high alert, as it had been since she'd left England. Her body might be ready to rest, but her mind was reluctant to relax. Thoughts of the past two weeks swirled around on a constant loop. Before they'd left France, Frédéric had received word that Jeanne and her children were all right, though their home had been thoroughly searched and all three of them had been questioned for over an hour. But the Germans had left without harming anyone – physically at least. Jeanne had managed to convince them that Madame Cussac was a gossip and troublemaker. Whether they believed her entirely or not, was another matter, but Jeanne was safe as were her children. Fitz was more than relieved to hear this.

As yet, Fitz hadn't heard anything about Philippe or Margot. When she'd asked Yvette what had happened, the little girl had only been able to give scant information. The morning after Fitz had been arrested, Margot had tried to take Yvette out of the château, to where she didn't know, but they had been stopped by the soldiers. When they found Yvette didn't have any relations in Josselin and had come from Saint Pierre, they had taken her away and put her in a hall along with other people. Fitz had no doubt Engel had been behind that order. After that Yvette had been bundled onto the truck. She cried as she relayed this to Fitz. The poor child was traumatised by events.

And now here they were in a foreign country where Yvette didn't speak the language and knew no one. Fitz consoled herself with the fact that Yvette was alive and safe.

Inevitably, her thoughts turned to Sam. He was never far from the front of her mind, but she realised with a deep sadness, that somewhere along the line, she had begun to prepare herself for the fact that he hadn't survived. The reality of life in France, the events she had experienced first-hand over the last few days, had been a sharp reminder that she had to now face the truth. Her romantic idea that Sam had somehow survived a plane crash and been found by the resistance and then made it back to England, seemed more fanciful than ever.

Eventually, she had fallen asleep but it had only been for a few short hours. When she woke the following morning, Yvette was already awake and sitting on her bed fully dressed.

'You're an early bird,' said Fitz. She looked at the end of

her bed and saw all her clothes set out. She looked back at Yvette properly and noted the anxious look on the child's face and the teddy tightly clutched to her.

'Do we have to leave?' asked Yvette.

Fitz pushed the covers back and slid out of bed, going to sit beside Yvette. She put her arm around her. 'We will be leaving, but not yet and not in a hurry. We're safe here. No one is coming who we have to hide from or run away from.'

Yvette looked up at her. 'But I heard voices downstairs. Men.'

'That will be Mr Bertram, who lives here or perhaps some of the other guests,' explained Fitz. 'Everyone here is our friend. The Germans aren't here in England. You know, sometimes Mr and Mrs Bertram have French people here.' She hoped this would help reassure her. 'Now, I'll get dressed and we can go down for breakfast together. How does that sound?' She made to sniff the air. 'In fact, I think I can smell breakfast. Eggs and bacon and toast.'

Yvette's eyes lit up and she jumped to her feet. 'Hurry up,' she urged.

Fitz laughed and did as she was told, getting dressed as fast as she could.

When they went into the dining room, two men were sitting at the table. They both rose and greeted Fitz and Yvette, who took their seats on the opposite side of the table.

They seemed a little surprised to see Yvette but no one asked questions and Fitz offered no explanation. The unwritten code of never giving anything away and never asking questions prevailing.

Yvette, however, wasn't accustomed to this code. After several minutes of glancing up at the men, her curiosity got the better of her. 'Are you French?' she asked.

The men exchanged a glance. The younger of the two, who Fitz thought couldn't be any older than twenty-five, replied. '*Oui*. We are. And you are too?'

'Yes. Are you going to France?' continued Yvette.

'We hope so,' replied the man. 'Maybe tonight.'

Yvette fiddled with the spoon. 'If you see my mother, can you tell her I'm here?'

The Frenchman looked up at Fitz and then back at Yvette. 'Of course. I will tell her you are safe and being looked after well. She will be happy to know that. What is your mother's name?'

'Edith Moreau. My name is Yvette. Yvette Moreau.'

'I will remember that, Yvette Moreau. And your mother Edith Moreau.' He tapped his temple with his forefinger. 'I won't forget.'

Fitz's promise to the doctor was reinforced further. She might not have Sam to live for now, but she had Yvette. She had a promise to fulfil and she embraced it. It gave her something to focus on.

Later that morning, Fitz was visited by someone from SOE, a Mr White – Fitz wasn't sure that was his real name but as ever it was a need-to-know basis. While Yvette played in the garden with the Bertram children, Fitz had spent three hours being debriefed. Every detail of her time in France scrutinised. She was exhausted when it was finally over.

'Thank you, Miss Fitz-Herbert,' said Mr White, placing the copious notes he'd made into his briefcase. 'Do you have any questions?'

'Will I be going back into the field?' Fitz needed to know, for Yvette's sake as much as her own.

'Do you feel able to go back?'

Fitz looked down. 'Not right now. But maybe in time.' Why did she feel like a traitor saying this?

'What is preventing you?' asked White.

Fitz looked out through the study window to the garden where Yvette was now helping Barbara Bertram feed the chickens. 'I made a promise and I can't break it.'

White followed her gaze. 'No one can force you to go back,' he said after a pause. 'It's not as if you can return anyway, until your injuries are fully healed. It might be the case that you won't be deemed medically fit.' He paused again as Fitz gave him a questioning look. He continued, 'Your back. With the possible scarring. If the Gestapo see it, they will guess you've already been of interest to them. It would make you much more vulnerable and ultimately the weak link in operations.'

'If there's anything I can do here in England, then I would be more than willing to help,' she replied.

'Of course, you could go back to ferrying planes,' said White. He tapped his finger on the edge of the briefcase. 'But, as I understand it, you have excellent linguistic skills in both French and German. We have certain, how shall we say, houses, where we have foreign guests. Listening to their conversations, spoken in their mother tongue, is very revealing. We're always on the lookout for linguists. Maybe something like that would interest you? Top secret, of course.'

'Yes, of course,' replied Fitz. This sounded like something she'd be able to do without leaving the country. She had heard a few rumours when she was training about a stately house that had been requisitioned by MI5 and MI6 and turned into a detention centre. 'That sounds something right up my street, Mr White.'

'Excellent. I shall put forward a recommendation,' said White. 'But, first, you need to recover from your latest exploits. I'll be in touch.'

'Thank you, sir,' said Fitz.

She saw White out and went over to where Yvette was playing a game of tag with one of the Bertram children. It was a frosty winter's morning and their breath formed puffs of air as they chased each other around. Fitz watched the scene, thinking it was the first time she'd heard Yvette laugh. It was a delightful infectious sound and warmed Fitz's heart. As she stood there, smiling to herself, an idea formed in her head. She didn't know why she hadn't thought of it before.

Barbara Bertram walked over to her. 'It's good to see them enjoying themselves,' she said.

'Yes. Definitely,' agreed Fitz.

'All finished with your visitor?'

'Yes, he's gone now. I'm to have a few weeks leave and then I might be able to resume duties here in England.'

'And what about Yvette?' asked Barbara.

'I was thinking, I'll take her with me to visit my father,' said Fitz. 'I have a half-brother Yvette's age. They might be good company for each other.'

'Oh, that sounds an excellent idea,' said Barbara.

'Yes. I just have to persuade my stepmother to go along with it.' That was the only fly in the ointment. Getting Camilla to agree to having Yvette there. 'Depending on where I'm posted, hopefully I can either return every night, I mean that would be perfect, or if too far to commute, then at weekends or days off.'

'That sounds very nice, except . . . do I detect some hesitation about your stepmother?'

Fitz shrugged. 'We haven't always got on. I think she found me challenging.'

'And are you?'

'No. I mean, at least I've never thought of myself as challenging.' Fitz paused and then relented 'Maybe a little. My mother died when I was eight. Camilla, that's my stepmother, she came along quite soon afterwards and I'm not sure I was ready for a replacement mother.'

'Yes, I can imagine it would be difficult,' said Barbara.

Yvette and Barbara's son, Tim, were now creating patterns and funny faces across the lawn by scuffing their feet through the damp grass and laughing at their results.

'Camilla tried to take my mother's place. She was always fussing over me. Asking me what I was doing. Would I rather do this, that or the other? She bought me clothes I didn't need. Even toys I didn't want. It felt false,' said Fitz. 'I don't think I understood when I was young and certainly wouldn't have been able to articulate it, but looking back, that's how it seemed.'

'Perhaps she was only trying to care for you? I take it she hadn't had any experience with children before that.'

'No. Michael, my half-brother, was born a couple of years later, when I was ten.'

'How was your father after your mother died?'

'He was very sad to start with but, you know what, we never spoke about our feelings. We just got on with life and the next thing, Camilla arrived on the scene.'

'Do you think perhaps Camilla was maybe trying a little too hard?' queried Barbara. 'Especially as she had no experience as a mother to call upon. Maybe she was trying to compensate and make you happy in other ways.'

Fitz bristled a little at this suggestion. No, Camilla didn't care about Fitz. She thought Fitz was a nuisance. She had just wanted to assert herself in the matriarchal role of the family. And then she was trying to convince Fitz's father to send Fitz away to Scotland. She wouldn't do that if she cared about her stepdaughter. 'I don't think she was trying to do anything like that,' replied Fitz, wishing the conversation would end.

She had inadvertently picked the scab from a wound that wouldn't quite heal properly. A wound she'd always believed was caused by someone else, but now it was being suggested that she herself might have contributed towards it. No, that wasn't how it was.

'So, what are your plans for the next few days?' asked Barbara. 'When Mr White arrived, he mentioned that you might be here for another night or two.'

Fitz was pleased with the change in direction of the conversation. 'I was wondering, would it be possible to stay for two nights? Tomorrow, I'd really like to try to catch up with a couple of friends from the ATA. They're down at Hamble.'

'Of course, that's not a problem,' said Barbara. 'If you're only going for the day tomorrow, then you can leave Yvette here with me. She and Tim seem to have hit it off rather well.'

'Thank you, that would be so kind of you,' said Fitz. 'I'll telephone Marjorie and Elsie later at the house they are billeted in.'

'Jolly good,' said Barbara. 'Now, I've got some chores to do.'

'Do you want any help?' asked Fitz.

'No, not at all. You need to recuperate. Watch the children if you want to do something useful.' Barbara smiled and went back into the house.

Fitz sat down on the wooden bench and gently stretched out her legs. The bruises were fading now. Her bones weren't as sore as they had been and when she leaned against the bench, there was no sharp sting to her back. She'd looked in the mirror that morning and the broken skin was healing well. She had Jeanne to thank for that.

It was a shame, Jeanne's balm couldn't soothe the damage to her heart.

Chapter 29

As luck would have it, both Marjorie and Elsie had the following day off work. Fitz had spoken to Marjorie on the phone the previous evening and amid squeals of joy, especially so from Elsie in the background, they had arranged to meet at ten o'clock the next morning.

Barbara had taken Fitz to the train station, and after promising Yvette it was only for the day, Fitz had boarded the train to Southampton.

She had been met with more squeals and hugging from her friends.

'Golly, Fitz, what's wrong with your eye?' asked Elsie, standing back and looking at her friend.

Fitz had attempted to hide the bruising with make-up. 'It's nothing,' she said. 'Now tell me about what you've been up to the last couple of months.'

'Erm, don't change the subject,' said Elsie. She was looking even closer at Fitz now. 'What have *you* been up to?'

Marjorie came to the rescue. 'I think whatever our darling Fitz has been up to, as you put it, it's something she probably can't tell us.'

Fitz offered her a grateful smile. 'Pretty much that.'

Elsie's eyes widened. 'Geraldine Fitz-Herbert, have you been spying in France?'

'Shh, keep your voice down,' scolded Marjorie. 'Even if

she had, she can't tell us.' She looked at Fitz. 'I'm assuming I'm saying all the right things.'

'I can neither confirm nor deny,' said Fitz.

'Oh my goodness,' gasped Elsie, this time in a whisper. 'You have, haven't you?'

'Whatever you think I've been doing,' replied Fitz. 'It won't be anywhere as glamorous or exciting as you think it is.' She couldn't help the reproachful tone in her voice.

'No, I'm sure it's not. Sorry, I didn't mean to sound frivolous about it,' said Elsie.

'So, tell me what you've been up to?' said Fitz.

They walked arm in arm out of the station and along the road to a nearby tea room. It was such a pleasure to see her friends again. Fitz hadn't realised just how much she had missed them. Listening to them talking about the aircraft they had been flying and some of the high jinks they'd been up to, was like a warm blanket around her.

'And Joyce Rigby was sitting on the tail of the Spit,' Elsie was saying, 'you know, how the pilots got us to sit on the tail while they taxied.'

'Of course I remember, I've only been away a few months, not years,' laughed Fitz.

'Well, the pilot only bloody forgot about her and took off!' Elsie swept her hand in an upward motion.

'Oh, my goodness! He never?' gasped Fitz. 'What happened?'

'Well, he soon realised when the rudder wasn't responding. Landed straight away,' said Elsie. 'Joyce held on for dear life. They both got in awful trouble for it.'

'Oh, poor old Joyce. I'm glad she's all right, though,' said Fitz.

'Don't you miss flying?' asked Elsie.

'Of course I do,' replied Fitz.

'Then why don't you come back?' Elsie asked.

Fitz dropped her gaze. 'I can't.'

'What do you mean you can't?' Elsie continued.

'I don't think we can ask,' said Marjorie after a moment.

'I don't think Fitz is allowed to say.' She looked at Fitz. 'Am I right?'

Fitz nodded. 'Sorry.' She wished she could tell them about Mr White's suggestion. She hated keeping secrets, but she knew they understood. 'It will do me good to do something different.'

'As opposed to flying?' Elsie again.

'Yes. Don't get me wrong, I love flying. Always will, but I've been asked to do something else.' She stirred her spoon around in her tea. 'And it will mean I don't have to think about Sam so much.'

'Oh, yes. Poor Sam,' said Elsie. 'That was awful what happened.'

'Honestly, I don't even want to think about it,' said Fitz. 'It's simply too upsetting. I think it's the not knowing that's the worst.'

She looked up at her friends who both had a puzzled expression on their faces.

'Not knowing?' repeated Elsie.

Fitz tamped down the little feeling of irritation. 'Yes,' she said. 'Not knowing exactly what happened to him.'

Marjorie reached across the table, resting her hand on Fitz's. 'But we do know what happened,' she said softly.

Fitz's breath caught in her throat. 'You do?'

'Yes, we do,' said Marjorie.

Fitz closed her eyes. She braced herself. Word must have got back to England. She thought of the graves in Josselin that Margot had taken her to. She hadn't wanted to believe it was Sam lying there, but a lot had happened since then and she was prepared for it now. She was ready to accept it. She opened her eyes. 'What happened?'

'His plane went down,' said Marjorie. 'The co-pilot didn't make it. Neither did the passenger they were taking. Sam survived.'

'He did?' Fitz gulped.

'Yes. He was found by the French resistance, thank God.

He was badly injured. He was treated out there and then two days later he was flown home after a supply drop.'

Fitz was sitting upright now. 'He made it back to England? He's . . . he's alive?' She could barely believe she was saying the words out loud. Her hands shook as she covered her face, taking a moment to catch her breath.

'Yes, my darling,' said Marjorie, taking Fitz's hands from her face. 'He's alive. Here in England.'

'No one told you?' asked Elsie.

Fitz shook her head. 'No. I haven't really seen anyone. I was taken straight to a safe house in the middle of the night. Debriefed yesterday. Here today.'

Her friends exchanged a look which Fitz couldn't quite decipher. 'There's something you're not telling me,' she said.

'He's at Goodwood House,' said Elsie. 'Just up the road from Tangmere. Westhampnett satellite airfield.'

'Yes, I know where Goodwood House is,' replied Fitz. It was a country house that had recently been requisitioned by the government and turned into a war hospital. The large rooms had been subdivided to make wards and the great ballroom had been converted into a surgical ward. 'Why is he there?'

Again, Marjorie's hand rested on hers. 'He's recovering. He needed surgery when he got back.'

'Surgery?' Fitz gulped. 'Please, tell me.'

'His leg was badly injured in the crash,' said Marjorie. 'The French did everything they could, but the treatment was rudimentary. He was in rather a state when he arrived back in England. Thank goodness it was only a matter of days, though. It could have been a lot worse.'

'How bad is the injury?' asked Fitz. Her heart, which had leapt with joy at the news Sam was alive, was now taking a slow descent to somewhere in the pit of her stomach.

'They had to amputate above the knee,' said Marjorie softly.

'Oh, no,' Fitz whispered. 'Oh, Sam. Sam. Sam.' She

dropped her head into her hands and cried silently for a moment. And then remembering they were in a tea room, she sat up and dabbed at her eyes with her napkin. She glanced around and saw the concerned look of a couple of women on a nearby table.

'Shall we leave?' suggested Elsie.

'Good idea,' said Marjorie. 'Take Fitz outside. I'll settle the bill.'

Fitz walked out of the tea room in something of a daze. She wasn't heartbroken for herself, but for Sam. He would hate it. She knew he would.

'At least he's alive,' comforted Elsie.

'I know,' said Fitz. 'I'm not crying for me. I'm crying for him.'

'He'll probably go back to America,' said Elsie.

'Do you know that?'

'Not exactly. I was just assuming.'

Fitz paced up and down the path as they waited for Marjorie. When their friend joined them, she had made up her mind what she was going to do.

'Look, I'm really sorry, but I need to go. I need to see Sam,' she said.

'Are you sure that's a good idea?' asked Elsie.

'I really don't know,' confessed Fitz. 'But I need to see him before he makes some stupid decision to leave England.'

'I don't think he'll be going anywhere soon,' said Marjorie. 'You don't need to be hasty.'

'I haven't got much time,' said Fitz. 'There's something I haven't told you.'

'What's that?' asked Elsie.

'Yes. Spill the beans,' urged Marjorie.

'You can't ask any questions. You just have to accept what I say,' said Fitz.

'Dib-dib and all that,' said Marjorie, making the Girl Guide promise sign.

'I have a nine-year-old French girl I'm looking after,' said

Fitz carefully. 'Only until the war is over but for now she's here with me in England.'

This piece of information took even the unflappable Marjorie by surprise. 'A nine-year-old French girl!'

'Yep,' said Fitz. She had to laugh at the stunned look on Elsie's face. 'I'll explain when I can, but I'm taking her to my father's tomorrow to see if she can stay there.'

Elsie suddenly found her voice. 'You've been to France, haven't you?' And then her face was one of concern. 'Oh, Fitz, your bruises . . .'

Fitz shook her head. 'Please don't ask.'

'Bloody hell,' muttered Marjorie. She gave Fitz a spontaneous hug. 'Gosh, what a brave stick you are.'

'I'm not sure I'm that,' said Fitz. 'Now, I'm sorry but I'm going to have to shoot off. I want to get to Goodwood House. I've got an American to find.'

'Yes you bloody well have,' said Marjorie. 'Come on, no time to lose.' She hooked Fitz's arm one side and Elsie grabbed the other and they all ran along the path back towards the train station.

Fitz's train arrived back in Barnham station nearly two hours later. She'd had to wait at Southampton for over thirty minutes for the next train and now she was standing at the bus stop, waiting to be taken to Tangmere. It was all she could do to stand still.

When she had landed back in Tangmere, two nights ago, she had totally forgotten about the letter from Sam she had left with Bob. She needed to know what it said before she hot-footed it up to Goodwood House. Although, she also knew that no matter what it said, whether Sam didn't want to see her again or not, she was going to see him. She needed to see him. She needed to tell him she'd made a mistake. It had taken nearly losing him and losing her own life to realise this.

Eventually, the bus turned up and it was another thirty minutes before she reached Tangmere.

Flashing her ATA pass at the guard, she hurried through the gates and headed towards the hangars, where she hoped to find Bob.

She breathed a sigh of relief as she spotted him. She called out to him and he turned. After a moment's hesitation as if he couldn't quite believe what he was seeing, he broke into a broad smile.

'Well, Fitz, I didn't expect to see you,' he said, wiping his hands on a grubby looking cloth. 'When did you get back?'

'Hello, Bob,' said Fitz with a smile, genuinely pleased to see the engineer. 'Got back the night before last.'

Bob frowned. 'That was you? I thought it was a woman and child. That's what I heard anyway.'

'You heard right. It was me. And a child.'

'Righty-o.' He took a longer look at her. 'They said you were . . .' He flicked his fingers to his face.

'Bruised and battered?' supplied Fitz. 'Yes. I'm all right, though. Nothing serious.'

'Glad to hear it.' He wiped his hands again and Fitz could tell he was deciding what to say next.

She saved him the trouble. 'I know about Sam.'

'Ah, right.' Bob shifted on his feet. 'He's not in a good way.'

'I know about his leg.'

'I meant in his head. Me and a couple of the lads went up to see him. He's taking it badly.'

'I can imagine,' replied Fitz, thinking how devastated Sam would be, especially if it meant he was grounded. 'I've actually come here to get that letter. You know, the one Sam wanted you to give to me?'

'Oh, yes. Of course. Wait there. I'll be back in a minute.'

Ten minutes later, Fitz was walking out of RAF Tangmere with Sam's letter in her pocket. She didn't want to stay at the airfield in case she got caught in a conversation with anyone. She walked down the road towards the duck pond and despite the coldness of the January day, she sat down on the bench, before opening the envelope.

Darling Fitz, my girl,

I don't know when you'll read this, but boy I hope it's soon. I miss you more than I ever thought would be possible.

When I told you I loved you, I meant it. I hoped you would find a way to trust yourself to love me back and let me into your life fully. You don't have to give up anything to be with me. You know I would never clip your wings. Hell, we could fly as high as we damn well like together. There would be no stopping us!

I've never felt like this about anyone before, Fitz. Never.

You're one in a million. I don't wanna lose you.

I know you're scared but you gotta believe it when I say you can trust me.

Come talk to me. Please.

Always yours

Sam

Fitz didn't need to read the letter again to know what she had to do. She jumped up from the bench and dashed back down to the airfield, where she found Bob.

'Back so soon,' he said, not seeming the least bit surprised to see her.

'I need a favour,' said Fitz.

'I'm just finishing my shift. Ask away.'

Ten minutes later, Fitz was on the back of Bob's motorbike as they sped up towards Goodwood House.

Fitz practically launched herself off the motorbike before it had come to a halt outside the country mansion. Built in the 1600s, Goodwood House was an impressive building. The main footprint was set out like three sides of a pentagon. Two round towers with green lead-domed rooftops, shouldered each end of the building, with two more identical towers in between. The entrance consisted of six stone pillars on the ground floor and six more directly above on the balcony,

The Girl in the Sky

which overlooked the front of the mansion. The symmetry of the building was perfection and established ivy covered the frontage, cut back around the twelve rectangular windows.

Fitz managed to stop herself from charging through the main entrance and curtailed her arrival to a brisk walk. 'I've come to see Flying Officer Sam Carter,' she said somewhat breathlessly in the reception hallway.

The nurse looked a little surprised to see Fitz. 'It's quite late in the day. There's only ten minutes of visiting time left.'

'Please, I need to see him,' said Fitz. She smiled to hide the impatience and desperation that was bubbling just below the surface. Not to mention the dread. She had no idea how Sam would react to seeing her. Especially not after what she'd said to him the last time she saw him.

With obvious reluctance, the nurse rose from her seat. 'What name is it? I'll have to ask him first.'

'Just say it's Fitz.'

The nurse raised her eyebrows but made no comment and headed across the black and white tiled hallway, disappearing down a corridor. Fitz wanted to shout at her to hurry up, but again, managed to control her emotions.

Eventually, the nurse returned. 'I'm sorry but he doesn't want to see you.'

'Pardon?' That couldn't be right. That's not what was supposed to happen.

'I'm sorry,' said the nurse.

'What exactly did he say?' asked Fitz.

For the first time, the nurse looked sympathetic as she answered. 'He said you should stay with the squadron leader, at least he could walk down the aisle with you.'

'He's a fool,' said Fitz angrily, tears stinging her eyes.

'We at least agree on that,' replied the nurse. 'Now, you really need to leave. Visiting times are over.'

'No, you don't understand. I need to see him,' said Fitz, panic racing through her. 'I have to see him.'

'I can't allow that.'

'Please.' She'd beg if she had to. 'I only need five minutes.'

'I'm afraid I'm going to insist that you leave,' replied the nurse, any sympathy she'd exhibited before having now vanished.

A hand touched Fitz on the arm. She spun around. It was Bob. 'Come on, Fitz,' he said gently.

'But I haven't seen Sam. I need to speak to him.' Fitz blinked hard as the tears gathered in her eyes. Surely Bob would understand. 'Tell her, Bob. Tell her I need to see Sam.'

'Fitz,' said Bob. 'Come on.' He shepherded her out of the building where she reluctantly took the crash helmet from him and climbed onto the back of the bike.

'Would you mind taking me up to Bignor, please?' asked Fitz, trying to cling to the last piece of dignity she had left.

'No problem.'

By the time they reached the Bertrams' house, Fitz had pulled herself together, at least outwardly. Inwardly, she was a wreck and didn't know how she was going to make it through the rest of the day without crumbling.

'Thanks, Bob,' she said as she dismounted from the Triumph.

Bob switched off the engine. 'I hope you're not going to let one little setback beat you.'

She gave a half-hearted smile. 'Did you know he didn't want to see me?'

'No, but I'm not surprised,' said the engineer. 'Like I said, Sam's pretty down. Don't give up on him just yet.'

'I'll see,' said Fitz, her gaze dropping to the ground.

'Hey, that's not like you. Where's that gung-ho spirit you're famous for?'

'It seems to have deserted me. Goodnight, Bob.'

Chapter 30

The following morning Fitz woke feeling much better than she had the night before. When she'd got back to Bignor House, she hadn't been able to stop thinking about Sam and his rejection of her. It truly was painful and, she had to admit, somewhat unexpected. Yes, she had been prepared for Sam to be feeling down and pretty sorry for himself, as he had every right to, but to point blank refuse to see her. That had not been on any horizon she'd been looking at.

When she'd gone to bed that night, she had lain awake for a long time going over and over the quite frankly ghastly situation. If only she'd let herself love Sam sooner and had told him how much she cared about him, then he might not have turned her away. But now, would she ever get the chance to tell him what a stupid fool she'd been and that he was the best thing to ever happen to her?

Fresh tears erupted. She hated feeling so helpless. Not being able to control the situation was her biggest fear and that fear had ironically led her to the very same point. She had gone full circle but missed her chance to break the cycle. Missed her chance to love and be loved.

Love. She loved Sam. Fact. She had never been in love with a man before so why was she squandering her chance at happiness now? He was the only man who'd made her feel like this and she had pushed him away. Now she'd come to her senses, he didn't think he was good enough. How wrong could a person be?

What was it Bob had said? Where was her gung-ho spirit?

Where, indeed? Geraldine Fitz-Herbert wasn't one to be beaten so easily. Fitz reminded herself of all the times she'd come up against adversity or authority. Had she just lain down and rolled over? No, she had not. She had always fought hard for what she believed in, for what she wanted and for what she loved. Why should Sam Carter receive any different treatment?

She had already booked her and Yvette two train tickets to Cambridge. They were off to Badcombe House to visit her father and Camilla.

Much as she was desperate to go back to try to see Sam, she had to think everything through. It would be her one and only chance to convince him they had a future together. She needed to ensure everything was in place so he couldn't argue with her.

Her mind was whirring furiously as she jumped out of bed, washed and dressed.

She wanted to be prepared for when MI6 got back in touch. If she wasn't going into France as a spy again, she still wanted to make a significant contribution to the war effort and working at one of their secret locations doing something so top secret, she really had no idea what, only that it involved her linguistic skills, then that's what she would do. It felt good to have a plan.

The train ride to Cambridgeshire took several hours, but her father had sent his car down to the station to collect her and Yvette. She had warned him she was bringing a guest with her but that was all she had said.

Now sitting in the Armstrong Siddeley, it glided through the gates of Badcombe House and up the gravel driveway. Fitz was surprised, not to mention flattered to see her father come out onto the steps to greet her.

'Geraldine,' he said warmly, embracing her in his

outstretched arms. Fortunately, the bruising on her face had gone down a lot and she hoped her father wouldn't notice. She'd applied a little more make-up than she had the day before and with his eyesight not quite as sharp as that of her friends, she hoped she'd get away without him noticing.

'Hello, Geraldine.' It was Camilla.

Fitz forced a smile to her face and greeted her stepmother. 'Hello, Camilla. How are you?'

'I'm very well, thank you. So nice to see you.' Camilla almost disguised the frown on her face as she looked at Fitz but didn't quite manage it. 'How are you?'

'Very well, too,' Fitz replied. 'I've got someone with me.'

'Oh, yes. Your father said you were bringing a guest. I wondered if it might be a young man,' said Camilla.

'It's not a young man,' corrected Fitz. 'It's a young girl. She's nine years old. She's French and her name is Yvette.'

Both adults looked bemused. 'Oh. Yes. Right. Jolly good,' blustered her father.

Fitz went back to the car. Hesitantly and gripping firmly onto Fitz's hand, Yvette stepped out onto the driveway. 'You'll have to speak French to her,' Fitz informed her father and Camilla. 'She doesn't know any English.'

'Welcome to Badcombe House,' said Fitz's father in his clear and fluent French. He stepped forward and held out his hand which Yvette dutifully shook.

'Hello, Yvette,' said Camilla. Her French wasn't quite as competent as Edward's, but it was good enough to be understood. 'How lovely to meet you. Do you like biscuits? Cook has just baked some.' She held out her hand and to Fitz's surprise, Yvette took it, seemingly happy to go with Camilla.

Fitz and her father exchanged a look as they followed on. Camilla was doing a sterling job of chatting away to the little girl. 'You'll have to meet Geraldine's brother, Michael,' she was saying.

Yvette turned and looked at Fitz. 'Oh, gosh,' said Fitz. 'I forgot, Yvette doesn't know my real name.'

Everyone paused in the doorway.

'Doesn't know your real name?' queried her father.

'Why doesn't she—' Camilla stopped mid-sentence. Her eyes wide as she looked at Fitz.

Fitz could tell Camilla had immediately put two and two together. She shook her head at her stepmother. 'I'll explain later.' Fitz knelt in front of Yvette. 'So, I should have told you before but now I'm in England, I can use my English name – Geraldine or some people call me Fitz. Do you think you can remember that?'

Yvette looked confused as if this was the most ridiculous thing she'd heard. 'You have three names?'

Fitz scrunched up her nose. 'Kind of. But mostly I'm simply called Fitz.'

As they went through to the sitting room, Fitz was nearly bowled right over as Michael ran at her, throwing his arms around her waist.

'Geraldine!' he cried.

'Michael! Oh, I've missed you. Let me see you.' She held her little brother at arm's length and then held her hand above his head, measuring his height against her. 'My goodness, I do believe you've grown since I last saw you.'

Michael beamed with pride. 'Soon I'll be taller than you.'

'You have a little way to go yet,' replied Fitz. 'Anyway, I'd like you to meet a friend I've brought with me.' She held out her arm towards Yvette, who shyly came over. 'Michael this is Yvette.' And then in French. 'Yvette this is Michael.'

'Hello,' said Michael.

'Darling, you will need to try to speak as much French as you can to Yvette,' said Camilla. 'She doesn't speak English.'

'*Bonjour,*' said Michael. '*Tu aimes les trains? J'ai mes trains dans la salle de jeux.*'

Fitz wasn't sure if Yvette would want to play with Michael's train set but after a moment's hesitation, Yvette smiled. '*Oui.*'

Michael gestured for her to follow him. Yvette looked at Fitz, who nodded. 'Go on. The playroom is upstairs.'

Yvette followed Michael out of the room and then Fitz heard their feet galloping up the stairs as Michael, who had slipped back into English, was excitedly telling Yvette about the new Dorchester Loco and coal tender he'd got for his birthday.

'I'm sure they will be fine,' said Edward. 'So, tell us about our surprise house guest.'

'Well, I can't go into too much detail,' warned Fitz, sitting down on the sofa. 'But I'm looking after Yvette until it's safe for her to go back to France. We don't know what happened to her family at this point. It's possible they aren't alive anymore.'

'Oh, the poor little mite,' said Camilla.

'That is terrible,' agreed Edward, picking up his pipe from the side table. He looked at his daughter. 'And what about you? I suspect you can't tell us your role in all this.'

'No. I'm sorry.'

'Are you still flying with the ATA?' asked Camilla.

'I was just coming to that,' replied Fitz, unsure of the concerned look her stepmother was giving her. 'I might be having a little change in direction. Working for the government, but I really can't say anything more. To be honest, I don't know much else.'

'It all sounds very secretive,' said Camilla. 'But then everything is these days. You don't know who you could be speaking to or who is listening. We keep being told to *Keep it under your hat* and *Mr Hitler wants to know*. There are posters on the village notice board.'

'And rightly so,' said Edward, lighting his pipe.

'So, going back to Yvette,' said Fitz. 'If I do take up this new position, or even if I do go back to flying for the ATA, I wondered if—'

Camilla held up her hand, cutting Fitz off before she'd finished. 'Stop,' she said.

'But you don't know what I was going to say,' protested Fitz.

'Sorry,' said Camilla. 'I didn't mean to interrupt. It was just purely to say yes.'

Fitz hesitated. 'To say yes?'

'Yes.' Camilla smiled somewhat uncertainly. 'Well, I assumed you were going to ask if you and Yvette could stay here.'

Fitz was taken by surprise. She looked at her father who gave a shrug, before he spoke. 'I was going to say, it goes without saying but, on reflection, maybe it does indeed need saying.' He smiled at Fitz. 'You know you always have a home here, Geraldine, and so does Yvette.'

'It will be lovely to fill the house with children's laughter,' said Camilla. 'When we had the two evacuee children here, I don't think I've ever heard Michael laugh so much. It was such a shame when they went home.'

Fitz was lost for words. She hadn't expected it to be that easy. She had already decided she wasn't going to beg. If her father had said no, or rather if Camilla had said no, then she would work something else out. But that didn't look like it was necessary. 'Thank you,' she said. 'That's very kind of you both.'

'You can stay as long as you like,' said Camilla. There was a look of happiness Fitz hadn't seen before on her stepmother's face and something else, almost gratitude.

'Claudine. Fitz!' It was Yvette calling from the top of the stairs. 'Come and look!'

'Oh, I'd better go and see what I need to look at,' said Fitz. 'Not that I haven't seen Michael's train set a million times.'

Fitz spent several minutes admiring the train set for Yvette's benefit and inspecting the new engine Michael had been given for his birthday, before heading back downstairs.

As she got to the last tread, she heard Camilla speaking. Fitz paused, more out of habit from when she lived at home and used to pause to eavesdrop on anything Camilla might be saying.

'I'm so glad Geraldine is back,' came Camilla's voice. 'I know you've been worried sick about her.'

'Yes. I think she might have been in France,' said Edward in a low voice.

Fitz strained to hear.

'Yes. I thought so too,' replied Camilla. 'Especially as she's now got Yvette. Heavens knows how that has come about. She seems a sweet child.'

'Yes. I'm going to have to brush up on my French,' said Edward.

'It will be nice company for Michael, too,' continued Camilla.

At that moment, footsteps from the kitchen sounded. Fitz looked around and there was dear Annie, carrying a tray of tea and sandwiches.

'Oh, Miss Geraldine, Cook said you were coming. How are you?'

'Annie! I'm very well, thank you.' Fitz smiled broadly at the young woman. 'You're looking well.'

'Thank you, Miss.'

'Here, let me get the door for you.'

The conversation between her father and stepmother had stopped and after telling Annie she'd come and see her later, Fitz sat down for what turned into a very civil hour. There was something different about Camilla that she couldn't quite work out. A thawing, maybe or had Camilla not changed? Was it Fitz who had changed and the angular corners of her younger-self been knocked off and smoothed a little after her experience of being away from home?

She could feel a warmth emanating from her stepmother. Was it a new thing, or had it always been there and Fitz had refused to see it?

The rest of the day passed happily. Fitz didn't see much of Yvette. Despite the language barrier between the two children, Michael knew enough French to communicate with Yvette and the two of them seemed to have hit it off. Fitz had taken them both for a walk in the afternoon, exploring the gardens, showing Yvette the stables where her father still had his horse, Colonel. A large chestnut hunter whose hunting days were over but Edward hadn't been able to part with him.

Fitz stroked the horse's velvety muzzle, thinking of the last colonel she'd come into contact with and wondering what had happened to Hoffmann. Had he been brought to England? Were they both on the same shores once again? Him now the one on enemy territory? She wouldn't ever know, of course. She was just a mere player in the game of war and espionage.

All too soon, it was time to think about leaving. The children had once again disappeared back to the playroom and Fitz had been chatting with Annie, catching up on all her latest news – mainly that Annie was getting married to her sweetheart the next time he was home on leave.

'I said she should wait until after the war,' said Cook, as she peeled potatoes at the large pine kitchen table. 'War can change a man. The man that left is not the soldier who returns.'

Annie rolled her eyes. 'She's a happy one, isn't she?'

'And you're the one with her head in the clouds full of romantic notions. Take those rose coloured specs off,' retorted Cook.

Fitz couldn't help laughing. The two women clearly were fond of each other even though they were often opposed. They had worked together for several years now and were probably more like mother and daughter.

A little pang of envy and hope shot through Fitz. Today, had been quite a strange day in lots of ways, but something had changed between her and Camilla, and it was for the better.

After saying her goodbyes to Cook and Annie, promising them she would be back again in a few days, she went off to find her father. She only got as far as the hallway. Camilla was standing there, waiting for Fitz.

'Is everything all right?' asked Fitz, wondering if something had happened.

'Geraldine . . . Fitz,' began Camilla. She fiddled with the pearls around her neck, clearly feeling uncomfortable. And she never called Fitz by anything other than her given Christian name. Fitz waited for the bombshell. 'Could I have a moment? In the drawing room?'

'Certainly,' said Fitz. She followed her stepmother into the room which overlooked the rose garden. It was a favourite place of Fitz's in the summer when she lived at home. The beautiful scent of the blooms and the glorious array of colours set out in a circle with inner circles of roses and a bench in the centre. This time of year though, all the roses had been pruned back for the winter. The garden was bare and stark. How fitting.

'Please, sit down,' said Camilla, taking the chair while Fitz sat on the sofa. 'I just wanted to ask if you really are all right,' she began. 'I know you can't say what happened, but I couldn't help noticing your eye. It looks a little bruised. I can only imagine what's happened. But I wanted to check.'

Fitz thought of the letter Camilla had sent her and reminded herself that her stepmother was actually a caring and compassionate woman. An observant one, too. She remembered Camilla looking at her strangely when she had first arrived, it must have been when she noticed Fitz's bruising.

'I thought I had covered the bruising, but it seems I'm not as good at it as I thought.' First Elsie and now Camilla. Fitz made a mental note to apply more face powder. Although hopefully in a day or two she wouldn't need to.

'I suspect you've been through something quite unimaginable for someone like me, sitting here in this big house, having the luxury of staff and plenty of food on the table,' said Camilla. 'I'm very aware of the privileged position I'm in and, I have to say, somewhat embarrassed given what's going on in the world.'

'You shouldn't be embarrassed,' said Fitz. 'And you could use your position to help others.'

'Yes. Indeed,' said Camilla. 'In fact, I've been thinking about that. I need to speak to your father first, but I thought about opening up the gardens to the villagers. Not to admire the flowers, but to share the produce. I'm turning the whole east side of the garden over to vegetables.'

'That's a great idea,' said Fitz. 'But the rose garden . . .'

'Oh, not that. I know it was your mother's creation and it's so beautiful, I really wouldn't want to destroy that. And I know how much you love it. I wouldn't take that from you.'

Fitz was quite stunned at this. She hadn't realised Camilla was aware of her attachment to the rose garden, but Fitz was beginning to realise just how much of Camilla's kindness she had refused to see. 'Thank you,' she said. 'I appreciate that.'

There was a small silence, before Camilla spoke again. 'I know things haven't always been easy between us—'

'Your letter,' Fitz said, before Camilla could continue.

'Ah, yes . . .'

'Thank you,' said Fitz.

Camilla met her gaze and gave a small nod. 'I . . .' she began uncertainly.

'It's all right,' said Fitz. 'You don't need to say anything. I just want you to know how sorry I am.'

Camilla looked a little surprised but then gave a sad smile. 'As am I,' she said. 'I haven't always been the kind of stepmother I've wanted to be. I'm not making excuses, but I had no idea how to help you and I think I made quite a mess of it at times. I am sorry.'

'It wasn't only you,' Fitz said. 'I know I wasn't always very nice to you. I'm sorry.'

'No don't apologise,' said Camilla hastily. 'You were a child. You'd lost your mother. You were angry and didn't understand why, and then I swanned into your life and quite frankly, tried too hard. And when you continued to be angry, it made me keep you at arm's length. I didn't know how to deal with your emotions.' She dipped her gaze for a moment before looking up again. 'While you were away, I can't tell you how worried both your father and I were about you. When I heard about your friend dying, it terrified me but it made me realise how much I cared for you. I had hidden those feeling away because I had been rejected. All rather immature of me.'

'I felt I was betraying my mother by accepting you,' said Fitz softly. 'It felt disloyal. That's why I rebelled. I didn't want anything to change but that day everything changed forever and it was outside of my control. I didn't know what to do. I see that now, but it's only recently I've understood myself.'

'You were hurting and your father and I didn't know how to help you. I should have done better.'

Fitz was stunned. Not only at Camilla's candid confession but at her own emotions – one of understanding and love. Something she never thought she'd ever feel for her stepmother. Without thinking, she rushed over to Camilla, who rose to her feet. They hesitated and then both hugged each other at the same time.

The years of misunderstanding, confusion and tension was squeezed out of them, to be replaced by this deeply buried love they hadn't realised they had for one another.

Chapter 31

In the end, Fitz had left Yvette at Badcombe House and returned on her own to Bignor and Mrs Bertram to collect their belongings and say goodbye.

'We thought seeing as Yvette was happy at my father's, it would be easier to leave her there,' explained Fitz.

'Oh, that is good news. I am pleased,' enthused Barbara. 'She's a dear little girl. I hope everything works out for her.'

'I'll do everything possible to make sure it does,' replied Fitz.

'So now, you just have to sort yourself out.'

'I do,' agreed Fitz. 'I'm determined to make every day count. I'm very lucky to have the chance to do that.'

'Indeed. As are we all.'

'Thank you so much for your kindness and good luck with everything.'

She parted from Barbara Bertram with a sense of contentment, something she had felt yesterday when she'd left Badcombe Hall. It was a fanciful thought, but she wondered if she was finally laying some of her past demons to rest. No, demons was too strong a word. Maybe her 'hang-ups'. It sounded awfully American to say that, but it was the best expression she could think of.

And of course, there was the issue of Sam. Another American hang-up – but one she was more than happy to have. All she had to do now was convince Sam of this.

Bob was very kind, he had offered to pick her up again and this time instead of two wheels, he arrived in four – a black Vauxhall staff car.

'Going up in the world, are we?' teased Fitz, climbing in beside him.

'I'm taking it for a test run,' said Bob. 'Problem with the spark plugs.' He winked at Fitz.

'You're such a dear,' said Fitz.

Soon they were pulling up outside the entrance to Goodwood House. Fitz took out her compact mirror and checked her hair, before touching up her red lipstick. 'There how do I look?'

'Perfect,' said Bob. 'And if he doesn't open his eyes and realise what he's got, then he's an arse.'

Fitz laughed. 'I agree.'

'Good luck, Fitz,' said Bob as she exited the car.

Fitz watched Bob drive off. He had to get the car back to the airfield before someone clocked what he was really up to. How she was going to get home, she didn't really care. At the moment, her main priority was to talk sense into a certain American. This was another mission she was determined to complete.

Thankfully, the nurse she'd seen earlier in the week wasn't on duty and a young one, who was much more welcoming, greeted Fitz.

'Flying Officer Sam Carter,' said the nurse after Fitz informed her who she had come to visit. 'I'll just go and see him.'

'Actually,' said Fitz quickly. 'Would you mind not telling him? I want to surprise him.'

The nurse looked at Fitz uncertainly. 'Surprise him. I'm not sure if that's a good idea.'

'Please,' said Fitz. 'He won't be cross. I promise.' She discreetly crossed her fingers as she spoke.

'All right, then. Just this once, seeing as Matron is busy on another ward.'

Fitz could have hugged the nurse. She followed her through the door which the previous nurse had used and along a corridor. 'There you are, bed five.'

'Thank you,' said Fitz. She could see Sam sitting up in the bed in the corner of the room. He had a good spot with the benefit of a large bay window which overlooked the west side of the building. Fortunately, he wouldn't have been able to see the front and so had not spotted Fitz arriving.

She approached the bed, aware she was drawing attention from some of the other patients. 'Hey, Miss. Have you come to see me?' called out one of them. 'I could do with cheering up.'

At that point Sam looked around. His eyes taking in Fitz approaching and then flitting to the bay where the remark had come from.

'Ah, Miss, don't disappoint me,' continued the man.

Fitz ignored him. Her gaze firmly fixed on Sam.

'Cut it out, Jones,' said Sam.

Jones muttered something indeterminable but then didn't say another word.

'Hello, Sam,' said Fitz as she reached his bed.

'Why are you here?'

'That's a nice way to greet someone who's come to see you.' Fitz sat down on the bedside chair. From her bag she took out a newspaper and a bar of chocolate.

'So, you're here to while away ten minutes to ask me how I'm doing and make pitying comments about my injuries?'

'My, we are feeling sorry for ourselves, aren't we?' said Fitz. She had prepared herself for Sam being bad-tempered but maybe not quite as hostile as he appeared to be.

'Don't start preaching about me being lucky to be alive,' said Sam, not looking at her. 'I may as well not be.'

'What on earth are you talking about?'

Now he looked at her. 'Are you serious? They did tell you what happened, didn't they? I have only got one leg. They had to amputate half the other one.'

Fitz could see the pain and anger in his eyes but there was something else under the surface, there was fear. 'I am fully aware of that,' she said evenly. 'You make it sound like your life is over.'

'It may as well be.'

'Why?'

Sam made a scoffing noise. 'Because I can't fucking walk.'

Fitz hadn't heard Sam swear before but undeterred she carried on. 'Don't be so ridiculous. Hundreds of men are amputees and you can get the most amazing prosthetics these days. There's nothing to stop you doing all the things you've always done. You're just being silly.'

Sam closed his eyes for a moment. 'If you're finished giving me a lecture, then you really should go.'

Fitz let out a gentle sigh. 'I'm not here to fight with you, Sam,' she said softly. 'I'm here to tell you I'm sorry for walking away from you. For not being honest with you. For not trusting you or myself.'

He took a deep breath before answering. 'You should have saved yourself the journey. Like I said before, go and marry your squadron leader boyfriend.'

Fitz sighed. 'There was no squadron leader. No boyfriend, at all,' she confessed.

'No boyfriend, huh?' For a moment she thought she saw a brief look of relief on Sam's face, but then it was gone, replaced by the scowl. 'It's irrelevant now anyway,' he said.

Fitz pushed on. She hadn't come here to be turned away at the first obstacle. That being Sam's stubbornness. 'When I heard your plane had been shot down, I was devastated,' she said.

'And it's taken you all this time to come here. You don't have to do this out of pity or any sense of loyalty.'

'I'm not,' said Fitz. 'I was asked to join SOE.' She probably wasn't supposed to tell him, but she didn't care. He deserved to know the truth.

He turned his head to look at her. 'SOE?'

'Yes, it's—'

'I know what it is.'

'The night I was flown out to France, I saw Bob and he had the letter you'd written. I told him to look after it until I got back. I couldn't take it with me. He told me you were MIA.'

She watched as Sam took in what she was telling him. 'He shouldn't have told you.'

'I made him. I'm glad he did,' said Fitz. 'It made me realise what an absolute idiot I'd been.'

'You went to France on a mission?' asked Sam, as if he couldn't quite believe it.

'Yes. And as you can see, I came back.'

'I had no idea.'

'That's the way it's supposed to work,' said Fitz. 'Need-to-know and all that.'

Sam studied her and she was grateful her bruising had all but gone. She'd also applied more face powder than she normally would. Sam didn't need to know what had happened to her, not yet anyway. In time, she hoped she would get the chance to tell him, but this wasn't about France. This was about her and Sam. Their future.

'All the time I was in France, you were on my mind,' she said. 'I couldn't stop thinking about how stupid I had been. When I returned to England, I got your letter from Bob. He had been looking after it for me.'

'You should rip it up. It doesn't mean anything now,' said Sam, bitterly.

'You're wrong,' replied Fitz. 'It means everything. I said just now that I had been an idiot. Do you want to know why?'

'Even if I say no, I get the feeling you're still gonna tell me.'

'Too bloody right I am,' said Fitz. 'And you'd better make sure you listen because if you don't, I'm simply going to keep repeating myself.'

Sam shook his head. She didn't miss the corners of his mouth tipping a fraction in amusement. Then he held up his hands in a get on with it, I'm waiting, gesture. 'If you must,' he said.

'You remember when I last saw you it was at Tangmere, right after that attack?'

'Like I would forget,' said Sam.

She didn't care that he was being snippy, he had every right to still be angry with her. 'You told me that our conversation wasn't over,' continued Fitz. 'So I'm here to continue it.'

'Is there a point to all this?' said Sam, looking at his watch. 'You know, I'm a busy man.'

He really was in a bad mood. Fitz wasn't put off, in fact, she relished the challenge. 'Have it your way,' she said. 'And listen up, Flying Officer Sam Carter.' She edged forward in her seat so she could lower her voice, aware that they were drawing quite a lot of attention. 'Ever since my mother died, I've wanted control. You know that, we've spoken about it before. I wanted control because with that came security. I needed to be in control of everything, what I did and what I felt.' She paused to catch her breath and forced herself to slow down. 'When you came along, you turned everything upside down. I loved being with you. When I wasn't with you, you were constantly on my mind. My first thought in the morning and my last thought at night.'

His face softened a little and he looked at her. 'It was the same for me. You don't have to explain it.'

'I had never felt like that about anyone before,' said Fitz, sensing she was making headway. 'I didn't know it was possible to feel that way. But that frightened me. Instead of embracing it, I shied away from it. Tried to deny it, even to myself. If I didn't acknowledge it, then it couldn't be happening. I couldn't be losing control . . .' She paused again, as her words caught in her throat. She had to get out everything she wanted to say before she started crying. 'I . . . I didn't want to call it what it was.'

Sam studied her face, as if trying to work something out. 'What was it?'

'Love,' replied Fitz. 'It was pure unadulterated love for you. And it terrified me.' She brushed away a tear that had managed to escape her eye. 'I was deeply in love with you and I ran, Sam. I ran from it because I was scared.' More tears breached the rim of her eyes. 'It was the biggest mistake of my life. It wasn't until I heard you were MIA that it hit me. That I had lost you and had never told you how I felt.'

She saw him move his hand as if he was going to reach out to her, but he stopped and curled his fingers around the edge of the mattress instead. 'You still haven't told me,' he said.

'I loved you, Sam. With all my heart. You were the best thing that had ever happened to me and I had pushed you away. I cannot tell you how sorry I am.'

The silence was thick and heavy between them. Fitz fumbled for a tissue from her pocket and wiped her face, sure she was smudging all her make-up, but she was beyond caring at this point.

Sam looked expectantly at her. 'Is that it? You came all this way to tell me that you loved me once and you're sorry you never told me? Well, sweetheart, that makes me feel a whole lot better.'

'Don't be so facetious,' said Fitz. 'I loved you then and I love you now. I will never stop loving you, Sam. Never. And I am never going to walk away from you again.' When he didn't say anything, she repeated her declaration. 'Did you hear me? I love you.'

'You should go,' said Sam.

'I should do nothing of the sort,' retorted Fitz. 'You love me. I know you do. I can see it in your eyes, and it is written all over your face. I can feel that love, even though you're pretending you hate me right now, I know you don't.'

She held her breath, as she waited for him to reply.

'It's not a case of not loving you,' he said at last. 'I loved you, right from the word go, but I have nothing to offer you now. I've nothing to give. I can't do anything.'

Fitz let out a sigh of relief that he had openly admitted to still loving her. 'You're being defeatist,' she said. 'You can still drive, swim, even fly a plane. Everything can be adapted. The only thing holding you back is you. You're Sam Carter. You love the challenge and the danger and risk. Why are you giving in?'

'I'm not giving in, I'm being realistic,' said Sam. 'I'm not the same man I was before.'

'Who told you that?' She waited dramatically for the pause. Sam didn't reply and she continued. 'No one told you that. Only you. I didn't fall in love with what you are, I fell in love with who you are and that's the difference. You're still the same man. The same heart. The same mind.'

He looked at her and Fitz stared right back at him. Honestly the man was making this so difficult.

Finally he spoke. 'You will get bored of me. You need to find someone who can give you the life you crave. The excitement and the adventure. It's in our blood, Fitz. I can't stand in your way. In fact, I can't stand at all, right now.'

'That's not funny,' said Fitz. She threw her hands up in exasperation. 'You're a stubborn fool. Stay here and wallow in self-pity, if that's what you want.' Then leaning closer to him, with as much self-control as she could muster, 'If you really want to do all the things you claim to love, then the Sam Carter I know will find a way and not make up lame excuses.'

With that she straightened up and began to stride away from his bedside. She wanted to throttle the stubborn fool.

Then she heard him call out. 'Lame excuses, huh? That's worse than my attempt at humour.'

She stopped but didn't turn around straight away. She was aware the whole ward was now watching them like they were some kind of theatre group who'd popped in to entertain them. Gosh, weren't her and Sam just excellent fun?

She turned to face Sam. 'Sorry, bad choice of words.'

'Oh, I don't know, love,' said Jones, who was sitting up in bed now, not even pretending he wasn't listening. 'You sounded spot on to me.'

'Shut up, Jones,' called out one of the other men. 'I want to hear how this ends.'

'If the Yank let's Blondie go, it's not just his leg he needs to worry about, it's his head,' said another, which caused a ripple of laughter around the ward.

Fitz raised her eyebrows at Sam. 'So, is the Yank letting Blondie go?'

Sam fixed her with those oh-so-beautiful blue eyes of his and for once Fitz couldn't read what she was seeing. She had an awful feeling she had misjudged the whole situation. She lifted her chin a fraction, to try to retain some sort of dignity. If this was a game of brinkmanship, she was about to fold.

'Godammit,' muttered Sam. 'No, he's not. The Yank was being an idiot.'

Fitz rushed back over to Sam's bed, throwing herself at him. She didn't care that the room was full of wounded servicemen who were all now cheering and whooping as she kissed him. It was only when the nurses hurried in to see what all the fuss was about that Fitz pulled away.

'Oh, you made that such hard work,' she scolded, wiping her smudged, red lipstick from his face. She kissed him some more before the ward sister descended on them and insisted Fitz should restrain herself and if she couldn't she should leave.

Sam grabbed Fitz's hand. 'She's not going anywhere just yet.'

'Well, kindly control yourselves,' said the ward sister. And then pulled the curtain around the bed. 'At least in front of the others,' she added, before bustling out through the curtain and back onto the rest of the ward.

Fitz collapsed on Sam, both of them giggling.

'Are you sure about this? About us?' asked Sam, once they had stopped laughing. 'It's not going to be easy.'

'I've never been more certain about anything in my life,' said Fitz. 'Although there is something I haven't told you about yet.'

'And that is?'

'When I came back from France, I didn't come back alone.'

'You didn't?'

'Let me explain.' Fitz gave him a slightly more detailed version of events than she'd told her father and Camilla. He deserved to know the truth. She looked at him once she'd finished. 'So, it's not just me. For a while, until the war is over, it's me and Yvette.'

He reached out and touched her face. 'I didn't think it would be possible to love you any more than I already do,' he said. 'But you've just taken my love to new heights. Way higher than any plane I've flown. You really are a remarkable woman, Fitz, and I don't know what I did to deserve you, but hell, I'm so glad you came into my life. And that you came back to me.'

'I was always coming back to you,' said Fitz. 'It simply took me a while to work it out, that's all.'

She hugged him, resting her head on his chest. For the first time in a long time, she felt contented. All her sharp edges had been smoothed and she liked this new improved version of her life.

Epilogue

October 1946

Fitz lifted Peter into his pram. 'Gosh, you're getting heavy,' she said, tucking the blankets around her eighteen-month-old son.

The clock in the hall of Badcombe House struck the hour and eight chimes rang out. Fitz went to the foot of the stairs. 'Yvette! Come on. You'll miss your bus.'

The young teenager trotted down the stairs, with her satchel hanging from her shoulder. 'Sorry, I was looking for my gloves.' She held them up in the air. 'Found them.'

The autumnal air of early October was already on the chilly side and Fitz fastened the button on Peter's knitted hat. His blue eyes looked even darker against the white of the wool. He looked so much like his father. Sam's mother had sent some photographs of Sam when he was a baby and they looked like two peas in a pod. Fitz hadn't yet been able to meet Sam's parents but now the war was over, they were hoping to be able to travel across the Atlantic the following year.

'Where's Michael?' asked Fitz as she slipped her hands into her own gloves.

'I'm here!' he called, coming through from the kitchen, biting into an apple.

'And eating as always,' sighed Camilla, following him out into the hall. She picked his cap up from the table and put it on his head, adjusting it and then making sure the collar of his blazer was turned down. 'There, that's better,' she said. 'Have a good day at school both of you.'

Both Yvette and Michael attended the local grammar school. They really had become firm friends. Yvette had grasped the English language with ease. There was no trace of a French accent, although they still often spoke French at home. She had thrived at school and had passed the Eleven Plus with flying colours.

'Isn't it wonderful how they've become such good friends?' said Camilla, leaning over the pram to smile at Peter and tickle him under the chin. 'They will miss each other when Michael goes to university next year.'

Camilla had turned into the most doting step-grandmother a person could wish for. Her love for children was glaringly apparent and Fitz had often wondered over the past few years why she had never seen it before. Maybe she hadn't been looking for it or hadn't wanted to find it.

Camilla delighted in having them at Badcombe House. When Fitz had first moved back, their relationship had most definitely improved, and then, once Fitz was married, Camilla had taken a step back and allowed her to be the grown woman she now was. Fitz couldn't deny her experience in France in the December of 1941 had changed her.

Taking care of Yvette hadn't come without its challenges, but Fitz found herself echoing the position Camilla had been in. She had become a mother to a child she hadn't given birth to. A child who already had a mother and didn't know what had happened to her. There had been resistance, tears, anger and confusion but no matter what, there had always been love.

It wasn't until then that Fitz really appreciated how much of a challenge it had been for Camilla to take her on. And just as Camilla had gone on to have her own child, Michael, Fitz had become pregnant and had Peter.

It was a chain of events no one could ever have predicted, and Fitz had grown very fond of Camilla, even seeking her out for advice on how to handle certain situations with Yvette. She regretted having made Camilla's life so difficult. Motherhood was no mean feat.

Their relationship now sat somewhere between parent and friend. Fitz didn't try too hard to define it, rather she tried to enjoy it for what it was.

Life had been full of challenges since Fitz had got back from France. Not only for her and Yvette but for Sam, too.

When Sam had been discharged from hospital, they had moved into Badcombe House, where there was space enough for his wheelchair, and for the first six months, they lived on the ground floor, using one of the sitting rooms as their bedroom.

Sam had approached his new life with the same gusto and enthusiasm as he did everything else in life. Never one to be half-hearted about anything he did, he faced everything head-on, with a fearless and contagious zest for life. He was never going to let being an amputee hold him back.

As Fitz had predicted, Sam had soon mastered the art of walking with his prosthetic leg, but he wasn't going to stop there. Sam had been back in an aeroplane within months.

Fitz had been so proud of him when they had adapted a plane for him to fly and he had joined the ATA. It wasn't his dream job, of course, but he had accepted his new circumstances with grace. Being at Badcombe House meant Fitz was able to work for the government in translating conversations enemy prisoners had among themselves. It had been fascinating work. She had only stopped once Peter was born, and now that the war was over, they were all adjusting to a new way of life.

With that, of course, came her promise to the doctor in France to find Yvette's mother or at the very least, close family. Sam had been in contact with the Red Cross, and they had given as much detail as they could about Yvette's mother in the hope the charity could locate her. Now they were waiting for any news.

Fitz fastened the top button on her coat and fussed with the blanket to make sure Peter was warm enough. The wind was colder than she expected. 'Do you want to walk with us to the bus stop?' she asked Camilla.

'I won't today,' replied Camilla. 'I'm speaking at the WI meeting this afternoon and I need to go over my notes.'

Since the end of the war, Camilla had become involved with a charity supporting war widows and their young families. Fundraising and speaking to local groups filled a lot of her time.

'Oh, yes, of course,' said Fitz, remembering Camilla had mentioned it at breakfast. 'Not that you need practice. I've been to your talks, and you are a wonderful speaker.'

Camilla waved them off from the doorstep and Fitz followed on as Yvette and Michael kicked through the fallen leaves that littered the grass verges of the drive. Peter was enchanted by the trees blowing giddily in the wind and squealed in delight as a large horse chestnut leaf floated down and landed on the apron of the pram.

They had just reached the end of the driveway when the sound of a bicycle bell caught Fitz's attention. She looked up to see Alf, the village postman pedalling towards them.

'Mrs Carter!' he called waving at her.

Fitz waited for him to reach her. 'Good morning, Alf. How are you?'

'Very well, thank you, Mrs Carter.' He dove his hand into the brown post sack on the front of his bike. 'There we are,' he said. 'Two for your father and one for you.'

'Oh, lovely. Thanks very much, Alf.'

She took the letters from him and tucked them into the foot of the pram.

'You might want to read that one sooner rather than later,' said Alf, as he began to pedal away.

Fitz watched him go, puzzled by his comment. She picked up the letters. As soon as she saw the Red Cross symbol in the left-hand corner of the envelope, with the George VI postage stamp in the opposite corner, she knew this was the letter they had been waiting for.

She looked up at Yvette, who was standing at the bus stop with Michael.

Fitz was desperate to open the letter but didn't dare in front of Yvette. Whatever the news, it had to be imparted with care. She also wanted Sam to be with her when they told Yvette the contents of the letter. He would be home that evening at around six o'clock.

Fitz tried to distract herself for most of the day by taking an extra-long walk with Peter in his pram both in the morning and the afternoon, but thoughts of the letter were never far away. She and Sam had previously agreed that when the Red Cross letter came, they would sit down and read it together. She was happy to wait. She didn't want to know the truth on her own.

Whatever the news was, whether they had found Yvette's mother, hadn't found her, or – the worst news – Yvette's mother had been confirmed as dead, Fitz was not looking forward to receiving it. If Yvette's mother was alive, it would very much be a double-edged sword for her and Sam. There was no doubt they had grown to love Yvette over the past five years. Even though Fitz knew it was possibly the road to heartbreak, she hadn't been able to help herself. It was almost as if, once she'd let Sam into her heart, her heart now knew no boundaries. It was wide open. To love and to be loved was truly a precious gift.

Eventually, six o'clock rolled around. Fitz was waiting on the doorstep as Sam arrived back. He climbed out of the car, lifting his prosthetic under the knee to swing his leg over the ledge.

He stopped as he saw her. 'Fitz? Is everything all right?' he asked. How well he knew her.

She held the letter out to him. 'The Red Cross,' she said.

Sam nodded and walked up the steps. He put his arms

around Fitz and held her closely to him, kissing the top of her head. 'Don't worry, sweetheart,' he soothed. 'We knew this day would come and whatever is in there, we'll face together. Yeah?'

She nodded. 'Camilla is looking after the children.'

'Come on, then. Let's go inside.'

They went into the study. Sam poured Fitz a port and himself a whisky. He sat down beside her on the sofa.

'Ready?' asked Fitz.

'As I'll ever be.'

She used the letter opener to slice through the flap of the envelope and withdrew the single sheet of paper. Sam took it from her and unfolded it, before reading out loud.

```
Dear Mr and Mrs Carter
   Further to your letter concerning the
whereabouts or fate of one Edith Moreau,
we are writing to advise you that we
have today heard from the Mairie of
Josselin in this matter.
   We are pleased to advise that Edith
Moreau did, indeed, survive the massacre
at Saint Pierre in December, 1941. We
understand that she hid under the bodies
of fellow villagers for twelve hours,
finally managing to escape with only
two other members of the community in
the middle of the night, via a hidden
doorway in the back of the crypt.
   Madame Moreau has been informed that
her daughter, Yvette Moreau is alive and
well in your care. She was overwhelmed
with the good news and is desperate to
be reunited with her daughter.
   As such, please could you contact
this office by return so we can arrange
```

```
to repatriate Yvette Moreau to France
and to her mother.
  Yours sincerely
  A. Akerman
  Welfare Officer, Wounded
  Missing and Relatives Department
```

Fitz closed her eyes as a tsunami of emotions washed over her. 'You all right?' asked Sam gently.

Fitz nodded. 'I think so.' She looked at Sam and saw the same conflict that she was feeling. 'We have to give her back. We're going to lose her, Sam. I shouldn't feel sad, but I do. So wretchedly sad my heart hurts.'

Sam wrapped her in his arms and she could hear him swallow hard as if he was fighting with his emotions. 'I know,' he said. 'But she's not ours to keep. Christ, I wish she could stay with us forever, but she has her own mother waiting for her.'

'We might never see her again,' sobbed Fitz. 'I don't know how I'm going to cope.' It was all well and good saying she knew Yvette might have to return to France, but it was something totally different when that notion turned into a reality.

'Whatever we're feeling right now about her leaving,' said Sam, 'her mother must have been going through it far worse.'

'I know. I honestly, do,' said Fitz. 'And I know I can't even compare what I'm feeling now to what her mother has gone through, but . . . I am going to miss her so much. And we may never see her again.'

'Don't think like that, sweetheart,' said Sam. 'Maybe her mother will let us go visit. We can write to her. We'll stay in touch for as long as she wants us to.'

Fitz sniffed. 'I'm so excited and yet I'm so very scared. It's going to be difficult for Yvette to adjust, too. She hasn't seen her mother for nearly five years.'

'We can prepare her as best we can but ultimately, that

is out of our hands,' said Sam. 'We need to present it as a positive thing. You think you can do that?'

'Yes. Of course. I just need a moment to get used to the idea,' said Fitz.

God, she was so lucky to have Sam there as her voice of reason, of calm and of comfort. She dabbed her face with her handkerchief and straightening herself up, she smiled at her husband.

'Ready?' asked Sam, squeezing her hand.

'Ready,' replied Fitz.

They crossed the hallway from the study to the living room. The door was ajar and Fitz could see Yvette sitting on the sofa with little Peter on her lap, while Michael pretended to tickle him with a cuddly toy. Peter was squealing in delight every time the toy went near him.

Fitz paused in the doorway, savouring the moment of domestic bliss. Her family – an odd complex blend of relationships, but oh, how beautiful that blend was. Fitz could never in her wildest dreams imagine she would find such contentment and happiness here at Badcombe House. She would miss Yvette so much, they all would, but she would always be a part of the Fitz-Herbert Carter clan. Always in their hearts and never far from their minds.

It was a fairy-tale ending for Yvette. The kind of ending Fitz had once imagined for herself as a child, where her mother came back and they all lived happily ever after but she realised that this was the best happy ever after she could ask for.

A Note from the Author

When I first set out to write a book about the ATA, I knew of the local connection to me at what was RAF Tangmere during the Second World War, but I had no idea of the other connections I was to unearth in my research.

One of those was Pilot Officer Billy Fiske – an American who joined the British Air Force at the beginning of the war. Prior to that he had achieved many things, including a gold medal at the Olympics. He encapsulated everything I imagined my character Sam to be, and more. Tragically, Billy Fiske died defending England and is buried in Boxgrove churchyard just a couple of miles away from me. A stained-glass window has been dedicated to him. He was only 29 years old but packed so much into his short life.

RAF Tangmere is now a museum and well worth a visit for anyone interested in aviation and especially its role during the war. The airbase was used to drop supplies and SOE operatives into France for covert missions. It played an important role in defending England against air attacks from Germany and was bombed several times but managed to stay operational throughout.

RAF Westhampnett, a satellite airfield to RAF Tangmere is mentioned in the book and was where Douglas Bader flew his last wartime flight in a Spitfire before being shot down over northern France.

Bignor Manor House, where the Bertrams lived, was used during the war as a secret base for Allied agents while they waited to be flown across the channel to France on clandestine missions. While they were at Bignor, the agents posed as wounded airmen, and it wasn't unusual for them to frequent the local pub.

Over the course of writing this book, and previous books where RAF Tangmere has been used as a setting, it's been fascinating finding out all the local history that's right on my doorstep.

Acknowledgements

As always, I couldn't have got this story to publication without the fantastic team at Embla and my agent, Hattie Grünewald.

Much thanks also to the Tangmere Military Aviation Museum, Tangmere for a wealth of information.

Read on for an extract from
The Dance Teacher of Paris...

Prologue

Fleur

West Sussex, October 2015

Fleur sat down in her grandmother's chair, placing the satin ballet shoe on her lap and her hands gently on the armrests. Closing her eyes, she brushed her thumbs across the sun-faded upholstery. Whenever Fleur thought of her grandmother, Lydia, she always pictured her sitting here, in the crook of the bay window, looking out across the green with the sound of the sea lapping at the shoreline just beyond the next row of houses that enjoyed their superior sea-fronted position.

Fleur drew in a deep breath and could detect the faintest trace of Lydia's favourite perfume – one Fleur had bought for her on many a birthday. It was Rive Gauche by Yves Saint Laurent. Lydia had been wearing the 1970s classic for as long as Fleur could remember. It was only in the last few months that Fleur understood the significance behind the name of the fragrance, which referred to the southern side of the river Seine – the Left Bank. But then Fleur hadn't known very much about her grandmother's past until recently, certainly not the time during the war when Lydia was a ten-year-old child living in Paris under the German occupation and attending the school opposite what was now the Musée d'Orsay in the Left Bank district of the city.

Fleur released her breath and opened her eyes, her gaze settling on the Pierre Valois miniature watercolour hanging in the alcove by the fireplace, depicting a ballerina at the barre. Another hidden connection to Lydia's past that had been in plain sight all these years.

Fleur's gaze travelled to the ballet shoe and her heart contracted as it had done ever since she'd found out the story behind it. The fabric was worn from hours of dancing and now delicate from the passing of time. The ribbon was frayed at the edges but still intact. It was a shoe that had graced the boards of the dance studio in Paris; pirouetting, skipping and hopping, rising and falling. It was a shoe that had held so much love and hope over many years. Another connection between past and present. A connection *for* Lydia and *to* Lydia. One Fleur knew she would always cherish, one that made her cry and made her smile, one that made her feel proud.

And, now that Fleur knew everything, it was also one that broke her heart.

Chapter 1

Adele

Paris, May 1942

Adele Basset looked up from the piano, calling out the sequence of steps to her dance class. Today was ballet and whilst her students aged between five and ten years old were probably never going to forge a career out of dancing, their unbridled enthusiasm and obvious delight made up for their lack of technical ability and natural grace.

Today the sun was shining in through the bank of full-length windows that lined the side of the studio, spotlighting the children and bouncing off the mirrored wall. The room could really do with a freshen up. The paint was peeling in one corner and two wooden floorboards needed replacing, having been repaired far too many times. However, paint and wood were scarce after two years of German occupation.

'*Et demi-plié*, knees over toes . . . Rise . . . *Et deuxième. Port de bras*, follow your arm to the side.' Adele called out the instructions above the sound of the piano. '*Excellent!* Daniel, *parfait!*' Strictly speaking, it wasn't excellent or perfect, but Adele had always been adamant her after-school dance lessons were not to reach perfection in performance, only perfection in joy.

What more could anyone ask for these children as the war in Europe raged on? The hour after school each day was an escape for them and for her after a long day teaching.

Here at the classes, through the medium of dance, they could be anything and anywhere they wanted. Goodness knows, they deserved the little pleasure and respite the hour brought – they had already witnessed horrors children had no right to see.

Adele rose from her position at the piano, gesturing with her hands for the children to carry on with the steps, just the way her own mother had taught her and her sister, Lucille. Their mother, Marianne, had been the most beautiful and skilled of dancers and trained with the *Ballet de l'Opéra national de Paris* – the Paris Opera Ballet. A career tragically cut short by a motor vehicle accident, and later her life by illness. Adele felt the familiar surge of grief that accompanied any thought of her mother. It had been nearly twelve years since Marianne died, a milestone as she had now been absent from Adele's life longer than she had been physically present. However, taking these classes and passing on the spirit and love for dance somehow made Adele feel closer to her mother and, in some ways, like she was still with her.

Adele smiled at her class. '*Bravo! Allez, tendu*. Remember your arms. Don't let them touch your body. Big circles. That's it, Margot. *Très bien.*'

With her back to the children, Adele joined in, demonstrating the steps for those less assured pupils. They weren't particularly co-ordinated or sharp in their foot placements, but the energy in the room was inspiring. She wasn't sure where they got their energy from and wished she had some of it. Today she felt tired, weary from being in a continual heightened state of anxiety, fearful of stepping out of line with the Germans. They were easy to rile and quick to retaliate. Adele caught sight of her reflection in the mirror. It shocked her to see the weariness on her face and grey circles under her green eyes. Her usually shiny brunette hair looked lacklustre, tied up in a bun, and she could see her collarbones; the ever-tightening supply of rations was doing nothing for her appearance.

The door to the classroom opened and Gérard Basset, her father and schoolmaster, popped his head around the doorway, pushing his spectacles up onto the bridge of his nose. His gaze travelled the room and he smiled an acknowledgement to his daughter. 'I'm leaving now,' he mimed more than spoke so as not to interrupt the class. Adele returned the smile and nodded as her father offered the class a small round of applause before waving a farewell and disappearing back into the corridor.

Forty-five minutes later, Adele brought the class to an end.

'*Bravo, mes enfants! Bravo!*' Adele gave a small curtsy to her class, who returned the gesture – a signal that dance class was officially over. As the children gathered excitedly around her, Adele lifted up the lid to the top of the piano and took out a small cloth bag. She put her finger to her lips to hush them.

Ten pairs of eyes looked eagerly up at her as she delved into the bag and brought out a string of apple rings dusted in cinnamon. Adele untied the string and handed out the little treats, watching as the children scoffed them down in seconds, dabbing the tiniest of crumbs from their laps and licking their fingers. They were always hungry these days, and Adele felt compelled to sacrifice some of her own rations to help stave off their hunger pains.

'Now, quickly change out of your shoes,' instructed Adele, once they had finished eating. 'Your mothers will be waiting downstairs for you.' She noticed one girl looking despondently at her shoe as she untied the ankle ribbons. 'What's the matter, Juliette?' Adele crouched down beside the eight-year-old.

'My shoe has a hole in the toe.'

'Oh, let me see.' Adele inspected the shoe. 'Hmm, yes, you've worn the toe right through. You'll have to tell your mother.'

'Maman doesn't know. She can't afford to buy another pair.'

Adele ran her hand gently over Juliette's head and down

her plaited hair. 'Don't worry, *ma petite puce*. I will fix it tonight.' She placed it on top of the piano so she wouldn't forget it later. Juliette's mother had three other children to look after and with her husband in a labour camp in Germany, she had no one to help her so fixing a ballet shoe probably wasn't high on her list of priorities.

She collected in the shoes from those children who weren't fortunate enough to own a pair. Adele and her younger sister, Lucille, had been dancing since they could walk, according to their parents, and over the years had gained a collection of dance shoes that now came into their own and enabled the little ones to participate.

As Adele helped the children change she picked up five-year-old Daniel's outdoor shoe and noticed it was nearly worn through on the sole. It was the same for the other one.

'One moment,' said Adele and nipped out of the classroom, returning a few minutes later with two pieces of stiff paper, once the cover of an exercise book, now repurposed as insoles. 'There, that should get you home.'

She went over to the cupboard and lifted out a basket of jazz shoes, sifting through until she found what she was looking for and handed the right-sized pair to the boy. 'For you.' She pushed a shoe into each pocket of Daniel's coat. 'These used to be mine when I was about your age. Tell your mother they're a gift.'

Once all laces and buckles were fastened, the children lined up along the barre. Adele was just about to lead them out when the door opened abruptly and to her horror, in marched two German soldiers, immediately followed by an officer and a French policeman.

'*Mademoiselle Basset?*' asked the German officer, removing his peaked cap and pushing it under his arm as he referred to his clipboard.

'*Oui*,' replied Adele, trying not to focus on the scar that ran from the German's lower lip and curved its way under his chin, as she placed herself between the officer and the children. She glanced towards the French policeman, who was clearly sweating, which she hoped was from embarrassment and shame. He looked away and Adele felt a small degree of satisfaction for his discomfort as the word 'traitor' rattled around inside her head.

The German officer looked up from his paperwork and paused for a moment before speaking. 'Do not worry, I am just here to gather some information.'

Adele nodded, not convinced she shouldn't worry. She felt the small hand of one of the children slip into hers. The little body huddled up to her leg. It was Daniel. Adele gave his hand a gentle squeeze of reassurance as she looked back at the officer. 'How can I help you?' she ventured.

'I need a list of all the Jewish children in your class. Names. Ages. Addresses.' He looked beyond Adele at the line of frightened faces. Then he swiped a piece of paper from his clipboard and held it out to Adele. 'Complete this form. I shall return for it in twenty-four hours. Do not miss off any names. It will be classed as subversive behaviour, something we will not tolerate. Do you understand?' He flapped the paper.

Adele nodded. '*Oui.*' She took the paper with a feeling of dread in both her heart and stomach. Only yesterday, Manu from the museum next door to the school had told her there were rumours circulating of a round-up of Jewish people. Surely, he didn't mean children too.

'Very good.' The officer looked at the children again as if memorising their faces, then gave a curt nod to Adele before striding from the room.

Adele's knees felt weak and she put out a hand, grasping the barre to steady herself. She took a deep breath and plastered on a smile as she turned to face the children. 'Well done for standing so nicely,' she said. 'Just wait here a moment.'

Adele poked her head out into the corridor to make sure the unwelcome visitors had left. She could hear their footsteps fading as they went down the stairs. She moved over to the window and watched the figures of the German officer, the two soldiers, and the French policeman leaving the building via the main entrance. A black saloon car was waiting and, once they were inside, it sped away.

Adele heaved a sigh of relief but couldn't get rid of the feeling of violation. She hated the thought of the German soldiers, not to mention the French policeman, inside the school. It was as if their mere presence could infect and pollute the air in the building, settling on the fixtures and fittings, seeping into the floors and ceilings, spreading like bacteria. She shrugged the thought from her mind.

The children were growing restless and, as she turned to face them, she once again ensured she at least looked like there was nothing to worry about. 'Is everyone ready to go home? Your parents are waiting for you.' Adele shepherded her flock of little swans from the classroom and down to the foyer where their mothers were most relieved to see them, except for two parents who seemed to be in the middle of a disagreement.

'It is getting too dangerous to come,' said Juliette's mother. She looked across at Daniel's mother, Madame Charon. 'It's people like you who are making it dangerous.'

Daniel's mother looked up. 'What is that supposed to mean?'

'Jews. You are making it difficult. You should not come here anymore. The Germans would leave us alone then.'

'Ladies, please,' interrupted Adele. 'We should stand together, not fight each other.'

'I was just stating a fact.' Juliette's mother was unrepentant.

'Please, everyone, go home now.' Adele adopted her friendly yet authoritative tone in an attempt to emulate her father. He somehow commanded respect without being confrontational.

It had the desired effect and soon the lobby was empty, much to Adele's relief. She looked at the form in her hand where she was to list the names. The urge to rip it to shreds was great and to avoid temptation, she dumped it on the reception desk. Madame Allard, the school secretary, would find it in the morning. Adele couldn't bring herself to do it.

The entrance door opened, making Adele jump. It was Manu.

'Sorry, I didn't mean to scare you,' he said, closing the door and briefly touching her arm.

'Manu.' She smiled, relieved to see her friend but hoping the small rise in colour to her cheeks went unnoticed. Tonight, his face was etched with concern. 'Is everything all right?' she asked.

'Yes. I was coming to ask you the same question. I saw your visitors.' His dark eyes looked intently at her.

'They want a list of names of our Jewish pupils,' Adele said. Although her father had warned her about speaking out of turn, she knew she could trust Manu. 'I don't know why they are targeting the children.'

Manu let out a sigh and rubbed the back of his neck. 'Maybe checking that no one has been missed from the list. There are rumours some families aren't listing their children. As I've mentioned, there are whispers around town that there will be a round-up of Jews soon. Some are talking about going into hiding or leaving the city before it happens.'

'Where are they taking them?'

'Work camps, apparently, but who knows what they are really going to do.'

'Every day I say I can't believe what is happening to the city I love.' Adele paced from one side of the foyer to the other and back again. 'Did you see the police officer today? They sent him along to make us think it is the French government doing this and not the Germans.'

'I know, but please, Adele, stay calm and do what they say.'

She stopped her pacing. 'I'm not so stupid as to blatantly go against them, but there are other ways.'

'Indeed. But for now, I suggest you comply. What use are you to anyone, let alone the children, if you're arrested?'

Adele knew he was right, but she hated the thought of

being so helpless. 'The parents were arguing this evening. I can't bear all the fear and mistrust that is around us.'

Manu took Adele's hand. 'I know, but you mustn't do anything rash. Now, I have to go. I too have a list to compile.'

Her heart beat a little faster at the touch of his hand holding hers, but she tried to appear nonchalant about it. 'You do?'

'Yes. They want a list of all the artefacts in the museum.'

'They're going to take them?'

Manu nodded. 'Steal them. Steal them from the people of Paris. I know they are not as valuable as your children, but still it fills me with a deep sadness.' He dipped his head and kissed Adele on each cheek. 'Goodnight, Adele. Lock the door behind me.'

'Goodnight, Manu.' She watched Manu leave, disappointed as always that he couldn't stay longer, then she slid the bolts into place before taking the key from the reception desk and turning the lock. She would go home soon. Her sister, Lucille, was preparing a meal for them tonight. Their father had gone to meet her where she worked as a secretary at one of the government buildings in the city, now under the rule of the Germans. Lucille working there concerned Gérard and it put his mind at rest to meet her every evening. Adele wasn't so sure her free-spirited sister totally appreciated this gesture of guardianship.

Back in the dance studio, Adele finished gathering up the ballet shoes into the basket and returned them to the store cupboard. She took a needle and thread from the sewing box and set about darning the toe of Juliette's shoe. The needle sliding through the pink satin, pulling the matching thread through and gradually healing the wound to the footwear. Adele thought of her mother; she thought of her fractured city, the children in her class and the wounds they would all be left to deal with. Like this shoe, they could be repaired but they would forever be scarred.

One brave woman will risk her life to save innocent Jewish children in occupied Paris.

Paris, 1942. During the dark days of Nazi occupation, **Adele Basset** continues to teach in her dance studio, providing a beacon of light and hope amongst so much terror and suffering.

When the Germans demand the names of her Jewish students, Adele realises they are in terrible danger. Only she can save them.

Hiding her Jewish pupils in the school attic, Adele puts her life on the line to keep them safe.

As the war rages, keeping her secret becomes more and more dangerous. Adele starts to question who she can trust and just how far she will need to go to protect the innocent children in her care.

She must find a way for them to escape, if they have a chance of making it out of Paris alive...

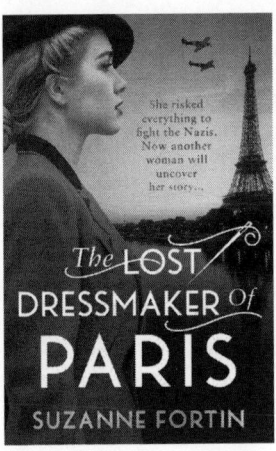

1942, Paris: Working as a tailor, **Nathalie Leroux** dreams of being a famous designer. But in occupied Paris, her dreams must be put on hold.

When the Germans take away the person she loves most, Nathalie accepts a dangerous Resistance mission. One that will use her dressmaking skills and put her at the heart of the Nazi high command.

With every stitch, Nathalie moves closer to avenging those she loves and freeing her country from tyranny. But also, to terrible danger...

2022, England: Darcie takes possession of a mysterious old suitcase, abandoned at a railway station. Inside, she discovers a beautiful vintage silk evening dress and a notebook of sketches. Written inside is the name: **Nathalie Leroux**.

Who was Nathalie? Why did she leave this at the station eighty years ago? What stopped her from returning?

Darcie's quest for answers will draw her into the dangerous world of the French Resistance. But is Darcie prepared for what she will find? And for Nathalie's secrets to change her world forever...

About the Author

Suzanne Fortin writes historical fiction and dual timeline and predominantly set in or partly in France. Her books feature courageous women in extraordinary circumstances with love and family at the heart of all the stories.

About Embla Books

Embla Books is a digital-first publisher of standout commercial adult fiction. Passionate about storytelling, the team at Embla publish books that will make you 'laugh, love, look over your shoulder and lose sleep'. Launched by Bonnier Books UK in 2021, the imprint is named after the first woman from the creation myth in Norse mythology, who was carved by the gods from a tree trunk found on the seashore – an image of the kind of creative work and crafting that writers do, and a symbol of how stories shape our lives.

Find out about some of our other books and stay in touch:

X, Facebook, Instagram: @emblabooks
Newsletter: https://bit.ly/emblanewsletter

Made in the USA
Columbia, SC
19 May 2025